2002

THE FILOSTRATO OF BOCCACCIO

THE FILOSTRATO OF
GIOVANNI BOCCACCIO

A Translation with Parallel Text by

NATHANIEL EDWARD GRIFFIN

and

ARTHUR BECKWITH MYRICK

With an Introduction by

NATHANIEL EDWARD GRIFFIN

BIBLO and TANNEN

Library of Congress Catalog Card Number 67-25164

ISBN 0-8196-0187-X

CARLETON · BROWN · VIRO · AMICO · ET · PRAECLARO
VENERABVNDI · DON · DED
N · E · G
A · B · M

PREFACE

THE Italian text used in this edition of the *Filostrato* is that of Ignazio Moutier, published as Vol. XIII of his edition of the *Opere volgari di Giovanni Boccaccio*, Florence, 1827-34. Differences in reading in the text of Paolo Savj-Lopez (*Bibliotheca Romanica*, 146-148, Strassburg) have been recorded in the footnotes.

The late Mr. Samuel Harper of Baltimore contributed substantially to laying the foundations of the present translation of the *Proemio* and of the first three cantos of the *Filostrato*. Helpful suggestions with regard to the translation of individual passages have been received from Professor C. H. Grandgent of Harvard University, President E. H. Wilkins of Oberlin College, Professor J. E. Shaw of the University of Toronto, Professor W. W. Lawrence of Columbia University, and others. Professors Domenico Vittorini and P. C. Kitchen of the University of Pennsylvania have compared the entire translation with the Italian and supplied a number of corrections and improvements. For their voluntary and unsparing services the translators owe these gentlemen a debt of gratitude that cannot be put into words.

The author of the introduction is indebted to Professors W. A. Nitze of the University of Chicago and Robert F. Seybolt of the University of Illinois and to Dr. P. W. Long of the *Webster's International Dictionary* for advice and correction. In particular he desires to

express his appreciation of the many courtesies of the officers and attendants of the Harvard College Library, without which the successful prosecution of his labors would have been impossible.

Finally it is to the author of the introduction a personal pleasure to acknowledge his appreciation of the good will of Professor A. C. Baugh of the University of Pennsylvania, who has been a friend to the book almost from its inception and has taken an active hand in securing its publication.

CONTENTS

INTRODUCTION

NO other work of Boccaccio combines so varied a range of interest as the *Filostrato*. The poem possesses an important autobiographical significance because of the parallel drawn by the author between the love of his hero for his heroine and his own love for the lady in whose honor it was written. From the poet's explanation in the *Proemio* of the applicability of the fable to his own case we obtain valuable information concerning this love relationship. The poem also possesses an important literary significance as an epoch-making contribution to the medieval story of Troy. For by enlarging and enriching the love episode of Troilus and Briseida and by separating it from the war narrative, by which in earlier versions of the Troy story it had been encompassed, Boccaccio virtually created a new story of his own. The poem also possesses an important cultural significance as exemplifying the well-recognized habit of late medieval writers of bringing, in so far as possible, older love stories of whatsoever provenience into conformity with the requirements of the contemporaneous code of Courtly Love. The extent to which the Italian poet has thus transformed his original fable makes of the *Filostrato* an interesting measure of the degree of authority exercised by Courtly Love in literary composition. Finally the poem possesses for students of English literature an important significance as inaugurating one of the most enduring love traditions in English poetry. As we all know, the *Filostrato* served Chaucer as the source of his

masterpiece, the *Troilus and Criseyde*, while Chaucer's poem furnished Shakespeare with the love plot of his play of *Troilus and Cressida*, subsequently imitated by Dryden.

I. Boccaccio and Maria d'Aquino

To the average reader Boccaccio is known only as one of the world's greatest story-tellers, as the author of the *Decameron*. Only the narrower circle of the professed students of humanism know him also as one of the pioneers of the Revival of Learning, as the author of the *De Genealogia Deorum*, of the *De Casibus Virorum Illustrium*, and of the *De Montibus, Silvis, Fontibus, et Lacubus*. Only the still smaller circle of those who have chanced to interest themselves in his biography, know him likewise, as they know Dante and Petrarch, as one of the world's greatest lovers, as the author of a series of romances in which, like his two great Italian contemporaries,[1] he turned his love experiences to literary account.[2]

The *Decameron* was the product of Boccaccio's middle age, when in the plenitude of his powers he gave, for a brief period only, free play to the highest capacities of his genius. In this, his supreme masterpiece, he relentlessly exposed the vices and follies of his age, draw-

[1] Dante was of course less strictly a contemporary of Boccaccio than Petrarch. Boccaccio was born in 1313, forty-eight years after the birth of Dante in 1265 and eight years before his death in 1321, whereas his lifetime almost exactly coincided with that of Petrarch, who was born in 1304, nine years before Boccaccio, and died in 1374, one year before Boccaccio's death in 1375.

[2] That Boccaccio was not unaware of his resemblance to Dante and to Petrarch in this regard is shown by the fact that in his *Sixtieth* and *Ninety-seventh Sonnets* (*Rime*, ed. Moutier, I., *Opere volgari di Giovanni Boccaccio*, Florence, 1827-34, XVI, 76, 95) he represents Fiammetta in Paradise by the side of Beatrice and Laura. See Torraca, F., *Per la biografia di Boccaccio*, Milan, 1912, pp. 82-83.

ing with the complete objectivity of the disinterested spectator incomparable pictures of the cunning artifices of lovers and revealing with the remorseless precision of the scientist the hypocrisies, knaveries, and deceits of the priesthood of an age in which he, like Chaucer, would have us believe that religion often served but as a cloak for folly. Boccaccio's learned treatises on the mythology, tragic histories, and geography of the ancients were the product of his old age, when coming as the result of a terrifying religious experience[1] to a conviction of sin by reason of the licentiousness of his "hundred tales of love," he vowed henceforth to abjure the vanities of vernacular composition and to devote himself, in emulation of the example of his much revered friend Petrarch, exclusively to the production of works of grave dignity and high seriousness. Boccaccio's romances,[2] on the other hand, were the product of his

[1] A Carthusian saint of Siena named Pietro Petroni, being about to die, summoned to his bedside a monk of the same order, one Gioacchimo Ciani, to inform him that he had beheld in a vision that Boccaccio would soon die and suffer eternal punishment unless he should abandon his profane studies and turn to a religious life. At Petroni's instigation Ciani conveyed this intelligence to Boccaccio. The latter, greatly agitated, had serious thoughts of forsaking his studies, selling his books, and destroying whatever he had written in the vernacular. But first he wrote to Petrarch for advice. In his reply Petrarch urged him to think twice before resorting to so desperate a remedy but added, with characteristic sagacity, that if he did indeed decide to sell his books, he would be glad to buy them himself for his own library. See Gaspary, A., *Giornale storico della letteratura italiana*, 1888, XII, 393-394; Graf, A., *Miti, leggende, e superstizioni del medio evo*, Turin, 1892-93, II, 169-195; Gaspary, A., *Storia della letteratura italiana*, Turin, 1900, II, 59-60; Segalla, S., *I sentimenti religiosi del Boccaccio*, Riva, 1909, p. 62; Hutton, E., *Life of Boccaccio*, London, 1909, pp. 198 ff.; Farnam, W., *Publications of the Modern Language Association*, 1924, XXXIX, 125-126.

[2] These romances, six in number, are edited by Ignazio Moutier in his *Opere volgari di Giovanni Boccaccio*, seventeen volumes, Florence, 1827-34, as follows: the *Fiammetta*, vol. VI; the *Filocolo*, vols. VII and VIII (herein referred to as *Filocolo* I and II); the *Teseide*, vol.

ardent and impetuous youth, being written while and
soon after he was, as lover of Maria d'Aquino, experi-
encing in his own person all the raptures and torments
of that passion of which he afterward gives us in the
Decameron such impersonal and dispassionate representations.

The scene of Boccaccio's courtship was the gay and
pleasure-loving city of Naples, *la dilettevole città di
Napoli*, as he never tires of calling it. Amid surround-
ings so well suited to appeal to his keen aesthetic sensi-
bilities, he spent the impressionable period of youth,
devoting to love and to beauty twelve golden years,[1]
the happiest years of a lifetime which shadows were
destined thereafter perpetually to darken.[2] To the

IX; the *Filostrato*, vol. XIII (herein referred to by canto and stanza);
the *Amorosa visione*, vol. XIV; and the *Ameto*, vol. XV.

[1] From 1328, when at the age of fifteen he first arrived in Naples, to
1349, when at the age of twenty-seven he was recalled to Florence by
the failure of his father in business. The date of Boccaccio's arrival in
Naples is determined by the date of his enamorment, since in the
Ameto (p. 153) Caleone, who represents Boccaccio (see p. 9, n. 2), says
that he fell in love with Fiammetta, who represents Maria d'Aquino,
seven years and four months after his arrival in that city. Wilkins,
E. H. (*Modern Philology*, 1913, XI, 54-55), dates the enamorment
March 30, 1336. For the date of his departure, see Della Torre, A., *La
giovinezza di Giovanni Boccaccio*, Città di Castello, 1905, pp. 342-345;
Young, K., "The Origin and Development of the Story of Troilus and
Criseyde," *Chaucer Society*, Second Series, 1908, XLI, 31, and n. 7;
Hutton, *op. cit.*, p. 59.

[2] Never afterward did life remain for Boccaccio what it had been
in those twelve youthful years at Naples. On his return to Florence he
found his father "old, cold, crabbed, and avaricious" and his house
"dark, silent, and forlorn" (see p. 6, n. 1). Henceforth he was obliged
to spend the greater portion of his life in a city "full of ostentatious
words and pusillanimous deeds" (*Fiammetta*, p. 43). Twice afterwards
he returned to Naples—in 1344 and again in 1362—but for short visits
only. On his first return he found the city under the distracted reign of
the unfortunate Joanna much changed from what it had been when
"joyous, peaceful, rich, magnificent, and under the rule of one king"
(*Fiammetta*, p. 43) and on his second visit he found the lady whose
obduracy he had sought so long in vain to overcome, dead, if, as Hutton supposes, she fell victim to the Black Death (see Hutton, *op. cit.*,

charms of Naples, of its delightful environs, especially Baia, he afterward repeatedly reverts in terms of the fondest recollection.[1]

To Naples Boccaccio had been sent at the age of fifteen by his father, Boccaccino, a prosperous Florentine money-lender, to engage in trade, perhaps as apprentice to a merchant.[2] But the youthful Boccaccio finding himself so suddenly placed in an aristocratic environment that presented so marked a contrast to the drab commercialism of his native Florence,[3] experienced an ever

p. 127, and "Some Aspects of the Genius of Giovanni Boccaccio," *Proceedings of the British Academy*, 1922, X, 4). Henceforth there remained nothing further in life for Boccaccio save the cold consolations of authorship.

[1] Thus in the *Fiammetta* (pp. 91-93) he speaks of Baia, of its famous baths, and of its soft languorous atmosphere, which Cupid found particularly favorable to his designs. Here hunting was engaged in and after the fatigue of the chase all manner of musical instruments were called into requisition and young men and maidens sang amorous songs in unison. Again (pp. 106-107) we read of rowing in the bay of Naples to the accompaniment of minstrelsy, of midday banquets spread on tables set on cliffs overlooking the sea, and afterward of outdoor dancing, of gliding along the shore in boats, of ladies' wading in the shallows, their shoes, stockings, and petticoats dispensed with, and searching, with sleeves rolled up, for sea shells, and, as they stooped to gather them, displaying bare bosoms to the wanton gaze of their masculine admirers.

[2] Boccaccio's words, "meque adolescentiam nondum intrantem arismetrica instructum maximo mercatori dedit [pater meus] discipulum" (*De Genealogia Deorum*, lib. XV, cap. 10), clearly refer to a Florentine, not to a Neapolitan, merchant. That in any case Boccaccio engaged in trade after reaching Naples is clear from the words of Idalagos (Boccaccio) in the *Filocolo* (II, 243): "io . . . in questi boschi venni l'apparato uficio a operare" (see p. 9, n. 2).

[3] Florence was not, strictly speaking, the poet's native city, since he was born in Paris, of a French lady whom his father had seduced while upon a business visit in that city. This he tells us through the lips of Idalagos (*Filocolo*, II, 240-242) and of Ibrida (*Ameto*, pp. 79-80) (see p. 9, n. 2). He was early carried to Florence, however, though presumably not by his father (see Hutton, *Life of Boccaccio*, p. 10; Hauvette, H., *Boccace*, Paris, 1914, p. 12), and in the *Prologue* of his *De Fluminibus* (a section of his *De Montibus, etc.*) speaks of the Arno as one of the earliest recollections of his childhood ("Arnus . . . flumen . . . mihi ante alios omnes ab infantia cognitus").

increasing distaste for trade, to which he afterward gives repeated expression in his writings,[1] and an ever growing passion for poetry "with strong aptitudes for which," as he tells us in a memorable autobiographical passage in his *De Genealogia Deorum*,[2] "Nature had drawn him from his mother's womb."[3] Having, as he goes on to say, "wasted six years of irrecoverable time" in a vain attempt to comply with his father's wishes and "as many more" in an equally futile effort to compromise with these wishes by studying for the "lucra-

---

[1] Aversion to trade was with Boccaccio an obsession. Generally he associates this aversion with his father, by whose sordid propensities it was evidently intensified. Thus upon his return to Florence after his father's failure in business, he thus describes his life under the parental roof (*Ameto*, p. 199):

> "Li non si ride se non di rado;
> La casa oscura e muta, e molto trista
> Mi ritiene e riceve mal mio grado;
> Dove la cruda ed orribile vista
> D'un vecchio freddo, ruvido ed avaro
> Ognora con affanno più m'attrista."

Again at a later period he represents his father as the original of the portrait of a man laboriously digging gold nuggets out of a mountain side with his nails (*Amorosa visione*, p. 58).

So inveterate did this loathing for trade become with Boccaccio that he often introduces allusions to it in his romances, sometimes most inappropriately, as when in the *Filostrato* he interrupts his description of the joys of Troilus and Criseida on their first night together by an altogether irrelevant digression upon the infinitely inferior delights of the miser (III, 38-39).

That there was a legitimate basis for Boccaccio's objections to his father's avarice appears to be borne out by the statement of the poet's contemporaneous biographer Filippo Villani in his second (enlarged) *Life of Boccaccio* (*Vita Dantis, Petrarchae, et Boccaccii*, Florence, 1826, p. 69) to the effect that "before he had completed the study of grammar Boccaccio was taken by his father from school and placed at a counting-desk" ("[Boccaccius] dum puer sub Ioanne magistro . . . non plene grammaticam didicisset, exigente, et impellente patre, lucri gratia servire calculis cogeretur, etc.").

[2] Lib. XV, cap. 10.

[3] In token of his lifelong devotion to poetry Boccaccio composed for his tombstone at Certaldo this epitaph: "Studium illi fuit alma poesis." See Hutton, *Life of Boccaccio*, p. 290.

tive" profession of the Canon Law, he determined at length to abandon entirely all occupations that savored of money-getting and to devote himself exclusively to poetry.[1] It was, according to the testimony of Villani,[2] while standing beside the tomb of Virgil[3] that he reached this momentous decision.

But it was while he was still engaged in fruitless efforts to pursue the study of the Canon Law[4] that Boccaccio beheld for the first time the lady who was destined to remain ever afterward the inspiration of his muse and the lodestar of his existence.[5]

[1] For which, during his study of the Canon Law, he had already been preparing himself by forming some preliminary acquaintance with astrology and classical mythology, studies which were at that time looked upon as propaedeutic to poetry. In the acquisition of astrology he was aided by Andalò di Negro, court astrologer to King Robert, whom in the *Filocolo* (II, 243) he describes, under the pastoral appellation *Calmeta*, as a shepherd well versed in the courses of the stars (see Hortis, A., *Studj sulle opere latine del Boccaccio*, Triest, 1879, pp. 516 ff.; Wilkins, E. H., *Modern Language Notes*, 1906, XXI, 212 ff.). Classical mythology he pursued under the encouragement of Paolo Perugino, learned librarian of King Robert, whose valuable collection of excerpts from Greek and Latin authors he tells us in the *De Genealogia Deorum* (XV, 6) he made use of in writing that work (see Hortis, *op. cit.*, pp. 494 ff.; *Giornale storico della letteratura italiana*, 1884, IV, 332-333; Zenatti, O., *Dante e Firenze*, Florence, 1903, p. 275, n. 1; Coulter, C. C., *Philological Quarterly*, 1926, V, 44).

[2] Since Villani (*op. cit.*, pp. 69-70) here represents Boccaccio as deploring only the years he had been forced to devote unwillingly to trade and makes no mention of his study of the Canon Law, it is impossible to determine just when this incident, if authentic, occurred. But since Villani goes on to say that Boccaccio resolved henceforth to devote himself exclusively to poetry, it is not improbable that it took place at or near the end of his legal studies.

[3] Near which, as appears from the subscription "apud busta Maronis Virgilii" of two of his Latin letters (Corazzini, F., *Le lettere edite e inedite di Giovanni Boccaccio*, Florence, 1877, pp. 440, 467), he took up his residence while at Naples.

[4] He refers to this study as occupying his attention at the time that he first met Maria, in the convent at Baia, soon after he first beheld her in the church at Naples (see pp. 14-16).

[5] The second of the two sonnets in which he represents Fiammetta in Paradise (see p. 2, n. 2), viz., the Ninety-seventh, was written in the next to the last year of his life (see Torraca, *op. cit.*, p. 83).

It is not of the beginning, however, but of one of the mid-stages of this courtship that the *Filostrato* gives us record. His lady, as appears from the *Proemio*, has recently left Naples for Sannio, plunging him into the deepest distress because of her departure. To ease his grief he determines to give it utterance in song and to compose "in light rhyme and in [his] Florentine idiom" (see p. 127) a little poem in the hope that he may thereby be able to induce her to "return" and to restore his "life" to its "first self-confidence" (pp. 129-130). To conceal his meaning from the vulgar eye, he has chosen to "relate [his sufferings] in the person of some impassioned one" and has selected "as a mask for [his] secret and amorous grief" the ancient story of the love of Troilus for Criseida, since "to [the] life [of Troilus], in so far as it was filled with sorrow by love and by the distance of his lady . . . after his much beloved Criseida was returned to her father Calchas, [his own], after [her] departure, hath been very similar" (p. 127).

Of his "nobilissima donna," as he styles her in the *Proemio* (p. 114), we know only as much as the poet, in passages intended primarily for her eyes alone, has chanced incidentally to disclose to us. The autobiographical implication of the passages in question is, as we shall see, attested by the constant recurrence in all of a single unvarying refrain of unhappiness in love, of which, at times, the poet makes direct application to his own case. The passages occur in six youthful romances, all written during or shortly after the courtship. These romances are, in the presumable order of their composition, the earlier portion of the *Filocolo*, the *Filostrato*, the *Teseide*, the *Ameto*, and the later portion of the *Filocolo*.[1]

[1] But two of these romances were written while the courtship was in

In no one of the six romances under consideration are Boccaccio's disclosures concerning his lady and his relations to her set forth in a full, clear, or consecutive fashion.[1] Fictitious characters, bearing all manner of fanciful pseudonyms,[2] represent Boccaccio and his lady

progress, viz., the *Filocolo* and the *Filostrato*. At the opening of the *Filocolo* (I, 7) Boccaccio mentions the commission given him by Maria to write that romance (see p. 16) and in the *Proemio* (pp. 117 and 125) states that the composition of the *Filostrato* was occasioned by his distress because of her absence in Sannio. Thus the *Filocolo*, in its earlier portion (see below), and the *Filostrato* synchronize with events which, as we shall see, constitute important landmarks in the courtship. It was not, however, until after his desertion that Boccaccio wrote the remaining four, viz., the *Teseide*, the *Fiammetta*, the *Ameto*, and the *Amorosa visione*. For in the first two of these romances he refers to his desertion (see p. 10, notes 2 and 3). Of these four romances the *Teseide* was apparently written first, because, being, like the *Filostrato*, based upon an ancient epic theme, it dovetails with it. For the order of the last three, see Wilkins, *Modern Philology*, XI, 44-45. To the desertion Boccaccio likewise refers in the *Filocolo* (see p. 21 and n. 5), a romance which, while the first to be begun, was, in all probability, the last to be completed. (See the words of the author in his envoy: "O piccolo mio libretto, a me più anni stato graziosa fatica," II, 376, and Young, *op. cit.*, p. 29 and n. 7.)

[1] To Vincentio Crescini belongs the credit of having been the first to recognize, to assemble, and to interpret these autobiographical allusions. This he has done in his *Contributo agli studi di Giovanni Boccaccio*, Turin, 1887.

[2] The pseudonym most frequently applied by Boccaccio to his lady is *Fiammetta*, meaning "little flame" and selected because of the "little darts of love" that flash from her eyes to his, as said of Lucia in the *Amorosa visione* (p. 63). Fiammetta appears as the queen of the court of love described in the *Filocolo* (II, 33-34), as titular heroine of the *Fiammetta*, and as one of the seven nymphs of the *Ameto* (p. 137).

Other pseudonyms applied by the author to his mistress are *Alleiram*, an anagrammatized form of *Mariella*, a Neapolitan diminutive of *Maria* (see Crescini, *Zeitschrift für rom. Philologie*, 1886, X, 20-21; *Fiammetta: Conferenza letta nella sala di Dante in Orsanmichele: Lectura Dantis*, Florence, 1913, p. 32), in the *Filocolo* (II, 259), and *Emilia*, another one of the seven nymphs of the *Ameto* (p. 70)—a reminiscence, no doubt, of the Emilia of the *Teseide*.

To himself, in like manner, Boccaccio assigns different soubriquets, varying as do those ascribed to his lady. It is *Panfilo* who makes love to Fiammetta in the romance of that name but Caleone in the *Filocolo* (II, 29) and in the *Ameto* (p. 156). Alleiram has as lover *Idalagos* in the *Filocolo* (II, 242) while the Emilia of the *Ameto* (p. 80) is the be-

and in what are ostensibly love confessions of their own, retell one or another of the love experiences of their author or of his inamorata.[1]

In the *Teseide* and in the *Filostrato* the author resorts to the device of selecting a love story that shall in some measure parallel his own, prefixing to each romance a dedicatory letter explaining the nature and the extent of the parallelism.[2] The *Fiammetta* promises, to be sure, in so far as wealth of detail is concerned, something of the satisfaction to be derived from formal autobiography. But in it *Dichtung* so largely replaces *Wahrheit* that it is only by reference to the other romances that we are enabled to determine to what extent it is autobiographical.[3] But it is in the other three ro-

loved of *Ibrida*, so named to indicate Boccaccio's hybrid origin, as the son of an Italian father and of a French mother (see p. 5, n. 3 and Crescini, *Fiammetta*, p. 12).

To this list of pseudonyms may, of course, be added, if we bear in mind that the identifications are but partial, *Criseida* for Maria and *Troilus* for Boccaccio in the *Filostrato*, and *Emilia* for Maria and *Arcita* for Boccaccio in the *Teseide*.

[1] This covert style of self-revelation occurs most frequently in the *Filocolo*, which, as we have seen (p. 8, n. 1), spans the entire period of the courtship. It is indeed, as Crescini has said (*Fiammetta*, pp. 9-10), possible to separate this romance into two shells, an outer and an inner shell. To the former of these Boccaccio has committed his prolonged and largely impersonal story of the adventures of Florio and Biancofiore while to the latter he has entrusted the secret and intimate history of his relations to his lady. But, as Crescini goes on to explain, what is true on a large scale in the case of the prolix *Filocolo* is also true on a smaller scale and to a greater or lesser extent in all the others.

[2] In the dedicatory letter prefixed to the *Teseide*, entitled *Lettera a Fiammetta*, Boccaccio explains to his lady (*Teseide*, p. 4) that by Emilia, the heroine of the poem, she is intended and by her unsuccessful suitor Arcita, himself, the inference, which she is discreetly left to draw, being that the successful suitor Palemone represents a rival lover who has already supplanted him in her affections.

[3] For in the *Fiammetta* Boccaccio takes an ungallant revenge upon Maria for having proved faithless to him by reversing the rôle which each has played in real life, representing her, under the soubriquet *Fiammetta*, as pining at home in Naples while he, the gay young Lothario, significantly named Panfilo, goes joyfully forth in search of fresh conquests in Florence.

mances, viz., the *Filocolo*, the *Ameto*, and the *Amorosa visione*, that Boccaccio has displayed the maximum degree of ingenuity in concealing from all save the initiate among his readers the full truth concerning his relations to his mistress. In the allegorical *Amorosa visione*, without, as a rule,[1] naming them, he allows various adumbrations of Maria to flit gracefully in and out among the several feminine figures, faintly drawn from the life of Florence, which, whether they be represented in portraiture or in the flesh, constitute so large a portion of the machinery of that fantastic poem. Even more carefully guarded are the poet's disclosures regarding his relations to his lady in the *Filocolo* and in the *Ameto*. In these romances his self-revelations frequently assume the form of brief narratives of the entire lives of himself or his lady up to and including the courtship, inserted at irregular intervals in stories which present, for the most part, no analogue to the experiences of either of them. Only by such tortuous and cryptic contrivances is it that in these two romances Boccaccio has seen fit to convey to his mistress—who alone was in a position to realize their full significance—a confidential record, as he saw them, of his relations to her and of hers to him.

By a comparison and a combination of what, in one form or another, Boccaccio has, in the course of his confidences to his lady in one or another of the six romances under consideration, incidentally divulged to the world at large, we obtain the following facts with regard to

---

[1] Twice only does Maria receive a name. Once, when introduced as one of the figures in a fresco of the Triumph of Love, she is called "Lucia" (p. 63) and again, when encountered by the poet in a beautiful garden, we are given to understand, though only in an elaborately periphrastic fashion, that her name is *Maria* (p. 175). See p. 12, n. 1.

her identity and career and with regard to the poet's relations to her.

Boccaccio's mistress was named Maria d'Aquino.[1] She was daughter to the Countess of Aquino,[2] in all probability by Robert, King of Naples and the Two Sicilies.[3] Not long after her birth the countess died and the count, whose death followed soon after, placed her

[1] In the *Filocolo* (I, 4), Boccaccio tells us that the lady with whom he fell in love bore the name of "her who held within herself the redeemer of the wretched loss which happened in consequence of the bold taste of the first mother" and, again, through the lips of Caleone (II, 30), makes, in a similar periphrastic fashion, the same assertion. Moreover it is to "madama Maria" that he dedicates his *Amorosa visione* (p. 1), in an elaborate acrostic, separately printed by Moutier immediately before the opening of his text of that poem (pp. 1-4).

Again in the *Amorosa visione* (p. 174) the author informs us that the lady he meets in a beautiful garden, whom (p. 175) he names, in the same periphrastic manner, Maria, belonged to the family of St. Thomas Aquinas ("del Campagnin") (see Antona-Traversi, C., *Studj di filologia romanza*, 1885, I, 438, n. 5; Crescini, *Contributo*, pp. 124-125). Crescini (*Fiammetta*, p. 21), remarks that Boccaccio would here have us believe that, "while carried to an extreme degree in the case of St. Thomas, holiness was not a habitual characteristic of that most noble house." That, however, the connection of Maria with the family of Aquino was, in all probability, only a connection by adoption, we shall see in what follows (p. 12, n. 3).

[2] The Countess of Aquino was by birth a Provençal lady, Sibilla Sabran by name, and was married to Tommaso IV of Aquino (see Antona-Traversi, *op. cit.*, p. 439, n. 2 and Bartoli, A., "Il Boccaccio," *Vita italiana nel trecento*, Milan, 1895, p. 271).

[3] We are informed by Fiammetta in the *Ameto* (p. 143) that on the occasion of a great festival, held a short time before his coronation, her mother drew from the king amorous glances, which afterward led to her seduction. Later, to be sure, Fiammetta adds (p. 144) that her mother informed her in childhood that she had been living with her husband at the time of her seduction by the king and was consequently in doubt as to which of the two was her daughter's father. Elsewhere, however, both when speaking through the person of Caleone in the *Filocolo* (II, 30) and in his own person (*ibid.*, p. 4), Boccaccio declares explicitly that she was daughter to the king. Moreover from the latter passage we learn that the countess "dwelt at the royal palace," presumably with her husband, who, according to Fiammetta (*Ameto*, p. 143), held "a high post" at court, as member of a family occupying "the highest position next the throne" of the king. At the same time Boccaccio tells us (*Filocolo*, I, 4) that the king, having in mind his

[12]

in a convent at Baia where he had relatives.[1] When she had grown up, her extreme beauty attracted the attention of an Italian nobleman and friend to King Robert, who sought her hand in marriage, but to her this union was distasteful and she was brought to consent to it only through the insistence of the king and then only on condition that she be granted the privilege of resuming her life in the convent, if so minded.[2] That she went back, not "to tend the sacred fires of Vesta," but to use the convent as a place of assignation, though not expressly stated, can be easily inferred from the fact that it was here that Boccaccio first became acquainted with her (see p. 16).

As to the personality of Maria we are left much in the dark. It seems likely, however, that she possessed beauty and a strong liking for tales of an amatory com-

own honor and that of her mother, gave her the name of her "adoptive" father, i.e., of the Count of Aquino.

The date of the festival at which the king fell in love with the countess is obviously of importance because upon it will depend the age of Maria. This festival is identified by Della Torre (*op. cit.*, p. 183) with one held in May or June, 1313, "probably in connection with the closing of Robert's first parliament." But since Robert was crowned at Avignon on September 4, 1310 (Della Torre, p. 182), the festival proposed by that critic must have followed the coronation. As we have already seen, however (p. 12, n. 3), Fiammetta expressly states that the festival in question preceded the coronation and this assertion is supported by a second statement, made by the author in his own person (*Filocolo*, I, 4), to the effect that Maria was "begotten" by the king before his ascent to the throne. Since the coronation occurred on September 4, 1310, Maria could not have been born later than the spring of 1311, which would make her two years older than Boccaccio.

[1] As told by Fiammetta in the *Ameto* (p. 144). The name of the convent in which she was placed by her putative father Fiammetta does not state. But that it was the Benedictine convent of S. Michele at Baia is clear from the fact that it was "in un santo tempio del principe de' celestiali uccelli nominato" that Boccaccio tells us that he first met her (*Filocolo*, I, 6). Concerning this convent, see Casetti, A. C., *Nuova antologia di scienze, lettere ed arti*, 1875, XXVIII, 575; d'Aloe, S., *Archivio storico per le province napolitane*, 1883, VIII, 132-133.

[2] *Ameto*, p. 146.

plexion.[1] That she was voluptuous does not admit of a doubt.[2]

Boccaccio first beheld Maria[3] on a Holy Saturday[4] in

[1] To her beauty Boccaccio pays tribute on numerous occasions. In the *Filocolo* (I, 4) we read that "as she grew up . . . she waxed so beautiful . . . that she was judged the daughter, not of man, but of God"; in the *Filostrato* (I, 27) Criseida is "tall and well proportioned"; and in the *Amorosa visione* (p. 63) Lucia has "two beautiful eyes which sparkle so that each seems to be a radiant little flame of love."

Of her interest in amatory literature he likewise often speaks. In his *Lettera a Fiammetta* (*Teseide*, p. 3), he reminds her that in the happy days now past he found her "desirous to hear and sometimes to read this story or that, particularly those that pertained to love." It was she who, because of her interest in the pitiful loves of Florio and Biancofiore, commissioned the poet to write his first romance, the *Filocolo* (*Filocolo*, I, 7). To her, moreover, he dedicated not only the *Filocolo* but also the *Filostrato*, the *Teseide*, and the *Amorosa visione*.

[2] Not only did Maria turn from her husband to accept the love of Boccaccio but she passed, as it seems (see p. 21 and n. 4), from Boccaccio onward to another lover later. It was probably not without warrant that, as Cook, A. S., has observed (*Publications of the Modern Language Association*, 1907, XXII, 537 and n. 1, 538 and n. 2, and 547), Boccaccio allows Fiammetta to make (*Fiammetta*, p. 54) a reference to Ovid and what is apparently a quotation from the *Remedia Amoris* (vv. 139-168) and places in her mouth (*Filocolo*, II, 79; *Fiammetta*, pp. 84, 139) sentiments concerning free love that remind one of the *Ars Amatoria* (III, 583-586) and of the discourse of the duenna in the *Roman de la rose* (vv. 14098 ff., 14208 ff.), although there seems to be little justification for the conclusion that he draws therefrom (pp. 538, 547) to the effect that Maria had herself read both Ovid and the French romance. Equally indicative of the character of Maria, as he likewise observes, are the indulgent theories of love cherished by Criseida in the *Filostrato* (II, 69-78).

[3] His first sight of his lady and almost simultaneous enamorment are most elaborately described by Boccaccio in almost identical language in five different passages in as many romances, viz., the *Filocolo* (I, 4-6), the *Filostrato* (I, 17-30), the *Fiammetta* (pp. 7-12), the *Ameto* (pp. 153-155), and the *Amorosa visione* (pp. 178-179). Of these the passages in the *Filocolo* and in the *Ameto* agree closely, the latter evidently having been modeled upon the former. See Wilkins, E. H., "The Enamorment of Boccaccio," *Modern Philology*, 1913, XI, 39 ff.

[4] As stated both in the *Filocolo* (p. 4) and in the *Ameto* (p. 153). In the *Ameto* (p. 154) Caleone returns to the church on the next day (Easter Sunday) and again beholds Fiammetta. In the *Fiammetta* it is the second visit only that is described.

the church of St. Lorenzo at Naples,[1] whither he had repaired, not for purposes of devotion, but to gaze, in compliance with a custom of the day, at the beautiful ladies, who, in their turn, resorted thither to be seen of men.[2] She is clad in black in token of the penitential season.[3] As he admires her beauty he experiences a per-

[1] Strikingly similar are Boccaccio's description of the circumstances under which he first beheld Maria and the description given by Petrarch in his *Third Sonnet* (*Il canzoniere di Francesco Petrarcha*, ed. Scherillo, M., Milan, 1925, parte prima, III, p. 115), of the circumstances attending his first sight of Laura. Just as it was on a Holy Saturday at the church of St. Lorenzo at Naples that Boccaccio first saw Maria, even so it was on a Good Friday at the church of St. Claire at Avignon that Petrarch first beheld Laura. See Mestica, G., "Il più giovanile sonetti del Petrarcha ed il suo primo innamoramento," *Fanfulla della domenica*, XXI, May 20, 1888.

[2] This is clear from the version of the enamorment given in the *Fiammetta*. This Boccaccio opens by describing (pp. 8-9), at considerable length and in terms that suggest that he has in mind a Neapolitan custom of the day, how a "crown" of admirers encircled each beautiful lady while at her prayers. In much the same fashion in the *Filostrato* (I, 20) Troilus makes, though in jest, pointed remarks concerning the Trojan ladies attending the sacrifices in honor of Pallas. The resort of young people of opposite sexes to religious ceremonies for the purpose of gazing upon one another, in itself and apart from the formation of the "crown" described by Boccaccio, was of course a custom by no means limited to Naples. It was in a church at Florence that Dante obtained one of his most memorable sights of Beatrice (*Vita nuova*, ed. Fraticelli, P., Florence, 1906, section V, pp. 56-57), and in a church at Avignon that Petrarch gained his first sight of Laura (see p. 15, n. 1). For interesting examples, beyond that in the *Filostrato*, of the anachronistic representation in medieval literature of a religious ceremonial as the occasion of the first sight had by lovers of their ladies, see Benoit de Ste. Maure, *Roman de Troie* (ed. Constans, L., *Société des anciens textes français*, Paris, 1904-1912), in which Paris first espies Helen at a festival in the temple of Venus at Cythera (vv. 4257-4372) and Achilles, Polyxena at the anniversary commemoration of the death of Hector (vv. 17489-17637), cited by Wilkins (*Modern Philology*, XI, 45).

[3] *Filostrato* (I, 26-27); *Ameto* (p. 154). In the *Ameto* Fiammetta is clad in black ("di bruna vesta coperta") on Holy Saturday, as appropriate to the penitential season, but when she returns on the next day (see p. 14, n. 4) she is appareled "in the finest green" ("di finissimo verde vestita"), as becomes the joyous Eastertide. Though, very natu-

vasive tremor of the limbs. At length a fiery shaft of gold leaps from her eyes to his and passes thence to his heart.[1] A short time ("più giorni") afterward, when on a visit with a friend to the Benedictine convent of S. Michele at Baia, he meets her for the first time in the convent parlor[2] and there receives from her a commission to retell in courtly style the rude tale of the pitiful loves of Florio and Biancofiore, which hitherto had circulated only on the lips of the ignorant.[3] The result of this commission was the composition of the *Filocolo*.[4]

At a considerable time after this meeting—how long we cannot say, though before the end of the spring[5]—

rally, no allusion is made to the day of the week in the *Filostrato*, Criseida is also dressed in black (I, 26, 7):

"Sotto candido velo in bruna vesta."

[1] *Filocolo*, I, 6; *Fiammetta*, p. 10. In the *Fiammetta*, because of the reversed relations between the lovers (see p. 10, n. 3), the shaft leaps in the opposite direction, from his eyes to hers.

[2] Although not so stated in the text, it was, according to Hutton (*Life of Boccaccio*, p. 32) and Ettore de Ferri ("Il Filocolo," *Collezione di classici italiani*, two vols., Turin, 1921-22, Introduzione, p. xi), in the parlor of the convent that he met her.

[3] *Filocolo*, I, 7.

[4] The *Filocolo* was so named because at the point of the story at which Florio undertakes his expedition in search of the missing Biancofiore, he assumes a new name, *Filocolo*, in token that he has now embarked upon a "labor of love." The name *Filocolo* is therefore, like *Filostrato*, a significant coinage of the author's own, being compounded, as he himself tells us (*Filocolo*, I, 354), of the Greek words "philos" ("love") and "colos" ("labor"). Κόλος (properly χόλος), means "anger," however, and was misused by Boccaccio for κόπος, which means "labor." Κόπος appears as an editorial correction in a few early editions bearing the etymologically correct title *Filocopo*. See Sorio, B., *Atti dell' I. R. Istituto Venuto di scienze, ecc.*, terza serie, 1861-62, VII, parte I, 604-605; 1864-65, X, parte I, 665; Gaspary, A., *Zeitschrift für rom. Philologie*, 1879, III, 395-396; Crescini, V., *Il cantare di Fiorio e Biancofiore*, Bologna, 1889, I, 355-366; Crane, T. F., *Italian Social Customs in the Sixteenth Century*, New Haven, 1920, p. 57, n. 6; Ettore de Ferri, *op. cit.*, Introduzione, pp. xi-xiv.

[5] Boccaccio says in the *Proemio* (pp. 117-118) that it was in the

occurred the event alluded to in the *Proemio* of the *Filostrato*. With a view possibly to testing the constancy of her lover's affections, Maria withdrew from Naples to Sannio, where was located the estate of her "adoptive" father, the Count of Aquino.[1] Her absence was, as we have seen, the immediate occasion of the composition of the *Filostrato* and there is every reason to believe that the poem was written rapidly and finished within a few months, quite clearly before her return to Naples.[2]

spring of the year ("nella più graziosa stagione dell'anno") that Maria left Naples for Sannio. The temple scene is dated by Wilkins (*op. cit.*, pp. 54-55) March 30, 1336. Young, who accepts this dating, places the composition of the *Filostrato* "perhaps in the summer of 1338" (*op. cit.*, p. 31, n. 10). This, for the reason just stated, would place the visit to Sannio in the spring of 1338, or approximately two years after the enamorment. It is, however, impossible to suppose with Young, that two years had gone by. For a letter in which Boccaccio announces to his friend Carlo, Duke of Durazzo, reverses in love (Corazzini, *ed. cit.*, pp. 439-440), is dated April 3, 1339. The dating of the visit to Sannio in the spring of 1338 would allow of but one year's interval at most between the visit to Sannio and the conclusion of the love affair. But this interval is too short. Time enough must have elapsed to allow Maria to return to Naples, to accept Boccaccio as suitor, to yield to him the final favors, and to live with him on terms of intimacy during a considerable interval of time before the separation. For Hutton has shown (*Life of Boccaccio*, pp. 39-40) that Boccaccio became the accepted suitor of Maria during the first of "three bathing seasons" at Baia, during the last of which occurred the betrayal (see p. 21, n. 2). The visit to Sannio must therefore have taken place later in the spring of 1336, shortly before he became her accepted suitor. The composition of the *Filostrato* may therefore be assigned with confidence to the year 1336.

[1] See Crescini, *Contributo*, p. 186, n. 4.

[2] No other romance of Boccaccio is so intimately and directly connected with any other stage of his courtship as is the *Filostrato* with the absence of his lady in Sannio. Upon the disastrous effects of this absence upon the mind of the poet and upon his purpose to give expression thereto in the *Filostrato*, the *Proemio* dwells throughout and exclusively. Nor is the promise given in the *Proemio* left unfulfilled in the poem that follows. The anguish that fills the breast of a lover bereaved of his mistress forms the *Leitmotif* of the entire poem. If in the first three cantos we are given a picture of the happy life of Troilus before the separation, it is only, as the author explains in the *Proemio*,

Subsequent to the visit to Sannio—and therefore to the composition of the *Filostrato*, Boccaccio obtained from Maria the final favors. Afterward he was deserted by her for another lover.

By a strange irony of fate both these events—the toward as well as the untoward—are, as it were, prophetically foreshadowed in the story of the *Filostrato*. For before her departure to the Greek camp Criseida granted to Troilus full possession of her person (III, 31) and after her departure abandoned him for Diomede (VI, 34). That he was destined in both these respects to follow in the footsteps of his protagonist Boccaccio could, however, at the time of writing the *Filostrato*, have had no foreknowledge. Both lay as yet hidden in the womb of time.

This is quite evident from the way in which in the *Proemio* the Italian poet undertakes to deal with occurrences in the career of his hero which, though for opposite reasons in the two cases, could not have failed to prove embarrassing to a lover anxious to obtain the good fortune of Troilus in winning full possession of his lady and to avoid his bad fortune in losing her to another.

To guard himself against the possible ill consequences of what his lady might construe as an act of presumption on his part in daring to present before her eyes an account of Troilus' success in winning full possession of Criseida, Boccaccio takes pains to assure her that he has recorded this portion of "his happy life . . . not because [he] desires that anyone should believe that

that we may, by contrast, be made the more acutely conscious of the "sorrow that followeth after." In the harmony of tone that springs from singleness of inspiration no other romance of Boccaccio equals the *Filostrato*. See Crescini, V., *Kritischer Jahresbericht über die Fortschritte der rom. Philologie*, 1897, Band III, Heft II, 384 ff.

[he] can glory in a like felicity . . . but . . . because when happiness hath been seen by anyone, much better is understood how great and of what nature is the misery that followeth after" (*Proemio*, pp. 127).[1] To protect himself, on the other hand, against the danger of arousing the resentment of his lady by seeming to imply that she could ever be so heartless as to treat him in the cruel manner in which Criseida treated Troilus, he requests that she apply to herself only those portions of the story in which "good looks, good manners, or other thing praiseworthy in a lady" are "said of Criseida," assuring her that he has retained the unfortunate remainder only "because the story of the noble young lover requireth it" (*Proemio*, p. 129).[2]

[1] It is at first sight tempting to suppose that at the time of writing his *Filostrato* Boccaccio had already won the last favors from Maria and that in the *Proemio* he was merely attempting to protect her reputation by concealing the truth under cover of courtly phrase. This is indeed the opinion of Novati, F. (*Istoria di Patroclo e di Insidorio*, Turin, 1888, Introduzione, p. xl, n. 1). But against such a supposition stands the following insuperable argument, advanced by Crescini (*Kritischer Jahresbericht, sup. cit.*, pp. 384 ff.), and repeated by Young (*op. cit.*, p. 30). In a number of other romances (see p. 20, n. 1), Boccaccio gives accounts of the surrender of a lady to her lover which, while agreeing substantially among themselves, differ essentially from the account given in the *Filostrato* of the surrender of Criseida to Troilus. Two of them, furthermore, are put into the mouths of Fiammetta and Caleone, respectively, and must be allowed the weight that attaches to the testimony of characters who are, as we have seen (p. 9, n. 2), fictitious embodiments of Maria and Boccaccio. Hence there can be no doubt that these later accounts are autobiographical and that the account given in the *Filostrato* is not. The chief point of difference between the two accounts is that in the former the lady is surprised in bed by a nocturnal visitor to whom she is at first indisposed to surrender, whereas in the *Filostrato* the surrender of Criseida to Troilus is carefully prearranged and she yields to him willingly.

[2] There appears good reason to suppose, however, that in this apparently innocent disclaimer of responsibility Boccaccio was less ingenuous than would appear on the surface. It is quite likely that he knew only too well the character of the lady with whom he was dealing and that in selecting the Trojan story as the basis of his *Filostrato* he was by no means unmindful of the opportunity it afforded him of

On an occasion somewhat later than the visit to Sannio—presumably about three months later—Boccaccio obtained complete possession of Maria by means of a nocturnal surprise. Of this nocturnal visit he has given us four separate accounts in four different romances.[1]

One night in the autumn[2] he went to her house in Baia,[3] while her husband was absent in Capua,[4] and surreptitiously wrested from her complete satisfaction of his desires,[5] though not, we may suppose, without

holding the dereliction of Criseida up before the eyes of Maria as an awful example of the havoc wrought by one who proved faithless to her vows of constancy.

[1] In the *Filocolo* (II, 167-183), the *Fiammetta* (p. 79), the *Ameto* (pp. 146, 156), and the *Amorosa visione* (p. 198).

In the *Filocolo* the account of the nocturnal surprise is made a part of the main narrative. Here it is the hero Florio who surprises the heroine Biancofiore in her bed, behind the curtain of which he has, before her entrance to the chamber, been concealed by her nurse Glorizia. The applicability of this account to Boccaccio is of course dependent upon the occurrence of similar accounts in the autobiographical *Fiammetta* and in autobiographical passages in the *Ameto* and in the *Amorosa visione*. Thus in the *Ameto* it is Fiammetta who tells of her surprise by Caleone (see p. 9, n. 2), and in the *Amorosa visione* Boccaccio, speaking, as always there, in his own person as dreamer, is, as is evident from an earlier identification (see p. 12, n. 1), relating, without naming her, experiences he had had with Maria.

[2] In the *Ameto* (p. 146) Fiammetta declares that she was visited by Caleone when the sun was in Scorpio ("temporante Apollo i veleni freddi di scorpione"). Since the sun entered Scorpio on October 17 and left it on November 14 (see Hutton, *Life of Boccaccio*, p. 36 and n. 3), the night of the seduction must have fallen between those two dates.

[3] That Maria was living with her husband at Baia seems to be borne out by the fact that Boccaccio frequently addresses her there in his sonnets (see Hutton, p. 39 and n. 1, p. 49 and n. 1).

[4] As stated by Fiammetta in the *Ameto* (p. 146).

[5] One can with difficulty avoid the conclusion that in choosing a nocturnal surprise as a means of overcoming the reluctance of Maria, Boccaccio was consciously impelled by a desire to conform to literary, if not perhaps also to social conventions of his day. In the love romances of the Middle Ages the nocturnal surprise is a device often resorted to by the lover to gain access to his lady. See the long list of examples given by Young, *op. cit.*, p. 151.

first having reason to believe that his advances would not be resented.[1]

After apparently something less than two years of living on intimate terms with Maria—or in the summer of 1338[2]—Boccaccio was deserted by her apparently for another lover.[3] It is chiefly to two episodes in the *Filocolo*[4] that Boccaccio has committed the story of the

[1] For in the *Amorosa visione* (p. 185) Boccaccio says that for one hundred and thirty-five days before the nocturnal surprise he had lived as her accepted suitor ("sotto la dolce signoria di questa [donna]"). Thus Boccaccio must have become accepted by Maria as suitor on some day between June 3 and July 1 (cf. p. 20, n. 2), or not long after her return from Sannio. See Hutton, *Life of Boccaccio*, pp. 35-40.

[2] The desertion took place before April 3, 1339, since in his letter of that date to the Duke of Durazzo (see p. 16, n. 5) Boccaccio complains bitterly of reverses in love. That it probably occurred early in the summer of 1338, or approximately two years after he had become accepted by Maria as suitor, appears from a letter of his to a fellow law student, opening "Sacrae famis," of date June 28, 1338 (Corazzini, *ed. cit.*, pp. 457-467), in which he writes how, after listening to compulsory lectures upon the "Decretals," he went home at night sick at heart to plunge into books in order that "by reading of the woes of others he might forget his own." The same period is indicated by his *Thirty-third Sonnet*, cited by Hutton (p. 39 and n. 2), in which he declares that Maria has forbidden him to follow her to Baia for the bathing season and has since betrayed him. A like conclusion is to be derived from his *Forty-seventh* and *Forty-eighth Sonnets*, cited by Della Torre (*op. cit.*, p. 207), in which he speaks of spending blissful hours with her at Capo Miseno and which both Della Torre and Hutton (p. 39) interpret to signify that there intervened between the summer in which he became her accepted lover and that at the opening of which she forbade him to accompany her to Baia, an entire bathing season of unalloyed happiness.

[3] Who this other lover was, we have no means of determining. But that some other admirer was the cause of the separation seems to be proved beyond any reasonable doubt by the words of the poet himself. Thus in the *Lettera a Fiammetta* he speaks of himself as thinking of "past joys in [present] miseries" (*Teseide*, p. 1), calls his "nobilissima donna" (*ibid.*, p. 6) "crudel donna" (*ibid.*, p. 1), and identifies himself with Arcita, the unsuccessful lover of Emilia (*ibid.*, p. 4). Again in the envoy of the *Filocolo* (II, 377) he expresses the hope that the perusal of that romance may "strengthen [his lady] to be satisfied with a single lover."

[4] Those of Idalagos (II, 238-254) and Caleone (II, 274-276). It is

desertion, particularly to the long and important episode of Idalagos.[1]

A question of commanding interest in connection with Boccaccio's courtship of Maria is this: how did it come to pass that he, a stranger in the city of Naples, the thriftless son of a Florentine money-lender, should ever have dared to aspire so high as to seek the love of one whom he believed to be a princess of the royal blood?

Attempts have been made to explain this seemingly extraordinary occurrence on the theory that Boccaccio had been presented at court either by his father or by one of his father's business associates.[2]

not unlikely that the stories of disappointment in love told respectively by the nameless youth whom Fileno meets after his flight from Montorio (I, 300-302) (see Young, *op. cit.*, pp. 102-103) and by Clonico, as his contribution to the "questioni d'amore" (II, 67-71) (Young, p. 44), may likewise possess autobiographical significance (see, in respect to the latter, p. 42, n. 2).

[1] The episode of Idalagos and of his desertion by Alleiram (*Filocolo*, II, 238-254) is by far the most elaborate of all the episodes inserted by Boccaccio in his romances to recall to the mind of his lady one or more of the incidents of the courtship. The story of the episode, which, needless to say, is lacking in all the earlier versions of the story of Floire and Blanchefleur (see p. 40, n. 1), is briefly this.

After rescuing Biancofiore, Filocolo, as he now calls himself (see p. 16, n. 4), on his return homeward through Naples, goes forth one day into a wood to hunt and there shoots by mistake an arrow into the bark of a tree. The tree, which was once a man, Idalagos by name, begins Polydorus-like, to speak and to the inquiring Filocolo relates the entire past history of his life, including in particular the misfortunes in love which, through the pitying intervention of Venus, have been the occasion of his transformation into his present shape. In the course of his disclosures he speaks in pastoral imagery, of a hen-pheasant ("fagiana") which so delighted him with the brilliancy of her plumage that he gave chase (II, 247) and which, later in the story, after the pastoral imagery has been discarded, turns out to be the heartless lady Alleiram (II, 259), who, because of her cruelty to him, has been transformed into a stone. As already explained (p. 9, n. 2), Idalagos represents Boccaccio and the flint-hearted lady Alleiram who deserts him, Maria. See Crescini, *Zeitschrift für rom. Philologie*, 1885, IX, 437-479; 1886, X, 1-21.

[2] Hutton (*Life of Boccaccio*, p. 5 and n. 1, p. 21) and Ettore de

But it was not, as we have seen, at court that Boccaccio first beheld Maria d'Aquino or that he first met her. When once the two had met, it may well be surmised that each was drawn to the other by their common interest in literature of an amatory character and, if we accept the royal parentage of Maria, by the strange coincidence that both were the illegitimate children of Italian fathers and French mothers (see p. 5, n. 3). Furthermore in an age when Courtly Love held sway and in a country where even so late as in the time of Byron it was customary "to serve the wife of another,"[1] what could be more natural than that a lady

Ferri (*op. cit.*, Introduzione, p. viii) conjecture that Boccaccio may have been introduced at court by his father after the latter came to Naples in 1327 to transact business with King Robert. Color is, in the opinion of Hutton (p. 21, n. 3), lent to this conjecture by the poet's own words in his *De Casibus* (lib. IX, cap. 26): "me adhuc adulescentulo versanteque Roberti . . . regis in aula." If Boccaccino was still in Naples at the end of 1338, the probable date of his son's arrival there (see p. 4, n. 1), there might perhaps, if such was the custom of the times, be no difficulty in supposing that Boccaccio was thus introduced. The words "adhuc adulescentulo" might, however, refer to some year later than 1338, since *adulescentia* began at the age of fourteen (Hutton, p. 21, n. 3) and lasted seven years (Hutton, p. 320). In harmony with this latter possibility is the suggestion of Symonds, J. A. (*Boccaccio as Man and Author*, London, 1894, p. 24), that Boccaccio may have been introduced by his father's business associate, the Florentine banker Niccolò Acciaiuoli. But since, according to Symonds (p. 27), Acciaiuoli did not arrive in Naples until 1331 and since we must allow for the passage of sufficient time to permit him to make his own acquaintance at court, we should, in this case, be obliged to postpone Boccaccio's introduction to a late date. In general it seems hardly probable that the youthful Boccaccio received, at any rate from a father anxious to have him succeed in the career of a merchant, any such formal presentation at court as the above mentioned critics conjecture. Nor need the poet's own words in the *De Casibus* imply more than that in the course of time he formed such friendships and associations at court as his known acquaintance with Andalò di Negro and Paolo Perugino might readily bring in its train.

[1] A phrase used by Lord Byron in a letter of June 29, 1819, from Ravenna to his publisher Murray to describe other relations in that city similar to his own with the Countess Guicciolli. See George

dissatisfied with her husband should have accorded to a youthful admirer with whom she had much in common, privileges which eventually culminated in the nocturnal visit to Baia? Nor is it indeed beyond the bounds of possibility that, as Gaspary intimates,[1] neither Boccaccio nor his lady were wholly unmoved by literary and historical precedent and that the Italian poet was encouraged to hope that a lady so far above him in social station might be led to comply with his wishes from a perception of the piquant parallelism between the relations in which he stood to her and those which the troubadour of old sustained to the lady of his affections. For, like the troubadour of old, Boccaccio was single while his lady was married, stood beneath her in social rank, came as a stranger from afar to court her, and depended for success upon his skill in song.

II. THE COMPOSITION OF THE FILOSTRATO

"The ancient story" to which Boccaccio refers in the *Proemio* (p. 127) and again in the *Filostrato* (I, 46; III, 90) as supplying him with the subject matter of his poem, is the elaborate version of the story of Troy found in the *Roman de Troie*[2] of the French trouvère

Gordon Byron's *Works: with his Letters and Journals and his Life* by Thomas Moore, seventeen vols., London, 1837-40, IV, 170, no. 333. Cf. the Courtly Love terms (Fr.) *chevalier servant*, (Ital.) *cavaliere serviente*, and (Eng.) *servant of love*, as used by Chaucer for example (*Troilus and Criseyde*, ed. Root, R. K., Princeton, 1926, book I, verse 15).

[1] *Storia della letteratura italiana*, II, 3.

[2] Edited by Joly, A. (two vols., Paris, 1870-71), and, critically, by Constans, *ed. cit.* All citations are made from the latter edition. The earlier portion of the *Roman de Troie* is based upon the *De Excidio Trojae Historia* of Dares Phrygius and the later portion upon the *Ephemeris de Bello Trojano* of Dictys Cretensis. At v. 24397 Benoit introduces the reader to Dictys and from this point forward follows this second author, with, however, occasional reversions to Dares (see Constans, *ed. cit.*, VI, 192).

Benoit de Ste. Maure[1] and in the *Historia Trojana* of his Latin translator, the Sicilian judge Guido delle Colonne.[2] To both of these works Boccaccio had recourse, though he mentions the author of neither of them by name.[3]

[1] Nothing is known of Benoit save his name, Benoit de Ste. Maure, which he gives in v. 132 of his poem. Constans believes that Benoit was born in the Ste. Maure near Poitiers, not in that near Troyes, and conjectures that the *Roman de Troie* was composed between 1155 and 1160 (*ed. cit.*, VI, 190).

[2] Guido made his translation, as stated in the colophon of the *Historia Trojana* (Strassburg 1486 edition), in 1287.

[3] In designating his immediate source by means of the general term "the ancient story," instead of naming specific authors, Boccaccio conforms to the usual medieval practice. Thus English redactors of the Troy story, while naming their ultimate sources, Dares and Dictys, with scrupulous care, generally refrain from naming their proximate sources, Benoit and Guido, save under such vague denominations as "as in the French" or "as in the Latin it is," "as the romance says," etc. Thus in the *Seege or Batayle of Troye* (ed. Wager, C. H. A., Macmillan, 1899, Introduction, p. xliii), we read in the Harleian version (v. 1522),

"Soo it is in Frenshe fownde"

and in the Lincoln's Inn version (v. 197),

"Þeo romaunce me doþ to vndurstande";

and in the *Laud Troy Book* (ed. Wülfing, J. E., *Early English Text Society*, Original Series, 1902, CXXI, v. 548),

"As the romaunce the sothe telles"

and (v. 3261),

"For I ffynde in prose and ryme";

and in Lydgate's *Troy Book* (ed. Bergen, H., *E.E.T.S.*, Extra Series, 1906, XCVII, *Prologue*, v. 115),

"As in latyn and in frensche it is."

It was perhaps from an instinctive obedience to this convention that Chaucer in his *Troilus and Criseyde*, while careful to name (I, 146) his remote sources, Dares and Dictys—with the first of whom, as Root has pointed out (*Modern Philology*, 1916, XV, 4), he adopts an earlier scribal blunder of identifying one of his immediate sources, Joseph of Exeter—has preferred, for some strange reason, to employ as a blanket designation for all his others, the still largely mystifying appellation Lollius (I, 394; V, 1653), which he states to be the name of the author of an ancient history of the Trojan war written in Latin (II, 14; III, 91).

The love story of Troilus and Cressida[1] appeared for the first time, so far as we know, as an episode in the *Roman de Troie* of Benoit. Whether Benoit invented the story or found it already present in one of his sources —perhaps in an enlarged version of the *De Excidio Trojae Historia* of Dares Phrygius—is still a mooted question.[2]

That Boccaccio derived the story of his *Filostrato* from Benoit or from Guido or from both authors, has

---

[1] The name *Criseida*, used by Boccaccio in place of Benoit's *Briseida*, occurs also in the *Florita* of Armannino, written in 1325, which contains a history of the Trojan war, based, according to Gorra, E. (*Testi inedite di storia trojana*, Turin, 1887, pp. 236-239), indirectly upon Benoit. In it, as Kittredge has pointed out (*Chaucer Society*, Second Series, 1909, XLII, 74-75), occurs the statement (quoted by Gorra, p. 555) that, according to certain accounts, the soothsayer brought back by Achilles from Mysia was "Calchas, father to Criseida." This substitution of *Calchas* in place of *Chryses* might have come, as has been shown by Kittredge (p. 17), simultaneously with Wilkins (*Modern Language Notes*, 1909, XXIV, 66-67), from Ovid's *Remedia Amoris* (vv. 467-478), where a hasty reading of the lines might create the impression that "pater" (v. 470) refers to "Calchas," named just below (v. 473), and not, as Ovid intended, to Chryses. Both Kittredge and Wilkins imply that the Italian poet changed Benoit's *Briseida* to *Criseida* independently of Armannino. But it seems quite as likely that Boccaccio, who wrote his *Filostrato* in 1336 (see p. 16, n. 5), adopted the altered form from his Italian predecessor.

[2] To the present writer it seems highly improbable that Benoit invented the love episode. Against the theory that he invented it, so ingeniously and persuasively championed by Kittredge (*op. cit.*, pp. 66-72), in pursuance of Dunger, H. (*Die Sage vom trojanischen Kriege*, 1869, pp. 35-36) and Joly (*ed. cit.*, I, 290), stand, among other objections, the following:

In the first place Benoit specifically declares at the opening of his poem (vv. 138-144) that he proposes to follow Dares throughout save when he may introduce some "bon dit" of his own. Hardly could an episode as long and as elaborate as this love story be dismissed as a mere "bon dit." Again Benoit entirely fails to record the first beginnings and subsequent growth of the love of Troilus for Briseida (see pp. 31-32) but refers to it (vv. 13261-13275) in terms that seem to imply that it was a matter of common knowledge to his reader. Joly (I, 290, n. 8) believes that Benoit "gives to his story all the development that it requires" because his main purpose was to reveal the perfidy of Briseida by relating at length her desertion to Diomede. But quite obviously some preliminary account of her love for Troilus would

long been recognized.[1] After a careful reëxamination of all the evidence Young concludes that Boccaccio utilized both authors but that, as we might expect, he made more extensive use of the vivid and picturesque narrative of the French trouvère than of the somewhat dull and pedestrian translation of the Sicilian judge.[2]

But while Boccaccio obtained the plot of his *Filostrato* from these two earlier writers, he followed neither of them consecutively or for long at a time. His borrowings from them[3] are of various kinds including brief descriptions of persons or of occurrences or brief

have served to emphasize by contrast her faithlessness in abandoning him for another. Moreover his words (v. 13270):

"Ço saveient tuit li plosur"

seem to imply that his reader was already acquainted with the earlier love story and could draw the contrast for himself. Still again Benoit's constant representation of love as a destructive agency in human society (see pp. 32-34) harmonizes much better with an antique or even with an early medieval conception of that passion than with the conception that we should expect to find entertained by the age to which he belonged. Finally it is difficult to believe that a medieval author would so far have disregarded the intense respect then paid to antiquity as to allow himself freedom of invention in dealing with the time-honored theme of Troy. The age for the free handling of this theme was the age of Nero, when, as we know, the medieval form of the story first sprang into existence and when, largely as a result of the interest taken in that subject by the emperor, Greek rhetoricians came to look upon their ancient epic traditions as plastic material to be remolded in such fashion as expediency might dictate (see my *Dares and Dictys*, Baltimore, 1907, p. 13, n. 2).

That an enlarged version of Dares formerly existed is the view of Benoit's later editor (see Constans in Petit de Julleville's *Histoire de la langue et de la littérature française*, Paris, 1903, I, 204-209, and Constans' edition of the *Roman de Troie*, VI, 224-234). May we not suppose not only that this enlarged version existed but that it contained a preparatory story of the love of Troilus for Briseida as well as Benoit's own story of the defection of Briseida to Diomede?

[1] First by Moland and D'Héricault, who in the Introduction to their edition of the French translation of the *Filostrato* by Pierre de Beauvau ("Nouvelles françoises en prose du XIVe siècle," *Bibliothèque elzévirienne*, Paris, 1858, LXVI, p. xciii) are uncertain as to which of the two authors Boccaccio was more largely indebted.

[2] *Op. cit.*, pp. 25-26.   [3] Listed by Young, pp. 7-25.

extracts from speeches, sometimes transferred from the lips of one character in his original to those of another in his own poem.[1] They are pretty evenly distributed throughout the *Filostrato*, save for the second and third cantos, in which he borrows practically nothing at all,[2] since his account of the development of the love of Troilus for Criseida, which fills these cantos, is entirely lacking in both his originals.

In so far as the obligations of Boccaccio to Benoit are concerned, Young finds a total of twenty passages in which the Italian is paralleled in the French.[3] One of these passages presents no verbal correspondences,[4] however, and one other passage, which does contain a

---

[1] As when, for example, he assigns to the Trojans (I, 10), to Hector (I, 13, *5-6*), and to Troilus (IV, 38) expressions of anger against Calchas for his treacherous desertion to the Greeks similar to those which in Benoit (vv. 5907-5911) the fugitive priest himself foretells that the Trojans will use against him when they learn of his flight to the Greeks. See Young, pp. 12-14.

[2] The only borrowing from either author which Young was able to discover is a very questionable case of indebtedness to Guido's use, by no means uncommon in Latin, of the verb *revolvere* to express mental action, as when (sig. i, 1, rect., col. 1, 11, 10-11) he writes of Briseida: "multa tamen in sua mente revolvit." Boccaccio uses the same verb *rivolvere* in the same sense, equally usual in Italian, both of Criseida (II, 68, *3-4*):

> "Seco nel cuor ciascuna paroletta
> Rivolvendo di Pandaro, ecc."

and again of Troilus (III, 54, *1-2*):

> "E giva ciascun atto rivolgendo
> Nel suo pensiero, ecc."

See Young, p. 12.

[3] Pp. 12-25. Young excludes from his comparison passages in the *Filostrato* drawn from Benoit's love episode of Achilles and Polyxena (see pp. 34-38), but includes a passage presumably taken from his love episode of Jason and Medea (see p. 36, n. 4).

[4] Viz., the passage in the *Filostrato* in which Troilus beholds in the possession of Deiphoebus a golden brooch which he had once given Criseida and Deiphoebus had captured from Diomede (VIII, 9, *7-9*), cited by Young, pp. 23-24.

verbal parallel,[1] might have been added, making the same total of twenty passages which present marked verbal resemblance to Benoit. These twenty passages occupy one hundred and six verses in the Italian. Since the total number of verses in the *Filostrato* is 5704, only one out of a little less than every fifty-four verses finds correspondence in the French poem.

Even less is the indebtedness of the Italian poet to Guido. Young finds a total of eight Italian passages which show the influence of the Sicilian writer.[2] These passages fill forty-four verses. Hence but one out of a little less than every one hundred and thirty verses of the *Filostrato* finds a parallel in the Latin history.

Thus the total indebtedness of Boccaccio to both authors runs to no more than one verse in approximately every thirty-eight. A showing so meager is little to be wondered at, however, when one comes to consider how ill suited the love stories of Benoit and of Guido are to the purposes which the Italian poet had in mind when he wrote the *Filostrato*.

In the first place Benoit[3] introduces his love story solely for the purpose of creating a diversion from the long and monotonous succession of encounters between the Greeks and Trojans. In order not to interrupt the

---

[1] Viz., the passage in the *Filostrato* (I, 21, *4-8*, 22), in which Troilus expresses scorn for men and women in love in terms that recall what Benoit himself says (vv. 13438-13456) with regard to the fickleness of womankind and the folly of those who trust in it. See Savj-Lopez, *Romania*, 1898, XXVII, 450-451.

[2] Pp. 7-12.

[3] Henceforth no reference will be made to Guido, whose version of the love story differs so slightly from Benoit's in plan and purpose that what is now to be said of the structure and motivation of the traditional love story might equally well be illustrated from either. Since, however, Boccaccio more frequently uses Benoit for particular passages, the illustrations may more properly be taken from the *Roman de Troie*.

onward progress of his war narrative he fits the love narrative into it piecemeal, a little at a time. Thus he opens his love story only to drop it again and return to the main war narrative. Nine times does he repeat this operation, so that the story is broken into nine sections[1] of varying length interposed at varying intervals in the main narrative.[2] Boccaccio, on the other hand, had, naturally, no direct interest in these battle engagements. What he was in search of was a story that should enable him to reveal to his lady the love that was consuming

[1] Of which the ninth has nothing to do with the love story, but is given here because allusion is made at the end of the *Filostrato* (VIII, 27, *8*) to the death of Troilus at the hands of Achilles.

These sections and their several topics are as follows: (1) the exchange of prisoners (*Roman de Troie*, vv. 13065-13120) ; (2) the grief of Troilus and Briseida at parting and the journey of the latter, under the escort of Diomede, to her father's tent (vv. 13261-13866) ; (3) the combat between Troilus and Diomede and the dispatch by the latter of the war steed of Troilus, which he has captured, as a present to Briseida (vv. 14268-14352) ; (4) Diomede's assiduous courtship of Briseida and her gift to him of her sleeve (vv. 15001-15186) ; (5) the second combat between Troilus and Diomede (vv. 15617-15658) ; (6) the third combat between Troilus and Diomede, in which the former wounds the latter and reproaches him for having robbed him of Briseida (vv. 20057-20118) ; (7) Briseida's grief at the wounding of Diomede and her determination to give him her love (vv. 20193-20340) ; (8) the displeasure of Troilus at the light-heartedness of Briseida and the maledictions pronounced against her by the Trojan damsels (vv. 20666-20682) ; (9) the treacherous slaying of Troilus by Achilles and the dragging of his dead body at the tail of Achilles' horse (vv. 21242-21512).

These nine sections combined occupy 1370 verses or about one twenty-second of the 30316 verses of which the entire poem consists.

[2] As Lawrence, W. W., has well said (*Shaksperian Studies by Members of the English Department at Columbia University*, 1916, p. 193), Benoit's love story "grew up about the tale of Troy like the ivy about the oak, attached somewhat loosely to the trunk to which it clung." At the same time the skill with which the French trouvère has, if we are to credit him with this particular invention, entwined his love story about his war narrative in such a manner that the intervention of the several battle engagements supplies the time intervals needed for a proper unfolding of the emotional changes in the hearts of the lovers, makes of the *Roman de Troie* a piece of narrative construction most unusual for the twelfth century.

his heart. Incumbent upon him, accordingly, was the necessity of making Benoit's intermittent love story contributory to his own needs by omitting the intervening battle narratives.[1] Needless to say it was by thus disengaging Benoit's love story from the encompassing war narrative that the Italian poet made possible the brilliant career that the love story, thus liberated, was destined to enjoy in subsequent English literature.

In the second place Benoit does not open his account of the love of Troilus for Briseida at the beginning, as we should expect, but in the middle. Of the hero's first falling in love with the heroine and of the subsequent growth of their passion he has nothing to say. We first learn of the affection between the two on the occasion of the request made by Calchas that his daughter be exchanged for the Trojan captive Antenor.[2] Thereupon we are informed that Troilus was filled with extreme grief because he loved the girl exceedingly.[3] No sooner, however, has Diomede arrived at the Trojan gate to escort Briseida to her father's tent than we largely[4]

---

[1] Boccaccio does not, however, allow us to forget that a war is all the time going on between the Greeks and Trojans. Reference to the martial deeds of Troilus are liberally intersprinkled throughout the *Filostrato* (I, 45, 46; III, 20, 90; VII, 80, 81, 104, 106; VIII, 27), thus paving the way for the large part Fate was to play in the *Troilus and Criseyde* of Chaucer (see Kittredge, *The Poetry of Chaucer*, Harvard University Press, 1914, p. 112). Particularly noteworthy, because of the Homeric reminiscences which the name evokes, is Boccaccio's representation of the visit of Troilus and Pandarus to the house of Sarpedon (V, 40-48), though the introduction therein of Trojan ladies who try to distract Troilus from his grief by playing upon musical instruments, appears to have been suggested to Boccaccio by the social practices of his own day (cf. p. 47, n. 3).

[2] *Roman de Troie*, vv. 13065-13120.

[3] *Roman de Troie*, vv. 13261-13275.

[4] Altogether, save for the two brief references which he makes to his faithless mistress, one on the occasion of the battle in which, after wounding Diomede, he warns him to beware of the fickleness of his newly won sweetheart, who will in the end, he says, betray her second

lose sight of Troilus in his capacity of lover and are henceforth called upon to assist at a series of scenes in the Greek camp through which is traced the gradual transference of the heroine's affections from her old lover to her new one. Obviously a story in which no attention at all has been paid to the origin and development of the passion of Troilus for Briseida and so little to his heartstricken condition after her departure, could have given but little assistance to Boccaccio, whose purpose in writing the *Filostrato* was, as he explains to his lady in the *Proemio*, to "relate" his "sufferings" "in the person of another" (p. 127). To make amends for these deficiencies in his French original Boccaccio has devoted the first three cantos of the *Filostrato* to a circumstantial account of the genesis, growth, and consummation of the love of Troilus for Criseida, and the last three to the anxieties of the hero as he impatiently awaits the heroine's return from the Greek camp and to the bitterness of his disillusionment when he beholds his hopes frustrated, the three intervening cantos only being occupied with the events treated by Benoit, viz., the news of the surrender of Criseida, the grief of the lovers on account of it, and the wooing of Criseida by Diomede.

In the third place Benoit's interest in his love story was essentially a cynical and a satiric one. He wished to relieve the monotony of his war narrative by providing a representation, not of the constancy of a faithful lover but of the inconstancy of a faithless mistress.[1] No

lover even as she has her first (vv. 20079-20102), and the other when, just before his death, he gives momentary expression to his chagrin over the manner in which she has treated him (vv. 20666-20670).

[1] Thus he explicitly declares (vv. 13471-13474) that he is relating his story of the defection of Briseida as a warning example to all men not to put their trust on womankind, for, as Solomon says, "he who can find a faithful woman ought to thank his creator."

doubt it was for this not altogether patent reason[1] that at the outset he so abruptly dismisses the story of the love of Troilus for Briseida to concentrate so largely thenceforth upon that of the love of Briseida for Diomede. For to Benoit love was not, as it afterward became to the disciples of Courtly Love—to Chrétien de Troyes and to the poets of the *dolce stil nuovo*—an elevating and regenerating influence in human society but a baneful and a destructive one, bringing about the ultimate undoing of those who allowed themselves to fall subject to its sway.[2] But to the still undisillusioned Boccaccio, filled with the impassioned yearnings natural to a youthful lover of his highly emotional temperament, the harsh and mordant aspects of love emphasized so exclusively by Benoit must have proved to the highest degree distasteful, if not actually repellent. More particularly to the wooer of a lady whose greatest offense thus far was her removal to Sannio, must it have proved embarrassing to repeat the story, told with such obvious relish by Benoit, of the gradual estrangement of the heart of Briseida and of her final surrender to Diomede. Accordingly for a short time only are we, in the sixth canto of the *Filostrato*, allowed to follow, with Benoit, the career of Criseida after her arrival in the Greek camp. No sooner does it become evident in

[1] Because it is hard to see why he could not have achieved his satiric purpose even better by opening with the story of the love of Troilus for Briseida so as to emphasize by contrast her fickleness in deserting him for Diomede (cf. p. 26, n. 2).

[2] To this pessimistic conception of love as a malign influence in human society—so strikingly suggestive of the typical clerical satire of the Middle Ages—Benoit gives expression not only in his Troilus and Briseida episode (*Roman de Troie*, vv. 13065-21512) but also in his two earlier episodes of the love of Medea for Jason (vv. 1210-2044) and of Paris for Helen (vv. 4219-4772) as well as in his concurrent episode of the love of Achilles for Polyxena (vv. 17489-22316). Cf. Joly, *ed. cit.,* I, 274.

what direction things are turning than, without being allowed a spectacle of her final surrender to Diomede, we are, at the opening of the seventh canto, recalled to Troy and Troilus that we may be made partakers of the alternate gleams of hope and paroxysms of despair that are his as he awaits the return of his lady to keep her tryst on the tenth day.

Finally if the Briseida of Benoit fell far short of the ideal of feminine constancy of which a lover would naturally have been in search to serve as a model to be imitated by his mistress, no less did his Troilus leave much to be desired in the way of providing him with a suitable image of what he would have liked her to believe he would be capable of proving as her lover. For the Troilus of Benoit has this in common with the other lovers of the French poet that he regards love but as a passing diversion from the serious business of fighting. He still retains traces of the hardy truculent gallant of the earlier *chansons de geste*,[1] who is "no more disconcerted by the infidelity of his mistress than he would be by a kick from his horse and as little surprised by it."[2]

Obviously, therefore, it was to models of a higher type of love-making that Boccaccio was under the necessity of turning if he would properly shadow forth the intensity of his devotion to Maria.[3]

It was, strange to say, to a second love episode of Benoit that, in the first instance, Boccaccio turned to

[1] See Joly, *ed. cit.*, I, 272 and Paris, G., *Romania*, 1883, XII, 519.

[2] Moland and D'Héricault, *op. cit.*, Introduction, p. lxxxix.

[3] In view of the foregoing considerations it is little wonder that Boccaccio's debt to Benoit was so small. The wonder rather is that he should have used his work at all. His reason for so doing was, as he tells us, the striking parallelism that the French story afforded to his own situation as a deserted lover. See p. 8.

remedy the deficiencies of the first. Largely enclosed within the limits of Benoit's episode of the love of Troilus for Briseida (vv. 13065-21512) there lay in the *Roman de Troie* another love episode, that of the love of Achilles for Polyxena (vv. 17489-22316), so that in turning the pages of the first love story Boccaccio could not have failed to discover the second. Notwithstanding the fact that this second love episode of the French poet shared with the first—and, indeed, with his others as well (see p. 33, n. 2)—a disastrous conclusion, it nevertheless possessed for Boccaccio's purposes important redeeming features. For Benoit's Achilles was in search of a wife, not of a mistress, and his formal negotiations by messenger with Hecuba for the hand of her daughter presented, at least from the standpoint of conventional propriety, a much more suitable model for Boccaccio to follow in his representation of a courtship that was to mirror his own than did the impudent effrontery of Diomede in his premature addresses to Briseida[1] in the first episode of the French trouvère.[2] Moreover the chaste maiden destined to suffer at the hands of the victorious Greeks so tragic an immolation at the tomb of her erstwhile lover[3] must have impressed Boccaccio as a much worthier representative of his lady than the fickle damsel who, like her two Homeric prototypes,[4] passes so readily from one warrior to another.

[1] In the *Roman de Troie* (vv. 13529-13616) Diomede does not hesitate to offer his love to Briseida as soon as the two have ridden out of earshot of Troilus. In this he shows less respect for the feelings of a girl just parted from her lover than does the Diomede of Boccaccio, who has the decency to postpone his addresses to a later and more auspicious occasion (*Filostrato*, VI, 9). See Savj-Lopez, *op. cit.*, p. 457.

[2] Which, by reason of his omission of the love-making of Troilus, was, in his first love episode, the only example of courtship that Benoit had to offer the Italian poet for imitation.

[3] *Roman de Troie*, vv. 26375-26552.

[4] I.e., Briseis and Chryseis. Joly (*ed. cit.*, I, 290) is of the opinion

Furthermore this second French episode was not, like the first, a torso but contained a full account of the courtship of Achilles from the first stirrings of love in his breast as he beholds Polyxena at the commemoration in Troy of the anniversary of Hector's death[1] to his treacherous murder at the hands of her brother Paris.[2] Here, therefore, was a love story from which Boccaccio might obtain materials for the filling out of that other story of the love of Troilus for Criseida which Benoit had omitted.

To Savj-Lopez[3] belongs the credit of having been the first to point out the indebtedness of Boccaccio to the Achilles and Polyxena episode of the *Roman de Troie*.[4] But Young has since succeeded, by a searching

that Benoit modeled his Briseida upon the Homeric Briseis. This view has, however, been effectually overthrown by Kittredge, who has shown (*Chaucer Society, sup. cit.*, pp. 66-67) that since later in the Dictaean portion of his *Roman de Troie* Benoit introduces the Homeric Briseis under the altered name of *Hippodamia* (v. 26899), he can hardly have understood that the two were identical. That Boccaccio, however—or, more probably, Armannino before him—felt that an identification with one of the two Homeric slave girls was intended but, not content with such associations as the name *Briseida* evoked, changed the name, under the influence of Ovid, to *Criseida* instead, we have already seen (see p. 26, n. 1).

[1] *Roman de Troie*, vv. 17552-17555.
[2] *Roman de Troie*, vv. 22235-22237.   [3] *Op. cit.*, pp. 452-453.
[4] Though there can be no doubt that Savj-Lopez's attention was first directed to this discovery by that most learned first editor of Benoit, Joly, who had already remarked (*ed. cit.*, I, 504 and n. 3) that Troilus' description of the omnipotence of Love in the *Filostrato* (II, 7, *1-2*):

> "Amore, incontro al qual chi si defende
> Più tosto è preso, ed adopera invano,"

had been suggested by "a phrase in which Benoit is speaking of the passion of Achilles." Just what phrase he had in mind Joly does not say, but he was probably alluding to the following description by Benoit of the effects of Love upon Achilles (vv. 17583-17584):

> "Force, vertu ne hardiment
> Nè valent contre Amors neient."

As Young has shown (p. 25), however, the Italian passage in question is more closely paralleled in an earlier passage in which Benoit is

comparison of the *Filostrato* with this second love episode, in discovering a number of correspondences unobserved by the earlier critic.[1] The results of Young's more penetrating analysis are these.

Boccaccio was influenced by Benoit in his treatment both of the enamorment of Troilus and of his love experiences immediately thereafter.

There are eight points of likeness between Boccaccio's description of the enamorment of Troilus and Benoit's description of the enamorment of Achilles. These eight points of resemblance are as follows: (1) Both Troilus and Achilles first behold their ladies at an annual religious festival in Troy, Troilus at the sacrifices in the temple of Pallas in honor of the Palladium, Achilles at the sacrifices in the temple of Apollo in commemoration of the death of Hector;[2] (2) The several classes of people who attend the ceremonies are similarly enumerated;[3] (3) Both Troilus and Achilles occupy themselves in gazing upon the various ladies in attendance;[4]

speaking of the powerlessness of Medea to resist the fascinations of Jason (vv. 1294-1295):

> "Dès or la tient bien en ses laz
> Amors, vers cui rien n'a defense."

That this is its derivation seems the more likely in that another Italian passage (I, 40, *1-5*, quoted by Young, p. 38) stands closer to the former French passage:

> "Non risparmiarono il sangue reale,
> Nè d'animo virtù ovver grandezza,
> Nè curaron di forza corporale
> Che in Troilo fosse, o di prodezza,
> L'ardenti fiamme amorose, ecc."

Young's observation is of peculiar interest as indicating how extensively Boccaccio had read in the *Roman de Troie* and how eclectic are the comparatively few borrowings he has made from it.

[1] Pp. 36-42.

[2] *Filostrato*, I, 17, *6-8*, 18, *5-8*; *Roman de Troie*, vv. 17489-17495, 22098.

[3] *Filostrato*, I, 18, *7-8*; *Roman de Troie*, vv. 17500-17501, 17505-17506.

[4] *Filostrato*, I, 20, *5-6*, 26, *3*; *Roman de Troie*, v. 17523.

(4) The heart of each beholder is suddenly smitten by a love dart;[1] (5) Each lover stands rapt in the contemplation of the beauty of his beloved as long as the service lasts;[2] (6) The irresistible power of love is commented upon similarly by both authors;[3] (7) Each lover leaves the scene of the enamorment with a heavy heart;[4] (8) Troilus compares the beauty of Criseida to that of Polyxena and Helen, just as Benoit names Helen as present with Polyxena in the temple of Apollo.[5]

There are six points of likeness between Boccaccio's account of the early love experiences of Troilus and Benoit's account of the early love experiences of Achilles. These are as follows: (1) On leaving the temple each lover languishes in his own room;[6] (2) Each lover thinks only of the great event of the morning;[7] (3) Both feel themselves differently disposed than formerly to the task of fighting;[8] (4) Both display the same love symptoms;[9] (5) Each thinks his case hopeless;[10] (6) Each has recourse to a trusted friend to act as intermediary between himself and his beloved.[11]

---

[1] *Filostrato*, I, 25, *6-8*, 29, *7-8*; *Roman de Troie*, vv. 17552-17568 (rather than the verses cited by Young, viz., 17534-17544), 17611-17614.

[2] *Filostrato*, I, 30, *5, 7*; *Roman de Troie*, vv. 17604-17605.

[3] *Filostrato*, I, 40, *1-5*; *Roman de Troie*, vv. 17579-17584.

[4] *Filostrato*, I, 31, *1-2*; *Roman de Troie*, vv. 17615-17616.

[5] *Filostrato*, I, 42, *6-8*; *Roman de Troie*, vv. 17511, 17514.

[6] *Filostrato*, I, 33, *1-3*; *Roman de Troie*, vv. 17625-17626.

[7] *Filostrato*, I, 33, *4-8*, 42, *4-5*; *Roman de Troie*, vv. 17621-17623.

[8] *Filostrato*, I, 44, *1-2*, 45, *1, 3-4*; *Roman de Troie*, vv. 17675-17683.

[9] Both Troilus (*Filostrato*, I, 47, *1-4*) and Achilles (*Roman de Troie*, vv. 17606-17607, 20770-20771) suffer from pallor, sleeplessness and loss of appetite. But since, as Young remarks (p. 39, n. 8), Benoit's Diomede also suffers from the same love symptoms (*Roman de Troie*, vv. 15005, 15016, 15059), it is not unlikely that in describing Troilus' love malady Boccaccio had both of Benoit's lovesick heroes in mind.

[10] *Filostrato*, I, 38-47, 49, *1-5* (rather than the verses [I, 48, *5-8*] cited by Young); *Roman de Troie*, vv. 17638-17647, 17712-17714.

[11] *Filostrato*, II, 1; *Roman de Troie*, vv. 17747-17753.

But to Boccaccio in his task of supplying the deficiencies of Benoit's love episode of Troilus and Briseida, a source of far greater usefulness than this second love episode of the French writer was, as Young has brilliantly demonstrated,[1] his own prose romance, the *Filocolo*.[2] Since the *Filocolo* was, as we have seen (p. 8, n. 1), begun before the *Filostrato* but not finished until after it, what, on a priori grounds, would have been a more natural thing for the Italian poet to do than to economize effort by reutilizing in the *Filostrato* those portions of the *Filocolo* already completed at the time that he began that work? We know moreover that it was a peculiar habit of the poet to repeat himself in his writings.[3] That, as a matter of fact, Boccaccio has made large use of the *Filocolo* in writing his *Filostrato*, Young has shown beyond a possibility of doubt. Since, however, it is not always possible to determine what portions of the *Filocolo* were finished before the *Filostrato* was begun, and since the portions of the *Filocolo* which show likenesses to the *Filostrato* contain inci-

[1] *Op. cit.*, pp. 26-105.

[2] In undertaking this demonstration Young was not, as he acknowledges (p. 27, n. 2), operating entirely without antecedent suggestion, Crescini having already called attention to resemblances between "the life and thoughts" of Florio and Biancofiore "when separated from one another" and those of Troilus and Criseida under like conditions. (*Contributo*, p. 204, n. 1.) But to Young belongs the credit of having followed up this casual observation of the earlier critic and of having, by bringing together a large number of small but striking resemblances between the love experiences of Troilus and Criseida as recorded in the *Filostrato* and of Florio and Biancofiore as set forth in the *Filocolo*, convincingly demonstrated the dependence of the former upon the latter.

[3] Thus the general idea of the *Decameron* is to be found in germinal form in the "questioni d'amore" of the *Filocolo* and in an intermediate state of development in the *Ameto*. See Gaspary, who points out (*Storia della letteratura italiana*, II, 6-7) that two of these "questioni" reappear in the *Decameron*, and Ettore de Ferri, *op. cit.*, Introduzione, p. xxvi.

dents which, in many instances, occur also in one or other of the extant versions of the old story of Floire and Blanchefleur,[1] which served Boccaccio as the source of his *Filocolo*, it may, at least in all such cases, be safer to allow for the possibility that the borrowing was made rather from the sources of the *Filocolo* than from the *Filocolo* itself.[2]

Those passages in the *Filocolo* with which Young brings the *Filostrato* into comparison occur in that earlier portion of the former work (I, 104-328) that has to

---

[1] The story of Floire and Blanchefleur survives in at least five versions, viz., (1) and (2) the French *Floire et Blanceflor*, in two versions, both ed. Du Méril, E., Paris, 1856; (3) the Italian *Cantare di Fiorio e Biancofiore*, ed. Crescini, two vols., Bologna, 1889, 1899; (4) the German *Flore und Blanscheflur*, by Konrad Fleck, ed. Sommer, E., Quedlinburg and Leipsic, 1846; and (5) the English *Floris and Blauncheflur*, ed. Hausknecht, E., Berlin, 1885. In so far as he used a written source and did not, as Maria's words suggest, rely upon oral tradition, Boccaccio depended in part upon the Italian *Cantare* and in part upon a lost Franco-Italian version, in both of which, the two (earlier) French and the (earlier) German versions were represented. From the possible sources of the *Filocolo*, therefore, the English version alone is to be excluded. See Young, pp. 187-188.

[2] Young (pp. 34-35) does not, in our opinion, make sufficient allowance for the extreme likelihood of this possibility. He cites (pp. 27-28) conclusions drawn by earlier scholars from a stylistic comparison between the two romances to the effect that the more artistically perfect *Filostrato* conveys the impression of a work written later than the more immature *Filocolo*. Since, moreover, all passages comparable with the *Filostrato* occur in the earlier portion of the *Filocolo*, it seems to him that they were the earlier composed and therefore the more likely to antedate the *Filostrato*. But since, as he recognizes (pp. 29, 30, 34), certain portions of the *Filocolo* were clearly written later than the *Filostrato* (see p. 8, n. 1), he seeks in the case of each parallel to find stylistic reasons for believing that the version in the *Filocolo* preceded that in the *Filostrato*. It is, however, not only conceivable but highly probable that an author who has read an old story for the purpose of reproducing it in one romance, should, upon coming to write a second romance before the first is finished, make simultaneous use of it in both. Moreover, in one instance mentioned by Young (p. 80) (see p. 49, n. 3), a detail found in the *Filostrato* reappears only in one of the sources of the *Filocolo*. In this case certainly and doubtless in many others as well, Boccaccio worked directly from the old story and not from a previous draft of that story in the *Filocolo*.

do with the separation between Florio and Biancofiore occasioned by the banishment of Florio to Montorio by his foster father Felice, King of Spain, to prevent the marriage of the young man to his daughter Biancofiore, with whom Florio is deeply in love.

By far the most significant of the results obtained by Young from his comparison of the two romances is that it was from the *Filocolo* that Boccaccio obtained a number of important hints for his conception of the character and activities of Pandarus. But the cogency of Young's demonstration will be better appreciated if, before proceeding to a consideration of the parallels upon which it is based, we, as he, pause first to pass in review certain earlier and less successful attempts to explain the genesis of Boccaccio's conception of that facile go-between, who, from sympathy with a companion in love, is willing to jeopardize the honor of his kinswoman that he may place his services at his disposal.

The name *Pandarus*, while perhaps called to the attention of Boccaccio by the "Pandarus de Sezile" mentioned by Benoit,[1] was used by him without reference to Benoit's presumable prototype, the Lycian archer Pandarus of Zeleia who, having (*Iliad*, IV, 125-126), shot an arrow in violation of the truce, "paid," in the words of Dictys (*Ephemeris*, II, 41), "the penalty for an accursed method of fighting" by losing his life at the hands of Diomede (*Iliad*, V, 94).[2] The Italian poet uses the name, as though it were a coinage of his own[3]

[1] *Roman de Troie*, v. 6667.

[2] Cf. Morf, H., *Romania*, 1892, XXI, 106; Root, *ed. cit.*, Introduction, p. xxvi, n. 40.

[3] Cf. Boccaccio's other similar coinages, viz., *Panfilo* (see p. 10, n. 3), *Filocolo* (see p. 16, n. 4), and *Filostrato* (see p. 115).

and with obvious reference to its fancied etymological meaning, to signify one who "gives all" for his friend.[1]

But the more interesting question regarding Pandarus concerns, not the name, but the content of qualities which Boccaccio assigns to the bearer of the name and the sources whence he derived his notion of these qualities.

That Boccaccio himself ever employed the services of an intermediary similar to Pandarus in the conduct of his courtship of Maria d'Aquino we have no certain evidence,[2] though his having done so would not necessarily have precluded his use of social custom or of literary models to embellish a reminiscence of actual experience.[3]

A character proposed by Savj-Lopez[4] as well qualified to serve Boccaccio as model for Pandarus is Governale, faithful servant to the titular hero of the Italian

[1] It is entirely in accordance with this etymology that Boccaccio is constantly representing Troilus as thanking Pandarus for his gifts. Cf. Hertzberg, W., *Jahrbuch der Shakespeare-Gesellschaft*, 1871, VI, 200, who cites *Filostrato*, IV, 52, from the Paris 1789 edition, which is III, 59 in that of Moutier. See also III, 16, 19, 57, 58.

[2] Noteworthy is it, however, that Clonico, in connection with his contribution to the "questioni d'amore" in the *Filocolo*, describes (II, 69) the coming of an adviser to comfort him after his betrayal in terms almost identical with those used by Boccaccio to describe the arrival of Pandarus to console Troilus after the enamorment (*Filostrato*, II, 1; see p. 21, n. 4 and Young, p. 44). That at all events Maria made use of a confidante to advise her in her relations with Boccaccio, seems placed beyond any reasonable doubt by the fact that the heroine of the autobiographical *Fiammetta* has an aged nurse to whom she confides respecting her relations with Panfilo (pp. 16-20) as well as a younger servant to whom both she and Panfilo at one time thought of entrusting the secret of their love (p. 31).

[3] Since we have found good reason to believe that he depended upon the one in certain of his versions of the temple scene (see p. 15 and n. 2), and upon the other in his account of the nocturnal surprise (see p. 20, n. 5).

[4] *Op. cit.*, pp. 459-461; Young, pp. 47-49.

metrical romance *Tristano*.[1] When Tristan is fearful of losing Isolt by reason of a dream he has had of a wound from a stag in hunting, Governale exhorts him to place no faith in dreams,[2] just as Troilus, when led by a vision of the body of his lady lacerated by the tusks of a wild boar to suspect her fidelity in love, is, in like manner, urged by Pandarus to repose no confidence in dreams.[3] But the Governale of the *Tristano* discharges, as Young objects,[4] the services of a mere "maestro" and in ability to sympathize with the anxieties of his master falls far short of the "courtly amico" who in the *Filostrato* associates with Troilus on terms of social equality.

In so far as meeting the conditions of social equality is concerned, Young,[5] acting very possibly upon a suggestion of Joly,[6] finds in the person of Galehout, who in the French prose romance *Lancelot du Lac*[7] arranges a meeting between the titular hero and Guinevere, a not unworthy counterpart to Pandarus. But there is no valid ground for supposing that Boccaccio was in any way influenced by Galehout in creating Pandarus. It is merely a curious, but irrelevant coincidence that the Lady of Mahout, who is present in the background

---

[1] *Il Tristano riccardiano*, ed. Parodi, E. G., Bologna, 1896. That Boccaccio was well acquainted with the Tristan story is shown by his reference both to Tristan and Isolt in the *Amorosa visione* (p. 46) and to the romance itself in the *Fiammetta* (pp. 185-186). See also Young, p. 49, n. 4.

[2] *Il Tristano, ed. cit.*, p. 187.   [3] *Filostrato*, VII, 40.

[4] P. 49.   [5] Pp. 49-53.   [6] *Ed. cit.*, I, 275.

[7] Of which an extract from a thirteenth century manuscript containing the interview is printed by Toynbee, P., *Dante Studies and Researches*, London, 1902, pp. 10-22. That Boccaccio was acquainted at least with the *Lancelot du Lac*, is clear from the comments he makes upon Dante's classical reference to it in the *Inferno* (V, 127-128, 137) in his *Comento sopra la commedia di Dante Aligheri* (ed. Moutier, *op. cit.*, 1831, XI, 60-62). See Young, p. 49, n. 5.

during the interview, coughs to inform the queen that her endearing words to Lancelot are being overheard,[1] just as Criseida uses the same signal to apprise Troilus of her whereabouts on the first night that the lovers spend together.[2] No such relation of intimacy exists between Lancelot and Galehout as between Troilus and Pandarus.

Young is, in the opinion of the present writer, on safer ground when he discovers[3] the germ of Boccaccio's Pandarus in the "ami" whom in Benoit[4] Achilles employs as messenger in his negotiations with Hecuba for the hand of her daughter Polyxena.[5] That, however, Boccaccio obtained from Benoit more than a first suggestion for the creation of Pandarus, we may not suppose because, aside from the scant attention paid to him by the French poet, the "friend" of Achilles "is in no sense a 'pander,' for the business in his hands is an honorable proposal of marriage."[6]

As supplying the means to an elaboration of the hint furnished Boccaccio by Achilles' "ami," Young adduces four characters in the *Filocolo*.[7] These four are Duke Feramonte, the uncle of Florio, to whose care he is committed when sent to Montorio, Ascalione, Florio's tutor, who accompanies him, Glorizia, nurse to Biancofiore, who remains behind at Montorio with her charge, and the "fedelissimo servidore" who bears letters between the two lovers after their separation.

---

[1] Toynbee, *op. cit.*, p. 17.   [2] *Filostrato*, III, 26, *1-3*.

[3] Pp. 53-56.   [4] *Roman de Troie*, vv. 17747-17750.

[5] That Boccaccio obtained from this incident in the *Roman de Troie* his first idea of creating such a figure as Pandarus, seems certain from his use of Benoit's Achilles and Polyxena episode in connection with his account of the beginning and earliest stages of Troilus' love for Criseida (see pp. 34-38).

[6] Young, p. 56.   [7] Pp. 56-66.

The specific actions with respect to which these four characters present parallels to Pandarus are as follows. Feramonte extracts from Florio a confession of his love for Biancofiore (*Filocolo*, I, 214-222), just as Pandarus extorts from Troilus an admission of his passion for Criseida (*Filostrato*, II, 1-20).[1] Ascalione bids Florio pay no heed to his dream of the birds (*Filocolo*, II, 26-27), just as Pandarus offers the same advice to Troilus respecting his dream of the wild boar (*Filostrato*, VII, 40).[2] Glorizia urges Biancofiore to restrain her tears on the occasion of Florio's departure on the ground that her excessive anguish will cause her lover to kill himself (*Filocolo*, I, 117-118), just as Pandarus uses the same argument with Criseida respecting Troilus (*Filostrato*, IV, 106-107).[3] Finally the "fedelissimo servidore" busies himself in bearing letters between Florio and Biancofiore (*Filocolo*, I, 267-275), just as Pandarus does between Troilus and Criseida (*Filostrato*, II, 107-110, 118, 119, 128).[4]

To illustrate the parallelism of phrase that is constantly recurring between the foregoing sets of corresponding passages, one example must suffice. In the *Filostrato* (II, 107, *2-5*), before handing his first letter

---

[1] Common to both cases are the five following circumstances attending the extraction of the confession: (1) The adviser finds the victim of love grieving alone in his chamber; (2) The adviser has difficulty in discovering the cause of the lover's grief; (3) the lover, after making the confession, falls prostrate; (4) The adviser acknowledges that he too has once been in love; (5) The adviser encourages the lover with hope of ultimate success but bids him restrain his amorous desires and seek other pleasures (see Young, pp. 57-59). Particularly significant is the fact that Feramonte finds Florio with "a dark blue circle around his eyes" ("i suoi occhi . . . di un purpureo colore intorniati") (*Filocolo*, I, 215), just as Pandarus finds Troilus' eyes encircled with "un purpurino giro" (*Filostrato*, IV, 100, *6*). (Young, p. 63.)

[2] Young, pp. 63-66.   [3] *Ibid.*, pp. 62-63.
[4] *Ibid.*, pp. 60-62.

to Pandarus for delivery to Criseida, Troilus wetted the seal against his tear-stained cheeks and then sealed it:

> . . . per ordin piegolla,
> E sulle guance tutte lagrimose
> Bagnò la gemma, e quindi suggellolla,
> E nella mano a Pandaro la pose.

In the *Filocolo* this highly sentimental mode of procedure is followed, if not in all respects by Florio, in all at least by Biancofiore. Of the former we read (*Filocolo*, I, 267-268): "Fatta la pistola, Florio la chiuse piangendo, e suggellolla, e chiamò a sè un suo fedelissimo servidore . . . e così gli disse: o a me carissimo, sopra tutti gli alteri servadori, te' la presente lettera . . . e con istudioso passo celatamente a Biancofiore la presenti." Of the latter we read (I, 274-275): "Colle amare lagrime bagnò la cara gemma, e suggellata quella, con turbato aspetto uscì della camera a sè chiamando il servo, che già per troppa lunga dimoranza che far gli pareva si cominciava a turbare, al quale ella disse: porterai questa al tuo signore. . . . E detto questo, piangando baciò la lettera, e posela in mano al fedel servo, il quale senza alcuna indugio . . . trovò Floria nella sua camera . . . a cui egli porse la portata pistola, dicendogli ciò che da Biancofiore compreso avea e le sue parole."

That the account given in the *Filocolo* of the services rendered Florio and Biancofiore by the four characters above mentioned supplied Boccaccio with hints for his account in the *Filostrato* of the similar services rendered Troilus and Criseida by Pandarus, can hardly be doubted when we bear in mind the following considerations. Two of the advisers of Florio, viz., Duke Feramonte and Ascalione, are the social equals and intimate

companions of Florio, occupying in these respects the
position of Pandarus in his relation to Troilus. Glorizia
and the "fedelissimo servidore," while lacking respectively in one or both of these qualifications, serve, by
the striking resemblance they bear to Pandarus in respect to the character of the services they render, to
corroborate the evidence furnished by Florio's social
equals. In the case of both romances it is to the heroine
that the argument with respect to the abatement of excessive lamentation is addressed. Finally the passages in
which the actions of the counselors are recorded, bear to
one another an impressive verbal resemblance.

In view of the unquestionable dependence of the
Filostrato upon the story of the separation between
Florio and Biancofiore for details regarding the activities of Pandarus, we need feel no surprise to discover
that those parts of the *Filostrato* that have to do with
the separation between Troilus and Criseida betray
even more numerous instances of indebtedness to this
earlier story of a separation between lovers. Young[1]
points out a large number of representations in the
Filostrato, both before[2] and after[3] the departure of Cri-

[1] Pp. 66-103.

[2] Before the departure of Criseida there are five parallels as follows: (1) Criseida, like Biancofiore, faints and Troilus, like Florio,
thinking her dead, prepares to commit suicide, when she revives; (2)
Troilus and (later) Cassandra comment upon the low birth of Criseida,
just as Felice and his queen, upon that of Biancofiore; (3) Troilus re-
fuses to act upon Pandarus' suggestion that he abduct Criseida, just
as Florio rejects Biancofiore's suggestion that he carry her off to Montorio; (4) Criseida promises to return to Troy in ten days to rejoin
Troilus, but he distrusts her ability to do so, just as Felice agrees
to send Biancofiore after Florio in ten days, but she distrusts his sincerity;
(5) Criseida warns Troilus to resist the allurements of other damsels,
just as Biancofiore arms Florio with the same advice. See Young, pp.
66-83.

[3] After the departure there are eight parallels as follows: (1)
Troilus seeks distraction by visiting Sarpedon, just as Florio is enter-

seida to the Greek camp (V, 14), which parallel, both in language and situation, representations in the corresponding story of the separation between Florio and Biancofiore, either as told in the *Filocolo*, or in its sources, or both.

Of these by far the most interesting by reason of the subsequent literary history of the incident in connection with which it arises, is that which concerns the promise given by Criseida to Troilus to return to Troy on the tenth day after her departure to the Greek camp.

tained by Duke Feramonte in the hopes of diverting him from thoughts of Biancofiore; (2) Troilus visits with Pandarus the deserted house of Criseida and then alone other spots in Troy with which she is associated, just as Florio slips out one night to behold the palace in Marmorina in which Biancofiore dwells and as Biancofiore herself revisits those parts of the palace in which she and Florio used to meet; (3) Troilus casts longing glances from the top of the Trojan gate toward the Greek camp, imagining that the breezes that blow against his face are Criseida's sighs, just as Biancofiore looks forth from the roof of her palace toward Montorio, imagining that the winds that blow from that quarter have touched her Florio; (4) Criseida looks out upon the abode of her beloved, just as Florio does upon the abode of his; (5) Troilus asks news of Criseida from those who come from the camp of the Greeks, even as Biancofiore asks news of Florio from those who come from Montorio; (6) Troilus believes that Calchas is preventing the return of Criseida, just as Florio believes that Felice is responsible for the nonarrival of Biancofiore; (7) Deiphoebus sends for ladies to cheer Troilus with their songs, but with no success, just as Feramonte and Ascalione employ Ednea and Calmena to seduce Florio, but to no effect; (8) Troilus, becoming jealous because of Criseida's failure to return on the tenth day and because of his dream of the wild boar, thinks to take his life, but is restrained by Pandarus, who counsels him to write Criseida a letter, to which he receives no reply and to letters subsequent to which, but evasive replies, until at length, convinced of her infidelity by the sight of the "fermaglio" on Diomede's vestment, he vows to take the life of his rival in battle, much as Florio, entertaining suspicions of Biancofiore's fidelity by reason of her failure to come to Montorio and beholding a veil which Fileno declares she has given him as a favor, meditates suicide, but after a reassuring vision writes Biancofiore a letter, to which he receives a reply assuring him of her eternal devotion but insufficient to cure his jealousy, so that he determines to slay Fileno, though the latter escapes by flight. See Young, pp. 83-103.

Young[1] proves conclusively that it was from the *Filocolo* and not from Benoit, as Savj-Lopez had previously surmised,[2] that the idea of such a return emanated.

Young analyzes the account given in the *Filostrato* of Criseida's projected return to Troy into the three following stages of development: (1) Criseida repeatedly assures Troilus of her determination to return to Troy on the tenth day (IV, 134, *7-8;* 135, *7-8;* 154, *5-8;* 159, *5-8*) and he anxiously awaits the fulfilment of her assurance (VII, 1, 13, 16, 54); (2) Troilus, however, doubts her ability to carry out her intentions (IV, 141, *2-8;* 142, *8*); (3) when on the evening of the tenth day Criseida has not yet returned, Troilus yields to despair (VII, 14, *8;* 15, *1-2*).

Each of these three stages in the development of the theme in the *Filostrato* is, with the inevitable change of persons, duplicated in the *Filocolo* as follows: (1) King Felice assures Florio that he will send Biancofiore to Montorio to rejoin him as soon as the queen shall have recovered from an illness (I, 97) and this assurance is in turn conveyed by Florio to Biancofiore (I, 109); (2) Biancofiore expresses to Florio her scepticism as to the good faith of the king (I, 104, 107); (3) when, after a considerable interval of time has elapsed, Biancofiore fails to arrive, Florio gives way to despair (I, 123-124).[3]

---

[1] Pp. 78-80.

[2] Savj-Lopez (p. 448) conjectured that Boccaccio might have derived his idea of the return of Criseida from the following verses of the *Roman de Troie* (vv. 13859-13861):

> "Anceis que veie le quart seie,
> N'avra corage ne voleir
> De retorner en la cite."

Cf. Young, p. 23.

[3] From the close parallelism between these two recitals one would at first sight be tempted to conclude that Boccaccio had simply trans-

In addition to the large number of miscellaneous bits of story material drawn by Boccaccio in part from Benoit's episode of Achilles and Polyxena and in part from the sources, or finished portions, of his own *Filostrato* to aid him in turning the French poet's defective episode of Troilus and Briseida into a well-rounded narrative, there remains to be considered a small but significant residuum of autobiographical matter derived from the poet's recollection of such events of the courtship as had preceded the composition of the *Filostrato*.

Strange indeed would it have been if a poet as fond as Boccaccio of weaving autobiographical incidents into the fabric of his romances, should not, in the case of a romance so much more intimately associated with his lady than any other as is the *Filostrato*,[1] have availed himself of such earlier incidents in his relations with Maria as could be made to fit into the design of his Trojan fable.

Of the two events which, as we have seen (pp. 14-16), antedated the courtship, but one was suitable for this purpose.[2] This was the initial event of the enamor-

ferred the entire story from the *Filocolo* into the *Filostrato*. But such a conclusion leaves unexplained the specification in the *Filostrato* (IV, 154, 7-8; VII, 13, 1; 16, 2; 54, 7) that it is within a period of ten days that Criseida is to return. For in the *Filocolo* no mention is made of any particular limit of time within which Biancofiore is to be sent to Montorio. Here, however, as Young has shown (p. 80), three of the four sources of the *Filocolo* step to our assistance. In the first French version (vv. 337-338) a fortnight is specified and in the second French version (vv. 349-350) four days. But in the German version, by Konrad Fleck, the requisite period of ten days is twice mentioned (vv. 109-111 and 1414-1415).

[1] Not only because the entire story of the *Filostrato* is built about the absence of Maria in Sannio (see p. 17, n. 2) but also because no other romance contains a letter of dedication to Maria at all so intimate and personal as the *Proemio*.

[2] The author's first meeting with his lady in the convent at Baia being entirely inapplicable to the Trojan story.

ment in the church of St. Lorenzo at Naples. Of this event we should accordingly expect to find reflection in the *Filostrato*.

That the poet's description of the first sight had by Troilus of Criseida at the Trojan sacrifices in honor of the Palladium may at the same time be looked upon as a description of his own first sight of Maria at the church at Naples, we have already stated (p. 14, n. 3). It now behooves us to look somewhat narrowly into Boccaccio's account of the enamorment of Troilus in the *Filostrato* to test the truth of that statement.

While, as already explained (pp. 34-38), certain particulars of this account were undoubtedly borrowed from Benoit's description of Achilles' first sight of Polyxena at the Trojan sacrifices in commemoration of Hector's death, there nevertheless remains a certain residuum of others which find no parallel in the French poem but reappear in one or other of the several versions[1] of the author's account of his own first sight of his lady in the church at Naples.[2]

---

[1] *Filocolo*, I, 4-6; *Fiammetta*, pp. 7-12; *Ameto*, pp. 153-155; *Amorosa visione*, pp. 178-179. Cf. p. 14, n. 3.

[2] Strictly speaking the sight had of Maria by Boccaccio in the church at Naples appears not to have been the first sight that he had had of her. According to the concurrent testimony of the *Filocolo* (II, 247-248), the *Ameto* (p. 154), and the *Amorosa visione* (p. 178), when the lover beholds his lady, he recollects having seen her before (see Crescini, *Contributo*, pp. 123-126). Apropos of these consonant representations, Wilkins (*Modern Philology*, XI, 45) quite properly remarks that Boccaccio may well have seen in Naples so "prominent [a] member of the court circle" as Maria before he beheld her at the church. But there is, in so far as the present writer can discover, no ground for Wilkins' further assertion (pp. 41-42) that "in the course of the story [of the *Filostrato*] it turns out that Troilus and Criseida have seen each other before the enamorment." To him it appears that, whatever may have been the occasion of this earlier glimpse had of Maria by Boccaccio, the story of the *Filostrato* afforded him no convenient opportunity for any parallel. Since no consequences seem to have resulted from this possible earlier sight of his mistress, we shall,

There can be little doubt that it was a recollection of the church of St. Lorenzo in which he first beheld Maria, and not Benoit, that prompted Boccaccio to employ the term "tempio" (*Filostrato*, I, 17, *4; 20, 3*) to designate the edifice in which the enamorment of Troilus occurred. In his account of the enamorment of Achilles (*Roman de Troie*, vv. 17489-17637) Benoit nowhere uses the word *temple* to name the building in which the sacrifices in honor of Hector were performed. Only in a passage far removed from this account (v. 22098) do we learn that the "temple of Apollo" was the place in which the Trojan dead were buried. On the other hand in the author's account of his own enamorment in the *Filocolo* (I, 5) we read that it was "in un tempio di Partenope" that he first beheld Maria[1] and in Caleone's version of the same event in the *Ameto* (p. 154) it is in "un tempio" that he sees Fiammetta.

Again it is specified in the *Filostrato* (I, 18, *1-6*) that the sacrifices in honor of the Palladium occurred in the spring of the year:

> Perchè venuto il vago tempo il quale
> Riveste i prati d'erbette e di fiori,
> E che gaio diviene ogni animale,
> E in diversi atti mostran loro amori;
> Li troian padri al Palladio fatale
> Fer preparare li consueti onori.

for brevity's sake, take the liberty henceforth, as we have done heretofore, of neglecting it.

[1] While, as Young in another connection suggests (p. 62, n. 3), it is not impossible that at the time of writing the earlier portion of the *Filocolo*, Boccaccio may already have formed the acquaintance of Benoit and while he may in that case have called the *chiesa* in which he first saw Maria "tempio" from a sense of what would seem appropriate to the antique ceremony described in the *Roman de Troie*, it is far more likely that he did so in accordance with his uniform habit in that romance of describing Christian rites under pagan formulae. See Gaspary, *Storia della letteratura italiana*, II, 5.

It can hardly be doubted that this specification is an autobiographical reminiscence of the springtime or Holy Saturday service at which the author himself beheld Maria at the church in Naples (see pp. 14-15).[1]

Boccaccio places marked emphasis upon the cynical attitude toward lovers maintained by Troilus immediately preceding his sight of Criseida, how he laughingly points out to his companions some lover vainly caught in the toils of some lady and comments to them upon the fickleness of womankind (*Filostrato*, I, 21, *4-8*, 22), how he rails at the anxious loves of others without suspicion of what heaven was soon to bring upon him (I, 25, *4-8*), and how he regrets these scornful remarks as soon as he is himself smitten with Love's arrow (I, 29, *5-6*).

This derisive point of view on the part of Troilus, while very possibly suggested in part by the caustic

[1] See Young, p. 42. It is to be noted that Young regards this and other resemblances which, as we shall see (p. 55, n. 1; p. 56, n. 1), he points out (pp. 41-42) between the accounts of Troilus' enamorment in the *Filostrato* and of Boccaccio's own enamorment in the *Filocolo*, primarily as evidence of the indebtedness of the former to the latter. Such indebtedness is, however, very improbable. It is not unlikely that Boccaccio's initial account of his own enamorment in the *Filocolo*, forming, as it does, with the subsequent account of his commission from Maria to write that romance, a sort of prefatory dedication to the whole work, was added after the *Filocolo* was completed. But assuming that this was not the case and that, as Young supposes (p. 41, n. 2) the account in the *Filocolo* was written before the *Filostrato* was begun, any resemblance between it and the story of Troilus' enamorment in the *Filostrato* can but prove, if it proves anything, that the account in the latter romance was also autobiographical. Certainly an occurrence as memorable as the occasion of the beginning of the courtship cannot have failed to stamp itself much more lastingly upon the mind of the author than a previous literary treatment of it in the *Filocolo* could have done. Hence it would appear more reasonable to regard those portions of the account of Troilus' first sight of Criseida in the *Filostrato* which resemble the *Filocolo* as freshly revived personal recollections rather than as reflections—at second hand—of an experience already recorded in the *Filocolo*.

animadversions upon the inconstancy of the female sex to which Benoit gives expression in connection with his prediction of Briseida's approaching change of heart toward Troilus (*Roman de Troie*, vv. 13438-13456),[1] was without doubt more largely prompted by unfortunate love experiences through which he had himself passed before seeing Maria in the church at Naples. For in the *Ameto* (p. 149) Caleone relates how, before beholding Fiammetta, he had rejected Pampinea for Abrotonia only to be jilted in turn by the latter.[2] From this passage it is clear that before the momentous event that marked the beginning of his grand passion, Boccaccio had himself "played with light love in the portals" to his own discomfiture. It may readily be inferred that it was the disillusioning experiences through which he had then passed that led him to ascribe to Troilus such cynical opinions about lovers.

Confirmation of this conjecture is afforded by the strikingly personal application made by Troilus of the foregoing cynical remarks to his own case (I, 23, *1-2;* 24, *1-4*):

> Io provai già per la mia gran follia
> Qual fosse questo maladetto fuoco.
>
> .   .   .   .   .
>
> Or ne son fuor, mercè n'abbia colui
> Che fu di me più ch'io stesso pietoso,
> Io dico Giove, iddio vero, da cui
> Viene ogni grazia, e vivommi in riposo . . .

Further evidence appears in what he says himself when,

[1] A parallel not noted by Young in his list of Boccaccio's borrowings from the Troilus and Briseida episode of Benoit (see p. 29, n. 1).

[2] See Wilkins, *Modern Language Notes*, 1908, XXIII, 111-116, 137-142.

speaking in his own person in his account of his own enamorment in the *Filocolo* (I, 5), he declares that after long gazing at the beautiful lady who stood before him in the church at Naples, he beheld "Amore in abito tanto pietoso, che me, cui lungamente a mia istanza avea risparmiato, fece tornare, desideroso d' essergli per così bella donna subieto, ecc."[1]

Still again there can be no doubt that Boccaccio's allusion to the dress worn by Criseida when first seen by Troilus in the temple of Pallas at Troy (*Filostrato*, I, 26, 7) is, in like manner, autobiographical. For this allusion, which describes her as wearing "a white veil" with her "black habit," is repeated verbatim in the same autobiographical passage in the *Filocolo*. Thus in the *Filostrato* (I, 26, 5-8) we read that Troilus, peering in and out among the bystanders, casts his eyes

> La dov'era Criseida piacente,
> Sotto candido velo in bruna vesta,
> Fra l'altre donne in sì solenne festa.[2]

Similarly in the *Filocolo* (I, 6) Boccaccio tells us that upon his visit, not long after the enamorment, to

---

[1] See Young (p. 41), who makes no comment upon the special autobiographical significance of both these passages.

[2] In the *Filostrato* (I, 38, 7) the words "sotto candido velo in bruna vesta" are repeated by Troilus in his thanks to the God of Love immediately after the enamorment and with obvious reference to the apparel of Criseida on that occasion. In another reference to the black attire of Criseida (I, 19, 2), which precedes the account of the enamorment, occur simply the words "bruna vesta." Here Boccaccio has in mind, not the penitential season, but the widowhood of Criseida, to which allusion has just been made (I, 11, 3). The same is true in the case of two references that follow the description of the enamorment, in both of which the shorter phrase is used, "vestimento bruno" (II, 54, 5) and "bruna vesta" again (II, 60, 1). In the two passages that relate directly to the enamorment the poet may thus be said to have had a double reason for clothing his heroine in black.

the convent at Baia, he found Maria conversing with the "sacerdotesse di Diana sotto bianchi veli e di neri vestimenti vestite."[1] Since, as remarked above (p. 13 and n. 2), Maria, when married, had reserved the right to resume her life in the convent, it is to be supposed that she had on this occasion donned the garb of a nun. That on the occasion of the enamorment she was similarly attired, we have no evidence in the *Filocolo*, no reference being made in that romance to the dress worn by Maria in the scene in the temple. But here the *Ameto* comes to our aid. For on the first of the two visits paid by Caleone to the church of St. Lorenzo, that on Holy Saturday (see p. 15, n. 3), Fiammetta is clad in "bruna vesta" (p. 154).

Finally, there are, as shown by the *Proemio*, three further representations in other parts of the *Filostrato* that seem to reflect experiences through which the author passed during the absence of his lady in Sannio.

The first of these representations is as follows. We read in the *Filostrato* (V, 54-55) that after the departure of Criseida to the Greek camp, Troilus was in the habit of revisiting spots in Troy associated in his mind with various marks of favor which she had deigned to bestow upon him. In like fashion Boccaccio writes his lady in the *Proemio* (p. 119) that "to suffer lesser miseries [his eyes] have abstained . . . from viewing the church, the loggias, the piazzas, and the other places in which they formerly sought eagerly and anxiously to see—and sometimes did see—[her] countenance."[2]

---

[1] See Young (p. 42), who, as above, regards the *Filostrato* passage mainly as an imitation of the corresponding passage in the *Filocolo*.

[2] This passage in the *Filostrato* Young (p. 88) derives from two

The second of the representations in the *Filostrato* the autobiographical nature of which is attested by the *Proemio* is this. In the *Filostrato* (II, 63, *5-8*) Troilus writes to Criseida that he takes delight in viewing that quarter of the heaven only under which he believes her to be:

> Sol quella parte del ciel mi diletta,
> Sotto la quale or credo che dimori,
> Quella riguardo, e dico: quella vede
> Ora colei da cui spero mercede.

In the *Proemio* (p. 120) we read: "ma io affermo solo una essere quella parte che alquanto la loro tristizia mitiga, riguardando quelle contrade, quelle montagne, quella parte del ciel, fra le quali e sotto la quale porto ferma opinione che voi siate."

The third of these representations is as follows. In the *Filostrato* (V, 70, *1-2*, *3-7*) Troilus imagines that the breezes that he feels in his face as he looks fondly

accounts given in the *Filocolo* (I, 120, 263) of similar visits paid by Biancofiore to parts of her father's palace in which she and Florio used sometimes to be together. We have, in pursuance of Young's derivation, included this among other *Filostrato* passages that betray dependence upon the *Filocolo* (see p. 47, n. 3) and are still disposed to regard it as written after, and therefore presumably not without consciousness of the passages in the *Filocolo*. Nevertheless it would appear probable that its inspiration is largely autobiographical, the more so since the *Filocolo* passages themselves seem to be of like origin, Young having failed to find warrant for them in the sources of that romance. Confirmation of this view is furnished by Antona-Traversi, who finds (*Propugnatore*, 1883, XVI, parte seconda, pp. 268-269, 406) similar representations in the autobiographical *Fiammetta*. Indeed it seems to us probable that the story of the separation between Florio and Biancofiore, though present, of course, in the sources of the *Filocolo*, was, like the *Filostrato*, written after the departure of Maria to Sannio and that no small part of the elaboration which the old story received at the hands of Boccaccio, owed its inspiration, no less surely than the parallel passages in the *Filostrato*, to the grief experienced by its author because of his lady's absence in Sannio.

toward the Greek camp, are sighs wafted from Criseida:

> El riguardava li Greci attendati
> Davanti a Troia . . .
>   . . . e ciò che soffiarsi
> Sentia nel viso, sì come mandati
> Sospiri di Criseida solea darsi
> A creder fosser, ecc.

This passage again is matched in the continuation of
the foregoing passage in the *Proemio* as follows:
"quindi ogni aura, ogni suave vento che di colà viene,
così nel viso ricevo, quasi il vostro senza fallo abbia
tocco."[1]

From what has already been said the conclusion
clearly emerges that what most appealed to Boccaccio
in Benoit's episode of the love of Troilus for Briseida
had lain in the provision by the latter of a story of the
separation between two lovers which he himself might
bend to purposes quite opposite to those contemplated
by the French trouvère by using as a vehicle to convey to his lady his sense of grief over her departure.
Benoit's interest had lain in the story of a woman, not
of a man, of a woman light in love, not of a man constant in affection. Boccaccio's special contribution to
the development of the story of Troilus and Cressida

---

[1] Undoubtedly dependent upon the same personal experiences of
the author as related in the *Proemio* and, if anterior, no doubt had in
mind by the poet when composing the above-quoted passage in the
Filostrato, is the following passage in the *Filocolo* (I, 120), quoted by
Young (pp. 89-90), in which Biancofiore, looking forth toward Montorio from the roof of her father's palace in Marmorina, takes, "dopo
molti sospiri," "alcun diletto, immaginando e dicendo fra sè medisima:
là è il mio disio e mio bene. E talvolta avvenia che stando ella sentia
alcuno suave e piccolo venticello venire da quella parte, e ferivala per
mezzo della fronte, il quale ella con aperte braccia riceveva nel suo
petto, dicendo: questo venticello toccò il mio Florio come egli fa ora
me avanti egli giungesse qui."

lay in the fact that he shifted the center of gravity of the story from the diverting activities of a frivolous and changeable heroine to the pathetic passivities of a patient and long-suffering hero.[1] The Italian poet interests himself in Criseida only in so far as her personality and actions affect Troilus. Throughout the first five cantos of the poem the fortunes of the two lovers are closely intertwined as their loves are reciprocal. But from the moment of Criseida's departure to the Greek camp Boccaccio's interest in her wanes. In the sixth canto he relates as rapidly as possible only enough of the story of her defection to Diomede to enable the reader to see what the outcome is to be. In the three remaining cantos his heroine passes entirely from view save as she abides in the mind of her lover or as he seeks news of her, now through letters and Pandarus, now through questionings of the chance wayfarer from the Greek camp. It is Troilus, therefore, who from the beginning to the end of the *Filostrato* holds the center of the stage and it is the vicissitudes of his fortune—as they pass "from woe to weal and after out of joy"— that form the primary business of the poem.

In thus concentrating interest upon Troilus, Boccaccio was, however, confronted with the inevitable difficulty of seeking to arouse interest in a hero who plays an essentially passive rôle. Initiative Troilus largely lacks. Whatever activity he may display in carrying out the instructions of Pandarus in the wooing of Criseida he largely ceases to display from the moment word is received of the contemplated surrender of

[1] Compare, for example, the utter prostration of spirits suffered by the Italian Troilus when at last he becomes convinced of the infidelity of Criseida (*Filostrato*, VIII, 11-21) with the light-hearted manner in which, as we have seen (p. 34), the French Troilus accepts his betrayal merely as one of the inevitable hazards in the game of love.

Criseida to the Greeks. From that point to the end of the poem his sufferings[1] increase and his activities diminish as he awaits in vain the return of his lady.

For these reasons it is inevitable that the *Filostrato*, while based upon an epic theme, should, especially toward the close, produce an essentially lyrical impression. Not infrequently the action of the poem halts and now through monologue and now through dialogue with Pandarus, we are enabled to perceive what is passing in the minds of the hero and of the heroine. According to Savj-Lopez,[2] "profound descent into the depths of the human heart, without regard to the external world, blind absorption in the sole thought of love manifest themselves in the *Filostrato* as nowhere else in the narrative poetry of Italy."

To find sentiments and images proper to the depiction of Troilus' grief, Boccaccio had recourse to sources that stand somewhat apart from those that supplied him with his story material. If for the latter he relied upon the chivalrous romances of the North of France,[3] for the former he depended upon the love lyric of the South of France, as it had established itself in the works of his own Italian predecessors, notably of the poets of

[1] In his explanation to his lady in the *Proemio* of his purpose in writing the *Filostrato* Boccaccio had naturally to make the most of the sufferings of Troilus as that part of the story in which he was most anxious to arouse her interest. Obviously, however, the demands of the Trojan story were such that it was not until toward the end of his poem that he was able to attend to them. We are disposed to agree with Gaspary (*Storia della letteratura italiana*, II, 10-11) in regarding this concluding portion of the poem as the least interesting and by no means with Hauvette (*op. cit.*, pp. 80-81) in taking the poet to task for not having fulfilled the promises of the *Proemio* by limiting himself exclusively to this theme.

[2] *Op. cit.*, p. 478.

[3] Viz., Benoit's *Roman de Troie* and versions of the story of Floire and Blanchefleur which ultimately ran back to a lost French original (see p. 40, n. 1).

the *dolce stil nuovo*.[1] Wherever in his representation of
the sorrows of Troilus, Boccaccio becomes most intimate
and personal, wherever in depicting his woes he seems
most clearly to have his own anguish in mind, the fact
is signalized by his more abundant use of the writings
of his own Italian predecessors.

First and foremost among the poets of the *dolce stil
nuovo* from whom Boccaccio borrowed hints and suggestions for his representation of the passion of Troilus
stands Dante.

Of Dante's poetry we meet constant echoes throughout the *Filostrato*.[2] Of the *Vita nuova* in particular, in

[1] A school of poetry which at its best was one of surpassing loveli-
ness. It had as its chief members Guido Guinizelli, Guido Cavalcanti,
and Dante, and is supposed to have derived its name from Dante's
praise (*Purgatorio*, XXVI, 112) of the "dolci detti" of its founder,
the Bolognese Guido Guinizelli. The poets of the *dolce stil* adopted
from antecedent Provençal poets—from Faidit, Vaqueiras, and Ventadorn—the conception of love as having an elevating and ennobling
effect upon the lover. But under the influence of theological and
philosophical teachings they carried this conception to mystic heights
undreamed of by their Provençal predecessors. The poets of the Italian
school retained, to be sure, the elaborately ritualistic formulae be-
queathed them by their Provençal forerunners but they turned them
to strictly supersensuous uses. So far, too, as initial inspiration was
concerned, the lady of the Provençal lyric had not in every case evapo-
rated into a symbol; her prototype was often, as in the case of Dante's
Beatrice, a lady in the flesh. But in the poetical representation this lady
was largely divested of bodily attributes and carried far in the direction
of a purely bloodless abstraction. See Salvadori, G., "Il problema
storico dello 'stil novo,'" *Nuova antologia di scienze, lettere, ed arti*,
quarta serie, 1896, LXV, 385 ff.; Azzolina, L., *Il "dolce stil nuovo,"* ecc.,
Palermo, 1903; Vossler, K., *Die philosophische Grundlagen zum "süs-
sen neuen Stil*," Heidelberg, 1904; Rossi, V., "Il 'dolce stil novo,'"
Conferenza letta nella sala di Dante in Orsanmichele: Lecture Dantis,
Florence, 1905; Pflaum, H., "Die Idee der Liebe," *Heidelberger Ab-
handlungen zur Philosophie und ihre Geschichte*, Tübingen, 1926, VII,
8 ff.

[2] Cf. *Filostrato*, II, 72, 6 with *Inferno*, canto II, verse 106; *Filo-
strato*, II, 80, 1-4 with *Inferno*, II, 127-130; *Filostrato*, II, 135, 8 with
Purgatorio, III, 78; *Filostrato*, III, 1 with *Paradiso*, I, 13-17; 22-27;
Filostrato, IV, 94, 1-2 with *Convivio*, trattato IV, canzone, verse 121;

which, more than in his other works, Dante shows himself to be a poet of the *new sweet style*, Boccaccio makes use in describing the effects of love upon Troilus. In illustration of this a single quotation must suffice.[1] Of the softening and humanizing effects of love upon Troilus, Boccaccio writes in the *Filostrato* (III, 93) as follows:

> Ed avvevna ch'el fosse di reale
> Sangue, e volendo ancor molto potesse;
> Benigno si faceva a tutti eguale,
> Come che alcun talvolta nol valesse:
> Così voleva Amor, che tutto vale,
> Che el per compiacere altrui facesse;
> Superbia, invidia, ed avarizia in ira
> Aveva, ed ognun dietro si tira.

Similarly Dante in the *Vita nuova* (section XI, *ed. cit.*, p. 63) writes thus of the uplifting influence exerted upon him by the presence of Beatrice: "Dico che quando ella apparia da parte alcuna, per la speranza dell'ammirabile salute nullo nemico mi rimanea, anzi me giungea una fiamma di caritade, la quale mi facea perdonare a chiunque m'avesse offeso: e chi allora m'avesse addimandato di alcuna cosa, la mia risponsione sarebbe stato, Amore, con viso vestito d'umilità."

Nor is it only in passages in which he is writing of the passion of Troilus, that Boccaccio turns to the poets of his own native country for inspiration. Of Dante he makes large use in his description, in the *Proemio*, of his own passion and of the state of mind in which the departure of his own lady has left him. Thus, to cite

---

Filostrato, VII, 24, 7-8 with *Vita nuova*, section III, Fraticelli, *ed. cit.*, p. 55, ll. 2-3; *Filostrato*, VIII, 17, 5-8 with *Purgatorio*, VI, 118-120.

[1] This passage, quoted by Savj-Lopez (*op. cit.*, pp. 463-464), is selected because it furnishes perhaps the best example of a fundamental tenet of the *dolce stil nuovo*, that of the conception of love as a regenerating influence in human life. (Cf. Savj-Lopez, pp. 462-463.)

but one example,[1] in the passage (p. 125) in which he represents himself as seeking an outlet for his grief over the departure of Maria for Sannio by giving expression to it in song, Boccaccio is imitating a passage in the *Vita nuova* (section XXXIII, *ed. cit.*, p. 101) in which, in like manner, Dante represents himself as anxious to secure relief from his affliction over the death of Beatrice by writing his sonnet beginning

Gli occhi dolenti per pietà del core.[2]

Nor is Dante the only poet of the *dolce stil nuovo* who can be identified as having supplied Boccaccio with inspiration in singing of the woes of Troilus. Another such, as shown by Volpi,[3] is Cino da Pistoja.[4] The first

[1] Another less evident example is, as pointed out by Savj-Lopez (p. 443), to be found in a passage in the *Proemio* (pp. 118, 120) opening "Dico adunque" and ending "m'e stato presso," in which the author speaks "with an almost mystic fervor" of his "weeping eyes" in a style that bears a general resemblance to that of the *Vita nuova*. Significant is it that in the midst of this passage Boccaccio makes the same quotation from *Lamentations* (I, 1) that Dante makes in the *Vita nuova* (section XXIX, *ed. cit.*, p. 98).

Again, as indicated by Korting, G. (*Boccaccio's Leben und Werke*, Leipsic, 1880, p. 568), when Boccaccio writes in the *Proemio* (p. 120): "ma quale sopra le cose unte veggiamo talvolta le fiamme discorrere," he is imitating Dante's *Inferno* (XIX, 28-29):

"Qual suole il fiammeggiar delle cose unte
Muoversi pur su per l'estrema buccia."

[2] This parallelism (cited by Savj-Lopez, p. 444) occurs between the passage in the *Proemio* opening "E conoscendo assai chiaramente" and ending "amorosa dolore" and the opening passage of section XXXII of the *Vita nuova*, from the beginning through "della anima mia." Particularly noteworthy is the marked verbal resemblance between Boccaccio's "pensai di volere con alcuno onesto rammarichio dare luogo a quello a uscire dell' tristo petto" and Dante's "pensai di voler disfogarla con alquante parole dolorose."

[3] Volpi, G., *Bullettino storico pistoiese*, 1899, I, 116-117.

[4] Whose actual name was Guittoncino de'Sinibuldi. On the death of Guido Cavalcanti in 1300, Cino succeeded him in the friendship of Dante. He was among the number of those to whom the Florentine poet sent the first sonnet of his *Vita nuova* for their criticism and to it he replied in a highly complimentary fashion in a sonnet of his own.

four ottave of the song of a disconsolate lover (*Filostrato*, V, 62-66), put into the mouth of Troilus when informed of the coming departure of Criseida, Boccaccio has lifted almost bodily out of a canzone of four nine-line stanzas by Cino opening:

> La dolce vista e 'l bel guardo suave.[1]

Of the four ottave based upon Cino, the third (*Filostrato*, V, 64), in which Troilus complains that every fair lady whom he greets puts him in mind of her who is absent, suggests the famous canzone of Guido Guinizelli,[2] whose doctrine of the "gentle heart" was so popular with the poets of the *dolce stil nuovo*:

> Quando per gentil atto di salute
> Ver bella donna giro gli occhi alquanto,
> Sì tutta si disfà la mia virtute
> Che ritener non posso dentro il pianto;

Cino's most beautiful poem is a sonnet written to console Dante on the death of Beatrice. See Rossetti, D. G., *Dante and His Circle*, London, 1874, pp. 15-20.

[1] Each of Boccaccio's four ottave opens with a line either identical or nearly identical with the opening line in the corresponding stanza of Cino and within Boccaccio's ottave occur close verbal resemblances to the interior of Cino's corresponding stanzas.

[2] The canzone in which Guido Guinizelli gives classical expression to his doctrine that only those of "gentle heart" are capable of loving, opens with the well-known line:

> "Al cor gentil ripara sempre amore."

See the edition of this canzone by Federzoni, G., Bologna, 1905.

The far-reaching influence of the phrase "cor gentil" is attested by its reappearance in Chaucer's "favorite line" (*Canterbury Tales*, A, 1761):

> "For pitee renneth sone in gentil herte,"

repeated almost verbatim three times (*ibid.*, E, 1986, F, 479, and *Legend of Good Women, Prologue*, B, 503). The phrase is also used by Chaucer in two other lines (*Canterbury Tales*, B, 660 and *Troilus and Criseyde*, III, 1, 5).

Root, in his comment on the Troilus line (*ed. cit.*, p. 463) and Manly, J. M., in his comment upon *Canterbury Tales*, A, 1761 (*Chaucer's Canterbury Tales*, Henry Holt, 1928, p. 549) are of the opinion that Chaucer took the phrase from Dante (*Inferno*, V, 100). But only in

Così mi van l'amorose ferute
Membrando la mia donna, a cui son tanto,
O lasso me, lontano a veder lei,
Che se 'l volesse Amor, morir vorrei.[1]

If in depicting the impassioned longing of his love-sick hero Boccaccio drew largely upon the lofty idealizations of the *dolce stil nuovo*, it was, obviously, to models of a less exalted and entirely non-lyrical strain that he was under the necessity of turning for his delineation of the aberrations of his inconstant heroine. In his representation of Criseida it was impossible to picture the life of Maria as faithfully as he had pictured his own life in his representation of Troilus. For while his hero was to a large extent flesh of his flesh and bone of his bone, his heroine sustained no such intimate ties of kinship to a lady who as yet had neither presented him with her love nor deserted him, as had Criseida, Troilus. In the treatment of Criseida, therefore, as contrasted with the treatment of Troilus, it was inevitable that, if the plot of the received story was not to be sacrificed, the influence of Benoit should have been paramount. And it cannot be doubted that however strange it may seem that as lover Boccaccio should not have been revolted at the thought of comparing his own Maria to the fickle heroine of the *Roman de Troie*,[2] as artist he "found," as

Guinizelli does the verb *riparare*, repeated by Chaucer in the Troilus line, appear. See also Tatlock, J. S. P., *Modern Language Notes*, 1920, XXXV, 443.

[1] The very phrase of Guinizelli appears in the following lines (*Filostrato*, III, 74, *5-8*) of the hymn in which Troilus, exultant over the newly won love of Criseida, apostrophizes Venus (III, 74, *6-9*):

> "Benigna donna d'ogni gentil core,
> Certa cagion del valor che mi muove
> A' sospir dolci della mia salute,
> Sempre lodata sia la tua virtute."

[2] If to the modern reader it may seem strange that Boccaccio should have put into the mouth of Troilus such glowing tributes to the high

Hauvette remarks,[1] "in the malicious sketch of the French trouvère courage to draw one of those profiles of frivolous and light-hearted women by whom he was always much diverted, as he observed them in Naples."[2] Moreover it cannot be denied that Boccaccio's treatment of the surrender of Criseida to Diomede, while much briefer than Benoit's, is not on the whole quite as unsparing in its reflections upon her conduct.[3]

Elsewhere occur scattered at random throughout the *Filostrato* and used without special reference either to hero or to heroine, echoes from a considerable number of lyrical poets other than those of the *dolce stil nuovo*.

In marked contrast to the practice observed by Boccaccio in his *Filocolo*, is the hospitality he has shown in

merits of a lady who was even then betraying him, the all-sufficient answer must be that such expressions but feebly voiced the subsequent sentiments of the poet himself toward his own lady, at whose shrine, despite his own betrayal, he continued, save in the *Fiammetta*, to burn incense ever afterward (see p. 7 and n. 5). Furthermore it was ever a marked characteristic of Boccaccio, in whom the man and the poet were ever struggling for mastery, that in the celebration of an essentially carnal passion he could avail himself of the mystic transports of a purely Platonic affection.

[1] *Op. cit.*, p. 48.

[2] That in his representation of Criseida Boccaccio was indulging his artist's fondness for portraying the lady of light virtue as he had come to see and to know the type in the contemporaneous life of Naples, while incapable of positive proof, may readily be conjectured from the presence of contemporaneous portraiture in his other works. On his sketches from Florentine life in the *Amorosa visione*, see Antona-Traversi, *Studj di filologia romanza*, 1885, I, 425 ff., and from Neapolitan life in the *Decameron*, Casetti, *Nuova antologia di scienze, lettere ed arti*, 1875, XXVIII, 558. On the likelihood that he was pursuing the same method in the *Filostrato*, see Gaspary, *Storia della letteratura italiana*, II, 8, 10, and De Sanctis, F., *Storia della letteratura italiana*, two vols., Bari, 1925, I, 284.

[3] Moland and D'Héricault maintain (*op. cit.*, Introduction, pp. lxxxviii-lxxxix) that whereas the Italian Criseida holds out longer against the importunities of Troilus than does the French Briseida against those of Diomede, she falls when she does fall, to earth and remains there. It is not her body simply that she sacrifices but her soul, for she has meditated long upon her fall and her surrender is deliberate.

the *Filostrato* to stray bits of verse from the popular muse of his own native country. A somewhat doubtful instance of such hospitality is found by Savj-Lopez in the reflections of Criseida, when debating with herself whether or not to accept the love of Troilus, upon the transitory character of youth and beauty and the impossibility of recovering lost opportunities of enjoyment when once old age has claimed her for its own (*Filostrato*, II, 69-71).[1] Less subject to question is the popular origin of a number of the distressful musings of Troilus after the departure of Criseida to the Greek camp. Not only are certain of the expressions used by the deserted lover in his letters to his absent mistress maintained to be suggestive of the messages sent by Pistoiese mountaineers to their distant sweethearts[2] but certain naïve ejaculations of despair seem to betoken popular influence.[3] Among these are a few that may well

[1] Savj-Lopez' attempted demonstration (*op. cit.*, p. 475) of the popular origin of Criseida's reflections is far from convincing. He points to the recurrence of a ballata of Boccaccio's—found not, as he says, in the *Filocolo* but in the *Rime* (Moutier, *ed. cit.*, Ballata II, p. 106)—opening:

> "Il fior che 'l valor perde
> Da poi che cade, mai non si rinverde,"

in four early editions of canzoni a ballo, in the last of which, according to Carducci, G., *Cantilene e ballate*, ecc., Pisa, 1871, pp. 171-172, the ballata in question undergoes variations not unlike those which one finds in popular poetry. It seems more probable, however, that the entirely human sentiments of Criseida were suggested to Boccaccio by Horace or some other exponent of ancient epicureanism.

[2] Savj-Lopez, p. 476.

[3] Savj-Lopez (pp. 475-476) cites four such passages in the *Filostrato* (II, 88, *7-8*; III, *58*, *1-2*; 86, *1-4*; VII, 64-65) and remarks that the last, in which Troilus apostrophizes the mountains and waters that enjoy the sight of Criseida, resembles a modern anonymous poem quoted by Tigri, G. (*Canti populari toscani*, Florence, 1860, p. 170):

> "O sol che te ne vai, che te ne vai,
> O sol che te ne vai su per que' poggi,
> Fammelo un bel piacer se tu potrai,
> Salutammi il mio amor, non l' ho visto oggi."

be of ultimately Provençal origin. A comparison made by Troilus between the return of love by one's mistress and the reanimating effects of spring upon a dead earth calls to mind a like simile in the poetry of Peire Vidal.[1] Again Boccaccio's idea in the *Proemio* (p. 120) and in the *Filostrato* (V, 70) that the breezes that blow upon the cheeks of a lover from that quarter of the heavens under which his mistress resides have touched her cheeks likewise, appears also in Bernart de Ventadorn.[2] Again Boccaccio's figure of "a leaf in the wind" occurs likewise in the same poet.[3]

[1] In the hope that his lady will turn upon him the eye of favor Troilus exclaims (*Filostrato*, I, 56, *1-2*):

> "Io tornerò, se tu fai, donna, questo,
> Qual fiore in nuovo prato in primavera."

Similarly Vidal (ed. J. Anglade, *Les poésies* de *Peire Vidal*, Paris, 1913, XVII, ix, p. 55), writes thus:

> "Na Vierna, lonjamen:
> Vos ai estat de bon sen
> Mas era mi renovel,
> Com bela flors en ramel."

[2] Thus in the *Proemio* (p. 120) Boccaccio writes: "Ogni aura, ogni suave vento che di colà viene, così nel viso ricevo, quasi il vostro senza niuno fallo abbia tocco." In much the same fashion Bernart de Ventadorn (ed. C. Appel, *Bernart de Ventadorn: seine Leider*, Halle, 1915, XXXVII, 1, p. 212) writes:

> "Can la frej' aura venta
> deves vostre päis,
> vejaire m' es qu' eu senta
> un ven de paradis
> per amor de la genta
> vas cui en sui aclis, etc."

[3] Of fickle damsels Boccaccio writes (VIII, 30, *7-8*):

> "Virtù non sente nè conoscimento,
> Volubil sempre come foglia al vento."

Similarly Bernart de Ventadorn (*op. cit.*, XXXI, vi, p. 190):

> "Cant eu la vei, be m'es parven
> als olhs, al vis, a la color,
> car aissi tremble de paor
> com fa la folha contra·l ven."

Similarly characteristic of the *Filostrato* as distinguished from the *Filocolo* is the much more limited use in the former work of ancient authors. While, as we have seen (p. 7, n. 1), when a student of the Canon Law, Boccaccio became an avid student of classical mythology and while in his *Filocolo* he is constantly making a pedantic and often highly irrelevant display of his newly acquired learning,[1] the *Filostrato* is refreshingly free of any forced or inartistic display of the fruits of this scholarship. A few reminiscences of Ovid appear in connection with Troilus' letters to Criseida. Thus he opens his first letter (*Filostrato*, II, 96, 7-8) as follows:

> Qui da me salutata non sarai,
> Perch' io non l' ho se tu non la me dai.

Even so Phaedra writes to Hippolytus (*Heroides*, IV, 1-2):

> Qua nisi tu dederis, caritura est ipsa salute,
> Mittit Amazonio Cressa puella viro.[2]

Most interesting of all the classical echoes in the *Filostrato* is, however, the prolonged simile in which Boccaccio likens the stricken condition of Troilus, when apprised of the decision of the Trojans to restore Criseida to Calchas, to the drooping lily of the field when upturned by the husbandman's plough (*Filostrato*, IV, 18):

> Qual, poscia ch' è dall' aratro intaccato
> Ne' campi il giglio, per soverchio sole
> Casca ed appassa, e 'l bel color cangiato
> Pallido fassi; tale, alle parole

[1] See Gaspary, *Storia della letteratura italiana*, II, 5.

[2] See Savj-Lopez (p. 477), who likewise cites two further instances of Ovidian imitation in the later letter written by Troilus to Criseida to remonstrate with her on her failure to return on the tenth day (cf. *Filostrato*, VII, 54 with *Heroides*, III, 5-6 and *Filostrato*, VII, 74 with *Heroides*, III, 3-4).

Rendute a' Greci dal determinato
Consiglio infra' Troian, in tanto mole
Di danno e di periglio, tramortito
Li cadde Troilo d' alto duol ferito.

While, as pointed out by Antona-Traversi,[1] the figure of a flower uprooted by the plough was a favorite one among ancient authors, occurring in Ovid (*Metamorphoses*, X, 4), in Virgil (*Aeneid*, IX, 435 ff.), and in Catullus (*Carmina*, XXII), the use of it most nearly resembling Boccaccio's is, as indicated by Landau,[2] to be found in the *Posthomerica* of the Greek writer Quintus of Smyrna (IV, 423-429), who unlike the aforementioned Latin writers, employs it, as does Boccaccio, in speaking of Troilus:

As when a gardener with new-whetted scythe
Mows down, ere it may seed, a blade of corn
Or poppy, in a garden dewy-fresh
And blossom-flushed, which by a water-course
Crowdeth its blooms—mows it ere it may reach
Its goal of bringing offspring to the birth,
And with his scythe-sweep makes its life-work vain
And barren of all issue, nevermore
Now to be fostered by the dews of spring;
So did Peleides cut down Priam's son, etc.[3]

III. The Filostrato as a Courtly Love Document

No poet of the later Middle Ages who undertook to compose a love story for the delectation of the upper circles of society could afford to neglect certain well-established rules of literary procedure which prescribed the nature of the relationship which should subsist be-

[1] *Giovanni Boccaccio del Dottor M. Landau: traduzione di C. Antona-Traversi*, Naples, 1881, p. 319.

[2] Landau, M., *Giovanni Boccaccio: sein Leben und seine Werke*, Stuttgart, 1877, p. 85, n. 2.

[3] Translated by Way, A. S., Macmillan, 1913, p. 199.

tween his hero and his heroine and the principles of conduct which should govern them therein.

There were in the circumstances in which Boccaccio found himself during his sojourn at Naples exceptionally urgent reasons why he in particular should have paid especial heed to the observance of these rules of Courtly Love,[1] as they were called.[2] For it was as the son of a Florentine money-lender that he had come there —not the best of recommendations for one who sought to win fame as a poet in that aristocratic environment. How better could he hope to overcome the prejudices certain to be cherished against one reared in the sordid atmosphere of trade than by showing himself a past master in the manipulation of a body of conventions with which only the gentle and highborn were supposed to be familiar?

More particularly incumbent upon Boccaccio must have been the obligation of respecting these conventions when he came to compose a love story so intimately connected with the progress of his own courtship as was the *Filostrato*. For as a court lady interested in tales of

[1] Prov. *domnei* ("lady-service"), It. *amore cortese*, F. *amour courtois*, G. *Frauendienst*.

[2] While ultimately derived no doubt, in large measure at least, from the actual practice of free love between the troubadour and the lady of the manor in the Provence of the eleventh and twelfth centuries, Courtly Love is, in the more generally accepted sense of the term, a literary, not a social phenomenon. It made its earliest appearance, at least on any considerable scale, about the middle of the twelfth century in Northern France, more particularly at Troyes in Champagne, where its principles were put into practice by Chrétien de Troyes in his *Cligès* and *Ivain* and particularly in his *Lancelot* and at much the same time elaborately codified by Andreas Capellanus in his *De Arte Amandi*. About a century later, largely under Provençal influence, operating either directly or through Sicily, it appeared, in a more idealistic form, in Italy, largely in connection with the rise of the poets of the *dolce stil nuovo*. It was, as we shall see (pp. 88 ff.), of this later and peculiarly Italian variety that Boccaccio has made much the larger use in the *Filostrato*.

amatory adventure,[1] Maria would naturally expect that a love poem written in her honor should show due regard for the rules of literary love-making that were largely observed in the writings with which he represents her as familiar.[2] It was evidently from a desire not to disappoint these expectations that in his love romance the *Filocolo*, which, as we have seen (p. 16), was written at her request, Boccaccio quite gratuitously inserted the elaborate incident of the court of love, over which her literary namesake Fiammetta is called upon to preside.[3] There can, moreover, be but little doubt that the Italian poet's interest in Courtly Love transcended the bounds of literature and that he sought as far as possible to order his relations with Maria in accordance with its principles (cf. p. 24).[4]

[1] See p. 14, n. 1.

[2] And with which no doubt, whether a "reading lady" or not, she professed familiarity. See p. 14, n. 2.

[3] On his journey south to seek his missing sweetheart Biancofiore, Filocolo is driven by contrary winds upon the coast of Naples. While strolling one day to the north of the city, in that region where "the ashes of Maro were interred," he meets a party of young people "holding festa" in a garden. They invite him to join them. After a time, because of the growing heat of the day, all repair to an adjoining meadow and there beneath a clump of shade trees and beside a fountain organize an impromptu court of love, over which Fiammetta, the favorite of their number, is called upon to preside. Thirteen "questioni d' amore," corresponding to the number of the party, are thereupon debated.

This court of love incident, which is entirely lacking in the earlier story of Floire and Blanchefleur, was clearly inserted by Boccaccio out of compliment to Maria, very much after the fashion in which the Italian painters of his day put contemporaneous figures into their pictures of the Holy Family.

[4] Hutton (*Life of Boccaccio*, pp. 25, 34 and *Some Aspects of the Genius of Giovanni Boccaccio*, pp. 4-5), following Crescini (*Contributo*, pp. 127 and 130 and n. 2) and Della Torre (*op. cit.*, pp. 192-210), distinguishes on the basis of two passages in the *Amorosa visione*, four stages in Boccaccio's courtship of Maria, which he designates as those of (1) uncertainty, (2) trial, (3) acceptance as suitor, and (4) acceptance as lover.

In the *Amorosa visione* (p. 179) Boccaccio declares that at first he

At the very opening of his *Proemio* Boccaccio refers
to a debate held in an assembly of "noble gentlemen
had not been able to regard the marvelous experience of his enamorment otherwise than as a jest but that after he had continued in this
state of scepticism for twenty-four revolutions of the sun,

> "Tanto, che quattro via sei volte il sole
> Con l' orizzonte il ciel coniunto avea,"

he received from his lady encouragement to hope that he might eventually win her love. This declaration on the part of the poet Hutton
agrees with the two afore-mentioned critics in interpreting to signify
that for a certain length of time after the enamorment Boccaccio was
so overpowered at the thought of the high rank of the lady with whom
he had fallen in love that he was quite unable to take what had happened seriously. The twenty-four solar revolutions he understands to
mean, not with Crescini twenty-four, but with Della Torre twelve days
—a period which the latter supposes (p. 213) to have been terminated
by the meeting with Maria in the convent at Baia.

Again in the *Amorosa visione* (p. 185) Boccaccio writes that for one
hundred and thirty-five days he dwelt under the "dolce signoria" of
his lady:

> "Cinque fiate tre via nove giorni
> Sotto la dolce signoria di questa
> Trovato m' era in diversi soggiorni,"

feeling that his grievous affliction ("molesta pena") was destined to
turn to delicious joy ("lieta festa"). This period of one hundred and
thirty-five days Hutton, in pursuance of Crescini and Della Torre,
regards as the period of Boccaccio's acceptance as suitor. It terminates
with the nocturnal surprise and so must have begun on or after June 3
(see p. 21, n. 1). This period Crescini understands, somewhat peculiarly, to have followed immediately after the period of uncertainty.
For since, according to his calculation, the enamorment occurred on
April 11, the period of uncertainty, which he counts as twenty-four
days, must have terminated on May 5, leaving an interval unaccounted
for before June 3. Hutton, therefore, following Della Torre, introduces between the period of uncertainty and the period of acceptance
as suitor, an intervening period, which he calls the period of trial.
Since, according to Hutton's reckoning, the enamorment fell on March
30 and the period of uncertainty lasted twelve days, this period of trial,
which he makes the second period, must have begun on April 11 (not,
as he says, on April 12) and lasted until June 3 or later—longer, however, in his opinion, than two or three months, for, contrary to Wilkins
(see p. 16, n. 5), he dates the enamorment in 1331 and so adds five
years, thus reaching the date June 3, 1336, or later. After this followed
the one hundred and thirty-five days of "dolce signoria," or period of
acceptance as suitor, the third period, which lasted until the nocturnal
visit, between October 17 and November 14 (see p. 20, n. 2). Thereupon
ensued the fourth and final period of acceptance as lover, or "cavaliere

and lovely ladies" which he has recently attended.[1]
The subject proposed for discussion was this: Which of
three things gives greatest delight to a lover, viz., to see
his lady, to talk of her among his friends, or to meditate
upon her in the secret recesses of his own thoughts?[2]

serviente," which continued until the betrayal in the summer of 1338
(see p. 21, n. 2).

Now the interesting point regarding these four stages in Boccaccio's
courtship, if correctly interpreted by Della Torre and Hutton, lies in
the conclusion inevitably to be drawn from them that the Italian poet
must have consciously or unconsciously modeled his procedure upon a
tradition passed downward from the troubadours, whose custom it was
to recognize a similar fourfold division in the progress of a love affair.
Thus in an anonymous "donnejeire" (or treatise on lady-service),
printed in Herrig's *Archiv* (1863, XXXIV, 425), we read:

> "Qatres scalos ha enamor
> Loprimiers es d' feignedor
> Elsecon es d' prejador
> Elo tersz es dentend'dor
> Ealqart es drutz apelasz."

These lines, as interpreted by L. Goldschmidt (*Die Doktrin der Liebe
in den italienischen Lyriken der XIII. Jahrhunderts*, Breslau, 1889, p.
3), mean that the lover must first be an "ogler" (*fenher*), secondly, a
"petitioner" (*preiaire*), thirdly, an "expectant" (*entendeire*), and
fourthly, a "lover" (*drutz*). How neatly these four stages in the traditional Provençal courtship fit the four stages in the love experiences
of Boccaccio deduced by Della Torre and Hutton from the two passages in the *Amorosa visione*, requires, if we disregard the somewhat
fantastic interpretation placed upon *fenher* by Goldschmidt, no extended demonstration.

[1] That Boccaccio actually attended such an assembly cannot be
doubted. Not only does he, as we have seen (p. 72 and n. 3), introduce,
out of compliment to Maria, a court of love scene in the *Filocolo* but,
as pointed out by Renier, R. (*Giornale storico della letteratura italiana*,
1889, XIII, 382), he again alludes to these gatherings in the *Corbaccio*
(Moutier, *ed. cit.*, V, 183).

The custom of holding courts of love (Lat. *curiae amoris*, Prov.
cortz d' amors), not as serious judicial tribunals clothed by law with
authority to enforce their decrees, but as purely festal assemblies for
social diversion, is abundantly attested by documentary evidence. Not
only have we the well-known instances cited by Andreas (see p. 75,
n. 1) of its occurrence in medieval France but, as shown by Renier
(*op. cit.*, pp. 382 ff.), many examples of its occurrence in Renaissance
Italy. See also p. 75, n. 1.

[2] It is of interest to observe that this question resembles another

The correct solution of this problem[1]—to a tardy realization of which, as Boccaccio tells his lady, only her absence from Naples could bring him—is that the delight that springs from the privilege of beholding one's lady in person far surpasses that which either of the other two privileges can afford.

This idea of the superior satisfaction to be derived from the immediate sight of one's lady, about which the

recorded as similarly debated in the fifteenth century in Spain. Thus in the *Cancionero de Baena* (ed. Michel, F., two vols., 1860, II, 83) the following question was submitted by Baena to Ferrant Manuel at the court of Don Juan II of Castile: "Which is better, to see one's beloved and never speak to her, or always to speak to her and never see her?" After many exchanges of opinion the dispute was finally referred to Fray Diego of Valencia, who (p. 89) pronounced in favor of the sight. See Crane, *op. cit.*, p. 17.

[1] In which we have, of course, a survival in fourteenth-century Italy of the Provençal tension, more properly called *partimen* when a subject of love is under discussion. See Crane, *op. cit.*, pp. 9-10.

These impromptu discussions of knotty problems of love casuistry are not, of course, to be confused with the carefully codified conventions of Courtly Love. The former had, long before Boccaccio's day, been brought from Provence to Italy, where they seem to have been engaged in by the clergy before they became, as in the case cited by Boccaccio, a pastime of the nobility (see Goldschmidt, *op. cit.*, pp. 17-19). The latter, on the other hand, had been a more recent importation, either from Provence or from Northern France, having in Italy, as well as in these other countries, remained from the beginning more largely a matter of interest to the strictly literary class.

An association of Courtly Love with the tension was, however, inevitable both because each had its ultimate origin in Provence and because a principal source of the rules of Courtly Love as codified by Andreas Capellanus (*De Arte Amandi*, ed. Trojel, E., Copenhagen, 1892, lib. II, cap. 8, pp. 310-311) were the decisions rendered by various noble ladies, who in consultation with other ladies of their court, adjudicated cases submitted to their jurisdiction by real or imaginary lovers, as recorded by Andreas (lib. II, cap. 7, pp. 271-295). Thus the well-known decision rendered by the Countess of Champagne in favor of a suitor who claimed the right to hold a married lady to a promise of love given before her marriage, to the effect that "love cannot exist between married people" ("amorem non posse suas inter duos conjugales extendere vires") (Trojel, *op. cit.*, p. 290), seems to have given rise to the first of the "regulae amoris," which declares that "marriage is not a valid excuse for not loving" ("causa coniugii ab amore non est excusio recta") (Trojel, p. 310).

entire argument of the *Proemio* revolves, though not emphasized by Andreas,[1] stands forth in the literature of the times as one of the leading principles of Courtly Love. It is ultimately derived from the old Provençal doctrine of "seeing and thence conceiving love."[2] To it Boccaccio gives repeated expression not only in the

[1] Who does not include it in his code of thirty-one rules (see p. 77, n. 4). At the opening of his *De Arte Amanti*, however, he defines love as "a certain innate passion proceeding from the sight and immoderate contemplation of the beauty of the opposite sex" (Trojel, *ed. cit.*, p. 3).

[2] This doctrine of the immediate visual perception of one's lady as a prerequisite to the birth of love originated among the *beaux esprits* of Provence. Aymerics de Pegulhan (ed. Mahn, C. A. F., *Gedichte der Troubadours*, four vols., Berlin, 1856-73, III, 40) writes thus:

> "Perque tuit li fin aman
> Sapchan quamors es fina beuolensa
> Que nays del cor e dels huelhs sens duptar."

In course of time a conventional description of the physiological process by which love was supposed to be engendered came into general use. According to this description love originates upon the eyes of the lady when encountered by those of her future lover. The love thus generated is conveyed on bright beams of light from her eyes to his, through which it passes to take up its abode in his heart. From Provence this conceit passed into other countries of Europe, there to be made the subject of further refinements and elaborations. Thus Chrétien de Troyes in his *Cligès* (ed. Forster, W., *Romanische Bibliothek*, Halle, 1910, I, 20, vv. 702 ff.) is at pains to explain how it is that love may penetrate the eyes without inflicting upon them the wound that it afterward inflicts on the heart. For further examples of this idea in Old French poetry, see Hofer, S., *Zeitschrift für französische Sprache und Literatur*, 1924, XLVII, 267-273. For three noteworthy early Italian examples, see D'Ancona, A., and Comparetti, D., *Le antiche rime volgari*, five vols., Bologna, 1875-88, nos. CCLXXVI, III, 221; DXVII, IV, 206; CMXLVIII, V, 252. Dante, of course, makes large use of this notion in the sonnets of his *Vita nuova* (sections XIX, Fraticelli, p. 78; XX, p. 81; XXI, p. 82; XXVI, p. 96). This same conception lies at the basis of Shakespeare's lines in the *Merchant of Venice* (III, 2, 63):

> "Tell me where is fancy bred
> Or in the heart or in the head?"

(see Baskervill, C. R., *Manly Anniversary Studies in Language and Literature*, Chicago, 1923, pp. 94-95).

Proemio[1] but also in the *Filostrato*[2] as well as in other
of his love romances.[3]

No one of the thirty-one "regulae amoris" of Andreas
Capellanus[4] enjoyed greater popularity in the polite
love fiction of the later Middle Ages than that which

---

[1] No fewer than six times in the course of the *Proemio* does Boccaccio allude to the sight of his lady, to her eyes, or to the passage of love
from her eyes to his heart. Thus he writes: (1) "I can clearly appreciate how great was the happiness . . . that came to me from the gracious
and beautiful sight of you" (p. 119); (2) . . . "an it please God soon
to replace mine eyes in their lost peace by the sight of your beautiful
countenance" (p. 119); (3) . . . "these eyes of mine, through which the
very gentle light of your love entered my mind" (p. 119); (4) . . .
"ever the better do I realize how great was the good . . . that proceeded
from your eyes" (p. 121); (5) "Now do I know . . . how much more
pleasure . . . dwelleth in the true light of your eyes . . . than in the
false flattery of my thoughts" (p. 123); (6) "Thus, therefore, O brilliant light of my mind, hath fortune, by depriving me of the love-
inspiring sight of you, dissipated the mists of error under which I formerly labored" (p. 123).

[2] In the invocation we read: "Thou, lady, art the clear and beautiful
light under whose guidance I live in this world of shadows" (I, 2) and
"Thou art imaged in my sad breast with such strength that thou hast
more power there than I" (I, 5). In the description of the enamorment
of Troilus is a singular blending of the Provençal conception of the
eyes as the birthplace of love with the classical idea of the God of Love
with his bow and quiver: "Nor did [Troilus] perceive that Love with
his darts dwelt within the rays of those lovely eyes . . . nor notice the
arrow that sped to his heart" (I, 29). This same combination of incon-
gruous elements appears again, after the enamorment, in Troilus' ad-
dress to the God of Love: "Thou takest thy station in her eyes as in a
place worthy of thy powers" (I, 39). Henceforth, however, it is the
eyes of his lady only that inspire Troilus' love. Thus he "imagined he
would draw from her fair eyes water soothing to his intense ardor"
(I, 41). See further II, 58, 86, 98; III, 36, 61; IV, 51; V, 53, 63.

[3] As in his account of his enamorment in the *Filocolo* (I, 6) and in
the *Fiammetta* (p. 10). See p. 16 and n. 1.

[4] These thirty-one rules of love (Trojel, *op. cit.*, pp. 310-318) are the
most numerous and the most sharply defined of those contained in three
codes in the *De Arte Amandi*. The other two codes are "the twelve
commandments of love" (Trojel, p. 106) and "the twenty-one judg-
ments of love" (Trojel, pp. 271-295). Nevertheless these thirty-one
rules of love form by no means a complete or logically arranged system. They bear every evidence of having been fortuitously assembled
from the equally fortuitous decisions rendered by the noble ladies to
whom Andreas elsewhere refers (see p. 75, n. 1).

enjoined secrecy upon the two participants in a Courtly Love intrigue. It runs thus: "Amor rare consuevit durare vulgatus."[1] All three of the principal actors in the love story of the *Filostrato* are acutely conscious of the need for secrecy in the conduct of their actions.

In the first instance (I, 31, 36) it is Troilus, who, after his departure from the scene of the enamorment, ponders the necessity of this precaution and later, in his first conversation with Pandarus (II, 8), beseeches him to observe it. In the second instance (II, 25-26, 28) it is Pandarus who, out of regard for the family to which he and his kinswoman belong, urges upon Troilus, albeit quite unnecessarily, the importance of this safeguard. In the third instance (II, 74) it is Criseida who, in debating with herself what course she shall pursue in relation to Troilus, regards a clandestine attachment as preferable to the less romantic possibilities of connubial bliss:

> L' acqua furtiva assai più dolce cosa
> È che il vin con abbondanza avuto:
> Così d' amor la gioia, che nascosa,
> Traspassa assai del sempre mai tenuto
> Marito in braccia.[2]

Nor are there wanting thereafter many other occasions on which the author, either directly or through one of his characters, counsels secrecy.[3]

Another important precept of Andreas provides that, however she may feel inwardly disposed toward her

---

[1] This precept is the thirteenth in Andreas' code (Trojel, p. 310). Cf. Andreas' other references to secrecy (pp. 175, 205, 247, 290-291, 294).

[2] It reflects no high degree of credit upon Boccaccio's Criseida that when Troilus, assisted by Pandarus, is taking thought to secrecy as a screen that will render his love for her safe, she thinks of it only as a sauce that will render it palatable.

[3] See *Filostrato*, II, 69, 77, 116, 140-141; III, 9-10, 15, 43; IV, 153.

lover, the lady should outwardly maintain toward him an indifferent, if not an actually disdainful attitude.[1] This requirement Andreas formulates thus: "Facilis perceptio contemptabilem facit amorem, difficilis eum carum haberi." In pursuance of this idea that "easy winning makes love despicable" Boccaccio writes thus of Criseida's indifference toward Troilus (I, 48):

> E qual si fosse non ci è assai certo,
> O che Criseida non se n' accorgesse,
> Per l' operar di lui ch' era coperto,
> O che di ciò conoscer s' infingesse,
> Ma questo n' è assai chiaro ed operto,
> Che niente pareva le calesse
> Di Troilo e dell' amor che le portava,
> Ma come non amata dura stava.[2]

Again the courtly lover should, according to Andreas, lose color and suffer from sleeplessness and loss of appetite. Regarding pallor he writes: "Omnis consuevit amans in amantis conspectu pallescere" and regarding sleeplessness and loss of appetite: "Minus dormit et edit, quem amoris cogitatio vexat."[3] In consonance with each of these three provisions Boccaccio describes the woebegone condition of Troilus as follows (I, 47, *1-4*):

> Aveagli già Amore il sonno tolto,
> E minuto il cibo, ed il pensiero
> Moltiplicato sì, che già nel volto
> Ne dava pallidezza segno vero.[4]

[1] She should possess, in other words, the quality denoted by Chaucer's adjective *daungerous* as used in the *Wife of Bath's Prologue* (v. 151),

"If I be daungerous, god geve me sorwe."

[2] In like manner Troilus in the course of his first love letter to Criseida (II, 103) begs her to "lay aside the lofty disdain of [her] great spirit and be condescending toward [him]."

[3] The precept regarding pallor is the fifteenth (Trojel, p. 310), that regarding sleeplessness and loss of appetite, the twenty-third in Andreas' list (Trojel, p. 311).

[4] For further references to Troilus' sleeplessness and loss of appe-

But despite these outward symptoms of distress, the effect of love upon the lover is to make him liberal toward others. This is negatively expressed by Andreas as follows: "Amor semper consuevit ab avaritiae domiciliis exsulare."[1] This effect of love upon Troilus Boccaccio records in the *Filostrato* (II, 84, *1-4*) as follows:

> Troilo canta e fa mirabil festa,
> Armeggia, spende, e dona lietamente,
> E spesso si rinnuova e cangia vesta,
> Ognora amando più ferventemente.

Finally Boccaccio may perhaps have had a further precept of Andreas in mind in connection with his references to Troilus' bravery in battle. Andreas writes: "Verus amans nil bonum credit nisi quod cogitat coamanti placere."[2] It is, says Boccaccio, to please Criseida that Troilus seeks fame in battle (I, 45, *5-8*; 46):

> . . . spesso ne' più perigliosi
> Assalti, innanzi agli altrui lui vedeano
> Mirabilmente nell' armi operare:
> Ciò disser quei che stavanlo a mirare.

tite, see *Filostrato*, VI, 19 and for further references to his pallor, II, 57; V, 60; VI, 20; VII, 90.

To this third symptom the heroine as well is no stranger. Criseida (II, 116) fears lest her "hidden desire" may appear in her colorless face, as later it actually does (VI, 1), though she does her best to conceal it.

[1] This is Andreas' tenth precept (Trojel, p. 310).

There can be no doubt that the positive side of this precept, viz., the production by love of liberality in the lover, which is recognized by Ovid and is made much of in the Latin metrical imitation of that author by Guiart (summarized by Le Grand d'Aussy, *Fabliaux ou contes du XIIe et du XIIIe siècle*, Paris, 1779, II, 61-65) and in the Latin prose Ovidian imitation entitled *Pamphilus* (ed. Baudouin, A., Paris, 1874) was known to Boccaccio and associated in his mind with Andreas. See on these Ovidian imitations, Gorra, E., *La teorica dell' amore* (pp. 206-207) in his *Fra drammi e poemi*, Milan, 1900, pp. 201 ff.

[2] This is the twenty-fifth rule in the code of Andreas (Trojel, p. 311). It is that virtuous effect of love technically known among the Provençal poets as *cortesia*. See Chaytor, H. J., *The Troubadours*, Cambridge, 1912, p. 17.

Nè a ciò l' odio dei Greci il rimovea,
Nè vaghezza ch' avesse di vittoria
Per Troia liberar, la qual vedea
Stretta da assedio, ma voglia di gloria
Per più piacer tutto questo facea;
E per amor se 'l ver dice la storia,
Divenne in arme sì feroce e forte,
Che gli Greci il temean come la morte.[1]

There is, moreover, apart from the "regulae amoris," one other important particular in respect to which Boccaccio is found to be in conscious or unconscious agreement with Andreas. This, as Young has pointed out,[2] is in the matter of his employment of Pandarus to act as intermediary between his hero and his heroine.

Contrary, as it might at first sight appear, to the cardinal doctrine of secrecy to admit any outside person whatsoever into the confidence of the two principals in a Courtly Love intrigue, Andreas grants permission to his two lovers to employ the services of no less than three confidants, viz., a *secretarius*, or "confidant," for the man, a *secretaria*, or "confidante," for the woman, and an *internuntius*, or "intermediary," to carry messages between them.[3]

That Boccaccio was aware of this privilege is quite evident from Troilus' proposal (I, 36) to hide his love from "every friend and attendant, unless it should be necessary." From this express reservation, made before the arrival of Pandarus, it is clear that the Trojan prince proposes, if need should arise, to avail himself of this right to employ one or more assistants to aid him in his courtship.

[1] Cf. also a later passage (III, 90) in which Boccaccio states that Troilus' unusual prowess on the field of battle was due to love.

[2] *University of Wisconsin Studies in Language and Literature,* Madison, 1918, no. 2, pp. 369 ff.

[3] *De Arte Amandi,* ed. Trojel, pp. 254 ff.

In respect to what privileges were accorded him by the rules of Courtly Love in this matter of an intermediary, Boccaccio could have received no hint from any of the sources he had used in composing the story of the *Filostrato*. Benoit had had nothing to say of the courtship of Briseida by Troilus. The French writer's Diomede had been far too forthright a suitor to take thought of any of the niceties of the game of love. The French account of the faithful "ami" employed by Achilles in his suit for the hand of Polyxena could have helped him not at all in adjusting the rôle of Pandarus to Courtly Love requirements, since Achilles' love was honorable and was not, therefore, amenable to these requirements. A like objection prevented him from making use of the several personages who in the *Filocolo* serve or attempt to serve Florio and Biancofiore in the solution of their love difficulties. For guidance in determining the activities of Pandarus, therefore, the Italian poet was compelled either to fall back upon his own resources or to have recourse to authorities other than those which supplied him with his story materials. That he chose the latter alternative and acted either in obedience to Andreas or to some well recognized Italian system founded upon Andreas, appears to be sufficiently borne out by the fact that he held himself well within the limits allowed by that writer.

The foregoing Courtly Love representations in the *Filostrato* complete our evidence of the direct or indirect use made by Boccaccio of the principles of that system as laid down by Andreas Capellanus. No doubt a prime reason why the author's debt to the French lawgiver was no greater is to be found in the unfortunate rôle played by the heroine of the ancient story

that he had undertaken to relate. We have already seen (pp. 18-19) that the defection of Benoit's Briseida to Diomede had proved an embarrassment to Boccaccio by reason of the peculiarly personal use he had proposed to make of the received fable as a vehicle through which to convey to a lady who had not as yet deserted him, his grief at her absence and hopes for her return. We have likewise seen (pp. 58-59) that the faithlessness of the French Briseida to her first lover prevented him from making use in his representation of Criseida's character and actions of those colors drawn from the poets of the *dolce stil nuovo* of which he had availed himself so abundantly in depicting the woes of Troilus. A like difficulty presented itself in his attempts to bring his received story into accordance with the principles of Courtly Love. For according to these principles infidelity in love was a most grievous offense, whether as committed by the hero or by the heroine. This is implicit in the precepts of Andreas[1] and explicit in the practices of the French romances.[2]

Criseida has, therefore, by reason of her desertion of

[1] Andreas is not particularly clear or precise on this point, no doubt because it was his aim less to specify the duties of the lover than what he supposed to be facts, rooted and grounded in the nature of love, upon which these duties rested. Nevertheless his third rule states "No one can be bound by a double love" ("Nemo duplici potest amore ligari") (Trojel, p. 310); the twelfth states "The true lover desires not the embraces of another than his co-lover" ("Verus amans alterius nisi sui coamantis ex affectu non cupit amplexus") (Trojel, p. 310); and the seventeenth states "A new love drives out the old" ("Novus amor veterum compellit abire") (Trojel, p. 311).

[2] Thus in the charming *Chatelaine de Vergi* (ed. Raynaud, G., *Romania*, 1892, XXI, 145 ff., summarized by Langlois, C. V., in his *Société française au XIII*e *siècle d'après dix romans d'aventure*, Paris, 1904, pp. 225 ff., and Englished by Kemp-Welch, A., Chatto and Windus, 1907) the heroine dies of a broken heart because falsely persuaded by her rival that her lover has been untrue to her. Again Machaut in his *Jugement du roi de Bohême* (ed. Höpffner, E., in his "Oevres de Guillaume de Machaut," *Société des anciens textes français*,

Troilus, no standing as a Courtly Love heroine. But since it was not the custom of Andreas or of the Courtly Love romancers to prescribe any definite penalties for infractions of the laws of love,[1] Boccaccio did all that he very well could have done under the circumstances, namely, permitted Troilus (*Filostrato*, VIII, 17) to adjure "divine justice" to have regard to his unmerited wrongs.

There is, moreover, one further particular with respect to which Boccaccio has, out of regard for his plot, violated the rules of Courtly Love in his representation of Criseida. This is in regard to the private station which she occupies. Criseida is not, as would seem to be required by Andreas,[2] a married woman but a

three vols., 1908-1921, I, 57 ff.) represents that monarch as passing judgment to the effect that it is better to be dead than to be faithless.

That a sense of the importance of faithfulness as an essential ingredient in Courtly Love had been felt from its beginnings in Provence is clear from the story related of the troubadour Barbeison, who, growing tired of his mistress' coldness, transferred his affections to a second lady but was ordered by the latter to return to his first lady, for since he had abandoned her, she could have no assurance that she would not be treated in the same way.

[1] As already implied (p. 74, n. 1), Courtly Love was not a juridical institution with a system of rewards and punishments. Penalties, as we learn from Andreas and others, were sometimes inflicted for infringement of its rules but each offense was judged upon its own merits and the penalties visited upon culprits were such as the arbitrary wish of the judge might, at the time, dictate. Generally the maximum penalty was social ostracism. As happens today in the case of the collection of gambling debts, a sense of honor had mainly to be relied upon to restrain those who might otherwise have been so disposed from disregarding their obligations.

[2] The first precept of that writer, "Causa coniugii ab amore non est excusio recta" (Trojel, p. 310), when read in the light of the decision upon which it evidently rests, viz., that of the Countess of Champagne to the effect that "love cannot exist between married people" (see p. 75, n. 1), presupposes marriage on the part of the lady.

While not all Courtly Love heroines were necessarily married and while Andreas nowhere specifies adulterousness on the lady's part as indispensable, it is clear that the relations of a heroine who is married to a hero who is single afford the best milieu for the practice of many

widow,[1] her husband having died before the action of
the poem begins.[2]

It might at first sight seem strange that since Boccaccio did not see fit to follow Benoit and represent his
heroine as a virgin,[3] he should not have remained content to move her but one step into the condition of a
married lady, as that of his mistress Maria,[4] instead of
carrying her onward two steps into the status of a
widow. Obviously the fact that in so doing he both
violated a rule of Courtly Love and sacrificed the ap-
parent advantage of placing her in the station of the
lady whom she is supposed to represent, demands explanation.

Young,[5] following Wilkins,[6] contends that Boccaccio's reason for this extreme shift of the pendulum
from virgin to widow is to be found in his own preference, as expressed through the lips of Fiammetta in the
ninth "questione d'amore" in the *Filocolo* (II, 94-
96),[7] for widowhood as the ideal state for a lover to
seek in his choice of a mistress. But to this theory it
may be objected that that portion of the question that

of the other principles of conduct that he does insist upon. Noteworthy
is it that the greatest of Courtly Love stories were based upon this
particular relationship, as the stories of Lancelot and Guinivere, of
Tristan and Isolt, and, in the sphere of the actual, of Paolo and Fran-
cesca and, on a more elevated plane, of Dante and Beatrice. There can
be no doubt that in this respect Courtly Love laid the foundations of
the "triangular" play, so popular on the modern stage.

[1] See *Filostrato*, I, 11 ; II, 27, 69.   [2] See *Filostrato*, II, 49 ; VI, 29.

[3] *Roman de Troie* (v. 13111), where she is spoken of as a "pucele."

[4] See p. 13.

[5] *University of Wisconsin Studies in Language and Literature*, pp.
379 ff.

[6] *Modern Philology*, XI, 48, n. 1.

[7] Here curiously enough, as though provoked by a comparison of the
three stations occupied severally by Benoit's Briseida, his own Maria,
and the Criseida of the *Filostrato*, Boccaccio proposes the three-
cornered question : Which is to be preferred, the love of a virgin, the
love of a married woman, or the love of a widow ?

relates to the preference expressed by Fiammetta in the *Filocolo* for widowhood over matrimony is a traditional solution of a traditional problem[1] and therefore neither the problem nor its solution can be regarded as the poet's own. Again it so happens that in the *Filostrato* (II, 69, 73-74) Criseida debates with herself this very same question as to the relative desirability of matrimony and widowhood, to arrive, to be sure, at the same conclusion as does Fiammetta in the *Filocolo*, but for quite different reasons.[2] If the arguments advanced in favor of widowhood by Criseida herself may be taken as indicative of the reasons why Boccaccio made her a widow, they effectually dispose of the contention of the above-mentioned critics that these reasons are to be sought in the arguments brought forward by Fiammetta in the *Filocolo*.[3]

A possible, though improbable reason for the widowhood of Criseida may have lain in the desire of the

[1] See Valeriano, L., and Lampredi, U., *Poeti del primo secolo della lingua italiana*, two vols., Florence, 1816, II, 395, 526-527; Boudet, T. J., Conte de Puymaigre, *La cour littéraire de Don Juan II, roi de Castille*, two vols., Paris, 1873, II, 137, n.; Knobloch, H., *Die Streitgedichte im Provenzalen und Altfranzösiscen*, Breslau, 1886, pp. 47, 68; Jeanroy, A., *Revue des langues romanes*, 1897, XL, 352; Gaspary, *Storia della letteratura italiana*, II, 396; Crane, *op. cit.*, pp. 17, 21, 82.

[2] Fiammetta—judging the matter somewhat strangely from the man's point of view—prefers widowhood on the ground that in loving a widow one is not breaking the commandment not to covet his neighbor's wife and that one may profit by a widow's previous amatory experiences as well as by her long suppressed desires. Criseida, on the other hand, bases her opposition to a second husband upon the freedom from domestic encumbrances which she now enjoys and upon the dangers that perpetually beset married ladies by reason of the jealousy of their husbands.

[3] Moreover the contention of Wilkins and Young derives its main force from the presupposition that the speech of Fiammetta, which occurs at a fairly advanced point in the *Filocolo*, was written before the *Filostrato*, whereas Young himself had already declared in his previous study (*Origin and Development of the Story of Troilus and Criseyde*, p. 34) that the later portion of the *Filocolo* followed the *Filostrato*.

author to avoid giving offense to Maria by providing opportunity for too ready an identification with herself should he picture Criseida as a married lady.[1] A much more probable, and in fact an all-sufficient reason for Criseida's widowhood is to be found in the plot of the *Filostrato*, as Boccaccio received it from Benoit. How with a husband dangling at her heels could Criseida have journeyed to the Greek camp and how, in this case, could Boccaccio have pitted Diomede against Troilus as her rival lover? Hence it seems best to conclude that, as in the case of his heroine's faithlessness so here again in that of her widowhood, Boccaccio has violated a Courtly Love principle out of regard for his plot.[2]

But if Boccaccio was prevented by the infidelity of

[1] Whether or not a side-glance at Maria was intended in Boccaccio's explicit statement (*Filostrato*, I, 13) that Criseida had no children, we cannot say. The statement is made in such a bald form as to suggest an allusion to reality. On the other hand one may argue that to preserve for his heroine the freedom of action that his plot required Boccaccio was compelled to relieve her of the chief of the domestic encumbrances to which she alludes (II, 69). For since Criseida is still young (II, 54; IV, 8; VI, 14) and since from her constant wearing of black it would appear that her husband had but recently died, maternity was not unnaturally to be looked for.

[2] Rarely if ever did it happen that any medieval author found himself so far unencumbered by the plot of his story that he could obey unreservedly one and all of the principles of Courtly Love. Hence it should not, in the opinion of the present writer, who has recently discussed this matter with others, be postulated that because an author violates any one—or indeed any considerable number—of these principles, he should, ipso facto, be excluded from the category of those who write on Courtly Love. To set up, for example, as a criterion even so unquestionably basic a principle as that of illicit love and to insist that no story in which the hero and heroine are wedded to one another can, for that reason, be included in the Courtly Love class, appears to him a purely arbitrary and non-scientific restriction. To his way of thinking a story in which regard is shown for any one of the principles enunciated by Andreas or by any other reputable lawgiver or, lacking that, for any principle found to be widely respected in love stories told or read at court, has a perfect right to be included in any list of Courtly Love documents.

the heroine of his received story from making as full use of the Courtly Love precepts of Andreas as he might otherwise have made, he was nevertheless enabled for this very reason to draw more heavily than he could otherwise have drawn upon the Courtly Love maxims of his own Italian predecessors. For the Courtly Love writers of the South, while as little disposed as Andreas to condone faithlessness in love, had an ampler store than he of doctrinal palliatives with which to alleviate, theoretically at least, the pains suffered by the victim of its oppressions. This happened incidentally, through the far greater emphasis laid by the writers of Italy upon love as an absolute good, regardless of the success of the lover in gaining or retaining the affections of his mistress. According to this Italian conception, largely entertained by the poets of the *dolce stil nuovo*,[1] love is of value subjectively, as a discipline of the soul, however it may objectively eventuate.[2]

Of this highly idealistic conception of love Boccaccio, by diverting attention from Criseida and her per-

[1] As, for example, by Dante in the *Vita nuova*, where, of course, the idea of the physical possession of Beatrice is entirely excluded.

[2] As already remarked (p. 61, n. 1), this idealistic conception of love had its ultimate origin in Provence, where the idea prevailed that love cherishes an end above and beyond that of the gratification of the senses. This is well brought out in the following lines quoted by Emma Calvé (*The Critic*, 1903, XLVII, 562) from Raimbaud de Vaqueiras, "He really knows nothing whatever of *domnei* who desires complete possession of his lady. The love that turns into reality is no longer love."

An interesting recrudescence of this idea in modern American fiction is to be found in the novels of Mr. Joseph Hergesheimer and of Mr. James Branch Cabell. Thus Hergesheimer in his *Preface* to Cabell's *Domnei* (1921) writes that the idea of the author is to bring again to light "the conception of the eternal feminine inherited by the Middle Ages from Plato" and Cabell in his *Rivet in Grandfather's Neck* (1921, p. 156) speaks of "that love which rather abhors than otherwise the notion of possessing its object."

fidy and concentrating it upon Troilus and his woes, succeeded in the *Filostrato* in availing himself to the full.[1]

This transforming and regenerating influence of love upon Troilus is represented in the *Filostrato* as cumulative. It is anticipated by the hero at the opening of the poem and experienced by him in ever fuller measure as the poem advances. After his first sight of Criseida at the sacrifices to Pallas, Troilus "thought it would be a great good fortune to love such a lady" (I, 34, *3-4*):

> . . . gran ventura
> Di cotal donna amar si riputava.

As he pursued his courtship he came to "[regard] everyone without love as lost, whatever his condition" (II, 92, *7-8*):

> E tenea senza amore ognun perduto,
> Di quale stato che si fosse suto.

Finally, and as though by way of climax, after love has had its perfect work and Criseida is about to pass

---

[1] Although it must be borne in mind, of course, that the love represented by Boccaccio in the *Filostrato* is never Platonic but always contemplates possession. So far, however, does he succeed in interweaving in the story of a purely carnal passion sentiments and reflections inspired by the conception of love as a spiritual force transcending the sphere of the physical that the reader is conscious of no essential incongruity between the two. Hardly so successful, at least to our modern ways of thinking, was Chaucer in his representation of Cleopatra as one of "Cupid's saints," though one familiar with the formulae of chivalric love may be less disposed to quarrel with Arcite's declaration in the *Knight's Tale* (vv. 1155-1156, Manly, *ed. cit.*, p. 179):

> "Love is a gretter lawe, by my pan,
> Than may be yeve of any erthely man,"

and certainly less with Malory's assertion (*Le Morte Darthur*, ed. Sommer, H. O., three vols., London, 1889-91, I, 505): "A kniȝt maye neuer be of prowesse but yf he be a louer."

to the Greeks, he declares to Pandarus (IV, 51, 6-8):
"[love] hath been the cause of every excellent thing
in me."

Nor, according to the Italian conception, was it the
lover only who was supposed to benefit by being a par-
ticipant in the gentle passion. Upon all who were in
any way associated with him, as abettors or counselors,
love was supposed to diffuse some measure of its benign influence. Thus it comes to pass that Pandarus,
by reason of the services that he renders Troilus, is not
without a certain share in love's benefits. He enjoys
the inward satisfaction of having served so worthy a
cause.[1] This it is that relieves his rôle in the *Filostrato*
of the odiousness that came later to attach to it at the
hands of Shakespeare.

It is chiefly of course by Troilus that love's salutary
effects are experienced.

One of the chief ways in which love operates benefi-
cially upon Troilus is in inducing in his soul extreme
humility toward all about him.[2] Thus we are informed
by Boccaccio (*Filostrato*, III, 93) that "despite his
high lineage and exalted privileges, Troilus became
kindly disposed to all men, even to the unworthy, and
held pride, envy, and avarice in hatred."

---

[1] It is not merely the motive of friendship that impels Pandarus to
aid Troilus. So impressed is he with the "high desires" proper to a
lover (II, 26) that he assures Troilus (II, 28) "I would do wrong if I
did not all in my power to aid thee."

[2] This idea of the humility incumbent upon a lover is likewise a
Provençal inheritance. Thus N'At de Mons, quoted by Matfre Ermen-
gaud in his *Breviari d'amor* (ed. Azaïs, G., two vols., Béziers, 1862-81,
II, 433, vv. 27878-27883) writes:

> "Sapchan li fin ayman
> Que per amor si fan
> L' ergolhos humilieu
> E lh' avol esforsieu
> Elh peresos espert
> Elh [pec] saben e cert, etc."

But it is more particularly toward his lady that Troilus assumes this attitude of humility. Even when seriously aggrieved by her failure to return to Troy to keep her tryst on the tenth day, he uses to her in his long letter of expostulation (VII, 52-74) no reproachful terms but only the gentlest and most forbearing of remonstrances (VII, 55, 1-4):

> Ma perchiocchè a me convien piacere
> Quanto a te piace, rammarcar non m'oso,
> Ma quanto umile posso, il parere
> Ti scrivo, più che mai d' amor focoso, ecc.

To enable Troilus the more forcibly to express his sense of inferiority to his mistress, Boccaccio, acting in compliance with a widespread custom among Courtly Love writers, represents him as using feudal imagery in addressing her.[1] Thus at the opening of the above-mentioned letter of humble remonstrance Troilus expresses himself as follows (VII, 54, 1-3):

> Se 'l servidore in caso alcuno potesse
> Del suo signor dolersi, fosse ch' io
> Avrei ragion se di te mi dolesse, ecc.[2]

[1] The use of feudal imagery by a lover in addressing a lady originated in Provence. Thus we find the exact formula employed by a vassal in paying homage to his suzerain pressed into service by Bernart de Ventadorn in his following declaration of love to Eleanor (quoted by Smythe, B., *The Trobador Poets*, Chatto and Windus, 1911, p. 38): "And therefore, lady, have pity on your true lover . . . with hands folded and head bent I give and deliver myself to you, and if there should be a fitting moment, give me a kind glance, for I have very great desire for it." For reasons for supposing this poem written to Eleanor, see Smythe, pp. 27, 52.

In the four stages of the Provençal courtship (see p. 72, n. 4) the recitation on bended knee of the above formula of "hands joined and head bent" was supposed to form one of the ceremonies attending the passage of the lover from the stage of "entendeire" ("accepted suitor") to that of "drutz" ("full-fledged lover").

See Wechssler, E., *Zeitschrift fur franz. Sprache*, 1902, Band XXIV, Heft 1 u. 3, 159-190.

[2] On three other occasions as well Boccaccio makes use of feudal

Because of this deep sense of his own unworthiness and his fear that because of it his lady will not deign to accept his love, Troilus, as above remarked (pp. 59, 60 and n. 1), plays throughout the *Filostrato* the rôle of a sufferer rather than that of an actor. It is not to be supposed that the sole reason for the extreme sentimentality of Troilus, for the grief in which, in Romeo fashion, he so persistently luxuriates, is to be found in the state of mind of the author at the time that the poem was written. It cannot be doubted that convention played a large part in the result and that Boccaccio discovered in contemporaneous ideas regarding the importance of suffering as essential to the work of regeneration which love accomplishes a concurrent reason for the insistence he places upon the many agonizing experiences of his hero.[1]

imagery in describing the services rendered Criseida by Troilus. Thus Troilus (I, 49, *2-5*) feared that Criseida had another lover and for that reason would not receive him as her servant:

> ". . . e per quello lui vilipendendo
> Ricever nol volesse a servidore."

Again in his hymn of thanksgiving to Venus for granting him success in love (III, 74-89) Troilus (III, 83, *3-7*) blessed the boy who had made him a true servant to Criseida:

> "E benedico il figlioul. . . .
> . . . che m' ha fatto a lei servo verace, ecc."

In like manner Diomede (VI, 25, *1-5*) prays Criseida to accept him as her servant:

> "Pregovi . . .
> Qual si conviene a vostra signoria,
> In servidor prendiate, ecc."

On one occasion this feudal allegiance is transferred from the lady to the love god himself, as when it is said of Troilus that Love, of whom he was faithful servant, granted him courage in battle (III, 90, *6-8*):

> ". . . questo spirto . . .
> . . . gli prestave Amore,
> Di cui egli era fedel servidore."

[1] As a necessary ingredient in this conception of love as a discipline of the soul much was made in Provence of the doctrine of *sufrirs*

Boccaccio makes occasional reference in the *Filostrato* to the God of Love with his bow and arrows. In the *Proemio* he thrice refers to this god, to whose service he has dedicated himself from his youth up (p. 115) and whose aid, in recompense therefor, he twice implores to ease him of his torments (pp. 129, 131). Again in the invocation of the *Filostrato* (I, 6) he begs all lovers to intercede for him with this god. Henceforth the love deity is represented as exercising his sovereignty over the author's hero instead of the author himself. Frequent reference to the God of Love is made in connection with the enamorment of Troilus. By a shaft from the god's bow the Trojan prince was "transfixed more than any other before he left the temple" (I, 25) and that so suddenly that he who had previously railed at the anxious loves of others did not "notice the arrow that sped to his heart until it struck him in very truth" (I, 29). After the enamorment Troilus gives thanks to the God of Love for having caused him to be enamored of so beautiful a lady (I, 38-91), though later he complains of the god for having subjected him

("suffering"). Thus Guiraut Riquier in his elaborate commentary (printed by C. F. A. Mahn, *Werke der Troubadours*, four vols., Berlin, 1846-53, IV, 210-232), upon the allegorical canzone of Guiraut de Calanson opening "A leis cui am de cor e de saber" (ed. Dammann, O., Breslau, 1891), interprets (p. 223) his "four steps to the Palace of Love" as *onrars* ("honor"), *selars* ("secrecy"), *seruirs* ("service"), *sufrirs* ("suffering"). See Goldschmidt, *op. cit.*, p. 3.

Not infrequently love's zealots, like religious fanatics, sought to prove their worthiness to their ladies by self-inflicted tortures. Thus Ulric von Lichtenstein tells us in his memoirs entitled *Frouendienst* (modernized by Michelangelo Baron Zois, Stuttgart, 1924), that "for his lady's sake he mangled his face, cut off one of his fingers, chopped away part of his upper lip, and jousted in motley with every knight from Venice to Styria." See Lee, Vernon, *Medieval Love*, a chapter in her *Euphorion* (two vols., London, 1884, II, 31).

See Vossler, K., "Der Trobador Marcabru und die Anfänge des gekünstelten Stiles," *Sitzungsberichte der K. B. Akademie*, 11 Abhandlung, Munich, 1913, p. 47.

to the danger of being derided by those of his victims whom he had previously scorned (I, 59) as well as censured by the war lords for having chosen so inauspicious an occasion for his passion (I, 52). Thereafter but occasional references are made to the God of Love, as when it is said to have been he who granted Troilus courage in battle (III, 90). From now on it is the eyes of the heroine that are invariably referred to as the source of the hero's love malady.

In view of what has been said of Boccaccio's representation of love as having been the cause of every excellent thing in Troilus, it would be natural to conclude that the reason of this lay in the divine origin of love as caused by the love deity. Plausible as this explanation may appear, however, it will hardly fit the case. For in Provençal poetry, where the conception of the beneficent effects of love originated (see p. 88, n. 2), love is less often represented as of divine origin and occasioned by the God of Love than as of human origin and occasioned by the eyes of the lady when gazed at by her future lover.[1] In Italy the newly imported Provençal idea of the physiological genesis of love came into conflict with the old idea of a God of Love, inherited from the ancients, and many were the learned tensions to which this conflict gave rise as to whether or no love possesses external existence.[2] It is entirely in keeping with this difference of Italian opinion that in

---

[1] Goldschmidt, *op. cit.*, p. 21.

[2] Goldschmidt (*op. cit.*, p. 17) describes a tension between Jacopo Mostacci, who maintained that love has no objective existence because it could not be seen, and Pietro della Vigna, who claimed it had, because it could be felt. Finally Jacopo da Lentino, the third party to the altercation, fell back upon the Provençal doctrine of "seeing and thence conceiving love" and so decided in favor of the physiological contention of Mostacci.

the *Filostrato* Boccaccio should so curiously blend the traditional anthropomorphic conception of a love deity with the more recent idea, imported from Provence, that love is generated upon the eyes of the lady, passes thence to the eyes of her future lover, and finally penetrates his eyes to take up its abode in his heart.

IV. The Bearing of the Filostrato upon English Literature

No detailed argument is needed to demonstrate the importance of a knowledge of Boccaccio's *Filostrato* to the student of English literature. The poem supplied Chaucer with the story of his masterpiece, the *Troilus and Criseyde*,[1] and, through Chaucer, furnished Shakespeare and, through Shakespeare, Dryden, with the love plots of their plays of *Troilus and Cressida*.[2] Thus the *Filostrato* became the starting point of

[1] On the indebtedness of Chaucer's *Troilus* to Boccaccio's *Filostrato* see Fischer, R., *Zu den Kunstformen des mittelalterlichen Epos*, Leipsic, 1899, pp. 217-370 ; Cook, *op. cit.*, pp. 531-547 ; Bardelli, M., *Qualche contributo agli studi sulle relazioni del Chaucer col Boccaccio*, Florence, 1911 ; Legouis, E., *Chaucer*, translated by Lailavoix, L., 1913, pp. 121-135 ; Kittredge, *Chaucer and his Poetry*, pp. 108-145 ; Root, *The Poetry of Chaucer*, Boston, 1922, pp. 87-134, and his edition of the *Troilus*, Introduction, pp. xxviii-xxxi.

[2] Shakespeare—or, more probably, some earlier playwright (Rollins, H. E., *Publications of the Modern Language Association*, 1917, XXXII, 388, cites a record of a lost pre-Elizabethan play of *Troylous and Pandor*), in which Ulysses appears among the dramatis personae—restored the enveloping war-narrative, in all probability, largely from Caxton, who in his *Recuyell of the Historyes of Troye*, followed the traditional form of the medieval story (see Tatlock, J. S. P., *Publications of the Modern Language Association*, 1915, XXX, 760 ff.). Shakespeare's love plot, however, retains much of the richness of elaboration given the love story by Boccaccio and Chaucer (see Lawrence, *op. cit.*, pp. 190 ff.). Dryden modernized the Shakespearean play, leaving the relative amount of space devoted to the war-narrative and to the love story substantially unchanged.

an English literary tradition that lived for three centuries and included the names of England's first great
poet and of her two foremost dramatists.[1]

It has long been recognized[2] that though he never

[1] Another non-dramatic treatment of the Troilus story is to be
found in the *Testament of Cresseid*, composed toward the end of the
fifteenth century, by the Scottish poet Robert Henryson. Henryson
broke fresh ground, however, writing his poem as a continuation of
Chaucer's *Troilus*. Although Henryson's *Testament*, by reason of the
carrying of the plot beyond the traditional limits, lies distinctly apart
from the main line of literary development, it was by no means without influence upon popular conceptions of the character of Cressida,
its representation of the heroine as visited with leprosy being directly
responsible for Shakespeare's "lazar kite of Cressid's kind" (*Henry V*,
II, i, 65-68).

In addition to Henryson's poem we have record of three pre-Elizabethan dramatizations of the Troilus story, one in Latin by Nicholas
Grimald of unknown date, and two in English, one presented at Eltham
(1516), and one at court (1517), as well as of later pre-Shakespearean
dramatizations. See Tatlock, *op. cit.*, p. 676 and Rollins, *op. cit.*, pp.
388-389.

[2] As early as 1530 if, as seems not unlikely, we may believe that
Lydgate was referring to the *Filostrato* when in the *Prologue* of his
Falls of Princes (ed. Bergen, H., *Early English Text Society*, Extra
Series, 1924-27, CXXI-IV, I, 8, vv. 283-287) he wrote of Chaucer:

> "In youthe he made a translacioun
> Off a book whiche called is Trophe
> In Lumbard tunge, as men may reede and see,
> And in our vulgar, longe or that he deide,
> Gaff it the name of Troylus and Cresseide."

Upon the insufficiency of W. W. Skeat's evidence (*The Complete
Works of Geoffrey Chaucer*, six vols., Oxford Press, 1900, V, 233) for
his identification of "Trophee," cited as an author by Chaucer (*Canterbury Tales*, ed. cit., B 3307) with Guido delle Colonne, see Kittredge,
"The Pillars of Hercules and Chaucer's Trophee," *Putnam Anniversary Volume*, The Torch Press, Cedar Rapids, 1909. See, also, Giulio
Bertoni, *Studj romanzi*, 1912, VIII, 252-254; Tupper, F., *Modern Language Notes*, 1916, XXXI, 11 ff.; Emerson, O. F., *Modern Language
Notes*, XXXI, 142 ff. It was not, however, until 1786, when parts of
Sir Francis Kinaston's *Commentary* upon Chaucer's *Troilus*, of which
the first two books of his Latin translation appeared in 1635, were published by F. W. Waldron, that Chaucer's dependence upon the *Filostrato* came to be generally known. See Eitner, K., *Jahrbuch der Shake-*

once mentions Boccaccio by name,[1] Chaucer[2] used his *Filostrato* as the main source of his *Troilus and Criseyde*, as he used his *Teseide* as the main source of his *Knight's Tale*.[3]

Chaucer has followed the main outline of Boccaccio's story throughout, not infrequently translating

speare-Gesellschaft, Berlin, 1868, III, 277; Spurgeon, C. F. E., *Five Hundred Years of Chaucer Criticism and Allusion*, three vols., Cambridge, 1925, I, 207.

[1] But always "Lollius" instead (*Troilus, ed. cit.*, V, 1653), or "myn auctour" (II, 18), or "myn auctour called Lollius" (I, 394). On possible reasons for Chaucer's reference to Lollius, who, as the author of an "old book on the Trojan war" (II, 14; III, 19), cannot possibly be identified with Boccaccio, whose *Filostrato* was neither "old," "in Latin," or specifically "on the Trojan war," see Kittredge, "Chaucer's Lollius," *Harvard Studies in Classical Philology*, 1917, XXVIII and Root, *ed. cit.*, Introduction, pp. xxxvi-xl.

[2] Of any direct use of the *Filostrato* by English writers other than Chaucer we have no certain evidence. We find in England, to be sure, three instances of the application of the love of Troilus for Cressida to the author's own love for his lady, which might seem to have been suggested by Boccaccio's similar practice in the *Proemio*. Thus in *Tottel's Miscellany* (1557) an anonymous writer entitles his poem "A comparison of his loue with the faithfull and painful loue of Troylus to Creside"; William Elderton in a ballad (1560) recommends "Cresseda's" pity for "Troylus" to his lady's attention; and in his *Enimi of Idlenesse* (1568) William Fulwood writes a poetical epistle, intended to serve as a model for lovers, in which he beseeches his mistress to grant him "grace, as Cressida did unto Troylus" (see Rollins, *op. cit.*, pp. 390-392). But in no one of these poems do we find reference to the later treachery of Cressida. Very interesting in this connection is the confession made by Pierre de Beauvau in the *Preface* to his fourteenth century French translation of the *Filostrato* entitled *Troilus (ed. cit.*, pp. 117-121) that he made his translation in order to warn ladies against acting toward their lovers as Criseida had acted toward Troilus, and as his own lady had acted toward him. With regard to one and all of these cases one may at least conclude that the writer felt that the story, whether as told by Boccaccio or by Chaucer, naturally lent itself to personal uses.

[3] Manly (*ed. cit.*, pp. 539-540) successfully disposes of Root's argument (*The Poetry of Chaucer*, p. 168) for the priority of the Troilus to the *Knight's Tale*. The fact that at the end of the Troilus (V, 1807-27) Chaucer paraphrases a passage in the *Teseide* dealing with the

single lines and at times whole stanzas almost verbatim.[1]

Nevertheless the English poem is something quite other than a mere paraphrase of the Italian. Very clearly Chaucer had views of his own as to what he wished to do with the story as he received it from Boccaccio and neither in content, nor in plot, nor in conception of character does he leave the narrative what he had found it in the *Filostrato*.

In respect to content, the *Troilus* is much longer than the *Filostrato*. The English poem contains 8239 lines as against the 5704 lines of the Italian, or 2535 more lines. Moreover, but 2730 of the 5704 lines of the *Filostrato* are used by Chaucer, leaving a balance of 5509 lines to the English poet's credit. Furthermore, the 2730 lines of the Italian used by Chaucer are condensed by him to 2583 lines, increasing the number of English lines not translated from the *Filostrato* to 5626, or more than double the number taken from the Italian poem.[2]

flight of Arcita's soul to heaven (see Root, p. 90), would seem to render it not unlikely that the English poet had written at least a preliminary draft of the *Knight's Tale* before the *Troilus*. Cf. Lowes, J. L. (*Publications of the Modern Language Association*, 1905, XX, 841-854), who argues in favor of the priority of the *Knight's Tale*.

[1] For a purely mechanical confrontation of the Italian passages translated by Chaucer with the English passages into which he translated them, see William Michael Rossetti, "Chaucer's *Troylus* compared with the *Filostrato* of Boccaccio," *Chaucer Society*, 1873, XLIV, 1883, XLV.

There is need of a more searching comparison of the two poems to determine the technique of Chaucer in handling an Italian original at the time he wrote the *Filostrato*. This, if then compared with a similar comparison of the *Knight's Tale* with the *Teseide*, would go far to determining the relative chronology of the two poems.

[2] See Rossetti, *op. cit.*, XLIV, iii; Root, edition of the *Troilus*, Introduction, p. xxx, n. 49. The foregoing computation includes, of

These 5626 lines not translated from the *Filostrato* owe their origin in part to Chaucer's use of supplementary sources, in part to inventions of his own, and in part to his use of a narrative method more leisurely and discursive than that employed by Boccaccio.

Of these lines the smallest number is attributable to Chaucer's borrowings from other sources. As a means of emphasizing the grief of Troilus at the departure of Criseyde to the Greek camp, the English poet, in pursuance of his customary method on such occasions,[1] puts into his mouth a long reflection from Boethius on the subject of predestination.[2] Later, in dealing with the wooing of Criseyde by Diomede, he makes frequent passing use of details from Benoit and perhaps Guido which Boccaccio had not seen fit to reproduce.[3]

course, only lines actually translated from Boccaccio, by no means all in which his influence was felt. Moreover, as Young has pointed out (*op. cit.*, p. 106), Rossetti has not succeeded in catching quite all even of the lines translated.

[1] As in three passages in the *Knight's Tale*. In the first of these (Manly, *Canterbury Tales, ed. cit.*, A, 1251-74) it is the exiled Arcite who calls out upon fortune; in the second (A, 1303-33) it is the still imprisoned Palamon; and in the third (A, 2987-3040) it is Theseus who cannot "with wisest sorrow" bestow Emily upon Palamon until he has first unbosomed himself of a long disquisition upon the inexorable destiny that has robbed the world of Arcite.

[2] *Troilus*, IV, 953-1085 (see Patch, H. R., *Journal of English and Germanic Philology*, 1918, XVII, 399-422). From Boethius Chaucer likewise took the substance of Troilus' hymn to love (III, 1744-71).

Root has discovered that these two passages from the *Consolation of Philosophy* were introduced by Chaucer only when he came to revise the *Troilus* (see his "Textual Tradition of Chaucer's Troilus," *Chaucer Society*, XCIX, London, 1916, pp. 155-157, 216-220; and his *Poetry of Chaucer*, p. 90).

See, further, B. L. Jefferson's admirable study of the influence of Boethius upon the *Troilus* in his *Chaucer and the Consolation of Philosophy of Boethius*, Princeton, 1917, pp. 120-130.

[3] From Benoit only could have come Chaucer's accounts of the early courting of Criseyde by Diomede on the way to Calchas' tent (V, 92-189; *Roman de Troie*, vv. 17529-17712), of Diomede's presentation to

A larger number of the lines in the *Troilus* not translated from the *Filostrato* is due to Chaucer's addition
of incidents introduced by the English poet in connection with his treatment of the later stages of Troilus'
courtship of Criseyde. Largely Chaucer's own is the
account of the banquet at Deiphoebus' house (II,
1394-III, 231),[1] where Troilus is granted his first interview with Criseyde and probably entirely his own is
the subsequent account of the supper party at the house

Criseyde of the war steed of Troilus which he had captured in battle
(V, 1037-1039; *Roman de Troie*, vv. 15079-15172), and of Criseyde's
gift to Diomede of a "pencel of hire sleve" (V, 1042-1043; *Roman de
Troie*, vv. 15176-15179). Either from Benoit or from Guido could have
come Chaucer's description of the changeable heart of Criseyde (V,
825; *Roman de Troie*, v. 5286; *Historia Trojana*, sig. e 2, rect., col. 2,
ll. 22-23), and his account of the theft of Criseyde's glove by Diomede
(V, 1013; *Roman de Troie*, 13709-13711; *Historia Trojana*, sig. i 2,
vers., col. 1, l. 42; col. 2, l. 3), and of the nursing of the wounded
Diomede by Criseyde (V, 1044-1050; *Roman de Troie*, vv. 20131-20146;
20202-20228; *Historia Trojana*, sig. l 1, rect. 1, 5-21).

See Skeat, W. W., *Works of Chaucer*, ed. *cit.*, 1894, II, Introduction,
lvi-lxii; Broach, J. W., *Journal of English and Germanic Philology*,
1899, II, 14-28; Hamilton, G. L., *Chaucer's Indebtedness to Guido delle
Colonne*, New York, 1903, pp. 83-85; Young, *op. cit.*, 105-139; Root,
ed. cit., pp. xxxv-xxxvi.

[1] Very reasonable is Root's surmise (*ed. cit.*, p. xxix) that the selec-
tion of Deiphoebus as Criseyde's host was suggested to Chaucer by the
fact that, at a later point in the story, he serves Troilus and Pandarus
in the same capacity in the *Filostrato* (VII, 77-85). Since Chaucer omits
this later representation of Deiphoebus' hospitality, he may very well
have decided to change its purpose and transfer it to this earlier
point. Significant is it in both cases that it is Pandarus who suggests that Deiphoebus play the host. It is, at the same time, instruc-
tive to observe how different is the use which Chaucer makes of the
hospitality of Deiphoebus from that made of it by the Italian poet. In
Boccaccio the visit was paid to divert Troilus from his grief at the non-
return of Criseida; in Chaucer it is paid so that Troilus may offer the
guest of honor his moral support against an unscrupulous lawyer, who,
in the absence of the heroine's father, has designs upon her estate.
Nothing could better illustrate Chaucer's detached and humorous attitude toward the story as contrasted with the serious and preoccupied
attitude of Boccaccio.

of Pandarus[1] (III, 505-1309), at which the final surrender takes place.[2]

By far the largest number of the lines in the *Troilus*
not taken from the *Filostrato* is to be ascribed to Chaucer's use of a narrative method more leisurely and circumstantial than Boccaccio's. By this means the tempo
of the Italian recital, slow as it may seem to the modern reader, is still further retarded. It is in passages in
the *Troilus* in which he thus embroiders upon a narrative background already supplied by Boccaccio that
Chaucer is most fully himself, even rising to higher
levels of originality than when treating incidents of
his own invention. This is well seen in his delineation
of Pandarus, a character whom he employs for the purpose of infusing into the Italian narrative a comic
spirit essentially English and essentially his own.
Chaucer's delight in the display of his characteristic

[1] The present writer is strongly inclined to agree with Cummings, H.
("The Indebtedness of Chaucer's Works to the Italian Works of
Boccaccio," *University of Cincinnati Studies*, 1916, vol. X, part 2, pp.
3-12) and with Root (*ed. cit.*, pp. xxix-xxx and n. 48) in their opposition to the theory advanced by Young (*op. cit.*, pp. 139-148) that Chaucer modeled his account of the meeting between Troilus and Criseyde
in the "litel closet" occupied by the latter at Pandarus' house (III,
512-1190) upon Boccaccio's account of the meeting between Filocolo
and Biancofiore in the latter's chamber in the tower of the ammiraglio
of the King of Babylon in the *Filocolo* (II, 165-183). Such parallelism
as may be said to exist between the two accounts seems to him, as to
them, no more than what might naturally be expected when two authors of the same epoch are dealing with the same situation, viz., a
nocturnal meeting between lovers. Furthermore it is certain from the
large number of earlier literary treatments of the nocturnal visit which
Young himself has listed (p. 151), that the situation must by Chaucer's
time have become a fairly stereotyped one.

[2] Entirely Chaucer's own, furthermore, are the song of Antigone
(II, 829-896), the song of the nightingale under Criseyde's window
(II, 918-924), and Criseyde's dream of the eagle that tears out her heart
(II, 925-931), incidents which serve the double purpose of providing
pleasing digressions from the main action and of indicating the emo-
tional changes that are taking place in the heroine's heart.

roguish humor, for which the appearance of Pandarus seems always to have supplied the occasion, accounts for the extended prolongation of the first scene between Pandarus and Troilus (I, 547-1064) and the first scene between Pandarus and Criseyde (II, 78-595).[1]

In the matter of plot Chaucer makes a notable departure from Boccaccio in not paying exclusive heed to Troilus and his woes but admitting Criseyde and her coquetries to at least an equal degree of attention. This distribution of interest he has effected by amplifying Boccaccio's successive accounts of the wooings of Criseyde by Troilus and by Diomede and by relatively curtailing his narrative of the anxieties of Troilus as he awaits in vain the return of Criseyde from Troy.[2] More particularly has he effected this distribution of interest by adding to Benoit's account of the betrayal

[1] The first of these scenes (*Filostrato*, II, 1-34) Chaucer has nearly doubled, expanding from 272 lines in the Italian to 517 lines in the English; the second (*Filostrato*, II, 35-67) he has more than doubled, expanding from 256 lines in the Italian to the same number of lines (517) in the English.

[2] Both in the *Troilus* and in the *Filostrato* Troilus' part in the wooing of Cressida is limited to the writing of letters. After the exchange of letters between the lovers Boccaccio devotes 88 lines to the successful efforts of Pandarus to persuade Criseida to allow Troilus to come to her house (*Filostrato*, II, 133-143). Instead of these 88 lines Chaucer has substituted 1400 lines, devoted in part (595 lines) to the dinner party at the house of Deiphoebus (*Troilus*, II, 1394-III, 231) and in part (1805 lines) to the supper party at the house of Pandarus (*Troilus*, II, 505-1309). Chaucer has lengthened his account of the wooing of Criseyde by Diomede from 272 lines in the *Filostrato* (VI) to 476 lines in the Troilus (V, 14-28, 99-114, 121-157). On the other hand the English poet has relatively shortened his account of the woes of Troilus after the departure of Criseyde to the Greeks from 1048 lines in the *Filostrato* (VII; VIII, 1-25) to 1064 lines in the *Troilus* (V, 29-98, 159-220, 225-227, 234-250). Cf. Fischer, *op. cit.*, pp. 236-239. Although Fischer's figures are impossible to follow because he fails to cite the passages out of which they are made up, his entire treatment of the relation of Chaucer to Boccaccio (pp. 217-370) is the most thoroughgoing yet made of the subject.

of Troilus by Briseida his own story of her remorse
thereafter.[1] Thus while allowing himself by no means
to lose sight of Boccaccio's exclusive preoccupation
with the sorrows of Troilus, even announcing at the
outset that his purpose is

> The double sorwe of Troilus to tellen,

Chaucer brightens his narrative immeasurably by re-
storing the colorful personality and varied activities
of the French Briseida to something of the position of
commanding interest which she originally occupied in
the histories of Benoit and Guido. Above all by following the career of Criseyde beyond the point at
which the French poet had taken leave of her to picture
her, if not as penitent, at least as fully alive to the
miseries which she has brought upon Troilus, the English poet has relieved Boccaccio's story of the unmiti-
gated tragedy of Troilus of much of its monotony by
supplying a counterpart in the tragedy of Criseyde,
thus adding greatly to the tragic effectiveness of the
story as a whole.

Of the wooing of Criseyde by Troilus Ten Brink

---

[1] It is possible that the seeds of a Cressida sensible of the havoc she
has wrought in the heart of her first lover are to be found in Benoit's
suggestive description of the regretful feelings with which Briseida
decides at length to present her love to Diomede (*Roman de Troie*, vv.
20318-20320):

> "Deus donge bien a Troilus!
> Quant nel puis aveir, ne il mei,
> A cestui me doing e otrei."

If out of these lines Chaucer obtained his ultimate hint for that pitiful
passage in which he represents Criseyde as pronouncing her own doom
through the prophecy that the bell of her infamy shall resound through
the ages (*Troilus*, V, 1054-1071), the credit for the result will have to
be divided between the one touch of tenderness that alone qualifies the
French trouvère's unsparing treatment of his erring heroine and the
perspicuity of the English poet in seizing upon it for the purpose of
so largely recasting the earlier writer's generally ruthless conception
of her character as to make of her a poignantly pathetic figure.

once pertinently remarked that the English heroine offers far more resistance to the overtures of her Trojan lover than does her Italian prototype, "a far greater concatenation of circumstances being needed to bring her to his arms."[1] While we cannot subscribe to the deduction thence drawn by the German critic, viz., that Chaucer meant thereby to represent Criseyde as "an injured innocent," we are nevertheless indebted to him for directing attention to the fact that by inventing the ruses whereby Pandarus decoys Criseyde into the presence of Troilus, Chaucer has succeeded most artfully in increasing our interest in his heroine by conveying the impression that she holds herself at a higher valuation than the Criseida of Boccaccio and that, if as willing, she is not at any rate as ready a victim as the latter. To balance the labors expended by Troilus and Pandarus upon the winning of Criseyde in the rising action, the English poet has out of an occasional hint from Benoit and Guido constructed a more circumstantial story than Boccaccio of the courtship of Criseyde by Diomede in the falling action. Thus by accumulating a larger weight of incident on both sides of the scales than had been gathered by Boccaccio and by giving it the happy balance that had been lacking both in Benoit and in Boccaccio, Chaucer has succeeded in imparting to his story its strongly marked dramatic quality.

In so far as the characters are concerned, Chaucer's Troilus remains the languishing, sentimental lover— seemingly a characteristically Italian type—that we find in the *Filostrato*. Diomede, in like manner, is still the forthright, masterful wooer of Boccaccio, Chaucer

---

[1] Bernard Ten Brink, *History of English Literature*, translated by W. C. Robinson, 1893, II, 92.

being at pains to emphasize his self-assurance by re-
verting to Benoit's representation of his wooing as begun during his escort of Briseida to her father's tent
instead of reproducing Boccaccio's postponement of
these advances to a later and more auspicious occasion.[1] In dealing with Criseyde and Pandarus, however, Chaucer has substantially altered the characters
handed down to him by his Italian forerunner.

In his portrayal of Criseyde the English poet holds
fast to the traditional conception of her instability and
changeableness as emphasized by Benoit and retained
by Boccaccio.[2] But this underlying traditional conception he, like Boccaccio before him, modifies in a manner
peculiarly his own. Moland and D'Héricault distin-
guish the nicer differences between the French, the Italian, and the English heroines by remarking that in Benoit's hands Cressida is "a slave girl," in the hands of
Boccaccio she becomes "a courtesan," and in the hands
of Chaucer somewhat of "a lady," though still with
"traces of her ancestors in her veins."[3] The distinction
thus strikingly phrased possesses a large measure of
truth. True to the hardy standards of an age still

[1] Cf. the *Troilus*, V, 92-189 with the *Filostrato*, V, 13 and with the
Roman de Troie, vv. 13529-13712. See, also, p. 35, n. 1.

[2] Throughout her entire career the constant element in Cressida's
character had been her inconstancy. Benoit evidently builded better
than he knew when upon his first introduction of Briseida, in his list
of Greek portraits, he said of her (*Roman de Troie*, vv. 5285-5286):

> "Molt fu amee et moult amot
> Mais sis corages li changot."

That Boccaccio in like manner conceived of Criseida's mutability as her
dominant characteristic may be inferred from the moral he draws from
the story he has just been relating when, at the end of his poem (*Filostrato*, VIII, 30), he advises young men not to put their trust in young
women, "inconstant ever as leaf in the wind." Finally Chaucer phrases
the matter quite as incisively as Benoit in his own portrait of Criseide
as "slydynge of corage" (*Troilus*, V, 825).

[3] *Op. cit.*, Introduction, p. xcvii.

largely heroic Benoit conceived of Briseida as a pure child of the senses, without moral responsibility, to be bandied about as a mere chattel from warrior to warrior in Homeric fashion. Boccaccio, in accordance with the more luxurious and less virile tastes of his own day, transforms the French heroine into the type of the sophisticated Neapolitan lady of pleasure. His Criseida is in no sense unconscious of the moral issue; she deliberately cherishes indulgent theories and sins with her eyes open; she is not seduced but seduces herself. Finally Chaucer, while forced to admit the damaging evidence of his authorities, does so with reluctance; he would spare Criseyde if he could.[1] As we have seen, he does what he can to make her appear more sinned against than sinning.

But it is even more conspicuously in his treatment of Pandarus that the English poet reveals his independence of his sources. In Chaucer Pandarus not only plays a far more extensive rôle than in Boccaccio but he plays a rôle of a quite different sort. The English Pandarus is no longer the youthful cousin of the heroine and the light-hearted companion of the hero but the middle-aged uncle of the heroine and the sage mentor of the hero. While Chaucer's Pandarus is still young enough to be a lover and to sympathize with Troilus on that account, he is at the same time sufficiently old and worldly-wise to take an objective and detached attitude both toward his own afflictions in love and those of his friend. He is, like Major Pendennis, a quixotic lover of the old beau type and at the same time, like him, the willing adviser in the more desperate passions of one younger than himself. Stronger than the obligations that bind him to his niece is the

[1] *Troilus*, V, 1093-1099.

bond of friendship that unites him to Troilus. The affection of Pandarus for Troilus is the affection of Falstaff for Prince Hal, not the affection of Arcite for Palamon. Pandarus contemplates Troilus with the delight with which an older man of more mature wisdom and riper experience beholds the fortunes of a youthful and still undisillusioned enthusiast—a visible reminder of his own vanished past and of the rôle which he himself would still play if he could. He is the outstanding example in literature of the man who finds a keener delight in the love affairs of another than in his own. That we have in Chaucer's Pandarus what Kittredge has happily styled "the sympathetic ironist" in place of the conventional "man about town" of Boccaccio, describes, if it does not explain, the nature of the transformation. Strange to say, it is through the agency of Pandarus, cynic though he be, that in one instance, at least, Chaucer has purged his poem of what the prurient might object to in the *Filostrato* as meretricious. The humorous remark of Pandarus on removing the lighted candle from the bedchamber of the two lovers (*Troilus*, III, 137) lets a wholesome draught of English comedy in upon a situation which in the *Filostrato* (III, 26) can hardly be said to have been handled in an altogether delicate manner.

BIBLIOGRAPHICAL NOTE

THE following is an alphabetical list of books and articles referred to more than once in the Introduction:

Andreas Capellanus, *De Arte Amandi*, ed. E. Trojel, Copenhagen, 1892.

Antona-Traversi, C., "Notizie storiche sull' Amorosa visione," *Studj di filologia romanza*, 1885, I, 425 ff.

Appel, C., *Bernart de Ventadorn: seine Lieder*, Halle, 1915.

Boccaccio, Giovanni, (1) *De Casibus Illustrium Virorum*, Venice, 1544.

(2) *De Genealogia Deorum*, Venice, 1472.

(3) *De Montibus, Silvis, Fontibus, et Lacubus*, Venice, 1473. See also under Moutier.

Casetti, A. C., "Il Boccaccio a Napoli," *Nuova antologia di scienze, lettere ed arti*, 1875, XXVIII, 557-595.

Constans, L., Edition of Benoit de Ste. Maure, "Roman de Troie," *Société des anciens textes français*, Paris, 1904-12.

Cook, A. S., "The Character of Criseyde," *Publications of the Modern Language Association*, 1907, XXII, 531 ff.

Corazzini, F., *Le lettere edite e inedite di Giovanni Boccaccio*, Florence, 1877.

Crane, T. F., *Italian Social Customs in the Sixteenth Century*, New Haven, 1920.

Crescini, V., (1) "Idalagos," *Zeitschrift für rom. Philologie*, 1885, IX, 437-479; 1886, X, 1-21.

(2) *Contributo agli studi di Giovanni Boccaccio*, Turin, 1887.

(3) *Il cantare di Fiorio e Biancofiore*, two vols., Bologna, 1889, 1899.

(4) "Boccaccio. Opere minori in volgare," *Kritischer Jahresbericht über die Fortschritte der rom. Philologie*, 1897, Band III, Heft II, 384 ff.

(5) *Fiammetta: conferenza letta nella sala di Dante in Orsanmichele: Lectura Dantis*, Florence, 1913.

Dante, *Vita nuova*, ed. P. Fraticelli, Florence, 1906.

Della Torre, A., *La giovinezza di Giovanni Boccaccio*, Città di Castello, 1905.

Ettore di Ferri, Edition of "Il Filocolo," *Collezione di classici italiani*, two vols., Turin, 1921-22, Introduzione.

Gaspary, A., "Il Boccaccio," *Storia della letteratura italiana*, 1900, II, 1-61.

Goldschmidt, T., *Die Doktrin der Liebe in den italienischen Lyriken des XIII Jahrhunderts*, Breslau, 1889.

Guido della Colonne, *Historia Trojana*, Strassburg, 1486.

Hauvette, H., *Boccace*, Paris, 1914.

Hortis, A., *Studj sulle opere latine del Boccaccio*, Triest, 1879.

Hutton, E., (1) *Life of Boccaccio*, London, 1909.

(2) "Some Aspects of the Genius of Giovanni Boccaccio," *Proceedings of the British Academy*, 1922, X, 3-20.

Joly, A., Edition of Benoit de Ste. Maure, *Roman de Troie*, Paris, 1870-71.

Kittredge, G. L., (1) "The Date of Chaucer's Troilus," *Chaucer Society*, Second Series, 1909, XLII.

(2) *The Poetry of Chaucer*, Harvard University Press, 1914.

Lawrence, W. W., "The Love Story in 'Troilus and Cressida,'" *Shaksperian Studies by Members of the English Department at Columbia University*, New York City, 1916, pp. 187 ff.

Manly, J. M., Edition of Chaucer's *Canterbury Tales*, Henry Holt, 1928.

Moland and D'Héricault, Edition of the "Troilus" of Pierre de Beauvau, "Nouvelles françoises en prose du XIV siècle," *Bibliothèque elzéverienne*, Paris, 1858, LXVI, Introduction.

Moutier, I., *Opere volgari di Giovanni Boccaccio*, Florence, 1827-34, seventeen vols.: *Fiammetta* (VI); *Filocolo* (VII, VIII); *Teseide* (IX); *Filostrato* (XIII); *Amorosa visione* (XIV); *Ameto* (XV); *Rime* (XVI).

Parodi, E. G., *Il Tristano riccardiano*, Bologna, 1896.

Renier, R., Review of Trojel, E., "Middelalderens elskovshoffer," *Giornale storico della letteratura italiana*, 1889, XIII, 371 ff.

Rollins, H. E., "The Troilus and Cressida Story from Chaucer to Shakespeare," *Publications of the Modern Language Association*, 1917, XXXII, 383 ff.

Root, R. K., (1) *The Poetry of Chaucer*, Houghton Mifflin, 1922.

(2) Edition of Chaucer's *Troilus*, Princeton, 1926.

Rossetti, W. M., "Chaucer's Troylus compared with Boccaccio's Filostrato," *Chaucer Society*, 1873, XLIV ; 1883, XLV.

Savj-Lopez, P., "Il Filostrato di Boccaccio," *Romania*, 1898, XXVII, 442 ff.

Tatlock, J. S. P., "The Siege of Troy in Elizabethan Literature," *Publications of the Modern Language Association*, 1915, XXX, 673 ff.

Torraca, F., *Per la biografia di Boccaccio*, Milan, 1912.

Toynbee, P., *Dante Studies and Researches*, London, 1902.

Villani, F., *Vita Dantis, Petrarchae, et Boccaccii*, Florence, 1826.

Wilkins, E. H., "The Enamorment of Boccaccio," *Modern Philology,* 1913, XI, 39 ff.

Young, Karl, (1) "The Origin and Development of the Story of Troilus and Cressida," *Chaucer Society*, Second Series, 1908, XLI.

(2) "Aspects of the Story of Troilus and Criseyde," *University of Wisconsin Studies in Language and Literature*, 1918, no. 2, pp. 367 ff.

THE FILOSTRATO OF BOCCACCIO

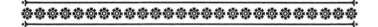

IL FILOSTRATO

DI

GIOVANNI BOCCACCIO*

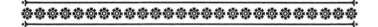

PROEMIO DELL' AUTORE

*Filostrato è il titolo di questo libro; e la cagione è, perchè
ottimamente si confà cotal nome con l'effetto del libro. Filostrato
tanto viene a dire, quanto uomo vinto ed abbattuto da amore,
come vedere si può che fu Troilo, dell' amore del quale in questo
libro si racconta; perciocchè egli fu da amore vinto sì forte-
mente amando Criseida,† e cotanto s'afflisse nella sua partita,
che poco mancò che morte non lo sorprendesse.‡*

MOLTE fiate già, nobilissima donna, avvenne,
che io, il quale quasi dalla mia puerizia insino
a questo tempo ne' servigi d' amore sono stato,
ritrovandomi nella sua corte tra li gentili uomini e le
vaghe donne, in quella con me parimente dimoranti, udii
muovere e disputare questa questione, cioè: Uno giovane

* Here and on the title-page of each "part" of the *Filostrato* Moutier
uses the old-fashioned form of the genitive *Boccacci* in place of *Boccaccio*. He uses the form *Boccaccio*, however, in the title-page of the
entire poem. This latter form we have employed consistently throughout.

† Griseida, the form of the heroine's name in Moutier's text, is here
and henceforth changed to Criseida, which was probably the form used
by Boccaccio. See E. H. Wilkins in *Mod. Lang. Notes*, XXIV, 65 ff.

‡ Moutier prints the preceding lines as the opening sentence of the
Proemio, of which it forms in reality no part, having been taken by
Moutier from a rubric which occurs in but one Riccardian manuscript.
See F. Corazzini, *Le Lettere Edite e Inedite di Boccaccio*, Firenze,
1877, p. 9, note 1.

THE FILOSTRATO

OF

GIOVANNI BOCCACCIO

THE AUTHOR'S PROEM

Filostrato is the title of this book and the reason is that this name comporteth excellently with the purport of the book. Filostrato is as much as to say a man vanquished and stricken down by Love, as can be seen was Troilus, the story of whose love is related in this book; for he was vanquished by Love in so strongly loving Cressida and so much grieved by her departure that little was wanting that death should come upon him.

MANY times already hath it happened, O most noble lady, that I, who well-nigh from my boyhood up to the present time have been in the service of Love, finding myself in his court among noble men and beautiful ladies, who equally with myself were attending it, heard proposed and discussed this question, to wit: a young man fervently loveth a lady as touching whom nothing else is granted him by Fortune except sometimes to see her, or sometimes to talk of her, or sweetly to meditate upon her in his thoughts. Which now of these three things giveth the greatest delight? Nor did it ever happen that each one of these three things—one by one person, another by another—was not defended by many zealously and with pointed arguments. And since to my love, more ar-

ferventemente ama una donna, della quale niuna altra cosa gli è conceduto dalla fortuna, se non il potere alcuna volta vederla, o tal volta di lei ragionare, o seco stesso di lei dolcemente pensare. Qual' è adunque di queste tre cose di più diletto? Nè era mai, che ciascuna di queste tre cose, da cui l' una da cui l' altra, non fosse da molti studiosamente e con acuti argomenti difesa: e perciocchè a' miei amori, più focosi che avventurati, pareva cotale questione ottimamente essere conforme, mi ricorda* la mente, che vinto dal falso parere, più volte mescolandomi tra' questionatori, tenni e difesi di gran lunga essere maggiore il diletto, potere della cosa amata talvolta pensare, che quello che porger potesse alcuna dell' altre due: affermando, tra gli altri argomenti da me a ciò indotti, non essere picciola parte della beatitudine dell' amante, potere secondo il disio di colui che pensa disporre della cosa amata, e lei rendere secondo quello benivola e rispondente, come che ciò solamente durasse quanto il pensiero, sì che del vedere nè del ragionare non poteva certamente addivenire. O stolto giudizio, o sciocca estimazione, o vano argomento, quanto dal vero eravate lontani! amara esperienza, me misero, me lo dimostra al presente. O speranza dolcissima dell' afflitta mente, ed unico conforto del trafitto core, io non mi vergognerò d' aprirvi con qual forza nel tenebroso intelletto m' entrasse la verità, contro alla quale io puerilmente errando avea l' armi prese; ed a cui il potre' io dire, che alcuno alleggiamento potesse porre alla penitenza datami, non so s' io mi dica da amore o dalla fortuna, per la falsa opinione avuta, se non a voi?

Affermo adunque, bellissima donna, esser vero, che poscia che voi nella più graziosa stagione dell' anno

Mi ricordo (all the Riccardiana Mss.; Corazzini, p. 9).

dent than fortunate, this question appeared excellently
to appertain, I recall that I, overcome by false appear-
ances, mingling many times among the disputants,
maintained and defended at great length the thesis that
the delight of being able to think at times of the object
loved was far greater than that which either of the
other two could afford, affirming among the other arguments adduced by me to this end, that it was no small
part of a lover's felicity to be able to dispose of the
object loved according to the desire of him who doth the
thinking, and in accordance therewith to render her
benevolent and responsive, even though it should last
only so long as the thought, in such wise as surely
could not happen in the case of seeing her and talking
of her. O foolish judgment, O ridiculous opinion, O
vain argument, how far were ye from the truth! Bitter
experience now proveth it to me, wretched one that I
am. O sweetest, hope of a mind distressed and sole comfort of a pierced heart, I shall not be ashamed to disclose to you with what force entered into my darkened
intellect the truth, against which I in my puerile error
had taken arms. And to whom could I tell this, to what
person capable of giving alleviation to the punishment
visited upon me—whether by Love or by Fortune I cannot well say—for the false opinion I held, if not to
you?

I therefore affirm it true, O most beautiful lady, that
after by departing from the delightful city of Naples
at the most charming season of the year and going hence
to Sannio, you suddenly removed from mine eyes, more
desirous of your angelic sight than of aught else, what I
ought to have known by your presence but did not, that,
by its contrary—that is, by the privation of it—I was
given instant knowledge of. And this hath saddened my

dalla dilettevole città di Napoli dipartendovi, e in Sannio andandone, agli occhi miei, più del vostro angelico
viso vaghi che d' altra cosa, mi toglieste subitamente
quello che io per la vostra presenza doveva conoscere,
non conoscendolo, per lo suo contrario prestamente mi
fece conoscere, cioè per la privazione di quella; la quale
tanto fuori d' ogni dovuto termine m' ha l' anima con-
tristata, che assai apertamente posso comprendere,
quanta fosse la letizia, allora poco da me conosciuta, che
mi veniva dalla vostra graziosa e bella vista. Ma perchè
alquanto appaia più questa verità manifesta, non mi fia
grave, nè il voglio intralasciare, come che altrove più
che qui si distenda, ciò che avvenuto mi sia, a dichiara-
zione di tanto errore, dopo la vostra partenza.

Dico adunque, se Dio tosto coll' aspetto del vostro
bel viso gli occhi miei riponga nella perduta pace, che
poichè io seppi che voi di qui partita eravate, e in parte
andatane, dove niuna onesta cagione a vedervi mi doveva mai potere menare, che essi, per li quali la luce soa-
vissima del vostro amore mi menò nella mente, oltre
alla fede che porger possono le mie parole, hanno assai
volte di tante e di sì amare lagrime bagnata la faccia
mia, ed il dolente seno riempiuto, che non solamente è
stata mirabil cosa onde tanta umidità sia ad essi da essi
venuta, ma ancora* non che in voi, la quale credo che
come gentile siete così siate pietosa, in niuno che mio
nimico fosse, e di ferro avesse il petto,† a forza avreb-
bono messa pietade. Nè solamente questo è avvenuto‡
quante volte ricordato mi sono d' avere la vostra piace-

* In place of *ma ancora* Corazzini reads *che* after MS. Riccardiana 6
(p. 11).

† Corazzini reads "ma in niuno mio nemico che di ferro fosse il petto"
without ms. citation (p. 11). The *ma* is an improvement.

‡ Corazzini supplies *a me* between *questo* and *è avvenuto* after MS.
Riccardiana 6. He also places a comma after *pietade* and a period after
avvenuto without ms. citation (p. 11).

soul so far beyond any proper limit that I can clearly appreciate how great was the happiness, though little realized by me at the time, that came to me from the gracious and beautiful sight of you. But to the end that this truth appear somewhat more manifest, it shall not irk me to tell, nor do I wish to pass over in silence, what happened to me, to the elucidation of so great error, after your departure, although it is told at greater length elsewhere than here.

I say therefore, an it please God soon to replace mine eyes in their lost peace by the sight of your beautiful countenance, that when I knew that you had departed hence and gone to a place whither no proper reason for seeing you could ever lead me, these eyes of mine, through which the very gentle light of your love entered my mind, have, beyond any assurance that my words may offer, many times bathed my face and filled my sorrowing breast with so many and so bitter tears that not only hath it been a wonderful thing that so much moisture hath come to my face and breast from mine eyes but also would my tears have bred pity, not only in you, whom I believe to be as pitiful as you are gentle born, but in one who had been mine enemy and had had a breast of iron. Nor hath this happened to me only as often as the recollection of the loss of your delightful presence hath made mine eyes sad, but whatever hath appeared before them hath been the occasion of their greater misery. Alas, how many times have they, to suffer lesser misery, abstained of their own accord from viewing the church, the loggias, the piazzas, and the other places in which they formerly eagerly and anxiously sought to see—and sometimes did see—your countenance! And how many times have they in their grief constrained my heart to repeat to itself that verse

vole presenza perduta gli ha fatti tristi, ma qualunque cosa è loro davanti apparita, di loro maggior miseria è stata cagione. Oimè, quante volte per minor doglia sentire, si sono spontaneamente ritorti dal guardare il tempio,* le logge, le piazze, e gli altri luoghi, ne' quali, già vaghi e desiderosi cercavano di vedere, e talvolta in essi videro la vostra sembianza; e dolorosi hanno il cuore costretto a dir seco quello verso di Geremia: "O "come siede sola la città, la quale in addietro era piena "di popolo, e donna delle genti!" Certo io non dirò ogni cosa parimente attristargli, ma io affermo solo una essere quella parte che alquanto la loro tristizia mitiga, riguardando quelle contrade, quelle montagne, quella parte del cielo, fra le quali e sotto la quale porto ferma opinione che voi siate; quindi ogni aura, ogni soave vento che di colà viene, così nel viso ricevo, quasi il vostro senza niuno fallo abbia tocco: nè è perciò troppo lungo questo mitigamento, ma quale sopra le cose unte veggiamo talvolta le fiamme discorrere, tal sopra l' afflitto cuore questa soavità discorre, fuggendo subita per lo sopravvegnente pensiero che mi mostra non potervi vedere, essendo di ciò senza misura acceso il mio disio.

Che dirò de' sospiri, i quali nel passato piacevole amore e dolce speranza mi soleano infiammati trarre dal petto? Certo io non ho altro che dirne, se non che moltiplicati in molti doppii di grandissima angoscia, mille volte ciascuna ora da quello per la mia bocca fuori sono sforzatamente sospinti. E similmente le mie voci, le quali già alcuna volta mosse, non so da che occulta letizia procedente dal vostro sereno aspetto, in amorosi canti, e in ragionamenti pieni di focoso amore, s' udirono sempre poi chiamare il vostro nome di grazia pieno

* Corazzini reads *i templi* without ms. citation (p. 11).

of Jeremiah: "O how solitary abideth the city that before was full of people and a mistress among the nations!" I will not indeed say that everything hath made them sad to an equal degree, but I do affirm that there is but one direction that somewhat qualifieth their sadness, and that is when they survey those countries, those mountains, that part of the heavens among which and under which I am persuaded that you are. Thence every breeze, every soft wind that cometh from there, I receive in my face as if without fail it hath touched yours. Nor, when I do so, is this alleviation of too long duration; but as upon things anointed we sometimes see flames flickering, so hovereth this sweetness above my afflicted heart, taking sudden flight because of the supervening thought that showeth me that I cannot see you, my desire thereof being enkindled beyond measure.

What shall I say of the sighs that in the past pleasing love and sweet hope were wont to draw inflamed from my breast? Naught have I indeed to say of them other than that, multiplied in many duplications of the greatest distress, they are a thousand times an hour violently forced thereby out of my mouth. And in like fashion my words, which in times past were sometimes stirred, I know not by what strange joy proceeding from your serene aspect, into amorous songs and discourses full of ardent love, thereafter have been heard ever calling upon your gracious name and upon Love for pity, and upon Death for an end of my sorrows, and the greatest lamentations may have been heard by anyone who hath been near me.

In such a life, therefore, I live far from you, and ever the better do I realize how great was the good, the pleasure, and the delight that proceeded from your eyes, though little appreciated by me in times past. And

e amore per mercede, e la morte per fine de' miei dolori, e i grandissimi rammarichii possono essere stati uditi da chi m' è stato presso.

In cotal vita adunque vivo da voi lontano, e sempre più comprendo quanto fosse il bene, e' l piacere e il diletto che da' vostri occhi per addietro male da me conosciuto procedeva: e come che tempo assai mi prestano e le lagrime e' sospiri a potere del vostro valore ragionare, e ancora al presente della vostra leggiadria, de' costumi gentili, e della donnesca altezza, e della sembianza vaga più ch' altra, la quale io sempre con gli occhi della mente riguardo tutta, e mentre perciò di tale ragionamento o pensiero non dico che alcuno piacere l'anima non senta, ma questo piacere viene mischiato con un disio ferventissimo, il quale tutti gli altri disii accende in tanta fiamma di vedervi, che appena in me regger gli posso, che non mi tirino, posta giù ogni debita onestà e ragionevole consiglio, colà dove voi dimorate; ma pur vinto dal volere il vostro onore più che la mia salute guardare, gli raffreno; e non avendo altro ricorso, sentendomi la via chiusa del rivedervi, per la cagione mostrata, alle lagrime tralasciate ritorno. Ah lasso, quanto m' è la fortuna crudele e nemica ne' miei piaceri, sempre stata rigida maestra e correggitrice de' miei errori! ora misero me il conosco, ora il sento, ora apertissimamente discerno, quanto di bene, quanto di piacere, quanto di soavità, più nella luce vera degli occhi vostri volgendola ne' miei, che nella falsa lusinga del mio pensier dimorasse. Così adunque, o splendido lume della mia mente, col privarmi della vostra amorosa vista, ha fortuna risoluta la nebula dell' errore per addietro da me sostenuto: ma nel vero sì amara medicina non bisognava a purgare la mia ignoranza, più lieve gastigamento m' avrebbe nella diritta via ritornato. Ora

even though tears and sighs give me time enough to speak of your worth, and even now of your grace, courteous habits, and womanly dignity, and appearance beautiful beyond any other, which I ever contemplate with the eyes of my mind in its entirety, and whereas I say not that my mind doth not, in consequence of such speech or reflection, experience a certain pleasure, yet this pleasure cometh mingled with a very fervent desire that kindleth all my other desires into such a longing to see you that I am hardly able to rule them within me that they do not draw me, despite every fitting duty and reasonable consideration, to that place in which you abide. But bound by the desire more to preserve your honor than my well-being, I repress them. And since I have no other recourse and feel the path to seeing you again, closed to me for the reason aforesaid, I return to my suspended tears. Alas, how cruel and adverse is fortune to me in my pleasures, always a rigorous mistress and corrector of mine errors! Now I know, wretched one that I am, now I feel, now I clearly perceive how much more good, how much more pleasure, how much more gentleness dwelleth in the true light of your eyes, as you turn it to mine, than in the false flattery of my thoughts. Thus, therefore, O brilliant light of my mind, hath Fortune, by depriving me of the love-inspiring sight of you, dissipated the mist of error under which I formerly labored. But there was in truth no need of such bitter medicine to purge my ignorance; a more gentle chastisement would have turned me again into the right path. What under these circumstances could my powers avail against those of Fortune? However much I may bring reason to bear, they cannot resist. And I have in any case, by reason of your departure, arrived at such a pass as my writing hath above declared unto you; and with

così vagliano le mie forze a quelle della fortuna? quantunque la mia ragione sia molta, non possono resistere. E come che si vada, io sono pure per la vostra partenza a tal punto venuto, qual di sopra v' hanno le mie lettere dichiarato; e con mia gravissima noia sono divenuto certo di ciò, che prima incerto disputava in contrario. Ma da venire è omai a quel termine, per lo quale scrivendo infino a qui son trascorso, e dico, che vedendomi in tanta e così aspra avversità per lo vostro dipartir pervenuto, prima proposi di ritenere del tutto dentro del tristo petto l' angoscia mia, acciocchè palesata non fosse per avventura di molto maggiore efficace cagione; e ciò sostenendo con forza, assai vicino a disperata morte mi fe' venire, la quale se pure venuta fosse, senza niun fallo allora cara mi sarebbe stata. Ma poi, non so da che occulta speranza mosso, di dovervi pure ancora quando che sia rivedere, e nella prima felicità ritornare gli occhi miei, mi nacque non solamente paura di morte, ma desiderio di lunga vita, quantunque misera non vedendovi la dovessi menare. E conoscendo assai chiaramente, che tenendo io del tutto, come proposto avea, la mia conceputa doglia nel petto nascosa, era impossibile, che delle mille volte che essa abbondante e ogni termine trapassante sopravvenia, alcuna non vincesse tanto le forze mie, già debolissime divenute, che morte senza fallo ne seguirebbe, e più in conseguenza non vi vedrei. Da più utile consiglio mosso mutai proposta, e pensai di volere con alcuno onesto rammarichio dare luogo a quello a uscire dal tristo petto, acciocchè io vivessi, e potessi ancora rivedervi, e più lungamente vostro dimorassi vivendo. Nè prima tal pensiero nella mente mi venne, che il modo con esso subitamente m'occorse; dal quale avvenimento, quasi da nascosa divinità spirato, certissimo augurio presi di futura salute. E il modo

my most grievous affliction I have become certain of that which at first in my uncertainty I disputed and denied. But I must now come to that end toward which I have been progressing in the writing that I have thus far done. And I declare that when I saw myself come into so great and so sharp adversity by reason of your departure, I first proposed altogether to retain my anguish in my sad breast lest it might perchance, if disclosed, be the effectual cause of a much greater. And the forcible sustaining of this made me come very near to desperate death, which, had it come, would then without fail have been dear to me. But afterward there was born in me, moved I know not by what secret hope of being destined once more at some time or other to see you again and again to turn my eyes to their first felicity, not only a fear of death but a desire of long life, however miserable should be the life I would have to lead without seeing you. And knowing very clearly that if, as I had proposed, I held the grief I had conceived altogether hidden in my breast, it was not possible that out of the thousand times it came forth, abounding and overrunning every limit, it should not sometime so overcome my powers, already very much weakened, that death would follow without fail and I should in consequence see you no more, moved by a more useful counsel, I changed my mind and decided to give it issue from my sad heart in some suitable lamentation, in order that I might live, and might be able to see you once more, and might by living remain the longer yours. Nor did such a thought enter my mind before the means, together with it, occurred to me. As a result of which event, as though inspired by a secret divinity, I conceived the surest augury of future well-being. And the means was this: in the person of some impassioned one,

fu questo, di dovere in persona di alcuno passionato, siccome io era e sono, cantando narrare i miei martirii. Meco adunque con sollecita cura cominciai a rivolgere l' antiche storie, per trovare cui potessi verisimilmente fare scudo del mio segreto e amoroso dolore. Nè altro più atto nella mente mi venne a tal bisogno, che il valoroso giovane Troilo, figliuolo di Priamo nobilissimo re di Troia, alla cui vita, in quanto per amore e per la lontananza della sua donna fu doloroso, se fede alcuna alle antiche storie si può dare, poichè Criseida da lui sommamente amata fu al suo padre Calcas renduta, è stata la mia similissima dopo la vostra partita. Per che dalla persona di lui e da' suoi accidenti ottimamente presi forma alla mia intenzione, e susseguentemente in leggiere rima, e nel mio fiorentino idioma, con stile assai pietoso i suoi e miei dolori parimente composi, li quali una e altra volta cantando, assai utili gli ho trovati, secondo che fu nel principio l' avviso. È vero, che dinanzi alle sue più amare doglie, in simile stilo parte della sua felice vita si trova, la quale posi, non perch' io desideri che alcuno creda che io di simil felicità gloriare mi possa, perocchè non mi fu mai tanto favorevole la fortuna, nè sforzandomi di sperarlo nol può in alcun modo concedere la credenza che ciò avvenga, ma per questo le scrissi, perchè la felicità veduta da alcuno, molto meglio si comprende quanta e qual sia la miseria sopravvenuta. La qual felicità nondimeno, in tanto è alli miei fatti conforme, in quanto io non meno di piacere dagli occhi vostri traeva, che Troilo prendesse dall'amoroso frutto che di Criseida gli concedea la fortuna.

Adunque, valorosa donna, queste cotali rime in forma d' un piccolo libro, in testimonianza perpetua a coloro che nel futuro il vedranno, e del vostro valore, del quale in persona altrui esse sono in più parti ornate, e della

such as I was and am, to relate my sufferings in song. I began therefore to turn over in my mind with great care ancient stories, in order to find one that would serve in all color of likelihood as a mask for my secret and amorous grief. Nor did other more apt for such a need occur to me than the valiant young Troilus, son of Priam, most noble king of Troy, to whose life in so far as it was filled with sorrow by Love and by the distance of his lady, if any credit may be given to ancient histories, after his much-beloved Cressida was returned to her father Calchas, mine, after your departure, hath been very similar. Therefore from his person and from what happened to him I obtained in excellent wise a form for my conceit and subsequently composed in light rhyme and in my Florentine idiom and in a very appealing style his sorrows as well as my own, which, as I sang from time to time, I found very useful, according to what was my expectation in the beginning. True it is that before his most bitter woes is found in style similar a portion of his happy life, which I have recorded not because I desire that anyone should believe that I can glory in a like felicity—for fortune never was so kind to me, nor by forcing myself to hope for it, can I in any way bring myself to the belief that it will come—but for this reason have I written it, because when happiness hath been seen by anyone, much better is understood how great and of what sort is the misery that followeth after. This happiness is nevertheless so far in conformity with the facts of my case as I drew from your eyes no less pleasure than Troilus derived from the amorous fruit that fortune granted him in the case of Cressida.

Therefore, worthy lady, I have brought these rhymes together in the form of a little book, in lasting testimony

mia tristizia, ridussi; e ridotte, pensai non essere onesta cosa, quelle ad alcuna altra persona prima pervenire alle mani che alle vostre, che d' esse siete stata vera e sola cagione. Per la qual cosa, come che picciolissimo dono sia da mandare a tanta donna quanto voi siete, nondimeno, perchè l' affezione di me mandatore è grandissima e piena di pura fede, vel pure ardisco a mandare, quasi sicuro, che non per mio merito, ma per vostra benignità e cortesia da voi ricevute saranno. Nelle quali se avviene che leggiate, quante volte Troilo piangere e dolersi della partita di Criseida troverete, tante apertamente potrete comprendere e conoscere le mie medesime voci, le lagrime, i sospiri e l' angosce; e quante volte le bellezze, i costumi, e qualunque altra cosa laudevole in donna, di Criseida scritto troverete, di* voi essere parlato potrete intendere: l' altre cose, che oltre a queste vi sono assai, niuna, siccome già dissi, a me non appartiene, nè per me vi si pone, ma perchè la storia nel† nobile innamorato giovane lo richiede: e se così siete avveduta come vi tengo, così da esse potrete comprendere quanti e quali siano i miei disii, dove terminino, e che cosa essi più che altro‡ dimandino, o se alcuna pietà meritano. Ora io non so se esse fieno di tanta efficacia, che voi leggendole con alcuna compassione possano toccare la casta mente, ma amore ne prego che questa forza a loro ne presti; il che se addiviene, quanto più umilmente posso prego voi, che alla vostra tornata mettiate sollecitudine, talchè la vita mia, la quale a uno sottilissimo filo è pendente, e da speranza con fatica tenuta, possa, vedendovi, lieta nella prima certezza di sè ritornare: e se ciò non può forse così

* Corazzini reads *tanto* before *di* after MS. Riccardiana 6 (p. 15).
† Corazzini emends to *del* (p. 16).
‡ Corazzini emends to *cosa più e altra* (p. 16).

to those who shall see it in the future, both of your worth, with which, in the person of another, they are in large part adorned, and of my sadness; and after they had been composed, I thought it not fitting that they should come into the hands of anyone before yours, since you are the true and only cause of them. Therefore although they be a very small gift to send to so exalted a lady as you are, nevertheless, since the affection of myself, the sender, is very great and full of pure loyalty, I venture to send them to you, confident that they will be received by you not because of my deserts but because of your kindness and courtesy. And if it chance that you read in them, how often you find Troilus weeping and grieving at the departure of Cressida, so often may you clearly understand and recognize my very cries, tears, sighs, and distresses; and as often as you find good looks, good manners, and other thing praiseworthy in a lady written of Cressida, you may understand them to be said of you. As to the other things, which in addition to these are many, no one, as I have already said, relateth to me, nor is set down here on my own account, but because the story of the noble young lover requireth it. And if you are as discerning as I hold you to be, you can from these things understand how great and of what sort are my desires, where they end, and what more than anything else they ask for, or if they deserve any pity. Now I know not whether these things will be of so great efficacy as to touch your chaste mind with some compassion as you read them, but I pray Love to give them this power. And if this happen, I pray you as humbly as I can, that you hasten your return, so that my life, which is hanging by a very slender thread and is with difficulty sustained by hope, may, when I behold you, return joy-

tosto come io desidererei avvenire, almeno con alcuno sospiro o con pietoso prego, per me fate ad amore che alle mie noie presti alcuna pace, e lei smarrita riconfortare. Il mio lungo sermone da sè medesimo chiede fine, e perciò dandoglielo, prego colui che nelle vostre mani ha posta la mia vita e la mia morte, che egli nel vostro cuore quello disio accenda, che solo esser può cagione della mia salute.

fully into its first self-confidence. And if this perchance cannot happen as soon as I should desire, at least with some sigh or some pitiful prayer speak to Love in my behalf that he may give some peace to my torments and recomfort my life in its dismay. My long discourse seeketh of its own accord an end, and therefore giving it one, I pray him who hath placed my life and death in your hands, that he may enkindle in your heart that desire which alone can be the occasion of my welfare.

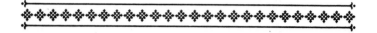

IL FILOSTRATO

DI

GIOVANNI BOCCACCIO

❖

PARTE PRIMA

ARGOMENTO

*Qui comincia la prima parte del libro chiamato Filostrato,
dell' amorose fatiche di Troilo, nella quale si pone, come Troilo
innamorossi di Criseida, e gli amorosi sospiri e le lagrime per lui
avuti, prima che ad alcuno il suo occulto amore discoprisse; e
primieramente la invocazione dell'autore.*

1.

Alcun di Giove sogliono il favore
 Ne' lor principii pietosi invocare;
 Altri d' Apollo chiamano il valore;
 Io di Parnaso le muse pregare
 Solea ne' miei bisogni, ma amore
 Novellamente m' ha fatto mutare
 Il mio costume antico e usitato,
 Poi fu' di te, madonna, innamorato.

2.

Tu donna se' la luce chiara e bella,
 Per cui nel tenebroso mondo accorto
 Vivo; tu se' la tramontana stella
 La qual' io seguo per venire al porto;
 Ancora di salute tu se' quella
 Che se' tutto il mio bene e 'l mio conforto;
 Tu mi se' Giove, tu mi sei Apollo,
 Tu se' mia musa, io l' ho provato e sollo.

THE FILOSTRATO

OF

GIOVANNI BOCCACCIO

FIRST PART

ARGUMENT

Here beginneth the first part of the book called Filostrato, of the amorous labors of Troilus, in which is recorded how Troilus became enamored of Cressida, and the amorous sighs and the tears that were his for her sake before he discovered to anyone his secret love. And in the first place the invocation of the author.

1.

Some are wont in their pious openings to invoke the favor of Jove; others call upon the might of Apollo. I was wont in my need to implore the muses of Parnassus, but Love hath recently caused me to change my long-accustomed habit, since I became enamored of thee, my lady.

2.

Thou, lady, art the clear and beautiful light under whose guidance I live in this world of shadows; thou art the lodestar which I follow to come to port; anchor of safety, thou art she who art all my weal and all my comfort; thou to me art Jove, thou to me art Apollo, thou art my muse; I have proved it and know it.

3.

Per che volendo per la tua partita,
   Più greve a me che morte e più noiosa,
   Scriver qual fosse la dolente vita
   Di Troilo, da poi che l' amorosa
   Criseida da Troia sen fu gita,
   E come pria gli fosse grazïosa;
   A te convienmi per grazia venire,
   S' io vo' poter la mia 'mpresa fornire.

4.

Adunque, o bella donna, alla qual fui
   E sarò sempre fedele e soggetto,
   O vaga luce de' begli occhi in cui
   Amore ha posto tutto il mio diletto;
   O isperanza sola di colui,
   Che t' ama più che sè d' amor perfetto,
   Guida la nostra man, reggi l' ingegno,
   Nell' opera la quale a scriver vegno.

5.

Tu se' nel tristo petto effigïata
   Con forza tal, che tu vi puoi più ch' io;
   Pingine fuor la voce sconsolata
   In guisa tal, che mostri il dolor mio
   Nell' altrui doglie, e rendila sì grata,
   Che chi l' ascolta ne divenga pio;
   Tuo sia l' onore, e mio si sia l' affanno,
   Se i detti alcuna laude acquisteranno.

6.

E voi amanti prego che ascoltiate
   Ciò che dirà 'l mio verso lagrimoso;
   E se nel cuore avvien che voi sentiate
   Destarsi alcuno spirito pietoso,
   Per me vi prego ch' Amore preghiate,
   Per cui siccome Troilo doglioso
   Vivo lontan dal più dolce piacere,
   Che a creatura mai fosse in calere.

3.

Therefore in undertaking because of thy departure—more grievous to me than death and more distressing—to write what was the sorrowful life of Troilus after the amorous Cressida had departed from Troy, and how, previous to that, she had been gracious to him, it is fitting that I come to thee for grace, if I am to finish my enterprise.

4.

Therefore, O fair lady, to whom I have been and ever shall be faithful and subject, O lovely light of those fair eyes in which Love hath set my whole delight, O sole hope of him who loveth thee more than himself, with perfect love, guide my hand, direct my invention in the work I am about to write.

5.

Thou art imaged in my sad breast with such strength that thou hast more power there than I. Drive forth from it my disconsolate voice in such manner that my sorrow may appear in another's woe, and make it so pleasing that he who heareth it may be moved to pity. Thine be the honor and mine be the labor, if these words shall acquire any praise.

6.

And ye lovers, I pray that ye hearken to what my tearful verse will say. And if it chance that ye feel any spirit of pity stir in your hearts, I beseech you that ye pray for me to Love, on whose account, like sorrowful Troilus, I live far from the sweetest pleasure that any creature ever cherished.

7.

Erano a Troia i greci re d' intorno
  Nell' armi forti, e giusta lor potere
  Ciascuno ardito, fiero, prode, e adorno
  Si dimostrava, e con le loro schiere
  Ognor la stringean più di giorno in giorno,
  Concordi tutti in un pari volere,
  Di vendicar l' oltraggio e la rapina
  Da Paris fatta d' Elena reina.

8.

Quando Calcas, la cui alta sciënza
  Avea già meritato di sentire
  Del grande Apollo ciascuna credenza
  Volendo del futuro il vero udire,
  Qual vincesse, o la lunga sofferenza
  De' Troiani, o de' Greci il grande ardire;
  Conobbe e vide, dopo lunga guerra
  I Troian morti e distrutta la terra.

9.

Per che segretamente dipartirsi
  Diliberò l' antiveduto e saggio;
  E preso luogo e tempo da fuggirsi,
  Ver la greca oste si mise in viaggio;
  Onde all' incontro assai vide venirsi,
  Che 'l ricevetton con lieto visaggio;
  Da lui sperando sommo e buon consiglio
  In ciascheduno accidente o periglio.

10.

Fu romor grande quando fu sentito
  Per tutta la città generalmente
  Che Calcas s' era di quella fuggito,
  E parlato ne fu diversamente,
  Ma mal da tutti, e ch' egli avea fallito,
  E come traditor fatto reamente,
  Nè quasi per la più gente rimase
  Di non andargli col fuoco alle case.

7.

The Greek kings were round about Troy, strong in arms, and each one, so far as in him lay, showed himself daring, proud, valiant, and gallant, and with their troops they ever pressed it more from day to day, all of accord in like desire to avenge the outrage and the rape committed by Paris on the person of Helen the queen.

8.

At this time Calchas, whose high science had already won the right to understand every secret of the great Apollo, wishing to hear the truth regarding the future, whether the long endurance of the Trojans or the great daring of the Greeks should prevail, discerned and saw, after a long war, the Trojans slain and their land destroyed.

9.

He therefore in his foresight and wisdom planned secretly to depart. And having chosen time and place to flee, he took his way toward the Greek host; whence he saw many come to meet him, who received him with joyful mien, hoping for most excellent counsel from him in every hap or danger.

10.

Great noise arose when it became known throughout the city generally that Calchas had fled therefrom. And comment was passed upon it diversely, but adversely by all, and it was agreed that he had done amiss and acted as a traitor wickedly. And the greater portion of the people barely refrained from going with fire to his house.

11.

Avea Calcas lasciata in tanto male,
   Senza niente farlene assapere,
   Una sua figlia vedova, la quale
   Sì bella e sì angelica a vedere
   Era, che non parea cosa mortale,
   Criseida nomata, al mio parere
   Accorta, savia, onesta e costumata
   Quanto altra che in Troia fosse nata.

12.

La qual sentendo il noioso romore
   Per la fuga del padre, assai dogliosa,
   Qual' era in tanto dubbioso furore,
   In abito dolente, e lagrimosa,
   Gittossi ginocchioni appiè d' Ettore,
   E con voce e con vista assai pietosa,
   Scusando sè, e 'l suo padre accusando,
   Finì suo dire mercè addimandando.

13.

Era pietoso Ettor di sua natura,
   Perchè vedendo di costei il gran pianto,
   Ch' era più bella ch' altra creatura,
   Con pio parlare la confortò alquanto,
   Dicendo: lascia con la ria ventura
   Tuo padre andar, che ci ha offeso tanto,
   E tu sicura e lieta senza noia,
   Con noi mentre t' aggrada ti sta' in Troia.

14.

Il piacere e l' onore il qual vorrai,
   Come Calcas ci fosse, abbi per certo,
   Sempre da tutti quanti noi avrai;
   A lui rendan gl' iddii condegno merto.
   Ella di questo il ringraziò assai,
   E più volea, ma non le fu sofferto,
   Ond' ella si drizzò, e ritornossi
   A casa sua, e quivi riposossi.

11.

In this evil plight, without informing her of his intentions, Calchas had left a daughter of his, a widow, who was so fair and so angelic to behold that she seemed not a mortal, Cressida by name, as amiable I am advised, as wise, as modest, and as well-mannered as any other lady born in Troy.

12.

Hearing the grievous outcry caused by her father's flight and much dismayed at the threatening tumult that surrounded her, in mourning habit and with eyes full of tears she threw herself on her knees at the feet of Hector, and with very pitiful voice and visage, excusing herself and accusing her father, ended her speech by imploring mercy.

13.

Hector was by nature full of pity. Therefore, hearing the lament of this lady, fairer than other creature, he comforted her somewhat with gentle words, saying: "Let thy father, who hath so greatly offended us, go forth with ill luck, and do thou remain with us in Troy as long as it pleaseth thee, safe, happy, and free from annoyance.

14.

"Be assured that thou shalt ever have, as if Calchas were here, the favor and honor that thou mayest desire from all of us. May the gods render him his merited deserts!" For this she thanked him greatly, and would have thanked him more, but was not permitted. Thereupon she arose, and returned to her house, and there remained quiet.

15.

Quivi si stette con quella famiglia
  Ch' al suo onor convenia di tenere,
  Mentre fu in Troia, onesta a maraviglia
  In abito ed in vita, nè calere
  Le bisognava di figlio o di figlia,
  Come a colei che mai nessuno avere
  N' avea potuto; e da ciascuno amata
  Che la conobbe fu ed onorata.

16.

Le cose andavan sì come di guerra,
  Tra li Troiani e' Greci assai sovente;
  Talvolta uscieno i Troian della terra
  Sopra gli Greci vigorosamente;
  E spesse volte i Greci, se non erra
  La storia, givano assai fieramente
  Fino in su' fossi e d' intorno rubando,
  Castella e ville ardendo ed abbruciando.

17.

E come ch' e' Troian fosser serrati
  Dalli greci nemici, non avvenne
  Che però fosson mai intralasciati
  Gli divin sacrificii, ma si tenne
  Per ciascun tempio quelli modi usati:
  Ma con maggiore onore e più solenne,
  Che alcuno altro, Pallade onoravano
  In ogni cosa, e più ch' altro guardavano.

18.

Perchè venuto il vago tempo il quale
  Riveste i prati d' erbette e di fiori,
  E che gaio diviene ogni animale,
  E in diversi atti mostran loro amori;
  Li troian padri al Palladio fatale
  Fer preparar li consueti onori;
  Alla qual festa e donne e cavalieri
  Fur parimente, e tutti volentieri.

15.

There she dwelt, while she was in Troy, with what household it befitted her dignity to maintain, singularly modest in habits and in life. Nor need she, as one who had never been able to have any, concern herself for son or daughter. And by everyone who knew her she was loved and honored.

16.

Things went on between the Trojans and the Greeks ever and anon as in time of war. At times the Trojans came forth from their city doughtily against the Greeks and oftentimes, if the story erreth not, the Greeks advanced valiantly even to the moats, pillaging on every side, firing and destroying castles and towns.

17.

Yet although the Trojans were hard pressed by their Greek enemies, it did not on that account come to pass that the divine sacrifices were ever remitted, but the accustomed rites were observed in every temple. To Pallas, however, they paid in every way honor greater and more solemn than to any other divinity and had regard to her more than to other.

18.

Therefore when was come the lovely season which revesteth the fields with herbs and flowers, and when every animal waxeth lusty and showeth its love in diverse acts, the Trojan fathers bade prepare the accustomed honors to the fateful Palladium. To this festival ladies and cavaliers repaired alike and all willingly.

19.

Tra' quali fu di Calcas la figliuola
    Criseida, la qual' era in bruna vesta,
    La qual, quanto la rosa la viola
    Di beltà vince, cotanto era questa
    Più ch' altra donna bella, ed essa sola
    Più ch' altra facea lieta la gran festa,
    Stando nel tempio assai presso alla porta,
    Negli atti altiera, piacente ed accorta.

20.

Troilo giva come soglion fare
    I giovinetti, or qua or là veggendo
    Per lo gran tempio, e co' compagni a stare;
    Or qui or quivi si giva ponendo,
    Ed ora questa ed or quella a lodare
    Incominciava, e tali riprendendo,
    Siccome quegli a cui non ne piacea
    Una più ch' altra, e sciolto si godea.

21.

Anzi talora in tal maniera andando,
    Veggendo alcun che fiso rimirava
    Alcuna donna seco sospirando,
    A' suoi compagni ridendo il mostrava,
    Dicendo: quel dolente ha dato bando
    Alla sua libertà, sì gli gravava,
    Ed a colei l' ha messa tra le mani:
    Vedete ben s' e' suo pensier son vani.

22.

Che è a porre in donna alcuno amore?
    Che come al vento si volge la foglia,
    Cosi in un dì ben mille volte il core
    Di lor si volge, nè curan di doglia
    Che per lor senta alcun loro amadore,
    Nè sa alcuna quel ch' ella si voglia.
    O felice colui che del piacere
    Lor non è preso, e sassene astenere!

19.

Among them was the daughter of Calchas, Cressida, appareled in black. And as much as the rose outdoeth the violet in beauty, so much fairer was she than other ladies, and she alone more than others made bright the great festival, standing in the temple, very near to the portal, dignified, gracious, and amiable.

20.

Troilus loitered about, as young men are wont to do, gazing now here, now there around the great temple, and took his station with his companions first in this spot then in that and began to praise now this lady and now that, and in like fashion to disparage them, as one to whom none was more pleasing than another, and took delight in his freedom.

21.

Nay, at times, while strolling about in this manner, upon catching sight of someone who gazed intently upon a certain lady and sighed to himself, he would laughingly point him out to his companions, saying: "Yonder wretched man hath parted with his liberty, so greatly did it burden him, and hath handed it over to that lady. Mark well how vain are his cares.

22.

"Why bestow love upon any woman? As the leaf turneth to the wind, so change their hearts a thousand times a day, nor care they for the anguish that a lover feeleth for them, nor doth any lady know what she wanteth. O happy that man who is not captured by their charm, and who knoweth how to abstain therefrom!

23.

Io provai già per la mia gran follia
Qual fosse questo maladetto fuoco.
E s' io dicessi che amor cortesia
Non mi facesse, ed allegrezza e giuoco
Non mi donasse, certo i' mentiria,
Ma tutto il bene insieme accolto, poco
Fu o niente, rispetto a' martirj,
Volendo amare, ed a' tristi sospiri.

24.

Or ne son fuor, mercè n' abbia colui
Che fu di me più ch' io stesso pietoso,
Io dico Giove, iddio vero, da cui
Viene ogni grazia, e vivommi in riposo:
E benchè di veder mi giovi altrui,
Io pur mi guardo dal corso ritroso,
E rido volentier degl' impacciati,
Non so s' io dico amanti o smemorati.

25.

O cecità delle mondane menti,
Come ne seguon sovente gli effetti
Tutti contrarii a' nostri intendimenti!
Troil va ora mordendo i difetti,
E' solleciti amor dell' altre genti,
Senza pensare in che il ciel s' affretti
Di recar lui il quale amor trafisse
Più ch' alcun altro, pria del tempio uscisse.

26.

Così adunque andandosi gabbando
Or d' uno or d' altro Troilo, e sovente
Or questa donna or quella rimirando,
Per caso avvenne che in fra la gente
L' occhio suo vago giunse penetrando
La dov' era Criseida piacente,
Sotto candido velo in bruna vesta,
Fra l' altre donne in sì solenne festa.

23.

"I once experienced by my own great folly what is this accursed fire. And if I said that love did not show me courtesy and give me gladness and joy, I should certainly lie; but all this pleasure that I took was but as little or nothing compared to my sufferings, since love I would, and to my woeful sighs.

24.

"Now I am out of it, thanks be to him who hath been more merciful to me than I myself, Jove, I mean, the true god, from whom cometh every favor, and I live my life in peace. And though it be to my advantage to watch others, I take care not to retrace the path I have trodden and gladly laugh at those who are ensnared, I know not whether to call them lovers or forgetful of the snare."

25.

O blindness of mundane minds! How often follow effects all contrary to our intentions! Troilus now raileth at the weaknesses and anxious loves of other people without a thought of what heaven hasteneth to bring upon him, whom Love transfixed more than any other before he left the temple.

26.

While Troilus was thus strolling about, making mock now at one now at another, and oft gazing intently now upon this lady again upon that, it chanced that his wandering eyes, glancing amongst the crowd, lighted where stood the charming Cressida, under white veil in black habit, among the other ladies at this so solemn festival.

27.

Ell' era grande, ed alla sua grandezza
 Rispondean bene i membri tutti quanti;
 Il viso aveva adorno di bellezza
 Celestïale, e nelli suoi sembianti
 Ivi mostrava una donnesca altezza;
 E col braccio il mantel tolto davanti
 S' avea dal viso, largo a sè facendo,
 Ed alquanto la calca rimovendo.

28.

Piacque quell' atto a Troilo, al tornare
 Ch' ella fe' in sè, alquanto sdegnosetto,
 Quasi dicesse: non ci si può stare;
 E diessi più a mirare il suo aspetto,
 Il qual più ch' altro degno in sè gli pare
 Di molta lode, e seco avea diletto
 Sommo tra uomo e uom di mirar fiso
 Gli occhi lucenti e l' angelico viso.

29.

Nè s' avvedea colui, ch' era sì saggio
 Poco davanti in riprendere altrui,
 Che amore dimorasse dentro al raggio
 Di que' vaghi occhi con gli strali sui;
 Nè rammentava ancora dell' oltraggio
 Detto davanti de' servi di lui,
 Nè dello strale, il quale al cuor gli corse,
 Finchè nol punse daddover s' accorse.

30.

Piacendo questa sotto il nero manto
 Oltre ad ogn' altra a Troilo, senza dire
 Qual cagion quivi il tenesse cotanto,
 Occultamente il suo alto desire
 Mirava di lontano, e mirò tanto,
 Senza niente ad alcun discoprire,
 Quanto duraro a Pallade gli onori,
 Poi coi compagni uscì del tempio fuori.

27.

She was tall and all her limbs were well proportioned to her height; her face was adorned with beauty
celestial, and in her whole appearance she showed a
womanly dignity. With her arm she had removed her
mantle from before her face, making room for herself
and pushing the crowd a little aside.

28.

As she recovered her composure, that act of hers—
somewhat disdainful, as if she were to say "one may
not stand here"—proved pleasing to Troilus. And he
continued to gaze upon her face, which seemeth to him
worthier of great praise than any other, and he took the
utmost delight in gazing fixedly 'twixt man and man
at her bright eyes and upon her angelic countenance.

29.

Nor did he who was so wise shortly before in finding
fault with others, perceive that Love with his darts
dwelt within the rays of those lovely eyes, nor yet did
he remember the outrageous words he had previously
uttered before his servants, nor notice the arrow that
sped to his heart, until it stung him in very truth.

30.

Since this lady beneath the dark mantle was above
all others pleasing to Troilus, without saying what kept
him there so long, he secretly gazed from afar upon the
object of his high desire, discovering naught to anyone,
and looked upon her so long as the honors to Pallas
lasted. Then with his companions he left the temple.

31.

Nè se n' uscì qual dentro v' era entrato
    Libero e lieto, ma n' uscì pensoso,
    Ed oltre al creder suo innamorato,
    Tenendo bene il suo disio nascoso,
    Per quel che poco avanti avea parlato
    Non fosse in lui rivolto l' oltraggioso
    Parlar d' altrui, se forse conosciuto
    Fosse l' ardor nel quale era caduto.

32.

Poi fu dal nobil tempio dipartita
    Criseida, Troilo al palazzo tornossi
    Co' suoi compagni, e quivi in lieta vita
    Con lor per lungo spazio dimorossi;
    Per me' celar l' amorosa ferita
    Di quei ch' amavan gran pezza gabbossi,
    Poi mostrando che altro lo stringesse,
    Disse a ciascun ch' andasse ove volesse.

33.

E partitosi ognun, tutto soletto
    In camera n' andò, dove a sedere
    Si pose, sospirando, appiè del letto,
    E seco a rammentarsi del piacere
    Avuto la mattina dell' aspetto
    Di Criseida cominciò, e delle vere
    Bellezze del suo viso annoverando,
    A parte a parte quelle commendando.

34.

Lodava molto gli atti e la statura,
    E lei di cuor grandissimo stimava,
    Ne' modi e nell' andare, e gran ventura
    Di cotal donna amar si riputava;
    E vie maggior se per sua lunga cura
    Potesse far, se quanto egli essa amava
    Cotanto appresso da lei fosse amato,
    O per servente almen non rifiutato.

31.

But he went not thence such as he had entered, free and light-hearted, but departed thoughtful and enamored beyond his belief, keeping his desire well hidden, in order that the abusive remarks about others to which he had formerly given utterance, might not be turned against him, if perchance the passion into which he had fallen were to become known.

32.

When Cressida had departed from the stately temple, Troilus returned with his companions to his palace and there in mirthful living long tarried with them. And in order the better to hide his amorous wound, he continued to mock at those that love. Then feigning that other matters constrained him, he bade each one go whither he listed.

33.

And after everyone had left, he went all alone into his chamber, and there sat down sighing at the foot of his couch. And he began to go over again in his mind the pleasure he had felt that morning at the sight of Cressida, enumerating the true beauties of her face and praising them one by one.

34.

Much he praised her movements and her stateliness and from her manners and carriage judged her a lady of very noble nature, and thought it would be a great good fortune to love such a lady, and a better still if by long attention he might bring it to pass that nearly as much as he loved her he might by her be loved, or at least not be rejected as suitor.

35.

Immaginando affanno nè sospiro
  Poter per cotal donna esser perduto,
  E che esser dovesse il suo disiro
  Molto lodato, se giammai saputo
  Da alcuno fosse, e quinci il suo martiro
  Men biasimato, essendo conosciuto,
  Argomentava il giovinetto lieto,
  Male avvisando il suo futuro fleto.

36.

Perchè disposto a seguir tale amore,
  Pensò volere oprar discretamente;
  Pria proponendo di celar l' ardore
  Concetto già nell' amorosa mente
  A ciascheduno amico e servidore,
  Se ciò non bisognasse, ultimamente
  Pensando, che amore a molti aperto
  Noia acquistava, e non gioia per merto.

37.

Ed oltre a queste, assai più altre cose,
  Qual da scuoprire e qual da provocare
  A sè la donna, con seco propose,
  E quindi lieto si diede a cantare
  Bene sperando, e tutto si dispose
  Di voler sola Criseida amare,
  Nulla apprezzando ogni altra che veduta
  Glie ne venisse, o fosse mai piaciuta;

38.

E in verso amore tal fiata dicea
  Con pietoso parlar: signore, omai
  L' anima è tua che mia esser solea,
  Il che mi piace, perciocchè tu m' hai,
  Non so s' io dico a donna, ovvero a dea,
  A servir dato, che non fu giammai
  Sotto candido velo in bruna vesta
  Sì bella donna, come mi par questa.

35.

Little foreseeing his future woes, the light-hearted youth thought in his imagination that neither labor nor sighs could be lost for such a lady, and that his desire, if ever known by any, must needs be greatly praised, and hence his anguish, if discovered, less blamed.

36.

Therefore being minded to pursue this love, he made up his mind to try to act with discretion, first proposing to hide the ardor conceived in his amorous mind from every friend and attendant, unless it were necessary, concluding that love disclosed to many bringeth vexation in its train and not joy.

37.

And beyond these he took thought upon many other matters, how to discover himself to the lady, and how to attract to himself her attention, and then he began joyfully to sing, high in hope and all-disposed to love Cressida alone, naught esteeming any other lady he might see or who had ever pleased him.

38.

And to Love at times he said with reverential words: "Lord, thine henceforth is the soul which used to be mine. This pleaseth me, for thou hast given me to serve I know not whether to say a lady or a goddess, for never was there under white veil in dark habit a lady so beautiful as this one appeareth to me.

39.

Tu stai negli occhi suoi, signor verace,
 Siccome in luogo degno a tua virtute:
 Perchè, se 'l mio servir punto ti piace,
 Da que' ti prego impetri la salute
 Dell' anima, la qual prostrata giace
 Sotto i tuoi piè, sì la ferir l' acute
 Saette che allora le gittasti,
 Che di costei 'l bel viso mi mostrasti.

40.

Non risparmiarono il sangue reale,
 Nè d' animo virtù ovver grandezza,
 Nè curaron di forza corporale
 Che in Troilo fosse, o di prodezza,
 L' ardenti fiamme amorose, ma quale
 In disposta materia o secca o mezza
 S' accende il fuoco, tal nel nuovo amante
 Messe le parti acceser tutte quante.

41.

Tanto di giorno in giorno col pensiero,
 E col piacer di quello or preparava
 Più l' esca secca dentro al cuore altiero,
 E da' begli occhi trarre immaginava
 Acqua soave al suo ardor severo;
 Perchè astutamente gli cercava
 Sovente di veder, nè s' avvedea
 Che più da quegli il fuoco s' accendea.

42.

Costui or qua or là che gisse, andando,
 Sedendo ancora, solo o accompagnato,
 Com' el volesse, bevendo o mangiando,
 La notte e 'l giorno ed in qualunque lato
 Di Criseida sempre gía pensando,
 E 'l suo valor e 'l viso dilicato
 Di lei, diceva, avanza Polissena
 D' ogni bellezza, e similmente Elena.

39.

"Thou takest thy station in her eyes, true lord, as in a place worthy of thy power. Therefore if my service at all pleaseth thee, I beseech thee obtain from them the healing of my soul, which lieth prostrate at thy feet, so wounded it the sharp arrows which thou didst hurl at it when thou didst show me the lovely face of this lady."

40.

The fiery flames of love spared not the royal blood, nor heeded they the strength or greatness of soul or the bodily power that was in Troilus or his prowess. But as flame kindleth in suitable substance, or dry or half-dry, so in the new lover did the members take fire, one and all.

41.

So much the more from day to day by thought and the pleasure he took therein, did he prepare dry tinder within his proud heart, and imagined he would draw from her fair eyes water soothing to his intense ardor. Therefore he made cunning attempt to see them often, nor did he perceive that by them the fire was kindled the more.

42.

Now whether he went hither or thither, walking or sitting, alone or in company, as he would, eating or drinking, night or day, wherever he might be, ever of Cressida were his thoughts, and he declared her worth and delicate features to be such that she surpassed Polyxena in every beauty and likewise Helen.

43.

Nè del dì trapassava nessun' ora
   Che mille volte seco non dicesse:
   O chiara luce che 'l cuor m' innamora,
   O Criseida bella, iddio volesse,
   Che 'l tuo valor che 'l viso mi scolora
   Per me alquanto a pietà ti movesse;
   Null' altra fuor che tu lieto può farmi,
   Tu sola se' colei che puoi atarmi.

44.

Ciascun altro pensier s' era fuggito
   Della gran guerra e della sua salute;
   E sol nel petto suo era sentito
   Quel che parlasse dell' alta virtute
   Della sua donna; e per questo impedito,
   Sol di curar l' amorose ferute
   Sellecito era, e quivi ogni intelletto
   Avea posto all' affanno, ed il diletto.

45.

L' aspre battaglie e gli stormi angosciosi,
   Ch' Ettore e gli altri suoi frate' faceano
   Seguiti da' Troian, dagli amorosi
   Pensier poco o niente il rimoveano;
   Come che spesso ne' più perigliosi
   Assalti, innanzi agli altri lui vedeano
   Mirabilmente nell' armi operare:
   Ciò disser quei che stavanlo a mirare.

46.

Nè a ciò l' odio dei Greci il rimovea,
   Nè vaghezza ch' avesse di vittoria
   Per Troia liberar, la qual vedea
   Stretta da assedio, ma voglia di gloria
   Per più piacer tutto questo facea;
   E per amor, se 'l ver dice la storia,
   Divenne in arme sì feroce e forte,
   Che gli Greci il temean come la morte.

43.

Nor did an hour of the day pass that he did not say to himself a thousand times: "O clear light which filleth my heart with love, O fair Cressida, may the gods grant that thy worth, which maketh my face to pale, might move thee to pity me a little! None beside thee can make me joyful; thou alone art she who canst help me."

44.

Every other thought, both of the great war and of his welfare, had fled and in his breast he gave sole audience to that which spake of the high virtue of his lady. By this burdened, he was anxious only to cure his amorous wounds, and to the task he now devoted his every thought and in it found his delight.

45.

The sharp battles and the woeful affrays of Hector and his brothers, followed by the Trojans, turned him little or naught from his amorous thoughts, although often in the most perilous encounters they saw him, before all others, work wonders in arms. So said they who stood watching him.

46.

Nor did hatred of the Greeks move him to this, nor the longing that he had for victory to liberate Troy, which he saw straitened by siege, but desire of glory, the more to please, effected all this. And for Love's sake, if the tale speaketh truth, he became so fierce and strong in arms that the Greeks feared him as death.

47.

Aveagli già amore il sonno tolto,
  E minuito il cibo, ed il pensiero
  Moltiplicato sì, che già nel volto
  Ne dava pallidezza segno vero;
  Come che egli il ricuoprisse molto
  Con riso infinto e con parlar sincero,
  E chi 'l vedea pensava ch' avvenisse
  Per noia della guerra ch' e' sentisse.

48.

E qual si fosse non ci è assai certo,
  O che Criseida non se n' accorgesse,
  Per l' operar di lui ch' era coperto,
  O che di ciò conoscer s' infingesse,
  Ma questo n' è assai chiaro ed aperto,
  Che nïente pareva le calesse
  Di Troilo e dell' amor che le portava,
  Ma come non amata dura stava.

49.

Di quinci sentia Troilo tal dolore
  Che dir non si poria, talor temendo
  Che Criseida non fosse d' altro amore
  Presa, e per quello lui vilipendendo
  Ricever nol volesse a servidore,
  Ben mille modi seco ripetendo
  Se veder puote di farle sentire
  Onestamente il suo caldo disire.

50.

Onde quand' egli aveva spazio punto
  Seco d' amor sen giva a lamentare,
  Fra sè dicendo: Troilo, or se' giunto,
  Che ti solevi degli altri gabbare,
  Nessun ne fu mai quanto tu consunto
  Per mal saperti dall' amor guardare;
  Or se' nel laccio preso, il qual biasmavi
  Tanto negli altri, e da te non guardavi.

47.

Already had Love taken from him his sleep, and diminished his food, and so increased his anxiety that now in his face pallor bore witness thereof, although much he concealed it with feigned smile and ingenuous speech, and whoever noticed it thought that it happened on account of the distress he felt because of the war.

48.

And how this was is not quite evident to us, whether Cressida was not sensible of his condition, because of the secrecy of his actions, or whether she feigned not to know of it. But this is sufficiently clear and manifest, that in no respect did she seem to care for Troilus and for the love that he bore her, but remained unmoved as one not loved.

49.

On this account Troilus felt such grief as could not be told, fearing at times that Cressida might be in love with another, and, despising him on this account, would not receive him as suitor. And he rehearsed to himself a thousand devices as to how he might in a proper manner find a way to make her sensible of his burning desire.

50.

Therefore when he had a moment of leisure, he went apart and complained of Love, saying to himself, "Troilus, now caught art thou who used to mock at others. No one was ever so consumed as thou art for ill-knowing how to guard thyself against Love; now art thou taken in the snare, a misadventure which thou hast so much blamed in others and hast not kept from thyself.

51.

Che si dirà di te fra gli altri amanti
    Se questo tuo amor fosse saputo?
    Di te si gabberanno tutti quanti,
    Fra lor dicendo: or ecco il provveduto
    Ch' e' sospir nostri e gli amorosi pianti
    Morder soleva, già ora è venuto
    Dove noi siamo; Amor ne sia lodato,
    Ch' a tal partito l' ha ora recato.

52.

Che si dirà di te fra gli eccellenti
    Re e signor, se questo fia sentito?
    Ben potran dir, di ciò assai scontenti:
    Vedi questi com' è del sonno* uscito,
    Che in questi tempi noiosi e dolenti
    Sì nuovamente d' amore è irretito,
    Dove alla guerra dovrebbe esser fiero,
    In amar si consuma il suo pensiero.

53.

Ed or fostu, o Troilo dolente,
    Poscia ch' egli era dato che tu amassi,
    Preso per tal, che un poco solamente
    D' amor sentissi,† onde ti consolassi;
    Ma quella per cui piagni nulla sente
    Se non come una pietra, e così stassi
    Fredda come al sereno interza il ghiaccio,
    Ed io qual neve al fuoco mi disfaccio.

54.

Ed or foss' io pur venuto al porto
    Al qual la mia sventura sì mi mena,
    Questo mi saria grazia e gran conforto,
    Perchè morendo uscire' d' ogni pena;
    Che se il mio mal, del qual nessun s' è accorto
    Ancora, se si scuopre, fia ripiena
    La vita mia di mille ingiurie al giorno,
    E più ch' altro sarò detto musorno.

* Savj-Lopez, *senno*
† Savj-Lopez, *sentisse*

51.

"What will be said of thee among other lovers, if this thy love should become known? They will all make mock at thee, saying among themselves: 'Behold now the well-guarded one, who used to rail at our sighs and our amorous plaints, hath even now come where we are. Praise be to Love, who now hath brought him to such a pass!'

52.

"What will be said of thee among the excellent kings and lords, if this become known? Well may they say, in ill-conceit thereat: 'Behold now how this man hath taken leave of his senses to be thus recently ensnared by Love in this time of sorrow and distress. Whereas he ought to be doughty in battle, his thoughts are consumed in loving.'

53.

"And now, O sorrowful Troilus, since it hath been decreed that thou shouldst love, would that thou wert caught by one sensible of just a little love, whence thou mightest derive consolation! But she for whom thou weepest feeleth naught any more than a stone, and remaineth as cold as ice which hardens beneath a clear sky, and I waste away like snow before the fire.

54.

"And were I now at last arrived at the port to which my misfortune thus leadeth me, this would be a mercy and great comfort to me, for by dying I should escape all pain. For if my trouble, of which no one is yet aware, be discovered, my life will be filled with a thousand insults each day and above all men shall I be called fool.

55.

Deh, aiutami amore! e tu per cui
  I' piango, preso più che altro mai,
  Deh sii pietosa un poco di colui
  Che t' ama più che la sua vita assai;
  Volgi il bel viso omai verso di lui,
  Da colui mossa che in questi guai
  Per te donna, mi tiene io te ne priego,
  Deh non mi far di questa grazia niego.

56.

Io tornerò, se tu fai donna questo,
  Qual fiore in nuovo prato in primavera,
  Nè mi fia poscia l' aspettar molesto,
  Nè il vederti disdegnosa o altera;
  E se t' è grave, almeno a me, che presto
  Ad ogni tuo piacer son, grida fera
  Ucciditi, che io 'l farò di fatto,
  Credendoti piacere in cotal atto.

57.

Quinci diceva molte altre parole,
  Piangeva e sospirava, e di colei
  Chiamava il nome, sì come far suole
  Chi soperchio ama, ed alli suoi omei
  Mercè non trova, che tutt' eran fole
  Che perdeansi ne' venti, che a lei
  Nulla ne perveniva, onde il tormento
  Moltiplicava ciascun giorno in cento.

55.

"Succor me, Love. And thou for whom I weep, caught more than other ever was, ah, have a little pity for him who loveth thee much more than his own life. Moved by him who on thine account, lady, holdeth me in these woes, turn now toward him thy lovely countenance. Ah, I beseech thee, do not deny me this favor.

56.

"If thou, lady, doest this, I shall revive as a flower in the fresh meadow in spring time. Nor will waiting then be irksome to me, nor seeing thee disdainful and haughty. And if it be grievous to thee, call out at least, in thy cruelty, to me, who am ready at thy every pleasure, 'Kill thyself,' for in truth I shall do it, thinking to please thee by that act."

57.

And then he spake many other words and wept and sighed and called upon her name, as he is wont to do who loveth to excess and findeth no compassion for his complaints. For they were all idle words lost in the wind and none did come to her. Thence his torment increased a hundredfold each day.

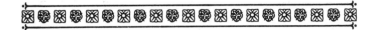

IL FILOSTRATO

DI

GIOVANNI BOCCACCIO

❀

PARTE SECONDA

ARGOMENTO

Comincia la seconda parte del Filostrato, nella quale Troilo manifesta il suo amore a Pandaro cugino di Criseida, il quale lui conforta, ed a Criseida scuopre l'occulto amore, e con preghe e con lusinghe la induce ad amare Troilo; e primieramente, dopo molti ragionamenti, Troilo a Pandaro, nobile giovane troiano, discuopre in tutto il suo amore.

1.

Standosi in cotal guisa un dì soletto
   Nella camera sua Troilo pensoso,
   Vi sopravvenne un troian giovinetto,
   D' alto lignaggio e molto coraggioso;
   Il qual veggendo lui sopra il suo letto
   Giacer disteso e tutto lagrimoso,
   Che è questo, gridò, amico caro?
   Hatti già così vinto il tempo amaro?

2.

Pandaro, disse Troilo, qual fortuna
   T' ha qui condotto a vedermi morire?
   Se la nostra amistade ha forza alcuna,
   Piacciati quinci volerti partire,
   Ch' io so che grave più ch' altra nessuna
   Cosa ti fia il vedermi morire;
   Ed io non sono per più stare in vita,
   Tant' è la mia virtù vinta e smarrita.

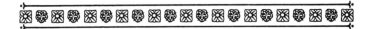

THE FILOSTRATO

OF

GIOVANNI BOCCACCIO

❀

SECOND PART

ARGUMENT

Here beginneth the second part of the Filostrato, in which Troilus maketh known his love to Pandarus, cousin of Cressida, who comforteth him and discovereth his secret love to Cressida and with prayers and with flattery induceth her to love Troilus. And in the first place, after much talk, Troilus discloseth wholly his love to Pandarus, a noble Trojan youth.

1.

While Troilus was thus one day quite alone in his room, engaged in thought, there suddenly arrived a young Trojan of high lineage and of abundant spirits, who, seeing him lie stretched out upon his couch and full of tears, cried: "What is the matter, dear friend? Hath the bitter time already thus vanquished thee?"

2.

"Pandarus," saith Troilus, "what fortune hath brought thee here to see me die? If our friendship hath any power, may it please thee to depart hence, for I know that to see me die will be more grievous to thee than aught else. And I am not to remain longer in life, so much is my vigor overcome and dissipated.

[163]

3.

Nè creder tu che l' assediata Troia,
  O d' armi affanno, o alcuna paura,
  Cagion mi sia della presente noia,
  Quest' è tra l' altre la mia minor cura;
  Altro mi strigne a pur voler ch' io muoia,
  Ond' io mi dolgo della mia sciagura;
  Che ciò si sia non ten curare amico,
  Ch' io 'l taccio per lo meglio e non tel dico.

4.

Di Pandar crebbe allora la pietade,
  Ed il disio di voler ciò sapere,
  Ond' el seguì: Se la nostra amistade,
  Come soleva, t' è ora in piacere,
  Discuopri a me qual sia la crudeltade
  Che di morir ti fa tanto calere;
  Ch' atto non è d' amico, alcuna cosa
  Al suo amico di tener nascosa.

5.

Io vo' con teco partir queste pene,
  Se dar non posso a tua noia conforto,
  Perciocchè coll' amico si convene
  Ogni cosa partir, noia e diporto;
  Ed io mi credo che tu sappia bene
  Se io t' ho amato a diritto ed a torto,
  E s' io farei per te ogni gran fatto,
  E fosse che volesse ed in qual atto.

6.

Troilo trasse allora un gran sospiro,
  E disse: Pandar, poscia che ti piace
  Pur di voler sentire il mio martiro,
  Dirotti brevemente che mi sface;
  Non perch' io speri che al mio disiro
  Per te si possa porre fine o pace,
  Ma sol per soddisfare al tuo gran priego,
  Al qual non so come mi metta niego.

3.

"Think not that Troy besieged or the travail of arms or any fear is the occasion of my present distress. This is among other things my least care. Something else constraineth me to wish to die, wherefore I grieve at my misfortune. That this is so, feel no concern, friend, for I conceal it for the best and do not tell it thee."

4.

Pandarus' pity then increased and his desire to know it. Wherefore he continued: "If our friendship, as was wont, is now a pleasure to thee, discover to me what is the cruelty that maketh thee so much wish to die. It is not the act of a friend to keep anything hidden from his friend.

5.

"I wish to share this affliction with thee, if I am not able to give comfort to thy distress, for it is fitting to share everything with a friend, both sorrow and delight. And I believe that thou knowest well whether I have loved thee in right and in wrong, and whether I would do for thee any great service, let it be what it will and in what act."

6.

Troilus then drew a deep sigh and said: "Pandarus, since it pleaseth thee to hear my sufferings, I will tell thee in a word what undoeth me, not because I hope that a peaceful end can be put by thee to my desire, but only to satisfy thy urgent entreaty, which I know not how to refuse.

7.

Amore, incontro al qual chi si difende
  Più tosto è preso, ed adopera invano,
  D' un piacer vago tanto il cor m' accende,
  Ch' io n' ho per quel da me fatto lontano
  Ciaschedun altro; e questo sì m' offende,
  Come tu puoi veder, che la mia mano
  Appena mille volte ho temperata,
  Ch' ella non m' abbia la vita levata.

8.

Bastiti questo, caro amico mio,
  Sentir de' miei dolori, i quai giammai
  Più non scopersi: e pregoti per Dio,
  S' alcuna fede al nostro amor tu hai,
  Ch' altrui tu non discopri tal disio,
  Che noia men potria seguire assai.
  Tu sai quel c' hai voluto, vanne, e lascia
  Qui me combatter colla mia ambascia.

9.

O, disse Pandar, come hai tu potuto
  Tenermi tanto tal fuoco nascoso?
  Che t' avrei dato consiglio o aiuto,
  E trovato alcun modo al tuo riposo.
  A cui Troilo disse: Come avuto
  Da te l' avrei, che sempre te doglioso
  Per amor vidi, e non ten sai atare?
  Me dunque come credi sodisfare?

10.

Pandaro disse: Troilo, io conosco
  Che tu di' il ver, ma spesse volte avviene,
  Che quei che sè non sa guardar dal tosco,
  Altrui per buon consiglio salvo tiene:
  E già veduto s' è andare il losco
  Dove l' alluminato* non va bene;
  E benchè l' uom non prenda buon consiglio,
  Donar lo puote nell' altrui periglio.

* Savj-Lopez, *illuminato*

7.

"Love, against whom he who defendeth himself the sooner is taken and laboreth in vain, so inflameth my heart with a fond delight that I have on his account put far from me every other god. And this so distresseth me that, as thou canst see, I have a thousand times with difficulty restrained my hand from taking my life.

8.

"Let it suffice thee, my dear friend, to hear of my sorrows, which will never more be disclosed. And I pray thee by the gods, if thou hast any fidelity to our love, that thou discover not this desire to anyone else, because much trouble might follow me on that account. Thou knowest what thou hast wished; go away, and leave me here to fight with my distress."

9.

"O," said Pandarus, "how hast thou been able to keep so great a fire as this hidden from me, for I would have given thee counsel or aid and found some means to thy peace?" And to him Troilus said: "How should I have had it from thee, whom I have always seen sorrowful for love, and who dost not know how to help thyself therein? How thinkest thou then to satisfy me?"

10.

Pandarus said: "Troilus, I know that thou speakest the truth. But oftentimes it happeneth that he who knoweth not how to protect himself from poison, by good counsel safeguardeth another. Of old the one-eyed man hath been seen to walk where the man of full vision walketh not well. Although a man taketh not good counsel, he can give it in another's peril.

11.

Io ho amato sventuratamente,
 Ed amo ancora per lo mio peccato;
 E ciò avvien, perchè celatamente
 Non ho, siccome tu, altrui amato.
 Sarà che Dio vorrà; ultimamente,*
 L' amore ch' io t' ho sempre mai portato,
 Ti porto e porterò, nè giammai fia
 Chi sappia che da te detto mi sia.

12.

Però ti rendi, amico mio, sicuro
 Di me, e dimmi chi ti sia cagione
 Di questo viver sì noioso e duro,
 Nè temer mai di mia riprensione
 D' amor, però che que' che savii furo
 Ne dichiarar con lor savio sermone,
 Ch' amor di cuore non potea esser tolto,
 Se non da sè per lungo tempo sciolto.

13.

Lascia l' angoscia tua, lascia i sospiri,
 E ragionando mitiga il dolore;
 Così facendo passano i martiri,
 E molto ancora menoma l' ardore,
 Quando compagni in simili desiri
 Colui si vede il quale è amatore;
 Ed io, come tu sai, contra mia voglia
 Amo, nè mi può tor nè crescer doglia.

14.

Forse fia tal colei che ti tormenta,
 Che 'n tuo piacer potrò operare assai,
 Ed io farei la tua voglia contenta,
 Se io potessi, più ch' io non fei mai
 La mia; tu il vederai: fa' ch' io senta
 Chi sia colei per cui questa pena hai;
 Leva su, non giacer, pensa che meco
 Ragionar puoi come con esso teco.

* Savj-Lopez, *Sarà che Dio vorrà ultimamente*

11.

"I have loved unhappily and to my sorrow still love. This happeneth because I have not, as thou, loved another secretly. What the gods will, shall at the last be done. The love that I have ever borne thee, I bear thee, and shall bear thee, nor ever shall he be who shall know what may be told me by thee.

12.

"Therefore have confidence in me, my friend, and tell me who is the cause of this thy so grievous and hard living, nor ever fear that I shall reprove thee for loving. For the wise of old have in their sage discourses declared as touching this matter that love of the heart could never be taken away, unless self-freed in the course of long time.

13.

"Leave thy anguish, leave thy sighs, and by talking assuage thy grief. The sufferings of those who do so, pass, and much too doth the intensity diminish when he who is the lover, seeth companions in like desires. I, as thou knowest, love against my will, nor can my suffering be removed nor increased.

14.

"Perhaps she that tormenteth thee will be such an one that I shall be able to work somewhat to thy pleasure—and I would satisfy thy wish, if I could, more than ever I would mine own. Thou shalt see it. Let me hear who she is for whom thou hast this pain. Arise, lie not down, consider that thou canst talk with me as with thine own self."

15.

Si stette Troilo alquanto sospeso,
  E dopo il trarre d' un sospiro amaro,
  E di rossor nel viso tutto acceso
  Per vergogna, rispose : amico caro,
  Cagione assai onesta m' ha difeso
  Di farti l' amor mio palese e chiaro,
  Perocchè quella che qui m' ha condotto
  È tua parente ; e più non fece motto ;

16.

E sopra il letto ricadde supino,
  Piangendo forte e nascondendo il viso.
  A cui Pandaro disse : amico fino,
  Poca fidanza t' ha nel petto miso
  Cotal sospetto ; orsù lascia il tapino
  Pianto che fai, che io non sia ucciso ;
  Se quella ch' ami fosse mia sorella,
  A mio potere avrai tuo piacer d' ella.

17.

Leva su, dimmi, di' chi è costei,
  Dillomi tosto sì ch' io veggia via
  Al tuo conforto, ch' altro non vorrei.
  È ella donna che sia in casa mia ?
  Deh dimmel tosto, che s' ella è colei,
  Ch' io vo meco pensando ch' ella sia,
  Non credo che trapassi il giorno sesto,
  Che ti trarrò di stato sì molesto.

18.

Troilo a questo nulla rispondea,
  Ma ciascun' ora più 'l viso turava ;
  E pure udendo ciò che promettea
  Pandaro, seco alquanto più sperava :
  E' volea dire, e poi si ritenea,
  Tanto d' aprirlo a lui si vergognava ;
  Ma stimolandol Pandaro, si volse
  Ver lui piangendo, e tai parole sciolse.

15.

Troilus stood somewhat in quandary. And after drawing a deep sigh and turning all a burning red in his face for shame, he replied: "Dear friend, a very honorable reason hath kept me from making my love manifest and clear to thee, for she who hath brought me to this pass is a relative of thine." And not a word more did he say.

16.

And he fell back flat upon his couch, weeping bitterly and hiding his face. And to him Pandarus said: "Well-tried friend, little faith hath planted such suspicion in thy breast. Come, cease this wretched plaint of thine, that I be not slain. If she whom thou lovest were my sister, to the best of my ability shouldst thou have thy pleasure of her.

17.

"Get up, tell me, say who she is, tell it me quickly, so that I, who would wish naught else, may find a way to thy comfort. Is she a lady of mine house? Tell me quickly, for if she is the one that I am thinking to myself that she be, I do not believe that the sixth day will pass before I shall deliver thee from so grievous state."

18.

Troilus answered nothing to this but each moment muffled his face the more closely. And yet when he heard what Pandarus promised, he conceived somewhat more hope in his breast, and felt inclined to speak, and then held back, so greatly ashamed was he of discovering it to him. But under Pandarus' urgency he turned toward him and gave vent to these words:

19.

Pandaro mio, vorrei esser già morto,
  Pensando a quel ch' amore m' ha sospinto,
  E s' io potessi senza farti torto
  Celarlo, già non men sarei infinto;
  Ma più non posso, e se tu sei accorto
  Siccome suoi, veder puoi che distinto
  Amor non ha che l' uomo ami per legge,
  Fuor che colei cui l' appetito elegge.

20.

Altri, come tu sai, amar le suore,
  E le suore i fratelli, e le figliuole
  Talvolta i padri, e' suoceri le nuore,
  Le matrigne i figliastri talor suole
  Anche avvenir; ma me ha preso amore
  Per tua cugina, il che forte mi duole,
  Io dico per Criseida: e questo detto
  Boccon piangendo ricadde in sul letto.

21.

Come Pandaro udì colei nomare,
  Così ridendo disse: amico mio,
  Per Dio ti prego non ti sconfortare;
  Amore ha posto in parte il tuo disio,
  Tal ch' el non lo potea meglio allogare,
  Perch' ella il val veracemente, s' io
  M' intendo di costumi, o di grandezza
  D' animo, o di valore o di bellezza.

22.

Nulla donna fu mai più valorosa,
  Nulla ne fu più lieta e più parlante,
  Nulla più da gradir nè più graziosa,
  Nulla di maggior animo tra quante
  Ne furon mai; nè è sì alta cosa
  Ch' ella non imprendesse tanto avante
  Quanto alcun re, e che 'l cuor non le desse
  Di trarla a fine, sol che si potesse.

19.

"My Pandarus, I would wish that I were already dead when I consider to what straits Love hath reduced me. Had I been able to conceal it without doing thee wrong, I would not indeed have dissembled. But I am no longer able. If thou art as discerning as thou art wont to be, thou canst see that Love hath not decreed that man love by rule, regardless of her whom his heart chooseth.

20.

"Others, as thou knowest, are wont to love their sisters, and sisters their brothers, and daughters sometimes their fathers, and fathers-in-law their daughters-in-law, and even, as is wont at times to happen, stepmothers their stepsons. But Love hath seized me for thy cousin, to my sore distress, for Cressida, I say." And when he had said this, he fell back upon his couch face-downward in tears.

21.

When Pandarus heard her named, he laughed and thus he spake: "My friend, I pray thee by the gods not to be disheartened. Love hath placed thy desire in a quarter such that he could not place it better. For she is truly worthy of it, if I am any judge of good qualities, or of greatness of soul, or of merit, or of beauty.

22.

"No lady was ever more deserving, none was ever livelier and more entertaining, none more pleasing nor more gracious, none of larger soul among all that ever have been. Nor is there task so lofty that she would not undertake as willingly as any king or would lack courage to carry to completion, provided only she had the power.

23.

Solo una cosa alquanto a te molesta
  Ha mia cugina in sè oltre alle dette,
  Che ella è più che altra donna onesta,
  E più d' amore ha le cose dispette:
  Ma s' altro non ci noia, credi a questa
  Troverò modo con mie parolette
  Qual ti bisogna; possi tu soffrire,
  Ben raffrenando il tuo caldo disire.

24.

Ben puoi dunque veder ch' amor t' ha posto
  In luogo degno della tua virtute;
  Sta' dunque fermo nell' atto proposto,
  E bene spera della tua salute,
  La quale credo che seguirà tosto,
  Se tu col pianto tuo non la rifiute;
  Tu se' di lei ed ella è di te degno,
  Ed io ci adoprerò tutto 'l mio ingegno.

25.

Non creder, Troilo, ch' io non vegga bene
  Non convenirsi a donna valorosa
  Sì fatti amori, e quel ch' a me ne viene,
  Ed a lei ed a' suoi, se cotal cosa
  Alla bocca del volgo mai perviene,
  Che, per follia di noi, vituperosa
  È divenuta, dove esser solea
  Onor, dappoi per amor si facea.

26.

Ma perciocchè 'l disio s' è impedito
  All' operare, e tutto simigliante
  Non conosciuto, parmi per partito
  Poter pigliar, che ciascheduno amante
  Possa seguire il suo alto appetito,
  Sol che sia savio in fatto ed in sembiante,
  Senza vergogna alcuna di coloro
  A cui tien la vergogna e l' onor loro.

23.

"Only one trait, somewhat troublesome to thee, hath my cousin beyond those mentioned, that she is more virtuous than other ladies, and holdeth matters of love more in contempt. But if naught else annoy us, believe me, I will with my soft words find a way to cope with this, to the relief of thy necessity. Possess thy soul in patience, curbing well thy warm desire.

24.

"Well canst thou then see that Love hath placed thee in a station worthy of thy mettle. Stand firm therefore in the act proposed and have good hope of thy cure, which I believe will follow soon, if thou do not forfeit it with thy plaint. Thou art worthy of her and she of thee, and I will employ all my cunning in this matter.

25.

"Think not, Troilus, that I do not fully realize that affairs so conducted are not becoming to a worthy lady and what may come therefrom to me, to her, and to hers, if such a thing ever reach people's ears as that she, on whose person honor was wont to dwell, hath, for thus obeying the dictates of Love, become, by our folly, an object of reproach.

26.

"But as long as desire hath been checked in its action and everything like unto it held secret, it seemeth to me reasonable to maintain that each lover may follow his high desires, provided only he be discreet in deed and in semblance, without causing any shame to those to whom shame and honor are matters of concern.

27.

Io credo certo, ch' ogni donna in voglia
Viva amorosa, e null' altro l' affrena
Che tema di vergogna ; e se a tal doglia,
Onestamente medicina piena
Si può donar, folle è chi non la spoglia,
E poco parmi gli cuoca la pena.
La mia cugina è vedova, e disia ;
E se 'l negasse nol gliel crederia.

28.

Poichè sentendo te saggio ed accorto,
A lei e ad amendue posso piacere,
E a ciascuno donar pari conforto,
Poscia che occulto il dovete tenere,
E fia come non fosse ; e farei torto,
Se in ciò non ne facessi il mio potere
In tuo servigio ; e tu sii saggio poi,
Nel tener chiuso tal' opera altroi.

29.

Udiva Troilo Pandaro contento
Sì nella mente, ch' esser gli parea
Quasi già fuor di tutto il suo tormento,
E più nel suo amor si raccendea.
Ma poichè alquanto stato fu attento,
A Pandaro si volse e gli dicea :
Io credo ciò che tu di' di costei,
Ma troppo ne par più agli occhi miei.

30.

Ma come mancherà però l' ardore
Ch' io porto dentro, ch' io non vidi mai !
Che ella s' accorgesse del mio amore ?
Ella nol crederà se tu il dirai :
Poi per tema di te, questo furore
Biasimerà, e niente farai ;
E se nel cuor l' avesse, per mostrarti
D' essere onesta, non vorrà ascoltarti.

27.

"I believe indeed that in desire every woman liveth amorously and that nothing but fear of shame restraineth her. And if to such anguish a full remedy may properly be given, foolish is he that doth not ravish her. And little in my opinion doth the punishment vex her. My cousin is a widow and hath desires; if she should deny it, I would not believe her.

28.

"Therefore, since I know thee wise and reasonable, I can please her and both of you and give you each equal comfort, provided you undertake to keep it secret, and it will be as though it were not. I would do wrong if in this matter I did not all in my power to serve thee. Be thou discreet then in keeping such doings concealed from others."

29.

Troilus listened to Pandarus so well satisfied in mind that he seemed to him to be already well-nigh delivered from his anguish. And he waxed again more ardent in his love. But after he had been silent for a while, he turned to Pandarus and said to him: "I believe what thou sayest of this lady but the difficulty appeareth to mine eyes all the greater on this account.

30.

"Furthermore how will the ardor that I bear within grow less since I have never seen her take notice of my love? She will not believe it, if thou tellest it to her. Moreover, for fear of thee, she will blame this passion and thou wilt accomplish naught. And if she had it in her heart, to show thee that she is honest, she would not be willing to listen to thee.

31.

Ed oltre a questo, Pandar, non vorria
Che tu credessi che io disiassi
Di cotal donna alcuna villania,
Ma che le fosse a grado ch' io l' amassi
Solamente vorrei, questo mi fia
Sovrana grazia se io la impetrassi;
Di questo cerca, e più non ti dimando;
E abbassò il viso alquanto vergognando.

32.

A cui ridendo Pandaro rispose:
Niente nuoce ciò che tu ragioni,
Lascia far me, che le fiamme amorose
Ho per le mani, e sì fatti sermoni,
E seppi già recar più alte cose
Al fine suo con nuove condizioni;
Questa fatica tutta sarà mia,
E 'l dolce fine tuo voglio che sia.

33.

Troilo destro si gittò in terra
Dal letto, lui abbracciando e baciando,
Giurando appresso che la greca guerra
Vincer nulla sariegli trionfando,
Appresso a quest' ardor che tanto il serra:
Pandaro mio, io mi ti raccomando,
Tu savio, tu amico, tu sai tutto
Ciò che bisogni a dar fine al mio lutto.

34.

Pandaro disioso di servire
Il giovinetto, il quale molto amava,
Lasciato lui dove gli piacque gire,
Sen gì ver dove Criseida stava;
La qual veggendo lui a sè venire,
Levata in piè da lunge il salutava,
E Pandar lei, che per la man pigliata,
In una loggia seco l' ha menata.

[178]

31.

"Furthermore, Pandarus, I would not have thee believe that I would desire of such a lady aught unbecoming, but only that she consent that I love her. This would be a sovereign favor to me, if I should obtain it. Seek for this, and more I do not ask of thee." Then he looked down somewhat abashed.

32.

And to him Pandarus laughingly replied: "There is no harm in what thou sayest. Leave the matter to me, for I have at hand love-enkindling words and speeches of like quality. Of old have I known, under unusual conditions, how to bring more arduous tasks to accomplishment. This labor will all be mine and the sweet result I wish to be thine."

33.

Troilus leaped nimbly to the ground from his couch, embracing and kissing him, swearing that to win in triumph the war against the Greeks would be naught to him when compared to this passion that so much bindeth him: "My Pandarus, I put myself in thy hands, thou philosopher, thou friend, thou knowest all that is needed to put an end to my distress."

34.

Pandarus, anxious to serve the youth, whom he loved much, left him to his own devices, and betook himself to where Cressida dwelt. As she saw him come toward her, she stood up and greeted him from afar, and Pandarus her, and he took her by the hand, and led her with him into an apartment.

35.

Quivi con risa e con dolci parole,
  Con lieti motti e con ragionamenti
  Parentevoli assai, sì come suole
  Farsi talvolta tra congiunte genti,
  Si stette alquanto, come quei che vuole
  Al suo proposto con nuovi argomenti
  Venire, se il potrà, e nel bel viso
  Cominciò forte a riguardarla fiso.

36.

Criseida che 'l vede, sorridendo
  Disse: Cugin, non mi vedesti mai,
  Che tu mi vai così mente tenendo?
  A cui rispose Pandaro: ben sai
  Ch' io t' ho veduta e di vederti intendo;
  Ma tu mi par più che l' usato assai
  Bella, ed hai più di che lodare Iddio,
  Che altra bella donna al parer mio.

37.

Criseida disse: che vuol dir codesto?
  Perchè più ora che per lo passato?
  A cui Pandar rispose lieto e presto:
  Perchè il tuo è il più avventurato
  Viso, che mai donna avesse in questo
  Mondo, s' io non mi sono ingannato;
  A sì fatto uomo ho sentito che piace
  Oltre misura sì, che se ne sface.

38.

Criseida alquanto arrossì vergognosa
  Udendo ciò che Pandaro diceva,
  E rassembrava a mattutina rosa;
  Poi tai parole a Pandaro moveva:
  Non ti far beffe di me, che gioiosa
  D' ogni tuo ben sarei; poco doveva
  Avere a far colui a cui io piacqui,
  Che mai più non m' avvenne poi ch' io nacqui.

35.

There he contented himself for a while with laughter and with sweet words, with many jests and with familiar talk, in the fashion usual at such times between relatives, as one who wisheth to come to his point with further arguments, if he may, and began to look into her lovely face very fixedly.

36.

Cressida, who observed this, said with a smile: "Cousin, hast thou never seen me, that thou art gazing at me so intently?" To her Pandarus replied: "Well thou knowest that I have seen thee and hope to continue to see thee. But thou appearest to me exceptionally beautiful and hast, as it seemeth to me, more to praise the gods for than any other fair lady."

37.

Cressida said: "What meaneth this? Why more now than in the past?" To her Pandarus replied gaily and promptly: "Because thine is the most fortune-favored face that ever lady had in this world, if I mistake not. I have heard that it pleaseth a very proper man so immeasurably that he is undone by it."

38.

Upon hearing what Pandarus said, Cressida blushed somewhat bashfully and looked like a morning rose. Then she addressed to Pandarus these words: "Mock not at me, for I should be glad of every good that should come to thee. The man I pleased must have had little to occupy his attention, for never on any other occasion did this happen to me since I was born."

39.

Lasciamo stare i motti, disse allora
  Pandaro : dimmi se' ten tu accorta ?
  A cui ella rispose : Non è ancora
  Più d' un che d' altro, s' io non sia morta ;
  È vero ch' io ci veggo ad ora ad ora
  Passare alcun, che sempre alla mia porta
  Rimira, nè so io se va cercando
  Di veder me, o d' altro va musando.

40.

Pandaro disse allora : Chi è colui ?
  A cui Criseida disse : veramente
  Io nol conosco, nè ti so di lui
  Più oltre dire. E Pandaro, che sente
  Che di Troilo non dice, ma d' altrui,
  Così seguì a lei subitamente :
  Non è colui il qual tu hai feruto,
  Uom che non sia da tutti conosciuto.

41.

Chi è dunque colui che si diletta
  Sì di vedermi ? criseida disse.
  A cui Pandaro allora : giovinetta,
  Poichè colui che il mondo circonscrisse,
  Fece il primo uom, non credo più perfetta
  Anima in alcun altro mai inserisse,
  Che quella di colui che t' ama tanto,
  Che dir non si potrebbe giammai quanto.

42.

Egli è d' animo altiero e di linguaggio,
  Onesto molto, e cupido d' onore ;
  Di senno natural più ch' altro uom saggio,
  Nè di scienza n' è alcun maggiore ;
  Prode ed ardito, e chiaro nel visaggio ;
  Io non potrei dir tutto il suo valore ;
  Deh quanto ell' è felice tua bellezza,
  Poichè tal uomo più ch' altra l' apprezza !

39.

"Let us dismiss all jests," said Pandarus then. "Tell me, art thou aware of him?" To this she replied: "No more of one man than of another, as I hope to live. It is true that I see pass here from time to time someone who ever gazeth at my door, nor know I if he come in search of a sight of me or be musing at something else."

40.

Then said Pandarus: "Who is this man?" To him Cressida said: "Truly I know him not, nor can I tell thee further of him." Pandarus, perceiving that she is not speaking of Troilus but of someone else, forthwith replied to her thus: "He whom thou hast wounded is not a man not known by all."

41.

"Who, then, is he who taketh such pleasure in seeing me?" said Cressida. To her Pandarus replied: "Lady, since he who circumscribed the world made the first man, I do not believe that he ever put a more perfect soul in anyone than is the soul of him who loveth thee so much that it would never be possible to tell thee how much.

42.

"He is lofty of soul and of speech, very virtuous, and jealous of honor, wise in native sense beyond another, and without a superior in knowledge, valiant and high spirited, and open in countenance. I could not tell thee all his worth. Ah, how fortunate is thy beauty, since such a man valueth it more than anything else!

43.

Ben' è la gemma posta nell' anello,
Se tu se' savia come tu se' bella.
Se tu diventi sua, così com' ello
È divenuto tuo, ben fia la stella
Giunta col sole ; nè mai fu donzello
Giunto sì bene ad alcuna donzella,
Come tu seco, se savia sarai :
Beata a te se tu 'l conoscerai.

44.

Sol una volta ha nel mondo ventura
Qualunque vive, se la sa pigliare ;
Chi lei vegnente lascia, sua sciagura
Pianga da sè senz' altrui biasimare :
La tua vaga e bellissima figura
La t' ha trovata, or sappila adoprare :
Lascia me pianger, che 'n mal' ora nacqui,
Ch' a Dio, e al mondo, ed a fortuna spiacqui.

45.

Tentimi tu, o parli daddovero,
Criseida disse, o se' del senno uscito ?
Chi deve aver di me piacere intero
Se già non divenisse mio marito ?
Ma dimmi, chi è questi, è istraniero
O cittadin, ch' è per me sì smarrito ;
Dimmel se vuoi, se pur dir me lo dei,
E non chiamar senza cagion gli omei.

46.

Pandaro disse : Egli è pur cittadino,
Nè de' minori, e mio amico molto ;
Del qual, per forza forse di destino,
Tratto ho del petto ciò ch' io t' ho disciolto ;
E' vive in pianto misero e meschino,
Sì lo splendor l' accende del tuo volto :
E perchè sappi chi cotanto t' ama,
Troilo è quei che cotanto ti brama.

[184]

43.

"Well is the jewel placed in the ring, if thou art wise as thou art fair. If thou become his, as he hath become thine, well will the star be joined with the sun. Nor ever was youth joined so well with maid as thou wilt be with him, if thou wilt be wise. Well for thee if thou wilt recognize it.

44.

"Once only hath everyone who liveth in the world fortune, if he knoweth how to seize it. Let him who abandoneth it when it cometh, bewail his misfortune by himself, without blaming another. Thy lovely and most beautiful face hath found it for thee. Know now how to use it. Let me weep, since I was born in an evil hour and was displeasing to the gods, to the world, and to fortune."

45.

"Dost thou tempt me or dost thou speak the truth," said Cressida, "or art thou out of thy senses? Who hath any right to have perfect pleasure of me, if he should not first become my husband? But tell me, who is this man? Is he who is so smitten with me a stranger or an inhabitant of our city? Tell me if thou art willing, if thou canst reconcile it with thy sense of duty to tell me, and do not cry 'ah me' without occasion."

46.

Pandarus said: "He is a citizen, nor of the lesser, and my great friend. From his breast, by the power, mayhap, of destiny, have I drawn what I have disclosed to thee. He liveth in wretched and miserable woe, so doth the splendor of thy countenance inflame him. And that thou mayest know who so much loveth thee, Troilus is he who desireth thee so much."

47.

Dimorò sopra sè Criseida allora
  Pandaro riguardando, e tal divenne
  Qual da mattina l' aere si scolora,
  E con fatica le lagrime tenne
  Venute agli occhi già per cader fuora:
  Poscia, come il perduto ardir rivenne,
  Un poco prima seco mormorando,
  Così a Pandaro disse sospirando:

48.

Io mi credea, Pandaro, se io
  In tal follía giammai fossi caduta,
  Che se Troilo venuto nel disio
  Mi fosse mai, tu m' avessi battuta
  Non che ripresa, sì com' uom che 'l mio
  Onor cercar dovresti: oh Dio m' aiuta!
  Che faran gli altri, poi che tu t' ingegni
  Di seguir farmi gli amorosi regni?

49.

Ben so che Troilo è grande e valoroso,
  E ciascuna gran donna ne dovria
  Esser contenta; ma poichè 'l mio sposo
  Tolto mi fu, sempre la voglia mia
  D' amore fu lontana, ed ho doglioso
  Il cuore ancor della sua morte ria,
  Ed avrò sempre mentre sarò in vita,
  Tornandomi a memoria sua partita.

50.

E se alcuno il mio amor dovesse
  Aver, per certo a lui il donerei,
  Sol ch' io credessi ched e' gli piacesse:
  Ma come tu conoscer chiaro dei,
  Che le vaghezze si trovano spesse
  Chente egli ha ora, e quattro dì o sei
  Durano, e passan poscia di leggiero;
  Cambiando amor così cambia il pensiero.

47.

Cressida then paused, looking at Pandarus, and turned such color as doth the air when in the morning it groweth pale, and with difficulty restrained the tears that came to her eyes ready to gush forth. Then, as her lost courage returned, she murmured to herself, and spake thus to Pandarus in sighs:

48.

"I would have thought, Pandarus, if I had ever fallen into such folly that Troilus had ever come into my desire, that thou wouldst have beaten me, not merely restrained me, as one who should seek my honor. O God help me! What will others do now that thou strivest to make me follow the precepts of Love?

49.

"Well I know that Troilus is great and brave and every great lady should be happy with him. But since my husband was taken away from me, my wishes have ever been far removed from Love, and I have still a heavy heart for his grievous death, and shall have whilst I live, calling to memory his departure.

50.

"And if anyone should have my love, certainly to him would I give it, provided only I thought that it would please him. But as thou shouldst clearly know, the fancies which he hath now, often occur, and last four or five days, and then pass lightly away, love changing as thought changeth.

51.

Però mi lascia tal vita menare,
    Chente fortuna apparecchiato m' have;
    Egli troverà ben donna da amare
    Al piacer suo, e umile e soave;
    A me onesta si convien di stare:
    Pandar, per Dio, deh non ti paia grave
    Questa risposta, e lui fa' che conforti
    Con piacer nuovi e con altri diporti.

52.

Pandaro seco si tenea scornato
    Udendo il ragionar della donzella,
    E per partirsi quasi fu levato,
    Poi pur ristette, e rivolsesi ad ella,
    Dicendo: io t' ho, Criseida, lodato
    Quel ch' io farei a mia carnal sorella,
    O a mia figlia, o a mia moglie s' io l' avessi,
    Se i miei piacer da Dio mi sien concessi;

53.

Perocch' io sento che Troilo vale
    Cosa maggiore assai, che non sarebbe
    Il tuo amore; e vidil' ieri a tale,
    Per questo amor, che forte me n' increbbe.
    Forse nol credi, e però non ten cale;
    Ben so che a forza te n' increscerebbe,
    Se sapessi ciò ch' io del suo ardore;
    Deh increscati di lui per lo mio amore.

54.

Io non credo ch' al mondo vi sia alcuno
    Più segreto uom di lui nè con più fede,
    Ed è leal quanto ne sia nessuno,
    Nè più oltre di te disia o vede;
    Ed a te stando in vestimento bruno,
    Giovane ancora, d' amar si concede;
    Non perder tempo, pensa che vecchiezza,
    O morte, torrà via la tua bellezza.

51.

"Therefore let me lead such a life as fortune may have prepared for me. He will easily find a lady, both submissive and gentle, to love at his pleasure. It is meet for me to remain virtuous. By the gods, Pandarus, pray do not let this reply seem grievous to thee. Strive to comfort him with new pleasure and with other diversions."

52.

Pandarus thought himself abused when he heard the remarks of the damsel and got up to leave. Then he stopped, turned to her, and said: "I have commended to thee, Cressida, one whom I would commend to my own sister, or to my daughter, or to my wife, if I had one, an I hope for the joys of Heaven.

53.

"For I believe that Troilus is worth a greater thing than thy love. Yesterday I saw him reduced to such straits because of this love that I pitied him greatly. Perhaps thou dost not believe it and therefore art not concerned about it. Well I know that thou wouldst perforce pity him, if thou knew what I know of his passion. Ah, have pity upon him for love of me.

54.

"I do not believe that there is in the world any man more worthy of confidence than he or more faithful. In loyalty he hath not his equal nor beyond thee doth he desire or look. And although thou art dressed in dark attire, thou art still young and hast the privilege of loving. Lose no time, consider that old age or death will take away all thy beauty."

55.

Oimè, disse Criseida, tu di' vero,
  Così ci portan gli anni a poco a poco:
  E' più si muoion prima che 'l sentiero
  Si compia dato dal celeste fuoco:
  Ma lasciam' ora di questo il pensiero,
  E dimmi, se d'amor sollazzo e giuoco
  Ancora io posso avere, e in che maniera
  T' avvedesti di Troilo la primiera.

56.

Sorrise allora Pandaro, e rispose:
  Io tel dirò, dappoi che 'l vuoi sapere;
  L' altrieri essendo in quiete le cose
  Per la tregua allor fatta, fu in calere
  A Troilo, ch' io con lui per selve ombrose
  M' andassi diportando; ivi a sedere
  Postici, a ragionar cominciò meco
  D' amore, e poi di lui a cantar seco.

57.

Io non gli era vicin, ma mormorare
  Udendol, ver di lui mi feci attento,
  E per quel ch' io mi possa ricordare,
  Ad amor si dolea del suo tormento,
  Dicendo: Signor mio, già mi si pare
  Nel viso e ne' sospiri ciò ch' io sento
  Dentro del cuor per leggiadra vaghezza,
  La qual m' ha preso colla sua bellezza.

58.

Tu stai colà dov' io porto dipinta
  L' imagine che più ch' altro mi piace;
  E quivi vedi l' anima che vinta
  Dalla folgore tua pensosa giace;
  La qual la tiene intorno stretta e cinta,
  Chiamando sempre quella dolce pace,
  Che gli occhi belli e vaghi di costei
  Sol posson dar, caro signore, a lei.

55.

"Alas," said Cressida, "thou speakest the truth. Thus do the years little by little bear us forward. The greater number die before the path granted by the celestial fire is completed. But let us now stop thinking of this, and tell me whether I may still have solace and joy of love, and in what way thou didst first take note of Troilus."

56.

Pandarus then smiled and replied: "I will tell it thee, since thou wishest to know it. The day before yesterday, while things were quiet because of the truce then made, Troilus desired that I should go with him for amusement through the shady woods. When we were seated there, he began to talk with me of love and then to sing to himself.

57.

"I was not near him, but hearing him murmur, I turned my attention toward him, and as far as I can remember, he complained to Love of his torment, saying: 'My lord, already in my visage and in my sighs appeareth that which I feel in my heart by reason of the gentle longing which hath seized me because of her beauty.

58.

" 'Thou takest thy station in that place where I bear pictured the image which pleaseth me more than aught else. There behold the soul which lieth pensive, conquered by thy radiance, which holdeth it bound about and engirded, whilst it calleth ever for that sweet peace which the fair and lovely eyes of this lady, dear lord, can alone give it.

59.

Dunque, per Dio, se 'l mio morir ti noia,
 Fallo sentire a questa vaga cosa,
 E lei pregando, impetra quella gioia
 Che suole a' tuoi soggetti donar posa;
 Deh non volere, signor mio, ch' io muoia;
 Deh fa 'l per Dio, vedi* che l' angosciosa
 Anima giorno e notte sempre grida,
 Tal paura ha che ella non l' uccida.

60.

Dubiti tu sotto la bruna vesta
 D' accender le tue fiamme, signor mio?
 Nulla ti fia maggior gloria che questa;
 Entra nel petto suo con quel disio
 Che dimora nel mio e mi molesta;
 Deh fallo, i' te ne prego, signor pio,
 Sicchè per te i suoi dolci sospiri,
 Conforto portino alli miei disiri.

61.

E questo detto, forte sospirando,
 Bassò la testa non so che dicendo;
 Poscia si tacque quasi lagrimando.
 In me di quel che era, ciò veggendo,
 Entrò sospetto, e proposi, che quando
 Tempo più atto fosse, un dì ridendo
 Di domandarlo ciò che la canzone
 Volesse dire e poi della cagione.

62.

Ma tempo prima a questo non m' occorse
 Che oggi, ch' io 'l trovai tutto soletto:
 Entrando nella sua camera, in forse
 Se el vi fosse, ed egli era in sul letto,
 E me vedendo, altrove si ritolse,
 Di che io presi alquanto di sospetto;
 E fattomi più presso, che piangea
 Il trovai forte, e forte si dolea.

* Savj-Lopez, *ve'*

59.

" 'Then by the gods, if my dying distresseth thee, make this fair creature sensible of it, and by supplicating her, obtain that joy which is wont to give relief to thy subjects. Ah, do not desire, my lord, that I die. Behold how my vanquished soul doth ever cry out day and night, such fear hath it lest she slay it.

60.

" 'Dost thou hesitate to kindle thy flames beneath her dark mantle, my lord? No greater glory will be thine than this. Enter into her heart with that desire which dwelleth in mine and tormenteth me. Ah, bring it to pass, I pray thee, merciful lord, that by thy mediation her sweet sighs may bring comfort to my desires.'

61.

"After he said this, he sighed deeply and bowed his head, saying I know not what. Then almost in tears he lapsed into silence. Into me, when I saw this, there entered a suspicion of what the matter was, and I made up my mind, when a more fitting opportunity should arise, to ask him some day smilingly what his song might mean and then of the occasion.

62.

"But only today did the time for this occur, when I found him all alone. I entered his room on the chance that he might be there. He was upon his couch, and seeing me, retired elsewhere. Wherefore I became somewhat suspicious, and came nearer, and found that he wept bitterly and bitterly lamented.

63.

Come io seppi il più lo confortai,
    E con nuova arte e con diverso ingegno
    Di bocca quel ch' avesse gli cavai,
    Datagli pria la mia fede per pegno,
    Ch' io nol direi ad alcun uom giammai.
    Questa pietà mi mosse, e per lui vegno
    A te, a cui in breve ho soddisfatto
    Di quel ch' e' prega in ogni modo e atto.

64.

Tu che farai? starai tu altiera,
    E lascerai colui, che sè non cura
    Per amar te, a morte tanto fiera
    Venire, a rio destino o ria ventura,
    Ch' un sì fatto uomo per te amando pera?
    Almanco della tua vaga figura
    Non gli fostu nè de' tuoi occhi cara,
    Forse il campresti ancor da morte amara.

65.

Criseida disse allora: di lontano
    Il segreto scorgesti del suo petto,
    Come ch' el fermo poi tenesse mano
    Quando il trovasti a pianger sopra il letto,
    E così 'l faccia Dio e lieto sano,*
    E me ancora, come per tuo detto
    Pietà me n' è venuta; i' non son cruda
    Come ti par, nè sì di pietà nuda.

66.

E stata alquanto, dopo un gran sospiro,
    Trafitta già, seguì: deh io m' avveggio
    Dove ti trae il pietoso disiro,
    Ed io 'l farò, poichè piacer ten deggio,
    Ed egli il vale, bastiti s' io 'l miro;
    Ma per fuggir vergogna, e forse peggio,
    Pregalo che sia saggio, e faccia quello
    Che a me biasmo non sia, nè anche ad ello.

* Savj-Lopez, *lieto e sano*

63.

"I comforted him as best I knew how. And with unaccustomed art and diverse artifice I extorted from him what was the matter, having first given my faith in pledge that I would never tell it to any man. This grief of his moved me and for his sake I come to thee, to whom I have in brief discharged his request in every particular.

64.

"What wilt thou do? Wilt thou remain proud and let him who loveth thee beyond any care for himself, come to so cruel death, to miserable destiny, or wretched hap, that so proper a man perish for loving thee? Wert thou only not dear to him for thy lovely figure and for thine eyes, thou mightest perchance still save him from bitter death."

65.

Cressida then said: "From afar didst thou discover the secret of his breast, although he held it in a firm grip what time thou didst find him weeping upon his couch. So may the gods make him well and happy and me also, as pity hath come to me by reason of what thou hast said. I am not cruel, as it seemeth to thee, nor so devoid of pity."

66.

She remained silent awhile and sighed deeply and then already wounded continued: "I perceive in what direction thy compassionate desire tendeth. I will do what thou asketh because I am sure to please thee thereby and he is worth it. Let it suffice thee if I see him. But in order to avoid shame and perhaps worse, pray that he be discreet and do what may not be a reproach to me nor to him as well."

67.

Sorella mia, allor Pandaro disse,
 Tu parli bene, ed io nel pregheraggio;
 Ver è che io non credo ch' el fallisse,
 Tanto il conosco costumato e saggio,
 Fuorchè per isciagura non venisse,
 Tolgalo Iddio, ed io ci metteraggio
 Compenso tal che ti sarà in piacere;
 Fatti* con Dio, e fa' il tuo dovere.

68.

Partito Pandar, se ne gì soletta
 Nella camera sua Criseida bella,
 Seco nel cuor ciascuna paroletta
 Rivolvendo di Pandaro e novella,
 In quella forma ch' era stata detta;
 E lieta seco ragiona e favella,
 E 'n cotal guisa spesso sospirando,
 Oltre l' usato Troilo immaginando.

69.

Io son giovane, bella, vaga e lieta,
 Vedova, ricca, nobile ed amata,
 Senza figliuoli ed in vita quieta,
 Perchè esser non deggio innamorata?
 Se forse l' onestà questo mi vieta,
 Io sarò saggia, e terrò sì celata
 La voglia mia, che non sarà saputo
 Ch'io aggia mai nel cuore amore avuto.

70.

La giovinezza mia si fugge ognora,
 Debbol' io perder sì miseramente?
 Io non conosco in questa terra ancora
 Veruna senza amante, e la più gente,
 Com' io conosco e veggo, s'innamora,
 Ed io mi perdo il tempo per niente?
 E come gli altri far non è peccato,
 E non può esser da alcun biasimato.

* Savj-Lopez, *statti*

67.

"Sister mine," said Pandarus then, "thou speakest well and I will make this request of him. Truly, I do not believe that he will fail, I know him to be so well-mannered and discreet, unless it happen by some unlucky accident. And this the gods forbid. I will contrive thee such recompense as shall be to thy pleasure. Fare thee well and do thy duty."

68.

After Pandarus departed, Cressida retired alone to her room, revolving in her heart every little word and message of Pandarus in the form in which it had been told. In joyful mood she discourseth and talketh with herself, and in so doing often sigheth, and pictureth Troilus in her mind beyond her wont.

69.

"I am young, fair, lovely, and carefree, a widow, rich, noble, and beloved. I have no children and lead an undisturbed life. Why should I not be in love? If perchance regard for my reputation forbid it me, I shall be prudent and keep my desire so hidden that it will not be known that I have ever entertained love in my heart.

70.

"Every hour my youth taketh flight. Am I to lose it so miserably? I do not know a single lady in this land without a lover. Most people, as I know and see, fall in love. Shall I lose my time for nothing? To do as others is no sin and I cannot incur the reproach of anyone.

71.

Chi mi vorrà se io invecchio mai?
  Certo nessuno, e allora a ravvedersi
  Altro non è se non crescer di guai;
  Niente vale il di dietro pentersi,
  O 'l dir dolente, perchè non amai?
  Buon è adunque a tempo provvedersi;
  Costui è bello, gentil, savio ed accorto,
  Che t'ama, e fresco più che giglio d'orto;

72.

Di real sangue e di sommo valore,
  E Pandar tuo cugin tel loda tanto:
  Dunque che fai, perchè dentro del cuore,
  Come egli ha te, lui non ricevi alquanto?
  Perchè non gli dai tu il tuo amore?
  Non odi tu la pieta del suo pianto?
  O quanto bene avrai ancor con lui,
  Se com' egli ama te tu ami lui!

73.

Ed ora non è tempo da marito,
  E se pur fosse, la sua libertade
  Servare è troppo più savio partito;
  L'amor che vien da sì fatta amistade
  È sempre dagli amanti più gradito;
  E sia quanto vuol grande la beltade,
  Che a' mariti tosto non rincresca,
  Vaghi d'avere ogni dì cosa fresca.

74.

L'acqua furtiva, assai più dolce cosa
  È che il vin con abbondanza avuto:
  Così d'amor la gioia, che nascosa
  Trapassa assai, del sempre mai tenuto
  Marito in braccio; adunque vigorosa
  Ricevi il dolce amante, il qual venuto
  T' è fermamente mandato da Dio,
  E sodisfa' al suo caldo disio.

71.

"Who will ever desire me, if I grow old? Certainly no one. And to regret then is naught but to suffer increase of woe. It doth no good to repent of it afterward or to say in grief: 'Why didst thou not love?' Well is it therefore to make provision in season. This lover of thine is handsome, well-bred, wise; and clever, and fresher than garden lily,

72.

"Of royal blood and of highest worth, and thy cousin Pandarus praiseth him so much to thee. What doest thou then? Why not receive him somewhat within thine heart, as he hath thee? Why not give thy love to him? Hearest thou not the pitifulness of his plaint? O how much happiness wilt thou have with him, besides, if thou love him as he loveth thee!

73.

"Now is not the time for a husband, and if it were, to keep one's liberty is a much wiser part. Love that springeth from so complete friendship is ever more pleasing to lovers. Beauty, however great, soon palleth upon married men, who desire to have every day something fresh.

74.

"Water acquired by stealth is sweeter far than wine had in abundance. So the joy of love, when hidden, ever surpasseth that of the husband held perpetually in arms. Therefore with zest receive the sweet lover, who hath come to thee at the certain behest of the gods, and give satisfaction to his burning desire."

75.

E stando alquanto, poi si rivolgea
  Nell' altra parte : misera, dicendo,
  Che vuoi tu far ? non sai tu quanto rea
  Vita si trae con esso amor languendo,
  Nella qual sempre convien che si stea
  In pianti, ed in sospiri, ed in dolendo ?
  Avendo poi per giunta gelosia,
  Che peggio è assai che non è morte ria.

76.

Appresso a questo, chi al presente t'ama,
  È di troppo più alta condizione
  Che tu non se' ; quest' amorosa brama
  Gli passerà, ed in abusíone
  Sempre t'avrà, e lasceratti grama,
  D'infamia piena e di confusíone :
  Guarda che fai ; che il senno da sezzo
  Nè fu, nè è, nè fia mai d'alcun prezzo.

77.

Ma posto pur che questo amor lontano
  Debba durar, come puoi tu sapere
  Che debba star celato ? assai è vano
  Fidarsi alla fortuna, e ben vedere
  Quanto uopo fa non può consiglio umano ;
  Che se si scuopre aperto, puoi tenere
  La fama tua in eterno perduta,
  La qual sì buona infino a qui è suta.

78.

Dunque cotali amor lasciali stare
  A cui e' piaccion : ed appresso il detto
  Incominciava forte a sospirare,
  Nè si poteva già dal casto petto
  Il bel viso di Troilo cacciare,
  Per che tornava sopra il primo effetto
  Biasimando e lodando, e in tale erranza,
  Seco faceva lunga dimoranza.

75.

She ceased awhile. Then she turned her thoughts in the opposite direction, saying: "What dost thou purpose to do, wretched one? Knowest thou not how bad is the life that one liveth with one's lover when passion languisheth, for there must ever be in it continuance of woes, of sighs, and grieving, with jealousy added, which is far worse than wretched death?

76.

"As for this man who now loveth thee, he is of much higher rank than thou. This amorous desire of his will pass and he will hold thee ever in abuse and will leave thee wretched, full of shame and confusion. Be careful what thou doest. Good sense, when it cometh too late, never was, nor is, nor ever will be of any avail.

77.

"But granting that this love be destined to last for a long time, how canst thou be sure that it is destined to remain concealed? 'Tis vain to trust to fortune and well to realize how impotent is human counsel when need ariseth. If it be discovered openly, thou canst regard thy reputation, which heretofore hath been excellent, as lost for ever.

78.

"Therefore leave such loves to those who delight in them." After she said this, she began to sigh violently, nor was she able to banish the fair image of Troilus from her chaste breast. Therefore she returned to her first impression, now blaming, now praising, and in such vacillation made with herself long delay.

79.

Pandar, che da Criseida dipartito
  S'era contento, senza altrove gire,
  A Troilo diritto se n'era ito,
  E di lontano gli cominciò a dire:
  Confortati fratel, ch' i' ho fornito
  Gran parte, credo, del tuo gran disire.
  E postosi a seder, gli disse ratto,
  Senza interpor, com'era stato il fatto.

80.

Quali i fioretti dal notturno gelo
  Chinati e chiusi, poi che 'l sol gl'imbianca,
  Tutti s'apron diritti in loro stelo;
  Cotal si fe' di sua virtude stanca
  Troilo allora, e riguardando il cielo,
  Incominciò come persona franca:
  Lodato sia il tuo sommo valore,
  Venere bella, e del tuo figlio Amore.

81.

Poi Pandaro abbracciò ben mille fiate,
  E baciollo altrettante, sì contento,
  Che più non saria fatto se donate
  Gli fosser mille Troie; e lento lento
  Con Pandar solo a veder la beltate
  Di Criseida n'andò, guardando attento
  Se alcuno atto nuovo in lei vedeva,
  Per quel che Pandar ragionato aveva.

82.

Ella si stava ad una sua finestra,
  E forse quel ch'avvenne ell' aspettava;
  Non si mostrò selvaggia nè alpestra
  Verso di Troilo che la riguardava,
  Ma tuttavolta in sulla poppa destra
  Onestamente verso lui mirava;
  Di che allegro Troilo se ne gio,
  Grazie rendendo a Pandaro ed a Dio.

79.

Pandarus, who after parting from Cressida had felt satisfied, had, without going elsewhere, repaired directly to Troilus, and began from afar to say to him: "Comfort thyself, brother, for I have, I believe, accomplished a great part of thy desire." And he sat down and straightway told him quickly what had happened.

80.

As little flowers, bowed and closed by the chill of night, when whitened by the sun, open all and straighten upon their stems, so at that moment did Troilus recover from his weary spirits, and glancing heavenward began as one enfranchised: "Praised be thy supreme power, fair Venus, and that of thy son Love."

81.

Then he embraced Pandarus fully a thousand times, and kissed him as much again, so happy that he would not have been made more so had he been given a thousand Troys. And very softly he went thence, with Pandarus alone, to behold the beauty of Cressida, watching intently if he saw any new behavior in her by reason of Pandarus' words.

82.

She was standing at one of her windows and was perchance expecting what happened. Not harsh nor forbidding did she show herself toward Troilus as he looked at her, but at all times cast toward him modest glances over her right shoulder. Troilus departed, delighted thereat, giving thanks to Pandarus and to the gods.

83.

E quella tiepidezza che intra due
  Criseida tenea, sen fuggì via,
  Seco lodando le maniere sue,
  Gli atti piacevoli e la cortesia;
  E sì subitamente presa fue,
  Che sopra ogni altro bene lui disia,
  E duolle forte del tempo perduto,
  Che 'l suo amor non avea conosciuto.

84.

Troilo canta e fa mirabil festa,
  Armeggia, spende, e dona lietamente,
  E spesso si rinnuova e cangia vesta,
  Ognora amando più ferventemente;
  E per piacer non gli è cosa molesta
  Amor seguir, mirar discretamente
  Criseida, la qual non men discreta,
  Gli si mostrava a' tempi vaga e lieta.

85.

Ma come noi, per continova usanza,
  Per più legne veggiam fuoco maggiore,
  Così avvien, crescendo la speranza
  Assai sovente ancor cresce l'amore:
  E quinci Troilo con maggior possanza,
  Che l'usato, sentia nel preso cuore
  L'alto disio spronarlo, onde i sospiri
  Tornar più forti che prima, e' martirj.

86.

Di che Troilo con Pandaro talvolta
  Si dolea forte: lasso me, dicendo,
  El m'ha Criseida sì la vita tolta
  Co' suoi begli occhi, che morir n'intendo
  Per lo disio fervente che s' affolta
  Sì sopra al cuor nel quale io ardo e incendo;
  Deh che farò? che contento dovria
  Solo esser della sua gran cortesia.

83.

And that indifference which was holding Cressida at cross-purposes with herself vanished, as she praised to herself his manner, his pleasing actions, and his courtesy, and so suddenly was she captivated that she desired him above every other good, and grieved much at the time lost when she had not known his love.

84.

Troilus singeth and maketh joyful, jousteth, spendeth, and giveth freely, and often reneweth and changeth his apparel, loving more fervently every hour. And for diversion's sake he findeth it not an irksome task to pursue love, to eye Cressida discreetly, and she, no less discreet, showed herself to him from time to time lovely and light-hearted.

85.

But as through continual experience we note the more the wood, the greater the fire, so if hope happeneth to increase, oft love increaseth too. From then on with greater force than usual felt Troilus in his captive heart the goad of high desire. Thenceforth sighs and torments came back stronger than before.

86.

Thereof Troilus did many times make plaint to Pandarus, saying: "Woe is me! Cressida hath with her fair eyes so taken away my life that I expect to die from the fervent desire that so presseth upon my heart that in it I glow and burn. Ah, what shall I do, I who alone ought to be satisfied with her great courtesy?

87.

Ella mi guarda, e soffera* ch'io guati
  Onestamente lei; questo dovrebbe
  Essere assai a' miei disii infiammati;
  Ma l'appetito cupido vorrebbe
  Non so che più; sì mal son regolati
  Gli ardor che 'l muovon, che nol crederebbe
  Chi nol provasse, quanto mi tormenta
  Tal fiamma, che maggiore ognor diventa.

88.

Che farò dunque? io non so che mi fare,
  Se non chiamarti Criseida bella;
  Tu sola se' che mi puoi aiutare,
  Tu valorosa donna, tu se' quella
  Che sola puoi il mio fuoco attutare,
  O dolce luce e del mio cuor fiammella;
  Or foss'io teco una notte di verno,
  Cento cinquanta poi stessi in inferno.

89.

Che farò, Pandar? Tu non di' niente?
  Tu mi vedi ardere in sì fatto fuoco,
  E vista fai di non aver la mente
  A' miei sospiri, dove ch' io mi cuoco;
  Aiutami, io ten prego caramente,
  Dimmi ch' io faccia, consigliami un poco;
  Che se da te o da lei non ho soccorso,
  Di morte nelle reti son trascorso.

90.

Pandaro disse allora: io veggio bene
  Ed odo quanto di', nè sonmi infinto,
  Nè mai m'infingerò alle tue pene
  Donare aiuto, e sempre son succinto
  A far non sol per te ciò che conviene,
  Ma ogni cosa senza esser sospinto
  O da forza o da prego: fa' tu ch' io
  Aperto veggia il tuo caldo disio.

* Savj-Lopez, *soffere*

87.

"She looketh at me and permitteth me to look modestly at her. This should suffice my inflamed desires. But my eager appetite would wish I know not what more. So poorly regulated are the ardors that excite it that he who should not experience it, would not believe how much this flame, which waxeth greater every hour, tormenteth me.

88.

"What shall I do then? I know not what to do, if not to call upon thee, fair Cressida. Thou alone art she who canst aid me, thou priceless lady; thou alone art she who canst quench my fire. O sweet light and dear flame of my heart! Might I pass a winter's night with thee, I would then remain an hundred and fifty in hell.

89.

"What shall I do, Pandarus? Sayest thou naught? Thou beholdest me glow in such a fire and dost appear to have no thought for the sighs wherein I burn. Help me, I pray thee dearly, tell me what I shall do, give me a word of advice. For if from thee or from her I have not succor, I am caught in the snares of death."

90.

Pandarus then said: "I see well and hear all thou sayest, nor have I feigned nor ever shall feign to give aid to all thy sufferings, and ever am I prepared to do for thee not only what is fitting, but anything, without being urged either by force or by prayer. Let me behold openly thy warm desire.

91.

Io so che in ogni cosa per un sei
   Tu vedi più di me, ma tuttavia
   S' io fossi in te, intiera scriverei
   Ad essa di mia man la pena mia;
   E sopra ciò, per Dio la pregherei,
   E per amore e per sua cortesia,
   Che di me le calesse, e questo scritto,
   Io glielo porterò senza rispitto.

92.

Ed oltre a questo, ancora a mio potere
   La pregherò ch' abbia di te mercede:
   Quel ch' ella rispondrà potrai vedere,
   E già di certo l'animo mio crede,
   Che sua risposta ti dovrà piacere;
   E però scrivi, e ponvi ogni tua fede,
   Ogni tua pena, ed il disio appresso,
   Nulla lasciar che non vi sia espresso.

93.

Questo consiglio a Troilo piacque assai,
   Ma come amante timido, rispose:
   Oimè, Pandaro, che tu vederai,
   Come si vede che son vergognose
   Le donne, che lo scritto che portrai,
   Criseida per vergogna, con noiose
   Parole rifiutarlo, e peggiorato
   Avremo oltre misura il nostro stato.

94.

A ciò Pandaro disse: se ti piace
   Fa' quel ch' io dico, e poi mi lascia fare;
   Che se amore mi ponga in la sua pace,
   Io te ne credo risposta recare
   Di sua man fatta; e se ciò ti dispiace,
   Timido e tristo te ne puoi stare.
   Ripeterai poi te del tuo tormento,
   Per me non rimarrà farti contento.

91.

"I know that in everything thou art six times as discerning as I. But nevertheless, if I were in thy place, I would write to her in mine own hand all about mine anguish, and, beyond this, I would beseech her by the gods, and by Love, and by her courtesy, that she should care for me. And if thou write this, I will bear it to her without delay.

92.

"And besides this, to the extent of my power I will pray her to have pity upon thee. What she will reply thou shalt see. Already my soul believeth of a certainty that her reply will be sure to please thee. Therefore write and put therein all thy faith, all thy grief, and then thy desire. Omit nothing; tell all."

93.

This advice pleased Troilus greatly, but as a timid lover he replied: "Ah me, Pandarus, thou shalt see, inasmuch as ladies are observed to be shamefaced, that Cressida for shame will reject with angry words the writing which thou shalt carry, and we shall be in a far worse plight."

94.

To this Pandarus: "If it pleaseth thee, do what I tell thee, and then leave matters to me. For, an Love be not my enemy, I will bring thee, I believe, a reply written in her own hand. If it displeaseth thee, timid and sad mayest thou remain because of it. If thou wilt persist in thy misery, it will not be my task to content thee."

95.

Allora disse Troilo: fatto sia
  Il piacer tuo; io vado e scriveraggio;
  Ed amor prego per sua cortesia,
  Lo scrivere, e la lettera, e il viaggio
  Fruttevol faccia. E di quindi s'invia
  Alla camera sua, e come saggio
  Alla sua donna carissima scrisse
  Una lettera presto, e così disse.

96.

Come può quegli che in affanno è posto,
  In pianto grave e in istato molesto,
  Come io son per te, donna, disposto
  Ad alcun dar salute? certo chiesto
  Esser non dee da lui; ond' io mi scosto
  Da quel che fanno gli altri; e sol per questo
  Qui da me salutata non sarai,
  Perch' io non l'ho se tu non la mi dai.

97.

Io non posso fuggir quel ch' amor vuole,
  Il qual più vil di me fe' già ardito,
  Ed el mi strigne a scriver le parole,
  Come vedrai, e vuol pure obbedito
  Esser da me, siccome egli esser suole;
  Però se per me fia in ciò fallito,
  Lui ne riprendi, ed a me perdonanza
  Ti prego doni, dolce mia speranza.

98.

L'alta bellezza tua, e lo splendore
  De' tuoi vaghi occhi e de' costumi ornati;
  L' onestà cara e' l donnesco valore,
  I modi e gli atti più ch' altri lodati,
  Nella mia mente hanno lui per signore,
  E te per donna in tal guisa fermati,
  Ch' altro accidente mai fuorchè la morte,
  A tirarline fuor non saria forte.

95.

Then said Troilus: "Be it as thou pleasest. I will go and write. And I pray Love of his courtesy that he make fruitful the writing, the letter, and the journey." And he went thence to his room, and like a wise man at once wrote to his dearest lady a letter. And thus he said:

96.

"How can he who is placed in torment, in heavy sorrow, and in grievous state, as I am for thee, lady, give good health to anyone? Certainly it should not be expected of him. Therefore I am departing from the practice of others. Thou shalt lack good health from me only for this reason, because I have it not to give, unless thou givest it to me.

97.

"I cannot escape what Love wisheth, who before now hath emboldened lowlier than I. He constraineth me to write the words, as thou shalt see, and wisheth to be implicitly obeyed by me, as he is wont to be. Therefore if I make a mistake in this letter, let his be the blame, and grant pardon to me, I pray thee, my sweet hope.

98.

"Thy lofty beauty, and the splendor of thy lovely eyes and of thine accomplished manners, thy dear modesty, and thy womanly worth, thy ways and actions, more praised than others, have in my mind so established him for lord and thee for lady that no other accident save death would ever be strong enough to pluck you out of it.

99.

E che ch' io faccia, l' imagine bella
  Di te sempre nel cor reca un pensiero,
  Che ogn' altro caccia che d' altro favella
  Che sol di te, benchè d' altro nel vero
  All' anima non caglia, fatta ancella
  Del tuo valor, nel quale io solo spero :
  E 'l nome tuo m' è sempre nella bocca,
  E il cor con più disio ognor mi tocca.

100.

Da queste cose, donna, nasce un fuoco
  Che giorno e notte l' anima martira,
  Senza lasciarmi in posa trovar loco ;
  Piangono gli occhi, e 'l petto ne sospira,
  E consumar mi sento a poco a poco
  Da questo ardor che dentro a me s' aggira ;
  Per che ricorrere alla tua virtute
  Sol mi convien, se voglio aver salute.

101.

Tu sola puoi queste pene noiose,
  Quando tu vogli, porre in dolce pace ;
  Tu sola puoi l'afflizïon penose,
  Madonna, porre in riposo verace ;
  Tu sola puoi con l' opere pietose
  Tormi il tormento che sì mi disface ;
  Tu sola puoi, siccome donna mia,
  Adempier ciò che lo mio cuor disia.

102.

Dunque, se mai per pura fede alcuno,
  Se mai per grande amor, se per disio
  Di ben servire ognora in ciascheduno
  Caso, qual si volesse o buono o rio,
  Meritò grazia, fa' ch'io ne sia uno,
  Cara mia donna ; fa' ch' io sia quell' io,
  Che a te ricorro, sì come a colei
  Che se' cagion di tutti i sospir miei.

99.

"And do what I may, the beautiful image of thee bringeth ever into my heart a thought which driveth forth any other which speaketh of anyone else than of thee alone, although of any other one my soul hath indeed no care, since it is made handmaid of thy worth, in which alone my hope is fixed. Thy name is ever on my lips, and toucheth my heart every hour with greater desire.

100.

"From all this, lady, there ariseth a fire which tortureth my soul day and night, without allowing me to find opportunity for rest. Mine eyes weep and my breast sigheth thereat, and little by little I feel myself consumed by this ardor that stirreth about within me. For this reason it behooveth me to have recourse solely to thy virtue, if I wish to have relief.

101.

"Thou alone, when thou wishest, canst give these sore torments sweet peace. Thou alone, my lady, canst give this painful affliction surcease. Thou alone with tender ministrations canst remove from me the torture that so undoeth me. Thou alone, as my lady, canst accomplish what my heart desireth.

102.

"Therefore if ever anyone by pure fidelity, if ever by great love, if by desire always to serve well in every case, whether good or evil, deserved grace, grant that I be one of them, dear my lady, grant that I be one of them, I who for refuge come to thee, as to her who is the cause of all my sighs.

103.

Assai conosco, che mai meritato
 Non fu per mio servir quel per che vegno;
 Ma sola tu che m'hai il cor piagato,
 E altro no di maggior cosa degno,
 Mi puoi far, quando vogli; o disiato
 Ben del mio cor, pon giù l'altero sdegno
 Dell' animo tuo grande, e sii umile
 Ver me, quanto negli atti se' gentile.

104.

Ora son certo che sarai pietosa
 Come se' bella, e la mia greve noia,
 Discretamente lieta e grazïosa,
 Senza volere ch' io misero muoia
 Per molto amarti, donna dilettosa,
 Ancora tornerà in dolce gioia.
 Io te ne prego, se 'l mio prego vale,
 Per quel'* amor del quale or più ti cale.

105.

Io come ch' io sia un piccol dono,
 E poco possa, e vaglia molto meno,
 Senza fallo nïun tutto tuo sono.
 Or tu se' savia, s' io non dico appieno,
 Intenderai assai me' ch' io non ragiono,
 E spero simil che l'opere fieno
 Migliori assai che mio merto, e maggiore;
 Amore a ciò sì ti disponga il cuore.

106.

El mi restava molte cose a dire,
 Ma per non farti noia il vo' tacere;
 E in questo fine prego il dolce sire
 Amor, che come te nel mio piacere
 Ha posto, così me nel tuo disire
 Ponga con quel medesimo volere,
 Sicchè com' io son tuo alcuna volta
 Tu mia diventi, e mai non mi sii tolta.

* Savj-Lopez, *quell'*

103.

"I know well that I have never deserved by my service that for which I come. But thou alone, who hast wounded my heart, thou and none other, canst, when thou wilt, make me worthy of a greater thing. O desired weal of my heart, lay aside the lofty disdain of thy great spirit, and be condescending toward me, in so much as thou art gentle in thine actions.

104.

"Certain I am that thou wilt be merciful as thou art fair, and that my sore distress, discreetly amiable and gracious one, who dost not wish that I perish in my misery for loving thee so much, will turn, delectable lady, to sweet joy. I beseech thee for it, if my prayer availeth, by that love for which thou mayest by now have more concern.

105.

"Although a small gift, with little ability, and much less worth, I am without fail all thine. Wise as thou art, thou wilt understand, if I do not speak adequately, that I am not a talker. In like manner I hope that thine acts will be much better and greater than my deserts. May Love dispose thine heart to this.

106.

"I had many more things in mind to say but in order not to annoy thee, I will suppress them. In conclusion I pray the sweet lord Love that, as he hath placed thee in my delight, so with the same willingness he place me in thy desire, that, as I am thine, so thou mayest at some time become mine and may never be taken away from me."

107.

Scritte adunque tutte queste cose
  In una carta, per ordin piegolla,
  E sulle guance tutte lagrimose
  Bagnò la gemma, e quindi suggellolla,
  E nella mano a Pandaro la pose,
  E cento volte e più prima baciolla:
  Lettera mia, dicendo, tu sarai
  Beata, in man di tal donna verrai.

108.

Pandaro presa la lettera pia
  N' andò verso Criseida; la quale
  Come 'l vide venir, la compagnia
  Colla qual' era lasciata, cotale
  Gli si fe' incontro parte della via,
  Qual pare in vista perla orïentale,
  Temendo e disiando; e' salutarsi
  Di lungi assai, poi per la man pigliarsi.

109.

Quindi disse Criseida: quale affare
  Or qui ti mena? hai tu altre novelle?
  Alla qual Pandar senza dimorare
  Disse: Donna, per te l' ho buone e belle,
  Ma non tai per altrui, come mostrare
  Ti potran queste scritte tapinelle
  Di colui, che per te mi par vedere
  Morir, sì poco te ne è in calere.

110.

Tolle, e vedralle* diligentemente,
  Ed alcuna risposta il farà lieto.
  Stette Criseida timorosamente
  Senza pigliarle, e un poco il mansueto
  Viso cambiò, e quindi pianamente
  Disse: Pandaro mio, se in quïeto
  Stato ti ponga amor, abbi rispetto
  Alquanto a me, non pure al giovinetto.

* Savj-Lopez, *vedraile*

107.

Then after writing all these things on a paper, he folded it in order, and wetted the seal against his tearful cheeks. Then he sealed it and put it in Pandarus' hands. First he kissed it a hundred times and more, saying: "Letter mine, how blissful wilt thou be, into the hand of such a lady shalt thou come!"

108.

Pandarus took the pitiful letter and went off to Cressida. When she saw him coming she left the company in which she was, and went part way to meet him, appearing in sight as doth an oriental pearl, overcome alike with fear and with desire. From afar they saluted one another and then took each other by the hand.

109.

Then said Cressida: "What business now bringeth thee here? Hast thou further news?" To her Pandarus replied: "Lady, for thee have I news good and favorable, but not for someone else, as can show thee these wretched writings of him whom I seem to see die for thee, so little dost thou care for him.

110.

"Take them away and peruse them diligently. Any answer will make him happy." Cressida stood timorously, without taking them, and her gentle aspect changed a little. Then she said softly: "My Pandarus, an I hope Love may give thee peace, have some little regard for me as well as for the youth.

111.

Guarda se quel che chiedi or si conviene,
  E tu stesso sii giudice di questo,
  E vedi se prendendole fo bene,
  E se 'l tuo domandare è tanto onesto,
  E se si vuol per alleggiar le pene
  Altrui, per sè far atto disonesto;
  Deh non le mi lasciar Pandaro mio,
  Portale indietro per l' amor di Dio.

112.

Pandaro alquanto di questo turbato
  Disse: Questo è a pensar nuova cosa,
  Che quel che più dalle donne è bramato,
  Di ciò ciascuna e ischifa e crucciosa
  Si mostra innanzi altrui: io t' ho parlato
  Tanto di questo, ch' omai vergognosa
  Non dovresti esser meco; i' te ne priego,
  Che or di questo non mi facci niego.

113.

Criseida sorrise lui udendo,
  E quelle prese, e messesele in seno:
  Quando avrò agio, poi a lui dicendo,
  Le vederò come saprò appieno;
  Se io fo men che ben questo facendo,
  Il non poter del tuo piacer far meno
  Me n' è cagion; Iddio dal cielo il vegga,
  Ed alla mia semplicità provvegga.

114.

Partissi Pandar poi glie l' ebbe date,
  Ed essa vaga molto di vedere
  Quel che dicesser, sue cagion trovate,
  L' altre compagne sue lasciò a sedere,
  Ne gì nella sua camera, e spiegate,
  Lesse e rilesse quelle con piacere,
  E ben s' accorse che Troilo ardea
  Vie più assai che in atto non parea.

111.

"Consider whether what thou now asketh is fitting, and do thou thyself be judge of this, and take thought whether in accepting these I do right, and whether thy request is altogether modest, and whether, in order to alleviate the pain of another, it is desirable to do that which is in itself an immodest act. Ah, do not leave them with me, my Pandarus, take them back for the love of the gods."

112.

Pandarus was somewhat disturbed by this and said: "A strange thing is this to consider that at what is most desired by her sex each lady should, in the presence of others, show herself annoyed and vexed. I have spoken to thee so much of this matter that thenceforth thou shouldst not play the prude with me. I beseech thee not to deny me this."

113.

Cressida smiled when she heard him, and took them, and thrust them into her bosom. Then she said to him: "When I have time, I shall peruse them to the best of my ability. If in doing this I do less than well, my inability to do less than thy pleasure is the reason. May the gods bear witness thereof from heaven and make provision for my simple-mindedness."

114.

Pandarus gave them to her and left. She was very eager to see what they said, and when she found opportunity, she left her other companions in their seats, and went away to her room, and after unfolding them, read and reread them with delight, and clearly perceived that Troilus was much more on fire than appeared in his outward demeanor.

115.

Il che caro le fu, perchè trafitta
   Esser sentissi l' anima nel core,
   Di che ella viveva molto afflitta,
   Come che punto non paresse fuore:
   E ben notata ogni parola scritta,
   Di ciò lodò e ringraziò amore,
   Seco dicendo: a spegner questo foco
   Conviene a me trovare il tempo e 'l loco:

116.

Che s' io il lascio in troppo grande arsura
   Moltiplicare, e' potrebbe avvenire,
   Che nella scolorita mia figura
   Si vederebbe il nascoso disire,
   Che mi saria non piccola sciagura;
   Ed io per me non intendo morire,
   Nè far morire altrui, quando con gioia
   Posso schifar la mia e l' altrui noia.

117.

Io non sarò per lo certo disposta,
   Siccome io sono infino ad ora stata;
   Se Pandar tornerà per la risposta,
   Io glie la darò piacevole e grata,
   Se mi costasse, come non mi costa:
   Nè da Troilo sarò mai dispietata
   Potuta dire; or foss' io nelle braccia
   Dolci di lui, stretta a faccia a faccia!

118.

Pandaro che da Troilo sovente
   Era studiato, a Criseida reddío,
   E sorridendo disse: donna, chente
   Ti par lo scriver dell' amico mio?
   Ella divenne rossa immantinente,
   Senza dir altro, se non: Sallo Iddio.
   A cui Pandaro disse: hai tu risposto?
   Al qual ella gabbando, disse: tosto?

115.

This was a comfort to her because she felt the soul in her heart transfixed. Wherefore she lived very disconsolate, although it did not appear at all outwardly. And after carefully noting every word that was written, she praised and thanked Love for it, saying to herself: "It is fitting that I find time and place to quench this fire.

116.

"For if I let it multiply into too great heat, my hidden desire might appear in my colorless face, which would be no small disgrace to me. And I on my part have no intent to die or to let another die, when with delight I can avoid my own and another's distress.

117.

"I shall certainly not remain so disposed as I have been up to the present. If Pandarus return for the answer, I shall give it to him amiably and agreeably, if it should cost me something, as it doth not. Nor can I ever more be called cruel by Troilus. Would that I were now in his sweet arms, pressed face to face with him!"

118.

After frequent promptings from Troilus Pandarus returned to Cressida and said with a smile: "Lady, what thinkest thou of my friend's writing?" She turned red at once and said naught save: "The gods know." Pandarus said to her: "Hast thou replied?" To him she said jestingly: "So soon?"

119.

S' io debbo mai potere adoperare
Per te, Pandaro disse, or fa' di farlo.
Ed ella a lui: io non lo so ben fare.
Deh, disse Pandar, pensa d' appagarlo,
E' suole amor saper bene insegnare;
I' ho sì gran disio di confortarlo,
Che tu nol crederesti in fede mia,
La tua risposta sol questo porìa.*

120.

Ed io 'l farò poichè t' aggrada tanto;
Ma voglia Iddio che ben la cosa vada!
Deh sì anderà, disse Pandaro, in quanto
Colui il vale, a cui più ch' altro aggrada.
Poi si partì: ed ella dall' un canto
Della camera sua, dove più rada
Usanza di venire ad ogni altro era,
A scriver giù si pose in tai maniera:

121.

A te amico discreto e possente,
Il qual forte di me t' inganna amore,
Com' uom preso per me indebitamente,
Criseida, salvato il suo onore,
Manda salute, e poi umilemente
Si raccomanda al tuo alto valore,
Vaga di compiacerti, dove sia
L' onestà salva, e la castità mia.

122.

I' ho avute da colui, che t' ama
Tanto perfettamente, che non cura
Già d' alcuno mio onor nè di mia fama,
Piene le carte della tua scrittura;
Nelle quai lessi la tua vita grama
Non senza doglia, s' io abbia ventura
Che mi sia cara e benchè sian fregiate
Di lacrime, pur l' ho assai mirate.

* Savj-Lopez, *poria*

119.

"If I am ever to go on thine errand," said Pandarus, "see now that thou do it." And she to him: "I do not know how to do it well." "Ah," said Pandarus, "try to satisfy him. Love is a good instructor. I have so great a desire to comfort him that upon my faith thou wouldst not believe it. Thy reply alone could do this."

120.

"I will do it because it pleaseth thee so much. But may the gods grant that matters go well!" "Ah, so they will," said Pandarus, "inasmuch as he, to whom it giveth more pleasure than anything else, is worth it." Then he departed. And in the least frequented corner of her room she sat down to write in the following manner:

121.

"To thee, discreet and powerful friend, whom Love greatly infatuateth for me, as a man unduly enamored of me, Cressida, her honor preserved, sendeth greeting, and thereafter humbly recommendeth herself to thy high worthiness, being anxious to please thee provided my honor and chastity be safe.

122.

"I have received from him who loveth thee so perfectly that he careth not any more for any honor of mine or for my good name, pages full of thy writing. In them I read thy wretched life not without grief, as I hope to have the fortune which is dear to me. Although they are adorned with tears, I have pondered them diligently.

123.

Ed ogni cosa con ragion pensando,
  E l' afflizione e 'l tuo addomandare,
  La fede, e la speranza esaminando,
  Non veggio com' io possa soddisfare
  Assai acconciamente al tuo dimando,
  Volendo bene e intiero riguardare
  Ciò che nel mondo più è da gradire,
  Ch' è in onestà vivere e morire.

124.

Come che il compiacerti saria bene,
  Se il mondo fosse tal chente dovrebbe;
  Ma perchè è tal qual è, a noi conviene
  Per forza usarlo; seguir ne potrebbe,
  Altro facendo, disperate pene;
  Alla pietà per cui di te m' increbbe,
  Malgrado mio pur mi convien dar lato,
  Di che sarai da me poco appagato.

125.

Ma è sì grande la virtù ch' io sento
  In te, ch' io so ch' aperto vederai
  Ciò ch' a me si conviene, e che contento
  Di ciò ch' io ti rispondo tu sarai,
  E porrai modo al tuo grave tormento,
  Che nel cor mi dispiace e noia assai;
  In verità, se non si disdicesse,
  Volentier farei ciò che ti piacesse.

126.

Poco è lo scriver, come puoi vedere,
  Ed arte in questa lettera, la quale
  Vorrei che più ti recasse piacere,
  Ma non si può ciò che si vuole avale,
  Forse farà ancor luogo il potere
  Al buon volere, e se non ti par male,
  Presta alla pena tua alquanto sosta,
  Perchè non ha ogni detto risposta.

123.

"And as I think everything over reasonably, and weigh thine affliction, and thy request, thy faith, and thy hope, I do not see how I can satisfy thy request very suitably, wishing as I do to have full regard to what is most to be desired in the world, namely, to live and die in good repute.

124.

"Although it would be well to please thee, if the world were what it ought to be, yet since it is what it is, we must perforce make the best of it. If we were to do otherwise, extreme suffering might follow. Despite myself must I put aside the pity I felt for thee, whereby thou wilt gain but little satisfaction from me.

125.

"But so great is the virtue which I perceive in thee that I know thou wilt see clearly what is proper for me, and that thou wilt be satisfied with my reply, and wilt moderate thy severe grief, which greatly displeaseth and troubleth my heart. In truth, if it were not unbecoming, willingly would I do what would please thee.

126.

"Of little worth, as thou canst see, is the writing and the art in this letter. I would wish that it might bring thee more pleasure but what is wished can do but little good. The power to do will perhaps sometime take the place of good intentions. If it doth not displease thee, give a little respite to thy sorrow at my not having replied to all thou hast said.

127.

Il proferir che fai, qui non ha loco,
Che certa son ch' ogni cosa faresti;
Ed io nel ver, come ch' io vaglia poco,
Vie più che mille volte mi potesti*
E puoi aver per tua, se 'l crudel fuoco
Non m' arda, il che son certa non vorresti;
Nè dico più, se non ch' io prego Iddio
Che ne contenti il tuo e 'l mio disio.

128.

E poi ch' ell' ebbe in cotal guisa detto,
La ripiegò, e suggellolla, e diella
A Pandaro, il qual tosto il giovinetto
Troilo cercando, a lui n' andò con ella,
E presentogliel con sommo diletto;
Il qual presala, ciò che scritto in quella
Era con fretta lesse, e sospirando,
Secondo le parole il cuor cambiando.

129.

Ma pure in fine, seco ripetendo
Bene ogni cosa che ella scrivea,
Disse fra sè: se io costei intendo,
Amor la stringe, ma siccome rea,
Sotto lo scudo ancor si va chiudendo;
Ma non potrà, pur che forza mi dea
Amore a sofferir, guari durare,
Ch' ella non vegna a tutt' altro parlare.

130.

E 'l somigliante ne pareva ancora
A Pandaro, col qual diceva tutto;
Per che più che l' usato si rincora
Troilo, lasciando alquanto il tristo lutto,
E spera in breve deggia venir l' ora
Che il suo martiro deggia render frutto;
E questo chiede, e dì e notte chiama,
Come colui che solamente il brama.

* Savj-Lopez, *protesti*

127.

"There is no need for the protestations which thou makest, for I am certain that thou wouldst perform everything. And me indeed, though of little worth, thou couldst and canst have for thine even more than a thousand times, an the cruel fire do not burn me, which I am certain thou wouldst not wish. I say no more, save to pray the gods to satisfy thy desire and mine."

128.

When she had spoken in such wise, she folded it, and sealed it, and gave it to Pandarus. Starting at once in search of the youth Troilus, he went off with it to him, and gave it to him with the greatest delight. He took it, read in haste what had been written therein, sighing the while and suffering change of heart according to the words.

129.

But at last, repeating to himself every thing she had written, he said to himself: "If I understand her, Love constraineth her, but as a guilty person she still goeth skulking behind the shield. But if Love give me strength to suffer, she cannot delay long before coming to quite different speech."

130.

And Pandarus, with whom he discussed the whole matter, agreed with him. Therefore he taketh fresh heart more than ever, leaving somewhat his sad affliction, and hopeth that the hour is soon to come that must bring reward to his suffering. This he imploreth and day and night beseecheth, as one whose heart is set on this alone.

131.

Crescea di giorno in giorno più l' ardore,
  E come che speranza l' aiutasse
  A sostener, pure era grave al core;
  E deesia creder* che assai il noiasse,
  Per che più volte dal suo gran fervore
  Stimar si può che lettere dittasse,
  Alle quai quando lieta e quando amara
  Risposta gli veniva, e spessa e rara.

132.

Per che sovente d' amor si dolea,
  E di fortuna cui tenea nemica,
  E spesse volte, oimè, seco dicea,
  Se un poco più la pungesse l' ortica
  D' amor, com' ella me trafigge e screa,
  La vita mia di sollazzo mendica
  Tosto verrebbe al grazïoso porto,
  Al qual prima ch' io vegna sarò morto.

133.

Pandaro che sentia le fiamme accese
  Nel petto di colui che egli amava,
  Era di preghi suoi spesso cortese
  A Criseida, e tutto gli narrava
  Ciò che di Troilo vedeva palese;
  La quale ancor che lieta l' ascoltava,
  Diceva: i' non posso altro, io gli fo quello,
  Che m' imponesti, caro mio fratello.

134.

Non basta questo, Pandar rispondea,
  Io vo' che tu 'l conforti e che gli parli.
  A cui Criseida all' incontro dicea:
  Cotesto non intendo io mai di farli,
  Che la corona dell' onestà mea
  Per partito nïun non vo donarli;
  Come fratel per la sua gran bontade
  L' amerò sempre, e per la sua onestade.

* Savj-Lopez, *deesi creder*

131.

From day to day his ardor increased, and although hope helped to sustain him, he was still heavy at heart. And it must be supposed that it troubled him greatly. Wherefore it may be guessed that many a time he wrote letters in great fervor. To these there came to him reply, now gentle and now harsh, now often and now seldom.

132.

Therefore he often complained of love, and of fortune, which he held his enemy. Oftentimes he said to himself: "Alas, if the nettle of love should a little more prick her, as it pierceth and tormenteth me, my life, bereft of solace, would quickly come to the gracious port to which before I come, I shall be dead."

133.

Pandarus, who perceived the flames enkindled in the breast of him whom he loved, was often liberal of his prayers to Cressida, and related to her without concealment all that he observed of Troilus. Although glad to hear it, she said: "I can do naught else; I am doing for him what thou didst enjoin upon me, my dear brother."

134.

"This is not enough," replied Pandarus. "I wish thee to comfort and speak to him." To him Cressida said in reply: "This mean I never to do for him, for the crown of my virtue I intend on no account to give him. As a brother shall I love him ever because of his great goodness and because of his noble nature."

135.

Pandaro rispondea : Questa corona
Lodano i preti a cui tor non la ponno,
E ciaschedun com' un santo ragiona,
E poi vi colgon tutte quante al sonno.
Di Troilo non saprà giammai persona ;
Or pena assai, e fa' pur ben del donno.
Assai fa mal chi può far ben nol face.
Che 'l perder tempo a chi più sa più spiace.

136.

Criseida dicea : La sua virtute
Tenera so che è del mio onore,
Nè da me altro che cose dovute
Domanderia, tant' è il suo valore ;
Ed io ti giuro per la mia salute,
Ch' io son, da quel che tu domandi in fuore
Sua mille volte più ch' io non son mia,
Tanto m' aggrada la sua cortesia.

137.

Se el t' aggrada, che vai tu cercando ?
Deh lascia star questa salvatichezza ;
Intendi tu che el si muoia amando ?
Ben potrai cara aver la tua bellezza
Se uccidi un tal uom ; deh dimmi, quando
Tu vuoi ch' ei venga a te ? cui e' più prezza
Che non fa il ciel, e dimmi come, e dove ;
Non voler vincer tutte le tue prove.

138.

Oimè lassa ! a che m' hai tu condotta,
Pandaro mio, e che vuoi tu ch' io faccia ?
Tu hai l' onestà mia spezzata e rotta,
Io non ardisco di mirarti in faccia ;
Oimè lassa ! misera, a che otta
La riavrò ? il sangue mi s' agghiaccia
Intorno al cor, pensando quel che chiedi,
E tu non te ne curi, e chiaro il vedi.

[230]

135.

Pandarus replied: "This crown the priests commend in those of you from whom they cannot take it. Each of them talketh like a saint and then surpriseth all of you that he can in sleep. No one will ever know about Troilus. He now suffereth much and hath only the prospect of thy gift to console him. Very ill doeth he who can act well and doth not, for the wiser a man is, the more doth the loss of time displease him."

136.

Cressida said: "I know that his virtue is tender of my honor, and that he would not ask of me other than he ought, so great is his worthiness. I swear to thee by my hope of salvation that I am, apart from what thou asketh of me, a thousand times more his than I am my own, so much doth his courtesy delight me."

137.

"If he pleaseth thee, what art thou in search of? Ah, lay aside this harshness! Dost thou intend that he die of love? Well wilt thou be able to hold thy beauty dear, if thou slay such a man. Ah, tell me, when dost thou wish that he come to thee, to whom this privilege is a greater prize than the heavens have to offer? Tell me, how, and where? Do not try to conquer all thy scruples."

138.

"Ah me, alas! To what hast thou led me, my Pandarus, and what dost thou wish that I do? Thou hast broken and shattered my sense of shame. I dare not look thee in the face. Ah me, wretched one that I am! When shall I have it again? My blood turneth ice about my heart, when I think of what thou askest, and thou hast no care thereat, and seest it clearly.

139.

Io vorrei esser morta il giorno ch' io
    Qui nella loggia tanto t' ascoltai;
    Tu mi mettesti nel cuore un disio,
    Ch' appena credo ch' el n' esca giammai;
    E che mi fia cagion dell' onor mio
    Perdere, o lassa, e d' infiniti guai;
    Or più non posso, poichè t' è in piacere,
    Disposta sono a fare il tuo volere.

140.

Ma se alcun prego val nel tuo cospetto,
    Ti prego, dolce e caro mio fratello,
    Che tutto ciascun nostro fatto o detto
    Occulto sia; tu puoi ben veder quello
    Che seguir ne potria, se tale affetto
    Venisse a luce: deh parlane ad ello,
    E fannel savio, e come tempo fia,
    Io farò ciò che 'l suo piacer disia.

141.

Rispose Pandar: Guarda la tua bocca,
    Che el per sè, nè io, mai il diremo.
    Ora hammi tu, diss' ella, per sì sciocca,
    Che vedi di paura tutta tremo
    Che non si sappia, ma poichè ti tocca
    L' onore e la vergogna che n' avremo
    Siccome a me, passerommene in pace,
    E tu ne fa' omai come ti piace.

142.

Pandar disse: Di ciò non dubitare,
    Che in ciò avremo ben buona cautela;
    Quando vuoi tu che ti venga a parlare?
    Tiriamo ormai a capo questa tela;
    Che 'l farlo tosto, poichè si dee fare,
    Fia molto meglio, e molto me' si cela
    Dopo il fatto l' amor, poscia ch' avrete
    Composto insieme ciò che far dovrete.

139.

"I would wish that I had been dead the day that I so much hearkened to thee here in this apartment. Thou didst put in my heart a desire that I believe will hardly ever depart from it. It will be the occasion of losing my honor, alas, and of infinite woes. I can do no more. Since it is to thy pleasure, I am disposed to do thy will.

140.

"But if any request have value in thy sight, I pray thee, sweet and dear my brother, that all that each of us hath said and done, be kept secret. Thou canst well see what might follow, if such a passion should come to light. Speak to him of it, and apprize him of it. As opportunity offereth, I will do what your pleasure desireth."

141.

Pandarus replied: "Guard thy lips, for neither he, on his part, nor I will ever tell it." "Dost thou now," she said, "consider me so foolish, because thou seest me tremble all over with fear lest it be known? But since the honor and the shame that we shall have from it toucheth thee as well as me, I shall dismiss the matter from my mind, and do thou henceforth in regard to it as it pleaseth thee."

142.

Pandarus said: "Do not doubt that in this matter we shall exercise very good caution. When dost thou wish that he come to speak to thee? Let us now draw this business to a head. To do it quickly, since it is to be done, will be much better. Love is much more easily hidden after the deed, when you shall have arranged together what you will need to do."

143.

Tu sai, disse Criseida, che in questa
 Casa son donne ed altra gente meco,
 Delle quai parte alla futura festa
 Devono andare ; ed allor sarò seco.
 Questa tardanza non gli sia molesta ;
 Del modo e del venire allora teco
 Favellerò ; fa' pur ch' egli sia saggio,
 E sappia ben celare il suo coraggio.

143.

"Thou knowest," said Cressida, "that there are ladies and other people with me in this house. Some of them are to go to the coming festival. Then I shall remain with him. I hope that this delay cause him no anxiety. Of the manner of his coming I shall then talk with thee. See only that he be prudent and know well how to conceal his desires."

IL FILOSTRATO

DI

GIOVANNI BOCCACCIO

※

PARTE TERZA

ARGOMENTO

Comincia la terza parte del Filostrato, nella quale, dopo l'invocazione, Pandaro e Troilo insieme ragionano di dovere occultare ciò che con Criseida si fa. Troilo vi va nascosamente, e dilettasi, e ragionasi con Criseida; partesi e ritorna; e ritornato, sta in festa e in canti; e primieramente invoca l'autore.

1.

Fulvida luce, il raggio della quale
  Infino a questo loco m'ha guidato,
  Com' io volea per l' amorose sale;
  Or convien che 'l tuo lume duplicato
  Guidi l' ingegno mio, e faccil tale,
  Che in particella alcuna dichiarato
  Per me appaia il ben del dolce regno
  D'Amor, del qual fu fatto Troilo degno.

2.

Al qual regno pervien chi fedelmente
  Con senno e con virtù può sofferire
  D'amor la passione interamente;
  Per altro modo, rado pervenire
  Vi si può mai. Adunque sii presente,
  O bella donna, al mio alto disire;
  Riempi della grazia ch' io dimando,
  Le lodi tue continuerò cantando.

THE FILOSTRATO

OF

GIOVANNI BOCCACCIO

※

THIRD PART

ARGUMENT

Here beginneth the third part of the Filostrato, in which, after the invocation, Pandarus and Troilus speak together of the need of keeping secret that which toucheth Cressida. Troilus goeth thither secretly and taketh delight and speaketh with Cressida. He departeth and returneth. And after returning he abideth in joy and in song. And in the first place the invocation of the author.

1.

O shining light, whose rays have thus far guided me, as through the halls of Love I took my wingèd way, now is it fitting that thy redoubled radiance guide my invocation and make it such that the benefits of the sweet reign of Love may in every particular appear set forth by me.

2.

To that kingdom cometh he who with discretion and with virtue can suffer faithfully the passion of Love to the full. By other method rarely may he ever come thither. Therefore, O fair lady, favor my desire. Grant an abundance of the grace that I ask and I will continue to sing thy praises.

3.

Troilo ancora benchè molto ardesse,
  Nondimen bene star pur gli parea,
  Pensando sol che a Criseida piacesse,
  E ch' ella umilemente rispondea
  Alle lettere sue quando scrivesse;
  Ed ancor più, che qualor la vedea,
  Ella il guardava con sì dolce aspetto,
  Che a lui parea sentir sommo diletto.

4.

Erasi Pandar, come ho detto avanti,
  Dalla donna in concordia dipartito,
  E lieto nella mente e ne' sembianti
  Di Troilo cercava, che smarrito
  Intra lieta speranza e tristi pianti
  Lasciato avea quando se n' era gito;
  E tanto el gì in qua e 'n là cercando,
  Ch' egli il trovò in un tempio pensando.

5.

Il qual tantosto ch'ad esso pervenne,
  Da parte il trasse, e cominciógli a dire:
  Amico mio, tanto di te mi tenne,
  Quando uguanno ti vidi languire
  Sì forte per amor, che 'l cor sostenne
  Per te gran parte in sè del tuo martire;
  Che per darti conforto, riposato
  Non ho giammai, fin ch'io non l'ho trovato.

6.

Io son per te divenuto mezzano,
  Per te gittato ho in terra il mio onore,
  Per te ho io corrotto il petto sano
  Di mia sorella, e posto l' ho nel core
  Il tuo amor; nè passerà lontano
  Tempo, che la vedrai con più dolzore,
  Che porger non ti può la mia favella,
  Quando avrai in braccio Criseida bella.

3.

Although Troilus still suffered much from the ardor
of Love, yet it seemed that all was well with him,
wholly intent upon pleasing Cressida, and bearing in
mind that she had replied humbly to all his letters and
had moreover, whenever he had seen her, looked at him
with a glance so sweet that it seemed that he experienced the utmost delight.

4.

Pandarus, as I have said above, had departed from
the lady with inward satisfaction and joyful in mind
and in face went in search of Troilus, whom, when he
had gone from him, he had left torn between cheerful
hope and sad plaints. And he went looking for him in
this place and in that until he found him in a temple
lost in thought.

5.

As soon as he reached him, he drew him aside and
began to say: "My friend, when lately I saw thee languish so bitterly for Love, so much did it affect me that
for thy sake mine own heart bore a great part of thy
suffering. Therefore, to give thee comfort, I have never
rested until I found her.

6.

"I have for thy sake become a go-between; for thy
sake have I cast mine honor to the ground; for thy sake
have I corrupted the wholesome breast of my sister,
and put thy love in her heart. Nor will long time pass
ere thou shalt see her with more relish than this speech
of mine can afford thee, when thou shalt have lovely
Cressida in thine arms.

7.

Ma come Iddio che tutto quanto vede,
    E tu che 'l sai, a ciò non m' ha indotto
    Di premïo speranza, ma sol fede,
    Che come amico ti porto, e condotto
    M' ha ad oprar che tu trovi mercede;
    Per ch' io ti prego, se non ti sia rotto
    Da ria fortuna il disiato bene,
    Che facci come a saggio far conviene.

8.

Tu sai ch' egli è la fama di costei
    Santa nel vulgo, nè si disse mai
    Da nullo altro che tutto ben di lei;
    Or venuto è che tu nelle man l' hai,
    E puogliel tor se fai quel che non dei,
    Benchè addivenir ciò non può mai
    Senza mia gran vergogna, che parente
    Le sono, e trattator similemente.

9.

Perch' io ti prego tanto quant' io posso
    Che occulto sia tra noi questo mestiero.
    I' ho del cuor di Criseida rimosso
    Ogni vergogna e ciaschedun pensiero
    Che contro t' era, ed hol tanto percosso
    Col ragionar del tuo amor sincero,
    Che ella t' ama, ed è disposta a fare
    Ciò che ti piacerà di comandare.

10.

Nè fuor che tempo manca a tale effetto,
    Il qual come l' avrai, nelle sue braccia
    Ti metterò a prenderne diletto;
    Ma per Dio fa' che tal' opra si taccia,
    Nè t' esca fuor per caso alcun del petto,
    O caro amico mio, nè ti dispiaccia
    Se molte volte ti prego di questo,
    Tu vedi che ben 'l mio pregare è onesto.

7.

"But as the gods who behold everything, know, and as thou knowest, not hope of reward but only fealty, which I bear thee as a friend, hath brought me to this and led me to act so that thou mayest find recompense. Therefore I pray thee, an the desired weal be not reft from thee by dire fortune, act as becometh a prudent man.

8.

"Thou knowest her reputation is sound among the people nor hath aught else than all good been said of her by anyone. It hath now happened that thou hast it in thy hands and canst take it away from her, if thou dost what thou shouldst not, though this can never happen without great shame to me, who am her kinsman and guardian as well.

9.

"Therefore I pray thee as earnestly as I know how, that this matter be kept secret between us. I have removed from Cressida's heart every shyness and every thought that was against thee, and have so plied her with talk of thy sincere love that she loveth thee and is disposed to do what thou shalt wish to command.

10.

"Nor to this outcome is there lacking aught but opportunity, and when it cometh, I will put thee in her arms to take delight therein. But by the gods, see that this business be conducted secretly nor in any case issue forth from thy breast, O dear my friend, nor be displeased if many times I make to thee this entreaty. Thou seest that my prayer is honorable."

11.

Chi potria dire intera la letizia
  Che l' anima di Troilo sentiva
  Udendo Pandar? che la sua tristizia
  Com più parlava più scemando giva:
  I sospir ch' egli aveva a gran dovizia
  Gli dieder luogo, e la pena cattiva
  Si dipartì, e 'l viso lagrimoso,
  Bene sperando, divenne gioioso.

12.

E sì come la nuova primavera,
  Di fronde e di fioretti gli arboscelli,
  Ignudi stati in la stagion severa,
  Di subito riveste e fagli belli;
  I prati, e' colli, e ciascuna riviera
  Riveste d' erbe e di be' fior novelli,
  Così di nuova gioia tosto pieno,
  Sì rise Troilo nel viso sereno.

13.

E dopo un sospiretto, riguardando
  Pandar nel viso, disse: amico caro,
  Tu ti dei ricordare e come e quando
  Già pianger mi trovasti nell' amaro
  Tempo, che io solea avere amando;
  Ed ancor simil, quando procacciaro
  Le tue parole di voler sapere,
  Qual fosse la cagion del mio dolere;

14.

E sai quant' io mi tenni a discoprirlo
  A te, che sol mi se' unico amico;
  Nè era alcun periglio però a dirlo,
  Benchè perciò non fosse atto pudico;
  Pensa dunque ora come consentirlo
  I' potrei mai, che mentre teco il dico,
  Ch' altri nol senta tremo di paura,
  Tolga Iddio via cotal disavventura.

11.

Who could tell fully the joy that the soul of Troilus felt when he heard Pandarus? For the more he spake, the more his sorrow diminished. The sighs that he heaved in great abundance ceased, and his wretched sorrow departed, and his tearful face, now that his hopes were fair, became joyful.

12.

And just as the fresh spring suddenly reclotheth with leaves and with flowerets the shrubs that were bare in the severe season, and maketh them beautiful, revesteth the meadows and hills and every river bank with grass and with beautiful fresh flowers, just so did Troilus, full at once of new joy, smile with calm visage.

13.

And after a little sigh he looked Pandarus in the face and said: "Thou shouldst bear in mind how and when thou didst of yore find me weeping in the bitter time I was wont to have in my loving and still had when thy words sought to discover what was the occasion of my woe.

14.

"Thou knowest how much I hesitated to disclose it to thee, who art my one and only friend. Nor on this account was there any danger in telling it to thee, although for this reason it was not a modest act. Think then how I should ever be able to consent to it, who, while I tell thee of it, tremble lest someone hear it. May the gods avert such a disaster!

15.

Ma nondimen per quello Dio ti giuro,
  Che 'l cielo 'l e modo egualmente governa,
  E s' io non venga nelle man del duro
  Agamennon, che se mia vita eterna
  Fosse, come è mortal, tu puoi sicuro
  Viver, che a mio poter sarà interna
  Questa credenza, e in ogni atto servato
  L' onor di quella che m' ha 'l cor piagato.

16.

Quanto per me tu abbi detto e fatto
  Assai conosco e manifesto veggio,
  Nè meritar giammai in ciascun atto
  Nol ti potrei, che d' inferno e di peggio
  In paradiso posso dir m' hai tratto;
  Ma per l' amistà nostra ti richieggio,
  Che quel nome villan più non ti pogni,
  Dove sovvien dell' amico a' bisogni;

17.

Lascialo stare alli dolenti avari,
  Cui oro induce a sì fatto servigio;
  Tu fatto l'hai per trarmi degli amari
  Pianti ov' io era, e dal duro litigio
  Che io avea co' pensieri avversarj,
  E turbator d'ogni dolce vestigio,
  Siccome per amico si dee fare,
  Quando l'amico il vede tribolare.

18.

E perchè tu conosca quanta piena
  Benevolenza da me t'è portata,
  I' ho la mia sorella Polissena
  Più di bellezza ch' altra pregïata,
  Ed ancor c' è con esso lei Eléna
  Bellissima, la quale è mia cognata;
  Apri il cuor tuo, se te ne piace alcuna,
  Poi mi lascia operar con qual sia l'una.

15.

"Nevertheless I swear to thee by the gods, who hold equal control over the heaven and the earth, that, an I hope not to fall into the hands of the strong Agamemnon, if my life were eternal as it is mortal, thou canst rest assured that in so far as in me lieth, this secret will repose within my breast and that in every act will be safeguarded the honor of that lady who hath wounded my heart.

16.

"How much thou hast said and done for me I well know and plainly see. Nor should I ever in any act be able to reward thee for it. For thou hast, I may say, drawn me from hell and worse to heaven. But I beg thee by our friendship that thou no more apply that ugly name to thyself, where it is a question of coming to the relief of a friend.

17.

"Leave it to the wretched misers whom gold prompteth to such service. Thou hast done it to draw me from the bitter lamentations which were mine and from the sore conflict which I had with distressful thoughts—disturbers of every sweet memory—as should be done for a friend when the friend seeth him suffer.

18.

"And that thou mayest know how much complete good will is borne thee by me, I have my sister Polyxena, more praised for beauty than any other lady, and also there is with her that loveliest Helen, who is my kinswoman. Open thy heart, if either of them please thee; then let me arrange matters with which one it be.

19.

Ma poichè tanto hai fatto, assai più ch'io
  Pregato non t'avrei, metti in effetto
  Quando tempo parratti il mio disio;
  A te ricorro, e sol da te aspetto
  L'alto piacere ed il conforto mio,
  La gioia, e 'l bene, e 'l sollazzo, e 'l diletto;
  Nè più farò se non quanto dirai,
  Mio fia il diletto, e tu 'l grado n'avrai.

20.

Rimase Pandar di Troilo contento,
  E ciascheduno a sue bisogna attese.
  Ma come che a Troilo ogni dì cento
  Paresse d'esser con quella alle prese,
  Pur sofferia, e con sommo argomento
  In sè reggeva l'amorose offese,
  Dando a' pensier d'amor la notte parte,
  E 'l dì co' suoi al faticoso marte.

21.

In questo mezzo il tempo disiato
  Da' due amanti venne, donde fessi
  Criseida a chiamar Pandaro, e mostrato
  Tutto gliel' ha; ma Pandaro dolessi
  Di Troilo, che 'l dì davanti andato
  Era con certi, per bisogni espressi
  Della lor guerra, alquanto di lontano,
  Bench' el dovea tornare a mano a mano.

22.

Disselo a lei, il che udir gravoso
  Molto le fu, ma questo non ostante,
  Pandar, siccome amico studïoso,
  Mandò tosto per lui un presto fante,
  Il qual senza pigliare alcun riposo
  In breve spazio a Troilo fu davante,
  Il quale udito ciò perchè venia,
  Lieto per ritornar si mise in via.

19.

"But since thou hast done so much—so much more than I would have asked thee—, bring my desire to pass when opportunity presenteth itself to thee. To thee do I turn and from thee alone do I await my high pleasure, and my comfort, my joy, and my well-being, and my solace, and my delight. Nor shall I act except as thou shalt say. Mine will be the pleasure and thou shalt have the gratification of it."

20.

Pandarus was pleased with Troilus and each went about his affairs. But although with that lady as prize every day seemed an hundred to Troilus, he endured meekly and with high argument controlled within himself his amorous impulses, giving the night to thoughts of love and the day to strenuous warfare with his followers.

21.

In the meantime the opportunity desired by the two lovers arrived. Thereupon Pandarus had Cressida summoned and explained everything to her. But Pandarus was anxious about Troilus, who the day before had gone with certain companions some little distance on important business of the war, although he was expected to return presently.

22.

This he told her and she was much distressed to hear it. But notwithstanding, Pandarus, as a diligent friend, at once sent after him a nimble servant, who, without taking any rest, was in short time in the presence of Troilus, who, after hearing what he came for, in joyful mood made ready to return.

23.

E giunto a Pandar, da lui pienamente
  Intese ciò che esso far dovea;
  Laonde esso assai impaziente
  La notte attese, la qual gli parea
  Che si fuggisse, e poi tacitamente
  Con Pandar solo il suo cammin prendea
  In ver là dove Criseida stava,
  Che sola e paurosa l'aspettava.

24.

Era la notte oscura e nebulosa
  Come Troilo volea, il quale attento
  Mirando andava ciascheduna cosa,
  Non fosse alcuna desse sturbamento,
  O poco o assai, alla sua amorosa
  Voglia, la qual del suo grave tormento
  Fosse sperava, ed in parte segreta
  Sol se n'entrò nella casa già cheta.

25.

E in certo luogo rimoto ed oscuro,
  Come imposto gli fu, la donna attese;
  Nè gli fu l' aspettar forte nè duro,
  Nè il non veder dove fosse palese;
  Ma baldanzoso con seco e sicuro
  Spesso diceva: la donna cortese
  Tosto verrà, ed io sarò giocondo,
  Più che se sol fossi signor del mondo.

26.

Criseida l' aveva ben sentito
  Venire, perchè acciò ch' egli intendesse,
  Com' era imposto, ell' aveva tossito;
  E perchè l' esser non gli rincrescesse,
  Spesso parlava con suono spedito,
  Ed avacciava che ciascun sen giesse
  Tosto a dormir, dicendo ch' ella avea
  Tal sonno, che vegghiar più non potea.

23.

After reaching Pandarus he heard from him in full what he had to do. Thereupon he very impatiently awaited the night, which seemed to him to flee, and then quietly alone with Pandarus took his way whither Cressida was staying, who alone and in fear awaited him.

24.

The night was dark and cloudy, as Troilus wished, and he advanced watching each object attentively that there might be no unnecessary disturbance, little or great, to his amorous desire, which he hoped would free him from his severe torment. And by a secret approach he made his entrance alone into the house, which was already quiet.

25.

And in a certain dark and remote spot, as ordered, he awaited the lady. Nor did he find the awaiting arduous or difficult or the obscurity of his whereabouts. But with a sense of courage and security he often said to himself: "My gentle lady will soon come and I shall be joyful, more than if I were the sole lord of the universe."

26.

Cressida had plainly heard him come, because, as had been agreed, she had coughed to make him hear. And that he might not be sorry that he had come, she kept speaking every little while in a clear voice. And she provided that everyone should go at once to sleep, saying that she was so sleepy that she could no longer keep awake.

27.

Poi che ciascun sen fu ito a dormire,
  E la casa rimasta tutta cheta,
  Tosto parve a Criseida di gire
  Dov' era Troilo in parte segreta,
  Il qual, com' egli la sentì venire,
  Drizzato in piè, e con la faccia lieta
  Le si fe' incontro, tacito aspettando,
  Per esser presto ad ogni suo comando.

28.

Avea la donna un torchio in mano acceso,
  E tutta sola discese le scale,
  E Troilo vide aspettarla sospeso,
  Cui ella salutò, poi disse, quale
  Ella potè: signor, se io ho offeso,
  In parte tale il tuo splendor reale
  Tenendo chiuso, pregoti per Dio,
  Che mi perdoni, dolce mio disio.

29.

A cui Troilo disse: donna bella,
  Sola speranza e ben della mia mente,
  Sempre davanti m'è stata la stella
  Del tuo bel viso splendido e lucente,
  E stata m'è più cara particella
  Questa, che 'l mio palagio certamente;
  E dimandar perdono a ciò non tocca;
  Poi l' abbracciò e baciaronsi in bocca.

30.

Non si partiron prima di quel loco,
  Che mille volte insieme s'abbracciaro
  Con dolce festa e con ardente gioco,
  Ed altrettante vie più si baciaro,
  Siccome que' ch' ardevan d' ugual foco,
  E che l'un l'altro molto aveva caro;
  Ma come l'accoglienze si finiro,
  Salir le scale e 'n camera ne giro.

27.

When everyone had gone to sleep and the house had become all quiet, Cressida thought it time to go at once where Troilus was in the hidden spot. When he heard her come, he stood up and with joyful countenance went to meet her, waiting in silence to be ready at her every command.

28.

The lady had in hand a lighted torch and descended the stairs all alone and beheld Troilus waiting for her in suspense. She greeted him and then said as well as she could: "My lord, if I have given offense by keeping thy royal splendor confined in such a spot as this, I pray thee by the gods, forgive me, my sweet desire."

29.

To her Troilus said: "Fair lady, sole hope and weal of my mind, ever have I had before me the star of thy fair visage in all its radiant splendor and of a truth more dear to me hath been this little corner than my palace. This is not a matter that requireth the asking of pardon." Then he took her in his arms and they kissed one another on the mouth.

30.

They did not leave that place before they had with sweet joy and ardent dalliance embraced one another a thousand times. And as many times more did they kiss one another, as those who burned with equal fire and were very dear to one another. But when the welcome ended, they mounted the stairs and went into a chamber.

31.

Lungo sarebbe a raccontar la festa,
  E impossibile a dire il diletto
  Che insieme preser pervenuti in questa:
  E' si spogliarono e entraron nel letto;
  Dove la donna nell' ultima vesta
  Rimasa già, con piacevole detto
  Gli disse: speglio mio, le nuove spose
  Son la notte primiera vergognose.

32.

A cui Troilo disse: anima mia,
  I' te ne prego, sì ch' io t' abbia in braccio
  Ignuda sì come il mio cor disia.
  Ed ella allora: ve' che me ne spaccio;
  E la camicia sua gittata via,
  Nelle sue braccia si raccolse avaccio;
  E strignendo l' un l' altro con fervore,
  D' amor sentiron l' ultimo valore.

33.

O dolce notte, e molto disiata,
  Chente fostu alli due lieti amanti!
  Se la scïenza mi fosse donata
  Che ebbero i poeti tutti quanti,
  Per me non potrebbe esser disegnata;
  Pensilo chi fu mai cotanto avanti
  Mercè d' amor, quanto furon costoro,
  E saprà in parte la letizia loro.

34.

E' non uscir di braccio l' uno all' altro
  Tutta la notte, e tenendosi in braccio,
  Si credeano esser tolti l' uno all' altro,
  O che non fosse ver che insieme in braccio,
  Siccome elli eran, fosse l' uno all' altro;
  Ma sognar si credean d' essere in braccio;
  E l' uno all' altro domandava spesso,
  O t' ho io in braccio, o sogno, o se' tu desso?

31.

Long would it be to recount the joy and impossible to tell the delight they took together when they came there. They stripped themselves and got into bed. There the lady, still keeping on her last garment, said to him: "Mirror mine, the newly wed are bashful the first night."

32.

To her Troilus said: "Soul of me, I pray thee remove it, so that I may have thee naked in my arms, as my heart desireth." And she replied: "Behold, I rid myself of it." And after casting off her shift, she quickly wrapped herself in his arms, and clasping one another fervently they experienced the last delight of love.

33.

O sweet and much-desired night, what wert thou to the two joyful lovers! If the knowledge that all the poets once possessed were given me, I should be unable to describe it. Let him who was ever before so much favored by Love as they, take thought of it, and he will know in part their delight.

34.

They did not leave one another's arms all night. While they held one another embraced, they thought they were separated, the one from the other, and that it was not true that they were locked together, one with another, as they were, but they believed they were dreaming of being in one another's arms. And the one often asked the other: "Have I thee in my arms? Do I dream or art thou thyself?"

35.

E' si miravan con tanto disio,
  Che l'un dall' altro gli occhi non torcea,
  E l' uno all' altro diceva : amor mio,
  Deh può egli esser ch' io con teco stea?
Sì, cuor del corpo, mercè n' abbia Dio,
  Sovente l' uno all' altro rispondea,
  E strignendosi forte spessamente,
  Si baciavano insieme dolcemente.

36.

Troilo spesso i begli occhi amorosi
  Baciava di Criseida, dicendo :
  Voi mi metteste nel cuor sì focosi
  Dardi d' amor, de' quali io tutto incendo ;
  Voi mi pigliaste ed io non mi nascosi,
  Come suol far chi dubita, fuggendo ;
  Voi mi tenete e sempre mi terrete
  Occhi miei bei nell' amorosa rete.

37.

Poi gli baciava e ribaciava ancora,
  E Criseida ancora i suoi baciava ;
  Poi tutto il viso e 'l petto, e nessun' ora
  Senza mille sospiri valicava,
  Non de' dolenti per cui si scolora,
  Ma di que' pii, pe' quai si dimostrava
  L' affezïon che giaceva nel petto,
  E dopo quei rinnovava il diletto.

38.

Deh pensin qui gli dolorosi avari,
  Che biasiman chi è innamorato,
  E chi, come fan essi, a far denari
  In alcun modo non s' è tutto dato,
  E guardin se tenendoli ben cari
  Tanto piacer fu mai da lor prestato,
  Quanto ne presta amore in un sol punto,
  A cui egli è con ventura congiunto.

35.

And they beheld one another with so great desire that the one did not remove his eyes from the other, and the one said to the other: "My love, can it be that I am with thee?" "Yes, soul of my life, thanks be to the gods," replied the other. And they exchanged sweet kisses together, ever and anon clasping one another tightly the while.

36.

Troilus often kissed the lovely amorous eyes of Cressida, saying: "You thrust into my heart darts of love so fiery that I am all inflamed by them. You seized me and I did not hide myself in flight, as is wont to do he who is in doubt. You hold me and ever will hold me in Love's net, bright eyes of mine."

37.

Then he kissed them and kissed them yet again and Cressida kissed his in return. Then he kissed all her face and her bosom, and not an hour passed without a thousand sighs—not those grievous ones by which one loseth color but those devoted ones, by which was shown the affection that lay in their breasts and which resulted in the renewal of their delight.

38.

Let now these wretched misers, who blame whoever hath fallen in love and who hath not, as they, devoted himself entirely in some way to the making of money, take thought and consider whether, when holding it full dear, as much pleasure was ever furnished by it as Love doth provide in a single moment to him to whom by good chance he is joined.

39.

Ei diranno di sì, ma mentiranno;
  E questo amor, dolorosa pazzia
  Con risa e con ischerzi chiameranno;
  Senza veder, che sola un' ora fia
  Quella che sè e' denari perderanno,
  Senza aver gioia saputo che sia
  Nella lor vita: Iddio gli faccia tristi,
  Ed agli amanti doni i loro acquisti.

40.

Rassicurati insieme i due amanti,
  Insieme incominciaro a ragionare,
  E l' uno all' altro i preteriti pianti,
  E l' angosce e' sospiri a raccontare;
  E tai ragionamenti tutti quanti
  Spesso rompean con fervente baciare,
  Ed isbandendo la passata noia,
  Prendeano insieme dilettosa gioia.

41.

Ragion non vi si fece di dormire,
  Ma che la notte non venisse meno
  Per bene assai vegghiare avean disire;
  Saziarsi l' un dell' altro non potieno,
  Quantunque molto fosse il fare e il dire,
  Ciò che a quell' atto appartener credieno;
  E senza invan lasciar correr le dotte
  Tutte l' adoperaron quella notte.

42.

Ma poich' e' galli presso al giorno udiro
  Cantar, per l'aurora che sorgea,
  Dell' abbracciar si rinfocò il disiro,
  Dolendosi dell' ora che dovea
  Lor dipartire, ed in nuovo martiro,
  Il qual nessuno ancor provato avea,
  Porli, per l'esser da lor seperati,*
  Vie più che mai d' amor ora infiammati.

* Savj-Lopez, *separati*

39.

They will say "Yes" but they will lie. With laughter and with jests will they call this love grievous folly, without perceiving that in a single hour they will lose themselves and their money, without having known in all their lives what joy is. May the gods make them sad and give their gains to lovers.

40.

Reassured in their union the two lovers began to talk together and to recount to one another their laments of the past, their anguish, and their sighs. And all this talk they often interrupted with fervent kissing and abandoning their past suffering, shared delicious joy.

41.

No talk was there of sleeping but they desired by keeping wide-awake to prevent the night from growing shorter. They could not have enough of one another, however much they might do or say what they believed to belong to that act. And without letting the hours run on in vain they used them all that night.

42.

But when near day they heard the cocks crow by reason of the rising dawn, the desire of embracing grew warm again, not unattended by sorrow on account of the hour which was to separate them and cast them into new torment, which no one had yet felt, because of their being separated, since they were inflamed more than ever with love.

43.

Li quai come Criseida cantare
 Sentì, dolente disse: o amor mio,
 Ora si fa da doversi levare,
 Se ben vogliam celar nostro disio;
 Ma io ti voglio, amor mio, abbracciare,
 Pria che ti levi, un poco, acciocchè io
 Men doglia senta della tua partita,
 Deh abbraccia tu me, dolce mia vita.

44.

Troilo l' abbracciò quasi piangendo,
 E strignendola forte la baciava,
 Il giorno che venía maledicendo,
 Che lor così avaccio separava;
 Poi cominciò in verso lei dicendo:
 Il dipartir senza modo mi grava;
 Come partir da te mi debbo mai,
 Che 'l ben ch' io sento, donna, tu mel dai?

45.

Non so com' io non mora pur pensando
 Ch' andar me ne convien contra il volere,
 E già di vita ch' io n' ho preso bando,
 E morte sopra me molto ha potere,
 Nè so del ritornar come nè quando;
 O fortuna, perchè da tal piacere
 Lontani me, che più d' altro mi piace,
 Perchè mi togli il sollazzo e la pace?

46.

Deh che farò? se già nel primo passo
 Sì mi strigne il disio di ritornarci,
 Che vita nol sostiene, oimè lasso?
 Deh perchè vien sì tosto a allontanarci
 O dispietato giorno? quando basso
 Sarai che io ti veggia ristorarci?
 Oimè che io non so! Quindi rivolto
 A Criseida baciava il fresco volto,

43.

When Cressida heard them crow she said in sorrow: "O my love, now is it time to arise, if we wish to conceal our desire. But I wish to embrace thee a little, my love, before thou arisest, that I may feel less grief at thy departure. Do thou embrace me, my sweet life."

44.

Troilus well-nigh in tears embraced her and clasping her tightly, kissed her, cursing the approaching day, which so quickly separated them. Then he began saying to her: "The parting grieveth me beyond measure. How am I ever to part from thee, since the happiness I feel, thou, lady, givest me?

45.

"I know not why I do not die when I consider that I must go away against my will and that I have already received banishment from life, and death hath much power over me. Nor know I how or when I shall return. O fortune, why dost thou take me afar from such pleasure, which pleaseth me more than aught else? Why dost thou take from me my consolation and my peace?

46.

"Alas what shall I do if at the first step the desire to return here so constraineth me that life may not bear it, wretched one that I am? Ah why, pitiless day, comest thou so soon to separate us? When wilt thou dip beneath the horizon that I may see thee bring us together again? Alas, I do not know." Then he turned to Cressida and kissed her fresh visage,

47.

Dicendo: s' io credessi in la tua mente,
　　Donna mia bella, sì com' io ti tegno
　　Dentro alla mia, star continuamente,
　　Più caro mi saria che 'l troian regno,
　　E di questo partir saria paziente,
　　Poscia che a quel contra mia voglia vegno,
　　E spererei tornarci a tempo e loco,
　　A temperar com' ora il nostro fuoco.

48.

Criseida gli rispose sospirando,
　　Mentre che stretto nelle braccia il tiene:
　　Anima mia, i' udii, ragionando
　　Già è assai, se mi ricordo bene,
　　Che amore è uno spirto avaro, e quando
　　Alcuna cosa prende, sì la tiene
　　Serrata forte e stretta con gli artigli,
　　Ch'a liberarla invan si dan consigli.

49.

Egli ha ghermito me in tal maniera
　　Per te, caro mio ben, che s'io volessi
　　Ritornarmi ora quale prima m'era,
　　Non ti cappia nel capo ch' io potessi;
　　Tu mi se' sempre da mane e da sera
　　Nella mente fermato; e s'io credessi
　　Così essere a te, io mi terrei
　　Beata più che chieder non saprei.

50.

Però sicuro vivi del mio amore,
　　Il qual mai per altrui più non provai;
　　E se 'l tornarci disii con fervore,
　　Io il disio vie più di te assai,
　　Nè prima mi fien date lecite ore
　　Sopra di me, che tu ci tornerai;
　　Cuor del mio corpo i' mi ti raccomando;
　　E così detto il baciò sospirando.

47.

Saying: "If I believed, my fair lady, that I should remain continually in thy mind, as I keep thee in mine, more dear would this be to me than the realm of Troy, and I would be patient at this parting, since I come to it against my will, and would hope to return here at time and place appointed to quench, as now, our fire."

48.

Cressida answered him in sighs, whilst she held him tight in her arms: "Soul of mine, I heard in conversation some time ago, if I remember correctly, that Love is a jealous spirit, and when he seizeth aught, he holdeth it so firmly bound and pressed in his claws that to free it, advice is given in vain.

49.

"He hath gripped me in such wise for thee, my dear weal, that if I wished to return now to what I was at first, take it not into thy head that I could do so. Thou art ever, morn and eve, locked in my mind. If I thought I were so in thine, I should esteem myself happier than I could ask.

50.

"Therefore live certain of my love, which is greater than I have ever felt for another. If thou desirest to return here, I desire it much more than thou. Nor when opportunity shall be given me, wilt thou return here sooner than I. Heart of my body, to thee I commend myself." After she said this she sighed and kissed him.

51.

Levossi Troilo contro a suo volere,
   Poi che baciata l'ebbe cento volte:
   Ma pur veggendo quel ch' era dovere,
   Si vestì tutto, e poscia dopo molte
   Parole, disse: io fo il tuo volere,
   Io me ne vo; fa' che non mi sian tolte
   Le tue promesse, e accomandoti a Dio.
   E teco lascio lo spirito mio.

52.

A lei non venne alla risposta voce,
   Tanta noia la strinse il suo partire
   Ma Troilo quindi con passo veloce,
   Ver lo palagio suo ne prese a gire;
   E' sente ben ch' amor vie più lo cuoce
   Che non faceva prima nel disire,
   Tanto ha da più Criseida trovata,
   Che seco non l' avea prima stimata.

53.

Tornato Troilo nel real palagio,
   Tacitamente se n' entrò nel letto,
   Per dormir se potesse alquanto ad agio;
   Ma non gli potè entrar sonno nel petto,
   Sì gli facean nuovi pensier disagio,
   Rammemorando il passato diletto,
   Pensando seco quanto più valeva
   Criseida bella, ch' el non si credeva.

54.

E giva ciascun atto rivolgendo
   Nel suo pensiero, e il savio ragionare;
   E seco spesso ancora ripetendo
   Il piacevole e 'l dolce motteggiare;
   L'amor di lei ancor giva sentendo
   Troppo maggior che nel suo immaginare;
   E con tali pensier più s' accendea
   In amor forte, e non se n' avvedea.

51.

Troilus arose against his will when he had kissed her an hundred times. But realizing what had to be done, he got all dressed and then after many words said: "I do thy will; I go away. See that what thou hast promised be not left unfulfilled. I commend thee to the gods and leave my soul with thee."

52.

Voice did not come to her for reply, so great sorrow constrained her at his departure. But Troilus set out thence with hasty steps toward his palace. He feeleth that Love vexeth him more than he did at first, when he longed for him, of so much more worth had he found Cressida than he had at first supposed.

53.

After Troilus had returned to the royal palace he went thence silently to bed, to sleep a little, if he could, for ease. But sleep could not enter his breast, so much did fresh anxieties disturb him, as he called to mind his past delight and thought with himself how much more worthy was fair Cressida than he had believed.

54.

He kept turning over each act in his thoughts, and the sensible talk they had had together, and often again repeated to himself their sweet and pleasing speech. He was constantly aware of far greater love for her than in his imaginings. And with such thoughts he burned the more violently in love and was not aware of it.

55.

Criseida seco facea il simigliante,
  Di Troilo parlando nel suo core;
E seco lieta di sì fatto amante,
  Grazie infinite ne rendea ad amore:
E parle ben mille anni che davante
  A lei ritorni il suo vago amatore,
E ch' ella il tenga in braccio e baci spesso,
Come la notte avea fatto d'appresso.

56.

Fu la mattina: Pandaro venuto
  A Troilo levato, e' salutollo,
E Troilo gli rendè il suo saluto,
  E con disio gli si gittò al collo:
Pandaro mio, tu sii il ben venuto!
  E nella fronte con amor baciollo;
Tu m' hai d' inferno messo in paradiso,
Amico mio, se io non sia ucciso.

57.

Io non potrei giammai operar tanto
  Se per te mille volte il dì morisse,
Che io facessi un atomo di quanto
  Conosco aperto ti si convenisse:
Tu m' hai in gioia posto d' aspro pianto;
  E da capo baciollo, e quindi disse:
Dolce mio ben, che contento mi fai,
Quando sarà ch' io più ti tenga mai?

58.

Non vede il sol, che tutto il mondo vede,
  Sì bella donna nè tanto piacente,
Se le parole mie meritan fede,
  Sì costumata, vaga ed avvenente,
Quanto lei, la cui buona mercede,
  Più ch' altro i' vivo allegro veramente;
Lodato sia amor che mi fe' suo,
E similmente il buon servigio tuo.

55.

Cressida on her part did likewise, speaking of Troilus in her heart. Inwardly happy because of such a lover she gave boundless thanks to Love. And it seemeth to her fully a thousand years before her sweet lover will return to her and she will hold him in her arms and kiss him often, as she had done the night just passed.

56.

It was morning. Pandarus came to Troilus, who was risen, and saluted him. And Troilus returned the salutation and threw himself upon his neck with eagerness. "Thou art welcome, my Pandarus," and kissed him lovingly on the forehead. "Thou hast, my friend, taken me from hell to usher me into paradise, as sure as I do live.

57.

"I would never be able to do for thee as much as an atom of what I clearly know is thy due, if I should die for thee a thousand times a day. Thou hast placed me in joy from bitter plaint." And he kissed him over again and said: "My sweet delight, how happy thou makest me! When will it be that I shall ever hold thee again in my arms?

58.

"The sun, which beholdeth the entire world, beholdeth not so fair a lady nor so pleasing, if my words deserve any belief, so well-mannered, lovely, and attractive as she, to whose tender mercies more than to aught else is it owing that I live truly happy. Praised be Love, who hath made me hers, and likewise thy good services.

59.

Dunque non m'hai poca cosa donata,
  Nè me a poca cosa donat' hai:
  La vita mia ti fia sempre obbligata,
  E ad ogni tuo piacer sempre l'avrai;
  Tu l' hai da morte a vita suscitata:
  E qui si tacque allegro più che mai.
  Pandaro uditol, stette alquanto, e poi
  Così rispose lieto a' detti suoi:

60.

S' i' ho, bel dolce amico, fatta cosa
  Che ti sia grata, assai ne son contento,
  Ed èmmi sommamente grazïosa;
  Ma nondimen più che mai ti rammento
  Che ponghi freno alla mente amorosa,
  E sii savio, che dove 'l tormento
  Hai tolto via con dilettosa gioia,
  Per favellar non ti ritorni in noia.

61.

Io 'l farò sicchè a grado sieti,
  Rispose Troilo al suo caro amico;
  Poi gli contò gli accidenti suoi lieti
  Con somma festa, e seguì: ben ti dico
  Ch' io non fu' mai d' amor dentro alle reti
  Com' io son ora, e vie più che l' antico
  Ora mi cuoce il fuoco che tratto aggio
  Degli occhi di Criseida e del visaggio.

62.

Io ardo più che mai, ma questo fuoco
  Ch' io sento nuovo, è d' altra qualitate
  Che quel di prima; or mi rinfresca il giuoco,
  Sempre nel cor pensando alla beltate
  Che n' è cagion; ma vero è che un poco
  Le voglie mie più calde che l' usate
  Fa di tornar nell' amorose braccia,
  E di baciar la delicata faccia.

59.

"Therefore thou hast not given me a little thing nor hast thou given me to a little thing. My life will ever be indebted to thee and thou shalt ever have it whenever it please thee. Thou hast raised it from death to life." Here he ceased speaking, more joyful than ever. Pandarus heard him, waited a little while, and then replied in high spirits to his words as follows:

60.

"If I have, fair sweet friend, done a thing that is pleasing to thee, I am very glad and it is highly gratifying to me. But nevertheless I remind thee more than ever to curb thy amorous desire and be wise, that now that thou hast driven away thy torment with delicious joy, thou mayest not by too much talk return to thy misery."

61.

"I shall do so to thy satisfaction," replied Troilus to his dear friend. Then he related to him in great gladness the joyful things that had happened to him and added: "I tell thee truly that I have never been enmeshed in the net of Love as I am at present and much more than formerly do I burn with the fire that I have caught from the fair eyes of Cressida and from her visage.

62.

"I burn more than ever, but this new fire that I feel is of another quality than what I felt before. Now the game refresheth me since there ever cometh to me in my heart thoughts of the beauty that is the occasion of it. But true it is that it maketh my wishes to return to her amorous arms and to kiss her delicate face a little more eager than they were wont to be."

63.

Saziar non si poteva il giovinetto
  Di ragionar con Pandaro del bene
  Il qual sentito aveva, e del diletto,
  E del conforto dato alle sue pene,
  E dell' amor che portava perfetto
  A Criseida, in cui sola la spene
  Aveva posta, e messone in oblio
  Ogni suo altro fatto e gran disio.

64.

Fra picciol tempo, la lieta fortuna
  Di Troilo, rendè luogo a' suoi amori;
  Il qual, poscia che fu la notte bruna,
  Del suo palagio solo uscito fuori,
  Senza nel ciel vedere stella alcuna,
  Per lo cammino usato a' suoi dolzori
  Nascosamente se n' entrò, e cheto
  Nel luogo usato e' si stette segreto.

65.

Come Criseida l' altra volta venne,
  Così a tempo venne questa volta,
  Ed il modo di prima tutto tenne;
  E poi che lieta e grazïosa accolta
  Fatta s' ebber fra lor quanto convenne,
  Presi per man con allegrezza molta
  Nella camera insieme se n' entraro,
  E senza indugio alcun si coricaro.

66.

Come Criseida Troilo in braccio ebbe,
  Così gioiosa cominciò a dire:
  Qual donna fu, o mai esser potrebbe,
  La qual potesse tanto ben sentire
  Quant' io fo or? Deh chi se ne terrebbe,
  Di non dovere a mano a man morire,
  Se altro non potesse, per avere
  Un poco sol di così gran piacere?

63.

The young man could not exhaust his desire to talk with Pandarus of the happiness he had felt and of the delight and comfort given his woes and of the perfect love that he bore Cressida, in whom alone he had placed his hope. And he forgot every other matter and every other great desire.

64.

Within a short time the good fortune of Troilus afforded opportunity for his amours. When the night had grown dark he issued forth alone from his palace, without beholding any star in the sky, entered to his pleasure stealthily by the path he had used before, and quietly and secretly took his station in the accustomed spot.

65.

Just as Cressida had come before, so in good season came she this time and followed altogether the practice she had used before. And after they had exchanged gentle and pleasing greetings as much as they saw fit, hand in hand they entered her room with great delight and lay down together without any delay.

66.

When Cressida had Troilus in her arms, she began joyfully as follows: "What lady ever was there or could there be who could experience such delicious sensations as I do now? Alas, who would shrink from meeting death immediately, if it could not be otherwise, in order to taste a bare morsel of so great pleasure?"

67.

Poi cominciava: dolce l' amor mio,
  Io non so che mi dir, nè mai potrei
  Dir la dolcezza e 'l focoso disio
  Che m' hai nel petto messo, ov' io vorrei
  Aver te tutto sempre sì com' io
  V' ho l' imagine tua; nè chiederei
  A Giove più, se questo mi facesse,
  Che sì com' ora sempre mi tenesse.

68.

Io non mi credo ch' el possa giammai
  Questo fuoco allenar, com' io credea
  Che el facesse, poi che insieme assai
  Fossimo stati, ma ben non vedea;
  L' acqua del fabbro su gettata ci hai,
  Sicchè egli arde più che non facea,
  Perchè mai non t' amai quant' ora t' amo,
  Che giorno e notte ti disio e bramo.

69.

Troilo a lei diceva il simigliante,
  Tenendosi amendue in braccio stretti;
  E motteggiando usavan tutte quante
  Quelle parole, ch' a cotai diletti
  Si soglion dir tra l' uno e l' altro amante,
  Baciandosi le bocche, gli occhi e' petti,
  Rendendo l' uno all' altro le salute,
  Che scrivendosi insieme eran taciute.

70.

Ma il nemico giorno s' appressava,
  Come per segno si sentiva aperto,
  Il qual ciascun cruccioso bestemmiava,
  Parendo lor ch' egli si fosse offerto
  Più tosto assai ch' offrirsi non usava,
  Il che doleva a ciascun per lo certo;
  Ma poi che più non si poteva, allora
  Ciascun su si levò senza dimora.

67.

Then he began: "My dear love, I do not know what to say nor should I ever be able to declare the sweet feelings and the fiery desires that thou hast placed in my breast, where I would wish always to have thee entire, as I have thine image, nor would I ask more of Jove, if he should grant me this, than that he should keep me ever as I am now.

68.

"I do not believe that he will ever temper this fire, as I believed he would, after we had been a number of times together. But I thought not well. Thou hast thrown upon it water such as blacksmiths use, so that it burneth more than it did. Wherefore I never loved thee as much as I love thee now; day and night I desire and long for thee."

69.

Troilus spake to her much as above, as they both held one another in close embrace, and falling into playful speech they used in their talk all those words which are customarily spoken between one lover and another to express such delights, kissing one another's mouths, eyes, and breasts, giving to one another the salutations which when they wrote to each other had been unexpressed.

70.

But the unfriendly day drew nigh, as was clearly perceived by signs, which each of them cursed angrily; for it seemed to them to come sooner than usual, which indeed grieved each of them. But since it could not be helped, each of them arose without delay.

71.

L' uno dall' altro fece dipartenza
    Al modo usato, dopo più sospiri,
    E nel futuro, ordinaron che senza
    Indugio si tornasse a que' disiri;
    Sicchè potesser colla lor presenza
    Rattemperar gli amorosi martirj,
    Ed operar sì lieta gioventute
    Mentre durasse in sì fatta salute.

72.

Era contento Troilo, ed in canti
    Menava la sua vita e in allegrezza:
    L' alte bellezze ed i vaghi sembianti
    Di qualunque altra donna nulla prezza,
    Fuor che la sua Criseida, e tutti quanti
    Gli altri uomin vivere in trista gramezza,
    A rispetto di sè, seco credeva;
    Tanto il suo ben gli aggradiva e piaceva.

73.

Esso talvolta Pandaro pigliava
    Per mano, e in un giardin con lui ne gia;
    E con el pria di Criseida parlava,
    Del suo valore e della cortesia;
    Poi lietamente con lui cominciava,
    Rimoto tutto da malinconia,
    Lietamente a cantare in cotal guisa,
    Qual qui senz' alcun mezzo si divisa.

74.

O luce eterna, il cui lieto splendore
    Fa bello il terzo ciel, dal qual ne piove
    Piacer, vaghezza, pietade ed amore;
    Del sole amica, e figliuola di Giove,
    Benigna donna d' ogni gentil core,
    Certa cagion del valor che mi muove
    A' sospir dolci della mia salute,
    Sempre lodata sia la tua virtute.

71.

The one took leave of the other in the usual manner, after many sighs. And they planned in the future to pass to their desires without delay, so that they might by being together temper their amorous sufferings and spend the joyful season of youth, while it lasted, in such happiness.

72.

Troilus was light-hearted and led a life of song and gaiety. The high beauty and alluring looks of any other lady—save only his Cressida—holdeth he in none esteem and believeth that as compared with himself all other men live in sad distress, so grateful and pleasing to him was his good fortune.

73.

Many a time he took Pandarus by the hand and went off with him into a garden and first spake with him of Cressida, of her worth and courtesy, then joyfully, with him as auditor, began, wholly free from sadness, to sing in joyful strains in such fashion as is here set forth without any alteration.

74.

"O light eterne, whose cheerful radiance maketh fair the third heaven, whence descendeth upon me pleasure, delight, pity, and love, friend of the sun and daughter of Jove, kindly mistress of every gentle heart, certain source of the strength which prompteth me to my health's sweet sighs, forever praised be thy power.

75.

Il ciel, la terra, lo mare e l'inferno,
Ciascuno in sè la tua potenzia sente,
O chiara luce; e s' io il ver discerno,
Le piante, i semi, e l' erbe parimente,
Gli uccei, le fiere, i pesci con eterno
Vapor ti senton nel tempo piacente,
E gli uomini e gli dei, nè creatura
Senza di te nel mondo vale o dura.

76.

Tu Giove prima agli alti effetti lieto,
Pe' qua' vivono e son tutte le cose,
Movesti, o bella dea; e mansueto
Sovente il rendi all' opere noiose
Di noi mortali; e il meritato fleto
In liete feste volgi e dilettose;
E in mille forme già quaggiù il mandasti,
Quand' ora d' una ed or d'altra il pregasti.

77.

Tu 'l fiero Marte al tuo piacer benegno
Ed umil rendi, e cacci ciascun' ira;
Tu discacci viltà, e d' alto sdegno
Riempi chi per te, o dea, sospira;
Tu d' alta signoria merito e degno
Fai ciaschedun secondo ch' el disira;
Tu fai cortese ognuno e costumato,
Chi del tuo fuoco alquanto è infiammato.

78.

Tu in unità le case e le cittadi,
Li regni, e le provincie, e 'l mondo tutto
Tien, bella dea; tu dell' amistadi
Se' cagion certa e di lor caro frutto:
Tu sola le nascose qualitadi
Delle cose conosci, onde 'l costrutto
Vi metti tal, che fai maravigliare
Chi tua potenza non sa riguardare.

[274]

75.

"The heavens, the earth, the sea, and the lower regions, each one feeleth in itself thy power, O clear light, and if I discern truly, plants, seeds, grass as well, birds, beasts, and fish feel thee with eternal vapor in the pleasing season, and men and gods; nor hath creature in the world without thee strength or endurance.

76.

"Thou first, O fair goddess, didst gently move Jove to the high effects whereby all things have life and existence and often dost incline him to pity the sorry actions of us mortals and dost turn the lamentations that we deserve into gentle and delicious rejoicings, and in a thousand forms didst of yore send him down here when thou didst beseech him now for one thing and now for another.

77.

"Thou makest, when thou wilt, the haughty Mars benign and humble and drivest forth every angry passion. Thou expellest villainy and fillest with high disdain him who sigheth for thee, O goddess. Thou makest each one according to his desires worthy and deserving of high sovereignty. Thou makest each one who is in any degree inflamed with thy fire courteous and well-mannered.

78.

"Thou, fair goddess, holdest houses and cities, kingdoms, provinces, and the entire world at one. Thou art the unfailing cause of friendships and their precious fruit. Thou alone knowest the hidden properties of things, out of which thou bringest such order that thou makest marvel whoever knoweth not how to regard thy power.

79.

Tu legge, o dea, poni all' universo,
 Per la qual esso in esser si mantiene;
 Nè è alcuno al tuo figliuolo avverso,
 Che non sen penta, se d' esser sostiene;
 Ed io che già con ragionar, perverso
 Li fui, aval, sì come si conviene,
 Mi riconosco innamorato tanto,
 Ch' esprimere giammai non potre' quanto.

80.

Il che, se avvegna ch' alcuno riprenda,
 Poco men curo, che non sa che dirsi:
 Ercole forte in questo mi difenda,
 Che da amore non potè schermirsi,
 Avvegna ch' ogni savio il ne commenda;
 E chi con frode non vuol ricoprirsi
 Non dirà mai che a me fia disdicevole
 Ciò che ad Ercole fu già convenevole.

81.

Adunque io amo, e intra' grandi effetti
 Tuoi, questo più mi piace e aggrada;
 Questo seguisco, in cui tutti i diletti
 Son (se diritto l' anima mia bada),
 Più che in altro compiuti e perfetti,
 Anzi da questo ogni altro si disgrada;
 Questo mi fa seguitar quella donna,
 Che di valore più ch' altra s' indonna:

82.

Questo m' induce avale a rallegrarmi,
 E farà sempre, sol che io sia saggio;
 Questo m' induce, o dea, tanto a lodarmi
 Del tuo lucente e virtuoso raggio,
 Per lo qual benedico che alcun' armi
 Non mi difeser dal chiaro visaggio,
 Nel qual la tua virtù vidi dipinta,
 E la potenza lucida e distinta.

79.

"Thou, O goddess, imposest laws on the universe, whereby it is held together, nor is anyone opposed to thy son but repenteth of it, if he persist therein. And I, who formerly opposed him in my talk, now, as is fitting, find myself so much in love that I should never be able to express the full sum of it.

80.

"For if anyone blameth me, little the less do I care, for he speaketh without knowledge. Let the strong Hercules in this be my strong defense, for he could not shield himself from Love, for which every wise man commendeth him. And he who doth not wish to involve himself in falsehood shall never say that what was once becoming to Hercules is unseemly for me.

81.

"Therefore I love and amongst thy grand effects this most pleaseth and gratifieth me. This I follow, in which, more than in anything else, if my mind heedeth justly, all delights are completed and perfected. In the presence of this everything else loseth quality. This causeth me to follow that lady who in worthiness beyond other holdeth sovereignty.

82.

"This induceth me now to rejoice and shall ever do so, if only I am prudent. This induceth me, O goddess, to glory so much in thy lucent and invigorating ray, because of which I rejoice that no arms defended me from thy radiant visage, in which I beheld thy virtues depicted and thy power bright and clear.

83.

E benedico il tempo, l' anno, e 'l mese,
  E 'l giorno, l'ora, e 'l punto, che costei
Onesta, bella, leggiadra e cortese,
  Primieramente apparve agli occhi miei;
E benedico il figliuol che m' accese
  Del suo valor, per la virtù di lei,
E che m'ha fatto a lei servo verace,
Negli occhi suoi ponendo la mia pace.

84.

E benedico i ferventi sospiri
  Ch' i' ho per lei cacciati già dal petto;
E benedico i pianti ed i martirj
  Che fatti m' ha avere amor perfetto;
E benedico i focosi desiri
  Tratti dal suo più bel che altro aspetto,
Perciocchè prezzo di sì alta cosa
Istati sono, e tanto grazïosa.

85.

Ma sopra tutti benedico Iddio,
  Che tanto cara donna diede al mondo,
E che tanto di lume ancor nel mio
  Discerner pose in questo basso fondo,
Che in lei, innanzi ad ogni altro disio,
  Io accendessi e fossine giocondo,
Talchè grazie giammai non si porieno
Render per uom, quai render si dovrieno.

86.

Se cento lingue, e ciascuna parlante,
  Nella mia bocca fossero, e 'l sapere
Nel petto avessi d'ogni poetante,
  Esprimer non potrei le virtù vere,
L' alta piacevolezza e l'abbondante
  Sua cortesia; chi n' ha dunque potere,
Prego divoto che lei lungamente
Mi presti, e me ne faccia conoscente;

83.

"And I bless the season, the year, the month, and the day, the hour and the very moment that one so virtuous, fair, graceful, and courteous first appeared to mine eyes. And I bless the boy who by his power kindleth me with love for her virtue and who hath made me a true servant to her, placing my peace in her eyes.

84.

"And I bless the fervent sighs which I have already heaved from my breast on her account, and I bless the plaints and tortures which perfect love hath caused me to suffer, and I bless the fiery desires drawn from her aspect, fairer than all else, because they have been the price of a creature so exalted and so gracious.

85.

"But before all I bless the gods, who gave so dear a lady to the world and who in this deep dungeon put so much light in my discernment that I burned because of her rather than any other desire and in her did take delight, so that the thanks that ought to be rendered, never can be rendered by man.

86.

"If there were an hundred tongues in my mouth and each were vocal, and if I had the cunning of every poet in my breast, I should never be able to express her true virtues, her lofty gentleness, and her abundant courtesy. Therefore I devoutly pray her who hath the power, to keep her long mine and to make me grateful for it.

87.

Che se' tu dessa, o dea, che far lo puoi,
    Sol che tu vogli, ed io ten prego molto;
Chi più felice si potrà dir poi,
    Se 'l tempo che con meco esser dee volto
Tutto disponi a' piacer miei e suoi?
    Deh fallo, o dea, poichè mi son raccolto
Nelle tue braccia, donde uscito m' era,
Non ben sapendo la tua virtù vera.

88.

Segua chi vuole i regni e le ricchezze,
    L' arme, i cavai, le selve, i can, gli uccelli,
Di Pallade gli studii e le prodezze
    Di Marte, ch' io in mirare gli occhi belli
Della mia donna e le vere bellezze
    Il tempo vo' por tutto, che son quelli
Che sopra Giove mi pongon, qualora
Gli miro, tanto il cor se ne innamora.

89.

Io non ho grazie quai si converrieno
    A te da me, o bella luce eterna,
Però prima tacer che non appieno
    Renderle: vuo'mmi tu chiara lucerna
Al desiderio mio non venir meno?
    Prolunga, cela, correggi e governa
Il mio ardore, e quel di questa a cui
Son dato, e fa' che non sia mai d' altrui.

90.

Nell' opere opportune alla lor guerra
    Egli era sempre nell' armi il primiero;
Che sopra' Greci uscia fuor della terra,
    Tanto animoso, e sì forte e sì fiero,
Che ciascun ne dottava, se non erra
    La storia; e questo spirto tanto altiero
Più che l' usato gli prestava amore,
Di cui egli era fedel servidore.

87.

"For thou art she, O goddess, who canst do this if only thou wilt, and I pray thee earnestly to do it. Who could then be called happier, if thou convert the time which is destined to be spent with me wholly to my pleasure and to hers? Do so, O goddess, since I have found myself again in thine arms, which I had left, not knowing well thy true virtue.

88.

"Let him who will, pursue power and wealth, arms, horses, wild beasts, dogs, birds, the studies of Pallas and the feats of Mars, for I wish to spend all my time contemplating the fair eyes of my lady and her true beauties, which, when I gaze at her, exalt me above Jove, so much is my heart enamored of her.

89.

"I have not the graces which should be rendered thee by me, O fair eternal light, and rather would I keep silent than not render them completely. Wilt thou none the less, clear light, come to the relief of my necessities? Prolong, conceal, correct, and govern my ardor and that of her to whom I am dedicated, and grant that she never belong to another."

90.

In the tasks belonging to their war he was always the first in arms, for he issued forth from the city upon the Greeks so full of spirits and so strong and so brave that each one was afraid of him, if the story erreth not. And Love, of whom he was faithful servant, granted him this courage, so much more dauntless than usual.

91.

Ne' tempi delle triegue egli uccellava,
  Falcon, girfalchi ed aquile tenendo;
  E tal fïata con li can cacciava,
  Orsi, cinghiali, e gran lion seguendo,
  Li piccoli animai tutti spregiava;
  Ed a' suoi tempi Criseida vedendo
  Si rifaceva grazïoso e bello
  Come falcon ch' uscisse di cappello.

92.

Era d' amor tutto il suo ragionare,
  O di costumi, e pien di cortesia;
  Lodava molto i valenti onorare,
  E simile i cattivi cacciar via:
  Piaceali ancora di vedere ornare
  Li giovani d' onesta leggiadria;
  E tenea senza amore ognun perduto,
  Di quale stato che si fosse suto.

93.

Ed avvegna ch' el fosse di reale
  Sangue, e volendo ancor molto potesse;
  Benigno si faceva a tutti eguale,
  Come che alcun talvolta nol valesse:
  Così voleva amor, che tutto vale,
  Che el per compiacere altrui facesse;
  Superbia, invidia, ed avarizia in ira
  Aveva, ed ognun dietro si tira.

94.

Ma poco tempo durò cotal bene,
  Mercè della fortuna invidiosa,
  Che in questo mondo nulla fermo tiene;
  Ella li volse la faccia crucciosa
  Per nuovo caso, sì com' egli avviene,
  E sottosopra volgendo ogni cosa,
  Di Criseida gli tolse i dolci frutti,
  E i lieti amor rivolse in tristi lutti.

91.

In times of truces he went fowling, holding falcons, gerfalcons, and eagles. And sometimes he hunted with dogs, pursuing bears, boars, and great lions. All small prey he disdained. And whenever he beheld Cressida, he put on a fair pleasing countenance, like an unhooded falcon.

92.

All his talk was of love or of gentle behavior, and full of courtesy. He delighted much to honor the valiant and likewise to cast forth the cowards. It ever pleased him to behold honors bestowed upon youths of modest grace. And he considered lost every one without love, of whatsoever station he might be.

93.

And though he was of royal blood and could, had he wished, have enjoyed much power, he made himself agreeable to all equally, although many a time a man did not deserve it. So wished Love, which is all-powerful, that he should act so as to please others. Pride, envy, and avarice he held in hatred and deferreth to everyone.

94.

But for a short time lasted this happiness, thanks to envious fortune, which in this world remaineth not stable. It turned toward him its bitter face, by a new chance, as it happeneth, and turning everything upside down, took from him the sweet fruits of Cressida, and changed his happy love into woeful mourning.

IL FILOSTRATO

DI

GIOVANNI BOCCACCIO

❖

PARTE QUARTA

ARGOMENTO

Comincia la quarta parte del Filostrato, nella quale si mostra primieramente perchè avvenisse che Criseida fosse renduta al padre Calcas. Dimandarono i Greci uno scambio de' prigioni; ègli conceduto Antenore: richiedesi Criseida, e deliberasi di renderla. Troilo si duole primieramente seco, e poscia con Pandaro ragionano insieme varie cose per consolazione di Troilo. Perviene la fama a Criseida della sua partita: visitanla donne, le quali partite, Criseida piagne. Pandaro ordina con lei che Troilo si vada la sera, ed egli vi va, e là tramortisce Criseida: Troilo si vuole uccidere; ella si risente, vannosi a letto piangendo, e ragionano di varie cose, e teneramente Criseida promette di tornare infra 'l decimo giorno. E primieramente come combattono i Troiani, dove molti sono presi da' Greci, e permutati i prigioni.

1.

Tenendo i Greci la cittade stretta
  Con forte assedio, Ettor, nelle cui mani
  Era tutta la guerra, fe' seletta
  De' suoi amici e ancora de' Troiani,
  E valoroso con sua gente eletta
  Incontro a' Greci uscì negli ampi piani,
  Come più altre volte fatto avea
  Con varii accidenti alla mislea.

THE FILOSTRATO

OF

GIOVANNI BOCCACCIO

FOURTH PART

ARGUMENT

Here beginneth the fourth part of the Filostrato, in which, in
the first place, is shown how it happened that Cressida was sent
back to her father Calchas. The Greeks requested an exchange
of prisoners. Antenor is surrendered. Cressida is asked for and
it is decided to give her up. Troilus at first grieveth inwardly,
and then he and Pandarus discuss many things for the comfort
of Troilus. The rumor of her coming departure reacheth Cressida. Ladies attend her and after their departure Cressida weepeth. Pandarus arrangeth with her that Troilus shall go to her
that evening. He goeth to her and Cressida there fainteth. Troilus wisheth to kill himself. She recovereth. They go to bed
weeping, and speak of various matters, and Cressida tenderly
promiseth to come back within the tenth day. And first of all
how the Trojans fight, where many are taken by the Greeks,
and how the prisoners are exchanged.

1.

While the Greeks held the city bound in close-girt
siege, Hector, in whose hands was placed the ordering
of the war, made choice among his friends and other
Trojans, and with his chosen men valiantly issued forth
against the Greeks on the broad plains, as he had done
many other times, with varying fortunes in the combat.

2.

Venner gli Greci incontro, e con battaglia
  Dura, quel giorno consumaron tutto;
  Ma de' Troiani alfine la puntaglia
  Non resse bene, onde opportuno al tutto
  Fu il fuggire con danno e con travaglia,
  E molti ne moriro in doglia e lutto;
  Ed assai ve ne furon per prigioni,
  Nobili re, ed altri gran baroni.

3.

Tra' quali fu il magnifico Antenorre,
  Polidamas suo figlio, e Menesteo,
  Santippo, Serpedon, Polinestorre,
  Polite ancora, ed il troian Rifeo,
  E molti più cui la virtù d' Ettorre
  Nel partirsi riscuoter non poteo,
  Sicchè gran pianto e cruccio fessi in Troia,
  E quasi annunzio di vie peggior noia.

4.

Chiese Priamo triegua, e fugli data;
  E cominciossi a trattare infra loro
  Di permutar prigioni quella fiata,
  E per li sopra più di donar oro.
  Il che Calcas sentendo, con cambiata
  Faccia si mise e con pianto sonoro
  Infra gli Greci, e per lo gridar fioco
  Pure impetrò che l' udissero un poco.

5.

Signori, cominciò Calcas, i' fui
  Troian, siccome voi tutti sapete;
  E se ben vi ricorda, i' son colui,
  Il qual primiero a quel per che ci sete
  Recai speranza, e dissivi che vui
  Al termine dovuto l' otterrete,
  Cioè vittoria della vostra impresa,
  E Troia fia per voi disfatta e accesa.

2.

The Greeks came forth against him and they spent all that day in savage battle. But at length the Trojans had the worst of the fighting. Wherefore all were forced to flee with hurt and pain and many perished in sorrow and in grief; and many noble kings and other great barons went thence as prisoners.

3.

Among them was the magnificent Antenor, Polydamas, his son, and Menestheus, Xanthippus, Sarpedon, Polymnestor, Polites, too, and the Trojan Ripheus, and many more whom Hector's valor could not rescue in the retreat, so that great grief and lamentation arose in Troy, a seeming prognostic of much greater woe.

4.

Priam besought a truce and it was granted him. And then debate began between them over exchanging prisoners at that time and giving gold to boot in ransom. And when Calchas heard this, with changed face and loud lament he mingled among the Greeks and by hoarse crying won their hearing for a while.

5.

"Good sirs," began Calchas, "I was once, as ye all know, a Trojan, and I am he who, if ye all remember, first brought hope to the errand on which ye are here, and I told you that ye would attain your destined end, which is to say victory in your undertaking, and that Troy would be destroyed by you and burned.

6.

L' ordine e 'l modo ancora da tenere
  In ciò sapete, ch' io v' ho dimostrato;
  E perchè tutte venissero intere
  Le voglie vostre nel tempo spiegato,
  Senza fidarmi in alcun messaggere,
  O in libello aperto o suggellato,
  A voi, com' egli appar, ne son venuto
  Per darvi in ciò e consiglio ed aiuto.

7.

Il che volendo fare, fu opportuno
  Che con ingegno, e molto occultamente,
  Senza ciò fare assentire a nessuno,
  Io mi partissi, e fello, di presente
  Che 'l chiaro giorno fu tornato bruno
  Me n' uscii solo, e qui tacitamente
  Ne venni, e nulla meco ne recai,
  Ma ciò che aveva tutto vi lasciai.

8.

Di ciò nel vero poco o nulla curo,
  Fuor d' una mia figliuola giovinetta
  Ch' io vi lasciai: oimè, padre duro
  E rigido ch' io fui, costei soletta
  Menata n' avess' io qui nel sicuro!
  Ma nol sofferse la tema e la fretta:
  Questo mi duol di ciò ch' io lasciai in Troia,
  Questo mi toglie ed allegrezza e gioia.

9.

Nè tempo ancor di richieder poterla
  Veduto ci ho, però taciuto sono,
  Ma ora è tempo di potere averla,
  Se da voi posso impetrar questo dono;
  E s' or non s' ha, giammai di rivederla
  Più non ispererò, e in abbandono
  La vita mia omai lascerò gire,
  Senza curar più 'l viver che 'l morire.

6.

"The method and procedure to be followed ye know, for I have clearly shown you. And that your desires may all be fulfilled at the time when I foretold they would, with no trust in messenger nor in open or sealed tablets, I have come to you, as ye well may see, to give you both counsel and aid in this matter.

7.

"In my desire to do this, I had to depart with much contriving and very secretly, without securing the consent of anyone. And this I did. Once the bright day had turned dark I went forth alone and hither came quietly. And naught brought I with me but left behind all that I had.

8.

"Truly I care little or naught for that, save for a youthful daughter of mine whom I left there. Alas, hard and unfeeling father that I was, would that I had brought this lonely little girl hither in safety! But fear and haste would not have it so. This grieveth me for what I left behind; this robbeth me at once of happiness and joy.

9.

"Nor yet have I seen a fitting time when I might ask her back; therefore have I held my peace. But now the time hath come when I may have her, can I but win this boon from you. And if it may not now be had, never shall I hope to see her more and henceforth in desolation shall I let my life pass by, with no more care for life than death.

10.

Qui son con voi di nobili baroni
   Troiani, ed altri assai, cui voi cambiate
Con gli avversarii pe' vostri prigioni;
   Un sol de' molti a me me ne donate,
In luogo delle cui redenzioni
   Io abbia mia figlia : consolate,
Per Dio, signor, questo vecchio cattivo,
Che d'ogni altro sollazzo è voto e privo.

11.

Nè d' aver or per li prigion vaghezza
   Vi tragga, ch' io vi giuro per Iddio,
Ch' ogni troiana forza, ogni ricchezza
   È nelle vostre man per certo; e s' io
Non me n' inganno, tosto la prodezza
   Fallirà di colui, che al disio
Di tutti voi tien serrate le porte,
Come apparrà per violenta morte.

12.

Questo dicendo il vecchio sacerdote,
   Umile nel parlare e nell' aspetto,
Sempre rigava di pianto le gote,
   E la canuta barba e 'l duro petto
Tutto bagnato avea : nè furon vote
   Le sue preghiere di pietoso effetto,
Che, lui tacendo, i Greci con romore
Tutti gridaron : diaglisi Antenóre.

13.

Così fu fatto; e Calcas fu contento,
   E la bisogna impose a' trattatori:
I quali, al re Priamo, il suo talento
   Dissero, ed a' figliuoli ed a' signori
Ch' ancora v'eran, onde un parlamento
   Di ciò si tenne, ed agli ambasciadori
Risposer breve : se gli addomandati
Rendesser loro, i lor fosser donati.

10.

"Here with you are noble Trojan barons, and many others, whom ye exchange with your foemen for your prisoners. One alone of many do ye give to me, that in return for his redemption I may have my daughter. Good sirs, in the name of the gods, console this wretched old man, destitute and bereft of every other solace.

11.

"Let no desire to have gold for the prisoners have weight with you, for I swear to you in God's name that all the might and wealth of Troy are assuredly within your grasp, and, if I mistake not, there will soon be an end to the prowess of him who holdeth the gates closed to the desire of all of you, as will appear by his violent death."

12.

As he said this, the aged priest with humility in speech and mien did ever streak his cheeks with tears, and his hoary beard and hard breast were all moist. Nor were his prayers without piteous effect; for when he held his peace, the Greeks all noisily shouted: "Let Antenor be given him."

13.

Thus 'twas done and Calchas was pleased. And he enjoined the business upon the negotiators. And the latter set forth his desire to King Priam and to his sons and to the lords who were there. Whereupon, a deliberation was held upon the matter. And to the ambassadors the lords made their brief response: if they should surrender the persons asked for, theirs would be given them.

14.

Troilo al domandare era presente
  Che fero i Greci, e Criseida udendo
  Richieder, dentro il cuor subitamente
  Per tutto si sentì ir trafiggendo,
  Ed una doglia sì acutamente,
  Che morir si credette ivi sedendo;
  Ma con fatica pur dentro ritenne
  L' amore e 'l pianto come si convenne.

15.

E pien d' angoscia e di fiera paura,
  Quel che fosse risposto ad aspettare
  Incominciò, con non usata cura
  Seco volgendo quel ch' avesse a fare,
  Se tanta fosse la sua sciagura,
  Se tra' fratei sentisse liberare
  Che a Calcas Criseida si rendesse,
  Come sturbarlo del tutto potesse.

16.

Amore il facea pronto ad ogni cosa
  Doversi oppor, ma d' altra parte era
  Ragion che 'l contrastava, e che dubbiosa
  Faceva molto quell' impresa altiera,
  Non forse che di ciò fosse crucciosa
  Criseida per vergogna; e in tal maniera,
  Volendo e non volendo or questo or quello,
  Intra due stava il timido donzello.

17.

Mentre che egli in cotal guisa stava
  Sospeso, molte cose ragionate
  Fur tra' baron, di quel che bisognava
  Ora al presente per le cose state;
  E come è detto, a chi quelle aspettava
  Fur le risposte interamente date,
  E che fosse Criseida renduta,
  Che mai non v' era stata ritenuta.

14.

Troilus was present at the Greeks' request, and hearing that they asked for Cressida, he suddenly felt his heart all transfixed within him and so sharp a pain that he thought he would die where he sat, but with difficulty he restrained the love and grief within, as was fitting.

15.

And full of anguish and cruel fear he began to await what answer should be made, turning over in his mind with no usual care what he must do, should his misfortune be so great; if he should hear opinion delivered among his brothers that Cressida be surrendered to Calchas, how he might altogether prevent it.

16.

Love made him ready as duty-bound to oppose everything but on the other side was Reason, who stood against it, and cast upon that lofty enterprise much doubt lest Cressida should perchance be angry on shame's account. And in such manner stood the timid youth between two courses, now willing this, now that, and then unwilling either.

17.

While he there stood irresolute, many things were in debate among the barons as to what must now be done in view of what had happened, and, as has been said, replies were given in full to those who awaited them and among them that surrender should be made of Cressida, who had never been kept as a prisoner there.

18.

Qual, poscia ch' è dall' aratro intaccato
Ne' campi il giglio, per soverchio sole
Casca ed appassa, e 'l bel color cangiato
Pallido fassi; tale, alle parole
Rendute a' Greci dal determinato
Consiglio infra' Troian, in tanta mole
Di danno e di periglio, tramortito
Lì cadde Troilo d' alto duol ferito.

19.

Il quale Priamo prese infra le braccia,
Ed Ettore e' fratei, temendo forte
Dell' accidente, e ciascun si procaccia
Di confortarlo, e le sue forze morte,
Ora i polsi fregando, ed or la faccia
Bagnandogli sovente, come accorte
Persone, s' ingegnavan rivocare,
Ma poco ancor valeva l' operare.

20.

Esso giacea fra' suoi disteso e vinto,
Che un poco di spirto ancor v' avea;
E 'l viso suo pallido, smorto, e tinto
Egli era tutto, e più morta parea
Che viva cosa, di pietà dipinto
In guisa tal, ch' ognun pianger facea;
Sì grave fu l' alto tuon che l' offese,
Quando di render Criseida intese.

21.

Ma poi che la sua anima dolente,
Per lungo spazio pria che ritornasse,
Vagata fu, ritornò chetamente,
Ond' esso, quale alcun che si svegliasse,
Stordito tutto, in piè subitamente
Si levò suso, e pria che 'l domandasse
Alcun che fosse ciò ch' avea sentito,
Altro infingendo, da lor s' è partito:

18.

Ev'n as the lily, after it hath been turned up in the fields by the plough, droopeth and withereth from too much sun and its bright color changeth and groweth pale, so at the message brought to the Greeks by the council concluded among the Trojans did Troilus 'neath so great load of harm and peril fall in a swoon, stricken with woe profound.

19.

Him did Priam, Hector, and his brothers take in arms, much terrified by this ill chance, and each one hasteneth to comfort him and his spent powers they sought to revive, now rubbing his wrists, now oft bathing his face, as experts in such mishap. But as yet their efforts were of slight avail.

20.

Outstretched and overcome he lay among his own, for breath of life yet faintly lingered. Pale and wan his visage was and he all livid, and seemed more dead than living, being so marked with affliction that he made everyone weep, so heavy was the lofty bolt that laid him low when he learned that Cressida would be surrendered.

21.

But after wandering far before return, his grieving spirit came quietly back. Wherefore all dazed, as one awake from slumber, he rose suddenly to his feet, and before any should ask him what it was that he had felt, feigning other business, he departed from them.

22.

E'n verso il suo palagio se ne gio,
  Senza ascoltare o volgersi ad alcuno,
E tal qual era sospiroso e pio,
  Senza voler compagnia di nessuno,
Nella camera ginne, e che disio
  Di riposarsi avea, disse; onde ognuno,
Amico e servitor quantunque caro,
N' uscì, ma pria le finestre serraro.

23.

A quel che segue, vaga donna, appresso,
  Non curo io guari se non se' presente,
Perciocchè il mio ingegno da sè stesso,
  (Se la memoria debol non gli mente)
Saprà il grave dolor, dal quale oppresso
  Per la partenza tua tristo si sente,
Ben raccontar senza alcun tuo soccorso,
Che se' cagion di sì amaro morso.

24.

I'ho infino a qui lieto cantato
  Il ben che Troilo sentì per amore,
Come che di sospir fosse mischiato,
  Or di letizia volgere in dolore
Conviemmi, perchè se da te ascoltato
  Non son, non curo, che a forza il core
Ti cangerà, facendoti pietosa
Della mia vita più ch' altra dogliosa.

25.

Ma se pur viene a' tuoi orecchi mai,
  Pregoti per l' amore il qual ti porto,
Che abbi alcun rispetto alli miei guai,
  E ritornando mi rendi il conforto
Il qual col tuo partir levato m' hai:
  E se discaro t' è 'l trovarmi morto,
Ritorna tosto, che poca è la vita,
La qual lasciato m' ha la tua partita.

22.

And thence he betook himself toward his own palace, without hearkening or turning to anyone, and sighing and dejected as he was, desiring no company, passed thence to his chamber and declared that he wished to rest. Wherefore everyone, friend and servant alike, however dear, went forth, but closed the windows first.

23.

To that which now followeth, lovely lady, I care not overmuch if thou dost not lend thy presence, since my understanding will of itself, if weak memory deceiveth it not, find a way, without any aid of thine, to tell the story of the heavy grief on account of which it feeleth oppressed because of thy departure, for thou art the cause of such bitter woe.

24.

Till now have I happily sung the joy that Troilus felt in his love, although with sighs 'twere mingled, but now from joy 'tis fitting to turn to grief. Wherefore, if thou listenest to me not, naught care I, for perforce thy heart will change, filling thee with pity for my life, more than any other grievous.

25.

But if indeed it ever come to thy ears, I pray thee by the love that I bear thee, have some regard for my woes and by thy return bring me back the comfort which thou didst take away from me by thy departure, and if it is displeasing to thee to find me dead, return at once, for short is the life which thy departure hath left me.

26.

Rimaso adunque Troilo soletto
　Nella camera sua serrata e scura,
　E senza aver di nessun uom sospetto,
　O di potere udito esser paura,
　Il raccolto dolor nel tristo petto
　Per la venuta subita sventura
　Cominciò ad aprire in tal maniera,
　Ch' uom non parea, ma arrabbiata fiera.

27.

Nè altrimenti il toro va saltando
　Or qua or là, dappoi c' ha ricevuto
　Il mortal colpo, e misero mugghiando
　Conoscer fa qual duolo ha conceputo,
　Che Troilo facesse, nabissando
　Sè stesso, e percuotendo dissoluto
　Il capo al muro, e con le man la faccia,
　Con pugni il petto e le dolenti braccia.

28.

I miseri occhi per pietà del core
　Forte piangeano, e parean due fontane
　Ch' acqua gittassero abbondevol fuore;
　Gli alti singhiozzi del pianto, e le vane
　Parole, ancor toglievano il valore;
　Le quali ancor delle passate strane,
　Null' altro fuor che morte gian chiedendo,
　Gl' iddii e sè bestemmiando e schernendo.

29.

Da poi che la gran furia diede loco,
　E per lunghezza temperossi il pianto,
　Troilo acceso nel dolente foco
　Sopra 'l suo letto si gittò alquanto;
　Non restando però punto nè poco
　Di pianger forte e di sospirar tanto,
　Che 'l capo e 'l petto appena gli bastava,
　A tanta noia quanta si donava.

26.

Now Troilus, who had remained alone in his locked and darksome chamber, mistrusting no man nor fearing lest he might be heard, began to give vent to the grief gathered in his sad breast by reason of his sudden mischance in such wise that he seemed not a man but a raging beast.

27.

Not otherwise doth the bull go leaping, now here now there, when once he hath received the mortal thrust, and bellowing in his misery maketh known the pain he hath conceived, than did Troilus, casting himself prone, and in a frenzy beating his head against the wall, and his face with his hands, his breast and aching arms with his fists.

28.

His wretched eyes through pity for his heart did weep right sore and they did seem two fountains throwing forth abundant jets of water. The deep sobs of his weeping and his vain words did ever sap his strength. Ever came forth his speech in strange outbursts, demanding naught else but death, cursing and mocking the gods and himself.

29.

When his great fury had spent itself and for long continuance his weeping had abated, Troilus, enkindled in the fire of sorrow, threw himself a little while upon his bed, not however ceasing for even so little from weeping sorely and sighing so much that head and breast scarce sufficed him for all the grief to which he gave way.

30.

Poi poco appresso cominciò a dire
 Seco nel pianto : o misera fortuna,
 Che t'ho io fatto, che ad ogni desire
 Mio sì t' opponi? Non hai tu più alcuna
 Altra faccenda fuor che 'l mio languire?
 Perchè sì tosto hai voltata la bruna
 Faccia ver me, che già t' amava assai
 Più ch' altro iddio, come tu crudel sai?

31.

Se la mia vita lieta e grazïosa
 Ti dispiacea, perchè non abbattevi
 Tu la superbia d' Ilïon pomposa?
 Perchè il padre mio non mi toglievi?
 Che non Ettor, nel cui valor si posa
 Ogni speranza in questi tempi grievi?
 Perchè non ten portavi Polissena,
 E perchè non Paris, ed anco Elena?

32.

Se a me fosse Criseida sola
 Rimasa, di nïuno altro gran danno
 Non curerei, nè ne farei parola;
 Ma li tuoi strali drittamente vanno
 Sempre alle cose d' onde s' ha più gola;
 Per mostrar più la forza del tuo inganno,
 Tu te ne porti tutto il mio conforto:
 Deh ora avessi tu me innanzi morto!

33.

Omè Amor, signor dolce e piacente,
 Il qual sai ciò che nell' anima giace,
 Come farà la mia vita dolente,
 S' io perdo questo ben, questa mia pace?
 Omè Amor soave, che la mente
 Mi consolasti già, signor verace,
 Che farò io, se m' è tolta costei,
 A cui per tuo voler tutto mi diei?

30.

Shortly after began he to say to himself in his plaint: "O grudging fortune, what have I done to thee that thou dost so oppose thyself to my every desire? Hast thou no longer aught else to busy thee save my grief? Why hast thou so quickly turned thy dark face toward me, who formerly loved thee far more than any god, as thou wotst well in thy cruelty?

31.

"If my happy and pleasing life was displeasing to thee, why didst thou not humble the stately pride of Ilium? Why didst thou not take from me my father? Why not Hector, on whose valor resteth every hope in these grievous times? Why didst thou not carry off from us Polyxena and why not Paris and Helen too?

32.

"If Cressida alone were left to me, I should care not for any other great loss nor should I complain of it. But thy shafts ever fly straight at the things whereof we have the greatest desire. The more to show the force of thy treachery, thou dost carry away from me all my comfort. Would indeed that thou hadst slain me first.

33.

"Alas, Love, sweet and pleasing lord, who knowest what lieth in my heart, how shall my sorrowful life find occupation, if I lose this happiness, this peace of mine? Alas, gentle Love, who didst once give comfort to my mind, what shall I do, true lord, if she to whom by thy will I gave myself wholly, be taken away from me?

34.

Io piangerò, e sempre doloroso
  Starò dove ch' io sia, mentre la vita
  Durerà in questo mio corpo angoscioso.
  O anima tapina ed ismarrita,
  Che non ti fuggi dal più sventuroso
  Corpo che viva? O anima invilita,
  Esci del corpo e Criseida segui:
  Perchè nol fai? Perchè non ti dilegui?

35.

O dolenti occhi, il cui conforto tutto
  Di Criseida nostra era nel viso,
  Che farete oramai? in tristo lutto
  Sempre starete, poi da voi diviso
  Sarà, e 'l valor vostro fia distrutto,
  Dal vostro lacrimar vinto e conquiso;
  Invano omai vedrete altra virtute,
  Se el v' è tolta la vostra salute.

36.

O Criseida mia, o dolce bene
  Dell' anima dolente che ti chiama,
  Chi darà più conforto alle mie pene?
  Chi porrà in pace l' amorosa brama?
  Se tu ten vai, oimè morir conviene
  A colui lasso che più che sè t' ama;
  E io morrò senza averlo meritato,
  De' dispietati iddii sia il peccato.

37.

Deh, or si fosse questo tuo partire
  Tanto indugiato, ch' apparato avessi
  Per lunga usanza, lasso, a sofferire;
  Io non vo' dir che io non m' opponessi
  A mio potere a non lasciarti gire;
  Ma se pur ciò addivenir vedessi,
  Per lunga usanza mi saria soave
  La tua partenza, che or mi par sì grave.

34.

"I shall weep and ever sorrowful shall I remain where'er I be, whilst life endureth in this distressful body of mine. O soul unhappy and dismayed, why fleest thou not from the wretchedest body alive? O dejected soul, flee forth the body and follow Cressida. Why dost thou not? Why not dissolve in air?

35.

"O wretched eyes, whose comfort was all in the visage of our Cressida, what will ye do now? In bitter mourning shall ye ever abide, since your comfort will be parted from you and your worth destroyed, o'erwhelmed and vanquished by your weeping. Vainly shall ye see other virtue now that your health is reft from you.

36.

"O Cressida mine, O sweet joy of the sorrowing soul that calleth upon thee, who will give further comfort to my woes? Who will quiet the yearnings of love? If thou departest hence, alas, 'tis fitting that the weary one who loveth thee more than himself should die. And die I shall, though I deserved it not—to blame be the pitiless gods.

37.

"Would indeed that this thy departure had been so delayed that I wretched one that I am might by long habit have learned to endure it. Sad as I should have been at the thought, I will not say that I would not have opposed letting thee go with all my might, but if I should still have seen it happen, thy going, which now seemeth so bitter to me, would by long habit have become sweet in mine eyes.

38.

O vecchio malvissuto, o vecchio insano,
   Qual fantasia ti mosse, o quale sdegno,
   A gire a' Greci essendo tu Troiano?
   Eri onorato in tutto il nostro regno,
   Più di te nullo regnicolo o strano.
   O iniquo consiglio, o petto pregno
   Di tradimenti, d' inganni e di noia,
   Or t' avess' io qual io vorrei in Troia!

39.

Or fostu morto il dì che tu n' uscisti;
   Or fostu morto a piè de' Greci allora
   Che tu la bocca primamente apristi
   A richieder colei che m' innamora!
   O quanto al mondo mal per me venisti!
   Tu se' cagion del dolor che m' accora:
   La lancia che passò Protesilao
   T' avesse nel cor fitta Menelao!

40.

S'tu fossi morto i' viverei per certo,
   Che chi cercar Criseida non sarebbe;
   S' tu fossi morto io non sarei diserto,
   Da me Criseida non si partirebbe;
   S' tu fossi morto, io veggio assai aperto,
   Quel che mi duole agual* non mi dorrebbe;
   Dunque la vita tua è di mia morte
   Trista cagione, e di dogliosa sorte.

41.

Mille sospiri più che fuoco ardenti
   N' uscivan fuor dell' amoroso petto,
   Misti con pianti e con detti dolenti,
   Senza dar l' uno all' altro alcun rispetto;
   E sì vinto l' avean questi lamenti,
   Che più non potea oltre il giovinetto,
   Ond' el s' addormentò, ma non dormio
   Guari di tempo, che si risentio.

* Savj-Lopez, *equal*

38.

"O wicked, O crazed old man, what fancy or what rancor moved thee, being a Trojan, to go to the Greeks? Thou wert honored in all our kingdom, none more so, native or stranger. O wicked counsel, O breast astir with treachery, deceit, and spite, would indeed that I had thee, as I should wish, in Troy!

39.

"Would that thou hadst been dead the day thou wentest forth. Would that thou hadst been dead at the feet of the Greeks when thou didst first open thy lips to require again her who stirreth my love. O in what an ill hour for me didst thou come into the world! Thou art the cause of the grief that afflicteth me. Would that Menelaus had thrust in thine heart the lance that pierced Protesilaus.

40.

"If thou wert dead I certainly should live, for none there would be to seek Cressida. If thou wert dead, I should not be disconsolate; Cressida would not be parted from me. If thou wert dead, clearly do I see it, that which afflicteth me now would not so distress me then. Therefore thy life is the sad cause of my death and doleful fate."

41.

Forth from his loving breast there issued, without waiting their turn, a thousand sighs, more burning than fire, mingled with tears and sorrowful words. And these laments had so o'erwhelmed him that the youth could weep no more. Whereupon he fell asleep, but slept not long before he awoke again.

42.

E sospirando, in piè si fu levato,
   Ginne alla porta che serrata avea,
   E quella aperse, e ad un suo privato
   Valletto, disse: fa' che tu non stea,
   Subitamente Pandaro chiamato,
   Fa' ch' a me venga: e quindi si tollea
   Al buio della camera doglioso,
   Pien di sospiri e tutto sonnacchioso.

43.

Pandaro venne, e già avea sentito
   Ciò che chiedeano i greci ambasciadori;
   E come aveano ancora per partito
   Preso, di render Criseida i signori;
   Di che nel viso tutto sbigottito,
   Ti Troilo seco pensando i dolori,
   Nella camera entrò oscura e cheta,
   Nè sa che dir parola o trista o lieta.

44.

Troilo, tosto che veduto l' ebbe,
   Gli corse al collo sì forte piangendo,
   Che bene raccontarlo uom non potrebbe;
   Il che il dolente Pandaro sentendo,
   A pianger cominciò, sì glie n' increbbe;
   E in cotal guisa, null' altro facendo
   Che pianger forte, dimoraro alquanto
   Senza parlar nessuno o tanto o quanto.

45.

Ma poi che Troilo ebbe presa lena,
   Pria cominciò a Pandaro: io son morto:
   La mia letizia s' è voltata in pena.
   Misero me, il mio dolce conforto,
   Fortuna invidïosa se nel mena,
   E con lui insieme il sollazzo e 'l diporto.
   Hai tu sentito ancor come ne sia
   Da' Greci tolta Criseïda mia?

42.

After rising in sighs to his feet he went to the door he had locked. This he opened and said to a servant of his: "Make haste, summon Pandarus quickly, and make him come to me." And then full of sighs and all heavy with sleep he withdrew in sadness to the darkness of his chamber.

43.

Pandarus came. Already had he heard what demands the Greek emissaries were making and also how the lords had already directed to give back Cressida. Whereat all disturbed in his visage, pondering Troilus' sorrows, he entered the dark and quiet chamber, nor knoweth he what word, sad or happy, to utter.

44.

Troilus, as soon as he had seen him, ran to his neck, weeping so sorely that no man could tell it aright. And when sorrowing Pandarus heard his sobs, he too began to weep, so sorry did he feel for him. And in such wise, doing naught else but weeping bitterly, they stood awhile, and neither spake, even though 'twere little.

45.

But when Troilus had taken breath, first he began to Pandarus: "I am dead, my happiness hath turned to pain. O wretched me, my sweet comfort envious fortune leadeth away and together with it my solace and my pleasure. Hast thou yet heard how my Cressida hath been taken hence by the Greeks?"

46.

Pandaro, il qual non men forte piangea,
  Rispose: sì, così non fosse 'l vero!
Oimè lasso, ch' io non mi credea,
  Che questo tempo sì dolce e sincero
Mancasse così tosto; nè potea
  Meco vedere che al tuo bene intero
Potesse nuocer fuor che palesarsi;
Or veggio tutt' i nostri avvisi scarsi.

47.

Ma tu, perchè tanta angoscia ti dai?
  Perchè tanto dolore e tal tormento?
Ciò che desideravi avuto l' hai,
  Esser dovresti sol di ciò contento:
Lasciagli a me e questi e gli altri guai,
  C' ho sempre amato, e mai un guatamento
Non ebbi da colei che mi disface,
E che potrebbe sola darmi pace.

48.

Ed oltre a ciò, questa città si vede
  Piena di belle donne e grazïose,
E se 'l ben ch' io ti vo' merita fede,
  Nulla ce n' è, quai vuoi le più vezzose,
Che a grado non le sia aver mercede
  Di te, se tu per lei in amorose
Pene entrerai, però se noi perdemo
Costei, molt' altre ne ritroveremo.

49.

E come io udii già sovente dire,
  Il nuovo amor sempre caccia l' antico;
Nuovo piacere il presente martire
  Torrà da te, se tu fai quel ch' io dico.
Dunque non vogli per costei morire,
  Nè vogli di te stesso esser nemico:
Credi per pianto forse riaverla?
O ch' ella non sen vada ritenerla?

46.

Pandarus, who was weeping no less bitterly, replied: "Yes, would it were not true. Ah! woe is me! for I did not believe that this time so sweet and untroubled should so soon be cut short. Nor for myself was I able to see that anything could harm your perfect bliss but its disclosure. Now I see how feeble were all our counsels.

47.

"But thou, why dost thou give thyself such anguish? Why such grief and torment? That which thou didst desire, thou hast had; thou shouldst be content with that alone. Leave both these and other woes to me, who have always loved and never had a glance from her who undoeth me and who alone could give me peace.

48.

"And beside that, this city is seen to be full of fair and gracious ladies, and if the happiness which I wish thee meriteth belief, there is not one among them—the fairest thou wilt—that will not gladly have pity upon thee, if thou wilt suffer the pangs of love for her. Therefore if we lose this lady, many others shall we find.

49.

"And as I have already often heard men say, 'the new love ever driveth away the old.' A new pleasure will take the present anguish away from thee, if thou doest what I tell thee. Then wish not to die for her, nor wish to be thine own enemy. Dost thou think perchance to have her back by weeping or to prevent her going away?"

50.

Troilo udendo Pandaro, più forte
  A pianger cominciò, dicendo appresso:
  Io prego Dio che mi mandi la morte,
  Prima che io commetta un tale eccesso;
  Come che belle leggiadre ed accorte
  Sian l' altre donne, ed io il ti confesso,
  Nulla cen fu mai simile a costei,
  A cui son dato, e tutto son di lei.

51.

Da' suoi begli occhi mosser le faville
  Che del fuoco amoroso m' infiammaro;
  Queste pe' miei passando a mille a mille,
  Soavemente amor seco menaro
  Dentro dal cor, nel quale esso sentille
  Come gli piacque; e quivi incominciaro
  Primiere il fuoco, il cui sommo fervore
  Cagione è stato d' ogni mio valore;

52.

Il qual perch' io volessi, che non voglio,
  Spegner non potre' mai, tant' è possente,
  E se più fosse ancor non me ne doglio,
  Stesse Criseida nosco solamente
  Del cui partir, non dell' amor cordoglio
  L' anima innamorata dentro sente;
  Nè altra c' è, non dispiaccia a nessuna,
  Ch' eguagliar le si possa in cosa alcuna.

53.

Dunque come potrebbe amor giammai,
  O d' alcuno i conforti, il mio desio
  Volgere ad altra donna? I' ho assai
  A sostener d' angoscia nel cor mio,
  Ma troppa più fino agli estremi guai
  Ve ne riceverei, prima che io
  In altra donna l' animo ponessi,
  Amore, Iddio, e'l mondo questo cessi.

50.

Troilus, hearing Pandarus, began to weep the more bitterly and then said: "I pray the gods to send me death before I commit such a sin. Although the other ladies are fair, winsome, and well-bred—and I confess to thee that they are so—never was there any like unto her whose slave I am, and I am entirely hers.

51.

"From her eyes darted the sparks that inflamed me with the fire of love. Passing by the thousands through mine eyes, they brought love with them gently into my heart, where it felt them to its pleasure. Here they first enkindled the fire the exceeding heat of which hath been the cause of every excellent thing in me.

52.

"Which even if I would, for I will not, I could never extinguish, so powerful is it, and if it were greater still, I grieve not at it, were Cressida only to remain with us, because of whose parting, and not on Love's account, the enamored soul feeleth sorrow within. Nor is there other—to none be it displeasing—who can in any way be compared to her.

53.

"How then could Love or the consolations of anyone ever turn my desire to another lady? Anguish enough have I to bear in my heart but much more, even to extremest woe, would I give lodgment to, ere I should set my heart upon any other lady. Love, the gods, and this world prevent it.

54.

E la morte e 'l sepolcro dipartire
  Questo mio fermo amor soli potranno;
  Che che di ciò mi si deggia seguire,
  Questi con lui la mia alma merranno
  Giù nell' inferno all' ultimo martire;
  Quivi insieme Criseida piangeranno,
  Di cui sempre sarò dove ch' io sia,
  Se per morire, amor non se n' oblia.

55.

Dunque, per Dio, il ragionar di questo
  Pandaro cessa, ch' altra donna vegna
  Nel cor, dov' io nel suo abito onesto
  Criseida tegno come certa insegna
  De' miei piacer; quantunque ora molesto
  Sia alla mente, ch' al suo mal s' ingegna,
  Il suo partir del qual fra noi si parla,
  Ch' ancor di quinci non veggiam mutarla.

56.

Ma tu favelli divisatamente;
  Quasi ragioni che men pena sia
  Il perder, che il non aver niente
  Avuto mai: ell' è chiara follia,
  Pandaro, se t' è questo nella mente:
  Ch' ogni dolor trapassa quel che ria
  Fortuna adduce a chi è stato felice,
  E partesi dal ver chi altro dice.

57.

Ma dimmi, se del mio amor ti cale,
  Poscia ch' egli ti par così leggiero
  Il permutare amore, come avale
  Mi ragionavi tu, perchè sentiero
  Non hai mutato? Perchè tanto male
  Di te si porta il tuo amor severo?
  Perchè non hai altra donna seguita,
  Ch' avesse in pace posta la tua vita?

54.

"Death and the tomb will alone have power to sever my constant love. Whatever must after happen to me on their account, they shall lead my soul down with them to Hell, to the extremest torment. There together shall they lament for Cressida, whose I shall ever remain, where'er I be, if love be not forgotten in death.

55.

"So for the love of the gods, Pandarus, cease urging that any other lady come into my heart, where I hold Cressida in her modest habit, as a sure token of my pleasures, however displeasing her departure—of which there is talk among us, for as yet we do not see her transported hence—may now be to the mind which is intent upon its woe.

56.

"But thou speakest in set terms, as who should say less pain it is to lose than never to have had anything. This is sheer folly, Pandarus, if this is in thy mind. For that sorrow which harsh Fortune bringeth to him who hath once been happy, surpasseth any other. He who sayeth otherwise, departeth from the truth.

57.

"But tell me, if in my love thou hast any concern, since, as thou hast just now been telling me, to change one's love appeareth to thee so slight a matter, why hast thou not changed thy course? Why doth thy cruel love bear manifest signs of thine ill-being? Why hast thou not followed another lady who would have brought peace to thy life?

58.

Se tu che viver suoi d' amor cruccioso,
   Non l' hai in altra potuto mutare,
   Io che con lui vivea lieto e gioioso,
   Come 'l potrò da me così cacciare
   Come ragioni? Perchè angoscioso
   Caso subitamente soprastare
   Ora mi veggia? Io son per altra guisa
   Preso, che la tua mente non divisa.

59.

Credimi Pandar, credimi che amore
   Quando s' apprende per sommo piacere
   Nell' animo d' alcun, cacciarnel fuore
   Non si può mai, ma puonne ben cadere
   In processo di tempo, se dolore,
   O morte, o povertà, o non vedere
   La cosa amata non gli son cagione,
   Com' egli avvenne già a più persone.

60.

Che farò dunque, lasso sventurato,
   Se io Criseida perdo in tal maniera
   Che l' ho perduta? perocchè cambiato
   A lei è Antenore: oimè che m' era
   La morte meglio, o non esser mai nato:
   Deh che farò? il mio cor si dispera:
   Deh, morte vieni a me che t' addimando,
   Deh vien, non mi lasciar languire amando.

61.

Morte, tu mi sarai tanto soave,
   Quant' è la vita a chi lieta la mena:
   Già l' orrido tuo aspetto non m' è grave,
   Dunque vieni e finisci la mia pena.
   Deh non tardar, che questo fuoco m' ave
   Incesa già sì ciascheduna vena,
   Che refrigerio il tuo colpo mi fia,
   Deh vieni omai che 'l cuor pur ti disia.

58.

"If thou, who art wont to live a love-vexed existence, hast been unable to change thy love to another, how shall I, who lived with love in happiness and joy, be able to drive it from me in the way thou sayest? Why do I see grievous calamity now suddenly threaten me? I have been taken captive in other fashion, which thy mind comprehendeth not.

59.

"Believe me, Pandarus, believe me that love when it taketh root in the mind of anyone for highest pleasure, can never be driven forth, but may well decline in process of time, if grief, or death, or poor estate, or not seeing the object beloved do not occasion it, as already hath happened to many an one.

60.

"What shall I do then, unhappy I, if I love Cressida in such manner? I have lost her because Antenor hath been exchanged for her. Alas, how much better were death or never to have been born! What shall I do? My heart despaireth. Ah, death, come to me who call thee. Come, leave me not to languish in my love.

61.

"Death, thou wilt be as sweet to me as is life to him who liveth a happy one. Already thy dreadful aspect is not fearful to me. Come, then, end my suffering. Tarry not, for this fire hath already so set each vein aflame that thy blow will be a cooling relief to me. Come now, for my heart indeed yearneth for thee.

62.

Uccidimi per Dio, non consentire
　Ch' io viva tanto in questo mondo, ch' io
　Il cuor del corpo mi veggia partire.
　Deh fallo morte, i' ten prego per Dio,
　Assai mi dorrà quel più che 'l morire,
　Contenta in questa parte il mio disio;
　Tu n' uccidi ben tanti oltre al volere,
　Che ben puo' fare a me questo piacere.

63.

Così piangendo si rammaricava
　Troilo, e Pandar facea similmente,
　E nondimen sovente il confortava,
　Quanto poteva il più pietosamente;
　Ma tal conforto nïente giovava,
　Anzi cresceva continovamente
　Il pianto doloroso ed il tormento,
　Tant' era di cotal cosa scontento.

64.

A cui Pandaro disse: amico caro,
　Se non t' aggradan gli argomenti miei,
　Ed ètti tanto quanto par discaro
　Il dipartir futuro di costei,
　Perchè non prendi in quel che puoi riparo
　Alla tua vita, e via rapisci lei?
　Paris andò in Grecïa e menonne
　Elena, il fior di tutte l' altre donne.

65.

E tu in Troia tua non ardirai
　Di rapire una donna chi ti piaccia?
　Tu fara' questo se mi crederai:
　Caccia via il dolor, caccia via, caccia
　L' angoscia tua e li dolenti guai;
　Rasciuga il tristo pianto della faccia,
　E l' animo tuo grande ora dimostra,
　Oprando sì che Criseida sia nostra.

62.

"For the love of the gods slay me, permit me not to live so long in this world that I see my heart depart from my body. Ah, do this, death, I pray thee in the name of the gods. Much more will that grieve me than dying. In this respect satisfy my desire. Thou slayest so many against their will that thou canst well do me this favor."

63.

Thus weeping did Troilus make lament and Pandarus did likewise. Nevertheless he often, when he could, comforted him most tenderly. But such comfort was of no avail; rather did the dolorous lament and anguish continually increase, so much was he distraught by this thing.

64.

To whom Pandarus said: "If my reasoning doth not please thee, dear friend, and the coming departure of this lady is as irksome to thee as it seemeth, why dost thou not take remedy for thy life in what way thou canst and ravish her away? Paris went into Greece and brought thence Helen, the flower of all other ladies.

65.

"And wilt thou in thine own Troy town not dare to steal a lady that pleaseth thee? This shalt thou do, if thou wilt heed my advice. Drive forth thy grief, drive it forth, drive forth thine anguish and thy grievous woes, dry the sad tears from thy face, and display now thy great courage, pursuing thy course so that Cressida may be ours."

66.

Troilo allora a Pandaro rispose:
Ben veggio amico ch' ogni ingegno poni
Per levar via le mie pene angosciose:
I' ho pensato ciò che tu ragioni,
E divisate ancor molt' altre cose,
Come ch' io pianga e tutto m' abbandoni
Nel dolore ch' avanza ogni mia possa,
Sì grave è stata la sua gran percossa;

67.

Nè mai però da consiglio dovuto
Potuto ho tor nel mio fervente amore;
Anzi pensando, ho con meco veduto
Che 'l tempo non concede tale errore,
Che se ciascun de' nostri rivenuto
Qui ritto* fosse, ed ancora Antenore,
Di romper fede i' non mi curerei,
Fosse ciò che potesse, anzi il farei.

68.

Poi temo di turbar con violenta
Rapina, il suo onore e la sua fama,
Nè so ben s' ella ne fosse contenta,
Ed io so pure ch' ella molto m' ama;
Per che a prender partito non s' attenta
Il cuor, che d' una parte questo brama,
E d' altra teme di non dispiacere,
Che non piacendol, non la vorre' avere.

69.

Pensato ancora avea di domandarla
Di grazia al padre mio che la mi desse;
Poi penso questo fora un accusarla,
E far palese le cose commesse;
Nè spero ancora ch' el dovesse darla,
Sì per non romper le cose promesse,
E perchè la direbbe diseguale
A me, al qual vuol dar donna reale.

* Savj-Lopez, *Quiritto*

[318]

66.

Troilus then made answer to Pandarus: "Well do I see, my friend, that thou dost bend thine every thought to take away my carking cares. What thou sayest I have thought, and devised many other plans, too, although I weep and despond utterly in the distress which is beyond every power of mind, so grievous hath been its heavy blow.

67.

"Never, however, have I been able in my fervent love to turn aside from the plan that duty hath impelled me to take. Rather have I, upon thinking the matter over, come to the conclusion that the times do not warrant such a departure, though were each of our men come back here straightway, and Antenor as well, I would care not about the breaking of our faith. Rather would I break it, let come what might.

68.

"Then too I fear to disturb her honor and good name by violently stealing her away, nor am I sure that she could consent thereto, though I know indeed that she loveth me much. On this account my heart ventureth not upon resolve, since while on the one hand it desireth this thing, on the other it feareth to give displeasure, for were it not pleasing to her, I would not wish to possess her.

69.

"I had thought even of asking as a boon of my father that he would grant her to me. But then I reflect that this would be a blaming of her and a disclosure of all that hath been done. Nor dare I hope even then that he would feel that he had any right to give her to me at the expense of a plighted troth, and because he would declare her beneath me, upon whom he desireth to bestow a lady of royal lineage.

70.

Così piangendo, in amorosa erranza
   Dimoro lasso, e non so che mi fare;
   Imperocchè 'l valor, se pure avanza,
   Forte d' amor, il mi sento mancare,
   E d' ogni parte fugge le speranza,
   E crescon le cagion del tormentare:
   Vorrei io esser morto il giorno ch' io
   Prima m' accesi in sì fatto desio.

71.

Pandaro disse allora: tu farai
   Come ti piacerà, ma s' io acceso
   Fossi, come tu mostri essere assai,
   Quantunque fosse grave questo peso,
   Avendo la potenza che tu hai,
   Se non mi fosse per forza difeso,
   Di portarla farei il mio potere,
   A cui ch' el si dovesse dispiacere.

72.

Non guarda amor cotanto sottilmente,
   Quanto par che tu facci, quando cuoce
   Ben da dover l' innamorata mente;
   Il qual, se quanto di' fiero ti nuoce,
   Seguita 'l suo volere, e virilmente
   T' opponi a questo tormento feroce,
   E vogli innanzi esser ripreso alquanto,
   Che con martír morire in tristo pianto.

73.

Tu non hai da rapir donna che sia
   Dal tuo voler lontana, ma è tale,
   Che di ciò che farai contenta fia;
   E se di ciò seguisse troppo male,
   O biasimo di te, tu hai la via
   Di riuscirne tosto, ch' è cotale,
   Renderla indietro: la fortuna aiuta
   Chiunque è ardito, e' timidi rifiuta.

70.

"Thus in tears do I bide aweary in amorous perplexity and know not what to do, because I feel the mighty power of Love, if indeed it is strong, is lacking in me, and on every hand hope taketh flight and the causes of my anguish increase. I would like to have died the day that I first felt the burning heat of such desire."

71.

Then said Pandarus: "Thou wilt do as it shall please thee, but were I burning, as thou dost very clearly show thyself to be, however heavy the burden might be, had I the power that thou hast, if I were not forcibly prevented, I would do my utmost to ravish her away, whomever it might displease.

72.

"Love doth not look so subtly as it seemeth thou dost, when the enamored mind burneth, as well it should. If Love harmeth thee so fiercely, follow his will, and, like a man, do thou oppose thyself to this cruel torment and choose rather to be somewhat blamed than to die with suffering in sad plaint.

73.

"Thou hast not to ravish a lady who is far from thy desire, but she is such that she will be content with whatever thou doest, and if too great evil or blame of thee should result therefrom, thou hast the means of putting an immediate end to it—that is, to bring her back again. Fortune aideth whoever is bold and turneth her back upon the timid.

74.

E se pur questa cosa a lei gravasse,
  In breve tempo ne riavrai pace.
  Non che io creda ch' ella sen crucciasse,
  Tanto l' amor che le porti le piace;
  Della sua fama, perch' ella mancasse,
  A dirti il ver men grava e men dispiace:
  Passisene ella come fa Elèna,
  Pur ch' ella faccia la tua voglia piena.

75.

Adunque piglia ardir, sii valoroso,
  Amor promessa non cura nè fede;
  Mostrati un poco al presente animoso,
  Abbi di te medesimo mercede.
  Io sarò teco in ciascun periglioso
  Caso, cotanto quanto mi concede
  Il poter mio; presumi pur di fare,
  Gl' iddii ci avranno poscia ad aiutare.

76.

Troilo il detto molto bene intese
  Di Pandaro, e rispose: io son contento;
  Ma s' elle fosser mille volte accese
  Le fiamme mie, e maggiore il tormento
  Che el non è, alla donna cortese,
  Per soddisfarmi, un picciol gravamento
  Io non farei; in pria vorrei morire,
  Però da lei il vo' prima sentire.

77.

Dunque leviamci quinci e più non stiamo;
  Lávati il viso, e ritorniamo a corte,
  E sotto il riso il dolore occultiamo;
  Di nulla ancor si son le genti accorte,
  Che stando qui, maravigliar facciamo
  Ciascun che 'l sa; or fa' che tu sii forte
  In ben celare, ed io terrò maniera,
  Che con Criseida parlerai stasera.

74.

"And even if this thing should displease her, in a short time thou shalt have again thy peace. Not that I believe that she would be angry thereat, so much pleaseth her the love that thou dost bear her. As to her reputation, that it should suffer diminution, is, to tell the truth, less grievous and displeasing. Let her do without it, as Helen doeth, provided she doeth thine entire will.

75.

"Then pluck up courage, be valorous; love careth not for promise nor for faith. Show thyself a little courageous now; have pity upon thyself. I shall be with thee in every perilous case, insomuch as my power alloweth. Dare to act; hereafter the gods will be constrained to aid us."

76.

Troilus gave close heed to what Pandarus said and replied: "I am content. But if my flame were a thousand times enkindled and my anguish greater than it is, I would not, to satisfy myself, do this courteous lady ever so little harm; rather would I die. Therefore I wish to hear it first from her.

77.

"Let us now go hence and abide no longer. Wash thy face and let us return to court, and conceal our grief beneath a smiling countenance. Nothing yet have people perceived. For by staying here we make everyone who knoweth it marvel. Now act so that thou be strong in wise concealment, and I will contrive that thou shalt have speech with Cressida this evening."

78.

La fama velocissima, la quale
   Il falso e 'l vero ugualmente rapporta,
   Era volata con prestissim' ale
   Per tutta Troia, e con parola sciolta
   Narrato aveva chente fosse e quale
   L' ambasciata de' Greci stata porta,
   E che Criseida data dal signore
   Alli Greci era in cambio d' Antenore.

79.

La qual novella siccome l' udio
   Criseida, che già non si curava
   Del padre più: Oimè tristo il cor mio!
   Disse fra sè, e forte le noiava,
   Come a colei ch' avea volto il disio
   A Troilo, il quale più che altro amava,
   E per paura ciò ch' udia contare
   Non fosse ver, non ardia domandare.

80.

Ma come noi veggiam che egli avviene,
   Che l' una donna all' altra a visitare
   Ne' casi nuovi va se le vuol bene,
   Così sen venner molte a dimorare
   Con Criseida il giorno, tutte piene
   Di pietosa allegrezza, e a raccontare
   Le cominciaron con ordine il fatto,
   Com' ell' era renduta, e con che patto.

81.

Diceva l' una: certo assai mi piace
   Che tu torni al tuo padre e sii con lui.
   L' altra diceva: E a me me ne dispiace
   Vederla dipartir quinci da nui.
   L' altra diceva: ella potrà la pace
   Nostra ordinare, e far con esso lui,
   Il qual sapete, come avete udito,
   Che prender fa qual vuol d' ogni partito.

78.

Fleetest fame, who reporteth impartially the true and the false, had flown with swiftest wings all over Troy, and had with nimble words related what and of what nature was the message brought by the Greeks and that Cressida was given to the Greeks by the king in exchange for Antenor.

79.

As Cressida, who had come by now to hold her father no longer in esteem, heard this news: "Alas, my sad heart!" said she to herself. And much it grieved her, as one who had turned her desire to Troilus, whom she loved more than any other. And for fear that what she heard related might be true, she dared not ask a question.

80.

But as we see that it happeneth that one woman goeth to visit another at some new happening, if she bear her affection, thus many came to pass the day with Cressida, all full of piteous joy, and they began to tell her the whole tale in due order, how she was surrendered and upon what agreement.

81.

Said one: "Certainly it pleaseth me much that thou dost return to thy father and that thou art to be with him." Another said: "And I am sorry to see her depart hence from us." Another said: "She will be able to lay plans for our peace and to arrange it with him who, you know by hearsay, carrieth into effect what resolution he wisheth."

82.

Questi e molt' altri parlar femminili,
  Quasi quivi non fosse, udiva quella,
  Senza risponder, tenendogli a vili;
  E non potea celar la faccia bella,
  Gli alti pensier ch' avea d' amor gentili,
  Venuti in lei per l' udita novella;
  Il corpo era ivi, e l' anima era altrove,
  Cercando Troilo senza saper dove.

83.

E queste donne che far le credeano
  Consolazione stando, sommamente
  Parlando seco assai le dispiaceano,
  Come a colei che sentia nella mente
  Tutt' altra passion che non vedeano
  Color che v' erano, ed assai sovente
  Donnescamente accomiatava quelle,
  Tal voglia avea di rimaner senz' elle.

84.

Non potea ritenere alcun sospiro,
  E tal fiata alcuna lagrimetta
  Cadendo, davan segno del martiro
  Nel qual l' anima sua era costretta:
  Ma quelle stolte che le facean giro
  Credevan, per pietà, la giovinetta
  Far ciò, ch' avesse d' abbandonar esse,
  Le quali esser solean sue compagnesse.

85.

E ciascuna voleva confortarla
  Pur sopra quello ch' a lei non dolea,
  Parole assai dicean di consolarla
  Per la partenza la qual far dovea
  Da loro, e non era altro che grattarla
  Nelle calcagne, ove 'l capo prudea;
  Ch' ella di lor niente si curava,
  Ma di Troilo solo il qual lasciava.

82.

This and much other womanish talk she heard almost as if she were not there, without answering, thinking it too base. And her fair face could not conceal the high gentle thoughts of love which she had, inspired in her by the news she had heard. The body was there and the soul elsewhere, seeking Troilus without knowing where.

83.

And these ladies, who thought they were giving her comfort by staying there, by overmuch talk highly displeased her, as one who felt in her mind quite another passion than the one seen by those who were present. And from time to time she would, in ladylike fashion, escort them to the door, such desire had she to avoid their company.

84.

An occasional sigh she could not check and now and again some little tear in its fall gave sign of the torment in which her soul was constrained. But these stupid ladies, who encircled her, believed that the maiden did this from sorrow, because she had to abandon them, who were her usual woman companions.

85.

And each did ever seek to comfort her only for that which grieved her not; many words they spake to console her for the departure which she was to make from them, and it was no different than scratching her in the heels for an itch in the head, for no thought took she for them, but for Troilus alone, whom she was leaving behind.

86.

Ma dopo molto cinguettare in vano,
  Come fanno le più, s' accomiataro,
  E girsen via ; ed ella a mano a mano
  Vinta e sospinta da dolore amaro,
  Nella camera sua piangendo piano
  Se n' entrò dentro, e senza far riparo
  Con consiglio nessuno al suo gran male,
  Tal pianger fe', che mai non si fe' tale.

87.

Erasi la dolente in sul suo letto
  Gittata stesa, piangendo sì forte,
  Che dir non si poria ; e il bianco petto
  Spesso batteasi, chiamando la morte
  Che l' uccidesse, poichè 'l suo diletto
  Lasciar le convenia per dura sorte ;
  E i biondi crin tirandosi rompea,
  E mille volte ognor morte chiedea.

88.

Ella diceva : lassa sventurata,
  Misera me dolente, ove vo io ?
  O trista me, che 'n mal punto fu' nata,
  Dove ti lascio dolce l' amor mio ?
  Deh or fuss' io nel nascere affogata,
  O non t' avessi, dolce mio disio,
  Veduto mai, poichè sì ria ventura,
  E me a te, e te a me or fura.

89.

Che farò io, dogliosa la mia vita,
  Allor che più non ti potrò vedere ?
  Che farò io da te, Troilo, partita ?
  Certo non credo mai mangiar nè bere ;
  E se per sè non sen va la smarrita
  Anima fuor del corpo, a mio potere
  Le caccerò con fame, perch' io veggio
  Che sempre mai andrò di male in peggio.

86.

But after a deal of foolish cackling, such as most women make, they took their leave and went their ways. And she, overwhelmed and stricken on the spot by bitter grief, entered her chamber, weeping softly, and without seeking remedy for her woe with any counsel, made such weeping that none was ever made like unto it.

87.

The grieving maiden had thrown herself upon her bed, weeping so bitterly that it could not be told. And ever and anon she beat her white breast, calling upon death to slay her, since by cruel fate she was constrained to leave her beloved. And plucking her blonde hair, she tore it out and a thousand times an hour she prayed for death.

88.

Often she said: "Alas, unhappy woman, wretched, woeful as I am, whither am I bound? O miserable me, who was born in an evil hour, where leave I thee, sweet my love? Would that I had been stifled at my birth or that I had never seen thee, my sweet desire, since cruel fortune now stealeth both me from thee and thee from me.

89.

"What shall I do, sorrowful life of mine, when I cannot see thee again? What shall I do separated from thee, Troilus? Certainly I believe I shall never eat nor drink again. And if of its own accord the bewildered soul parteth not from the body, as much as ever I may, shall I drive it forth with hunger, since I see that I shall always go from bad to worse?

90.

Or vedova sarò io daddovero,
  Poichè da te dipartir mi conviene,
  Cuor del mio corpo, e 'l vestimento nero
  Ver testimonio fia delle mie pene.
  Oimè lassa, che duro pensiero
  È quello in che la partenza mi tiene!
  Oimè, come potrò io sofferire,
  Troilo vedermi da te dipartire?

91.

Come potrò io senza anima stare?
  Ella si rimarrà qui per lo certo
  Col nostro amore, e teco a lamentare
  Il partir doloroso, che per merto
  Di tanto buono amor ci convien fare;
  Oimè Troilo, or fia egli sofferto
  Da te vedermi gir, che non t' ingegni,
  Per amore o per forza mi ritegni?

92.

Io me n' andrò, nè so se fia giammai
  Ch' io ti riveggia, dolce mio amore;
  Ma tu che tanto m' ami, che farai?
  Deh potra' tu sostener tal dolore?
  Io già nol sosterrò, perocchè guai
  Soperchi mi faran crepare il core;
  Deh foss' egli pur tosto, perchè poscia
  Io sarei fuor di questa grave angoscia.

93.

O padre mio, iniquo e disleale
  Alla patria tua, sia tristo il punto
  Che nel petto ti venne sì gran male,
  Qual fu volere a' Greci esser congiunto,
  E li Troian lasciar! nell' infernale
  Valle fustu, volesse Iddio, defunto
  Te iniquo vecchio, che negli ultimi anni
  Della tua vita hai fatti tali inganni.

90.

"Now shall I be a widow in very sooth, since it behooveth me to part from thee, heart of my body, and black attire shall bear true witness to my sorrows. O woe, alas, what a hard thought is that in which the parting holdeth me! Alas, how shall I be able to suffer seeing myself parted from thee, Troilus?

91.

"How shall I be able to endure without a soul? Surely it will tarry here with our love, and with thee to lament the grievous parting which it behooveth us to make in return for love so good. Alas, Troilus, wilt thou now suffer seeing me go from thee and not strive by love or by force to stay me?

92.

"Set forth I shall, nor do I know if 'twill ever be that I may see thee again, sweet my love. But thou who dost so love me, what wilt thou do? Canst thou bear such pain as this? Of a truth I shall not bear it, since too many woes will cause my heart to break. Would that it were but soon, since afterward I would be beyond this heavy sorrow.

93.

"Oh father mine, wicked and faithless to thine own land, accursed be the moment when into thy heart came evil as great as was thy wish to join the Greeks and desert the Trojans! Would God thou wert dead in the vale of Hell, wicked old man, who in thy life's declining years hast wrought such guile!

94.

Oimè lassa, trista e dolorosa,
  Ch' a me convien portar la penitenza
Del tuo peccato, che tanto noiosa
  Vita non meritai per mia fallenza.
O verità del ciel, luce pietosa,
  Come sofferi tu cotal sentenza,
Ch' un pecchi, e l' altro pianga, com' io faccio,
Che non peccai, e di dolor mi sfaccio?

95.

Chi potrebbe giammai narrare a pieno
  Ciò che Criseida nel pianto dicea?
Certo non io, che al fatto il dir vien meno,
  Tant' era la sua noia cruda e rea.
Ma mentre tai lamenti si facieno,
  Pandaro venne, a cui non si tenea
Uscio giammai, e 'n camera sen gio,
Là dov' ella faceva il pianto pio.

96.

El vide lei in sul letto avviluppata
  Ne' singhiozzi, nel pianto e ne' sospiri;
E 'l petto tutto e la faccia bagnata
  Di lacrime le vide, ed in disiri
Di pianger gli occhi suoi, e scapigliata,
  Dar vero segno degli aspri martirj;
La qual come lui vide, fra le braccia
Per vergogna nascose la sua faccia.

97.

Crudele il punto, cominciò a dire
  Pandar, fu quel nel quale i' mi levai;
Che dovunque oggi vo doglia sentire,
  Tormenti, pianti, angoscie, ed altri guai,
Sospiri, noia, ed amaro languire
  Mi par per tutto: o Giove, che farai?
Io credo che dal ciel lacrime versi,
Tanto ti son li nostri fatti avversi.

94.

"Alas, weary, sad, and disconsolate woman that I am, for I must bear the punishment of thy sin, though I did not deserve so wearisome a life for any fault of mine! O Heaven's truth, O light of pity, how sufferest thou such a judgment that one sin and the other weep, as do I, who sinned not and am undone with grief?"

95.

Who could ever narrate in every part the words of Cressida in her lament? Surely not I, for speech falleth short of the fact, so fierce and cruel was her grief. But whilst such lamentations were in progress, came Pandarus, whom doors never halted, and entered the room where she was making her piteous plaint.

96.

And he saw her in bed, enveloped in sobs, in tears, and in sighs; he saw her whole breast and face bathed in tears and her eyes longing to weep and herself disheveled, giving true sign of bitter torment. When she saw him, she hid her face between her arms for shame.

97.

"Cruel the moment was," began Pandarus, "in which I rose, for where'er I go today, methinketh I perceive on every hand grief, torments, weeping, anguish, and other woes, sighs, pain, and bitter languishing. O Jove, what canst thou mean to do? I believe that thou dost shed tears from Heaven, so adverse are our actions to thee.

98.

Ma tu isconsolata mia sorella,
  Che credi far? credi cozzar coi fati?
Perchè disfar la tua persona bella
  Con pianti sì crudeli e smisurati?
Levati su, e volgiti, e favella,
  Leva alto il viso, e gli occhi sconsolati
Rasciuga alquanto, ed odi quel ch' io dico,
A te mandato dal tuo dolce amico.

99.

Voltossi allor Criseida, facendo
  Un pianto tal che dir non si poria,
E rimirava Pandaro, dicendo:
  Oh lassa me! che vuol l' anima mia?
La qual conviemmi abbandonar piangendo,
  Che così vuole la sventura ria;
Vuol ei sospiri, o pianti, o che domanda?
Io n' ho assai s' egli per questi manda.

100.

Ell' era tale a riguardar nel viso,
  Qual' è colei ch' alla fossa è portata;
E la sua faccia, fatta in paradiso,
  Tututta si vedea trasfigurata,
La sua vaghezza e 'l piacevole riso
  Fuggendosi, l' aveano abbandonata;
E intorno agli occhi un purpurino giro,
Dava vero segnal del suo martiro.

101.

Il che vedendo Pandaro, ch' avea
  Con Troilo pianto il giorno lungamente,
Le lagrime dolenti non potea
  Tener, ma cominciò similemente,
Lasciando star quel che parlar volea,
  A pianger con costei dogliosamente;
Ma poi ch' ebber ciò fatto insieme alquanto,
Temperò prima Pandaro il suo pianto,

98.

"But thou, disconsolate sister of mine, what thinkest thou to do? Dost thou believe that thou canst contend with the fates? Why wreck thy fair person with weepings so cruel and unmeasured? Rise up and turn and speak, lift up thy face and dry somewhat thy downcast eyes, and hear what I, sent thee by thy sweet friend, do tell thee."

99.

Then Cressida turned, making such weeping as no words could tell of, and upon Pandarus she gazed, saying: "O woe is me, what doth my soul desire? Him must I abandon in tears, for such is cruel fate's will. Wisheth he sighs or tears, or what doth he demand? I have enough, if for these he sendeth."

100.

Such was she to look at in her face as is one borne to the grave; and her face, shaped in paradise, was seen to be quite transformed; its beauty and its pleasing smile had taken flight and abandoned it; and round about her eyes a purple circle bore true witness of her suffering.

101.

When Pandarus, who had wept all the day long with Troilus, saw this, he could not restrain painful tears, but likewise began sorrowfully to weep with her, forgetting what he wished to say. But when they had somewhat indulged their grief together, Pandarus first moderated his weeping,

102.

E disse: donna, io credo ch' abbi udito,
  Ma ne son certo, come se' richesta
  Dal padre tuo, e preso è già il partito
  Di renderti dal re, sicchè di questa
  Semmana ten dei gir, s' ho 'l ver sentito;
  E quanto questo sia cosa molesta
  A Troilo, appien non si potrebbe dire,
  Il qual del tutto in duol ne vuol morire.

103.

Ed abbiam tanto pianto oggi egli ed io,
  C' ho maraviglia donde egli è venuto;
  Ora alla fine pel consiglio mio
  Alquanto s' è di pianger ritenuto,
  E par che d' esser teco abbia desio,
  Per ch' io a dir, siccome gli è paciuto,
  Tel son venuto, pria che vi partiate,
  Acciocchè insieme alquanto vi sfoghiate.

104.

Grande è, disse Criseida, il mio dolore,
  Come di quella che più che sè l'ama,
  Ma 'l suo m' è di gran lunga maggiore,
  Udendo che per me la morte brama;
  Or s' aprirà, s' aprir si dee mai cuore
  Per fera doglia, il mio; ora si sfama
  La nemica fortuna in su' miei danni,
  Ora conosco i suoi occulti inganni.

105.

Grave m' è la partita, Iddio il vede,
  Ma più m' è di veder Troilo afflitto,
  E incomportabil molto, per mia fede,
  Tanto ch' io ne morrò senza rispitto,
  E morir vo' senza sperar mercede,
  Poichè 'l mio Troilo veggio sì trafitto;
  Di' quando vuol venir, questo mi fia
  Sommo conforto nell' angoscia mia.

102.

And said: "Lady, I believe thou hast heard—but certain am I not—how thou art demanded of thy father, and already hath it been resolved by the king to yield thee up, so that thou must go hence within this week, if I have heard aright. And it could not be told to the full how grievous is this thing to Troilus, who desireth wholly to die in grief thereat.

103.

"And he and I have wept so much today that I marvel whence it hath come. Now by my counsel hath he finally restrained himself somewhat from weeping and it seemeth that he desireth to be with thee. Wherefore, before thou departest, I have come to tell it to thee, as he desired, in order that ye may vent your sorrow somewhat together."

104.

"Great is my grief," said Cressida, "as of her who loveth him more than herself; but his for me is by far greater, when I hear that he yearneth for death on account of me. Now will my heart rend, if ever a heart should rend for bitter grief. Now doth hostile fortune glut itself upon my woes; now do I know its hidden deceits.

105.

"Grievous is the departure to me, God knoweth, but more grievous to me is the sight of Troilus in affliction and so insupportably, by my faith, that I shall die thereof without respite. And die I shall without hope of succor, since I see my Troilus so affected. Tell him to come when he desireth; this will be to me greatest comfort in my anguish."

106.

E questo detto, ricadde supina,
 Poi 'n sulle braccia ricominciò il pianto:
A cui Pandaro disse: oimè, meschina,
Or che farai? Non prenderai alquanto
Di conforto, pensando che vicina
Si è l'ora già, che quel ch' ami cotanto
Ti sarà in braccio? Leva su, racconcia
Te, ch' esso non ti trovi così sconcia.

107.

Se el sapesse che così facessi,
 Esso s' uccideria, nè il potrebbe
Ritenerlo nessuno; e s' io credessi
Che così stessi, el non ci metterebbe
Credimi il piè, se io far lo potessi,
Ch' io so che noia ne gli seguirebbe:
Però levati su, rifatti tale,
Che tu alleggi e non cresca 'l suo male.

108.

Va', Criseida disse, io ti prometto,
 Pandaro mio, io me ne sforzeraggio;
Come partito ti sarai, dal letto
Senza indugio nïun mi leveraggio,
Ed il mio male e 'l perduto diletto
Tutto nel cor serrato mi terraggio:
Fa' pur ch' el venga, e venga al modo usato,
Che troverà qual suol l' uscio appoggiato.

109.

Ritrovò Pandar Troilo pensoso,
 E sì forte nel viso sbigottito,
Che per pietà ne divenne doglioso,
Ver lui dicendo: or se' tu sì invilito
Come tu mostri, giovin valoroso?
Ancor non s' è da te il tuo ben partito;
Perchè ancora cotanto ti sconforti,
Che gli occhi in testa ti paion già morti?

106.

And when she had said this she fell back at full length. Then resting on her arms she began again to weep. And to her Pandarus said: "Alas, poor woman, what wilt thou do now? Wilt thou not take a little comfort, when thou dost consider that the hour is already so near when he whom thou lovest so greatly will be in thine arms? Rise up, compose thyself, that he may not find thee in such disarray.

107.

"If he knew that thou wert acting thus, he would slay himself nor could anyone restrain him. And if I believed that thou wouldst remain as thou art, believe me, he would not set foot here, if I could prevent it, for I know that harm would come to him as a result. Therefore rise up, compose thyself, so that thou mayest relieve and not augment his woe."

108.

"Go," said Cressida, "I promise thee, my Pandarus, I shall make this effort. As soon as thou hast gone I shall rise from my bed with no delay and my woes and my lost delight shall I keep tightly locked in my heart. Make him come then and come in the usual way, for he shall find the door ajar, as it is wont to be."

109.

Pandarus found Troilus disheartened and so utterly despondent in his visage that for pity he became sorrowful on his account. And then he said to him: "Hast thou now, valorous youth, become such a coward as thou seemest? Thy love hath not yet departed from thee. Why art thou still so discomforted that thine eyes seem already dead in thy head?

110.

Tu se' vissuto assai senza costei,
　　Non ti dà 'l cuor poter vivere ancora?
　　Nascesti tu al mondo pur per lei?
　　Dimostrati uomo, e alquanto ti rincora,
　　Caccia questi dolori e questi omei
　　Almeno in parte: io non fe' poi dimora
　　In altro luogo se non qui con teco,
　　Ch' io le parlai e fui gran pezza seco.

111.

E per quel che mi paia, tu non senti
　　La metà noia che la donna face;
　　E' suoi sospiri son tanto cocenti,
　　E sì questa partenza le dispiace,
　　Che trapassano i tuoi per ognun venti;
　　Dunque con teco datti alquanto pace,
　　Che almen puoi tu in questo caso amaro
　　Conoscer quanto tu a lei se' caro.

112.

I' ho con esso lei testè composto
　　Che tu ad essa ne vadi, e stasera
　　Sarai con seco, e quel c' hai già disposto
　　Le mostrerai per più bella maniera
　　Che tu potrai; tu t' avvedrai ben tosto
　　Quel che a grado le fia con mente intera:
　　Forse che troverete modi i quali
　　Fian grandi alleggiamenti a' vostri mali.

113.

A cui rispose Troilo sospirando:
　　Tu parli bene, ed io così vo' fare:
　　Ed altre cose assai disse, ma quando
　　Tempo gli parve di dovere andare,
　　Pandaro sopra ciò 'l lasciò pensando.
　　Ed el sen gì, e mille anni gli pare
　　D' essere in braccio al suo caro conforto,
　　Il qual fortuna poi gli tolse a torto.

110.

"Thou hast lived a space of time without her; doth not thy heart give thee power to live still longer? Wert thou born into the world for her alone? Show thyself a man, and take courage somewhat, drive forth these sorrows and these troubles, at least in part. In no place did I tarry since, save here with thee, and I had speech with her and was with her a long time.

111.

"And as it seemeth to me, thou feelest not half the sorrow that thy lady doth. So hot are her sighs and so doth this departure grieve her that they surpass thine twenty to one. Give thyself a little peace, then, for at least thou canst know in this bitter case how dear thou art to her.

112.

"I have just arranged with her that thou shalt go to her, and thou shalt be with her this very night and what thou hast already contrived thou shalt set forth to her in the best way thou canst. Right soon shalt thou see what will be entirely to her pleasure. Perhaps ye shall find means which shall be of great solace to your woes."

113.

To whom Troilus responded with a sigh: "Thou sayest well and it is my will to do so." And many other things he said. But when it seemed time to go, Pandarus left him meditating thereon, and went away. And it seemeth to him a thousand years before he be in the arms of his dear love, whom fortune after did wickedly ravish away from him.

114.

Criseida, quando ora e tempo fue,
  Com' era usata con un torchio acceso
  Sen venne a lui, e nelle braccia sue
  Il ricevette, ed esso lei, compreso
  Da grave doglia, e mutoli amendue
  Nasconder non poteano il core offeso,
  Ma abbracciati senza farsi motto
  Incominciaro un gran pianto e dirotto.

115.

E forte insieme amendue si strignieno,
  Di lagrime bagnati tutti quanti,
  E volendo parlarsi non potieno,
  Sì gl' impedivan gli angosciosi pianti,
  E' singhiozzi e' sospiri, e nondimeno
  Si baciavan talvolta, e le cascanti
  Lacrime si bevean, senza aver cura
  Ch' amare fosser oltre lor natura.

116.

Ma poscia che gli spiriti affannati,
  Per l' angoscia del pianto e de' sospiri,
  Furon nelli lor luoghi ritornati
  Per l' allentar de' noiosi martirj,
  Criseida ver Troilo levati
  Gli occhi dolenti per gli aspri disiri,
  Con rotta voce, disse: o signor mio,
  Chi mi ti toglie, e dove ne vo io?

117.

Poi gli ricadde col viso in sul petto
  Venendo meno, e le forze partirsi,
  Da tanta doglia fu il suo cor costretto,
  Ed ingegnossi l' alma di fuggirsi;
  E Troilo guardando nel suo aspetto,
  E lei chiamando, e non sentendo udirsi,
  E gli occhi suo* velati e lei cascante,
  Che morta fosse gli porser sembiante.

* Savj-Lopez, *suoi*

114.

When the hour and moment arrived, Cressida came forth, as was her wont, with a lighted torch to meet him, and received him in her arms, and he, oppressed with heavy sorrow, her in his. And both falling silent were unable to conceal the wounds in their hearts, but in close and silent embrace fell to shedding great floods of tears.

115.

And both clasped one another tightly, bathed both in tears, and though they would, they could not speak, so did the agonizing tears and sobs and sighs prevent. And nevertheless they ever and again exchanged kisses and drank the falling tears, without care that they were bitter beyond their nature.

116.

But when their spirits, exhausted by the anguish of tears and sighs, were restored by the abating of their bitter pains, Cressida raised to Troilus her eyes sad with cruel yearnings and said in broken accents: "O lord of mine, who taketh me from thee and where am I to go?"

117.

Then she fell in a swoon with her face upon his breast and her strength departed from her, with so sore grief was her heart wrung. And her spirit sought this way and that to make its escape, Troilus the while gazing upon her face and calling her name, though it seemed to him that he was not heard. And the veiling of her eyes as she fell gave him the impression that she was dead.

118.

Il che vedendo Troilo, angoscioso
  Di doppia doglia, la pose a giacere,
  Spesso baciando il viso lacrimoso,
  Cercando se potesse in lei vedere
  Alcun segno di vita, e doloroso
  Ogni parte tentava, ed al parere
  Di lui, di vita così sconsolata,
  Dicea piangendo, ch' era trapassata.

119.

Ell' era fredda e senza sentimento
  Alcun, per quel che Troilo conoscesse,
  E questo gli parea vero argomento
  Che ella i giorni suoi finiti avesse;
  Per che dopo lunghissimo lamento,
  Prima che ad altro atto procedesse,
  L' asciugò 'l viso, e 'l corpo suo compose,
  Come si soglion far le morte cose.

120.

E fatto questo, con animo forte
  La propria spada del fodero trasse,
  Tutto disposto di prender la morte,
  Acciocchè il suo spirto seguitasse
  Quel della donna con sì trista sorte,
  E nell' inferno con lei abitasse,
  Poichè aspra fortuna e duro amore
  Di questa vita lui cacciava fuore.

121.

Ma prima disse acceso d' alto sdegno:
  O crudel Giove, e tu fortuna ria,
  A quel che voi volete ecco ch' io vegno;
  Tolta m' avete Criseïda mia,
  La qual credetti che con altro ingegno
  Tor mi doveste; e dove ella si sia
  Ora non so, ma il corpo suo qui morto
  Veggio da voi a grandissimo torto.

118.

Which when Troilus saw, distressed by a double grief, he laid her down, ever and anon kissing the tear-stained face, seeking whether he might perceive in her any sign of life. In his grief he lightly touched every part, and in his opinion, he said weeping, she had passed from so wretched life.

119.

Cold she was and quite without feeling, as far as Troilus might know. And this appeared to him a certain proof that she had ended her days. Wherefore after prolonged weeping, and before he proceeded to any other act, he dried her face and composed her body, as we are wont to do with the dead.

120.

This done with a firm will he drew his sword from its scabbard, entirely disposed to welcome death in order that his spirit might follow that of his lady in so sad a fate and dwell with her in hell, since cruel fortune and implacable love were driving him out of this life.

121.

But first he said, burning with noble wrath: "O cruel Jove, and thou, harsh fortune, lo I come to do your will. Ye have bereft me of my Cressida, whom I thought ye were destined to steal away from me with trickery of another sort. Wherever she may be now, I know not, but here I see her body most unjustly done to death by you.

122.

Ed io lascerò il mondo, e seguiraggio
   Con lo spirito lei poichè 'l vi piace;
   Forse di là miglior fortuna araggio
   Con lei, avendo de' miei sospir pace,
   Se di là s' ama, sì come udito aggio
   Alcuna volta dir che vi si face;
   Poichè vedermi in vita non volete,
   L' anima mia almen con lei ponete.

123.

E tu città, la qual' io lascio in guerra,
   E tu Priamo, e voi cari fratelli,
   Fate con Dio, ch' io me ne vo sotterra,
   Di Criseida dietro agli occhi belli;
   E tu, per cui tanto il dolor mi serra,
   E che dal corpo l' anima divelli,
   Ricevimi, Criseida volea dire,
   Già colla spada al petto per morire;

124.

Quand' ella risentendosi, un sospiro
   Grandissimo gittò, Troilo chiamando;
   A cui el disse: dolce mio disiro,
   Or vivi tu ancora? E lagrimando,
   In braccio la riprese, e 'l suo martiro,
   Come potea, con parole alleggiando,
   La confortò, e l' anima smarrita
   Tornò al core, onde s' era fuggita.

125.

E stata alquanto tutta alïenata
   Si tacque; e poscia la spada veggendo,
   Cominciò: quella perchè fu tirata
   Del foder fuori? A cui Troilo piangendo,
   Narrò qual fosse la sua vita stata:
   Ond' ella disse: che è ciò ch' io intendo!
   Dunque s' io fossi stata più un poco,
   Tu ti saresti ucciso in questo loco.

122.

"And I shall leave the world and follow her in spirit, since it pleaseth you. Perchance from the world beyond I shall have better fortune with her, when I shall have a truce to my sighs, if there one loveth, as I have heard say one doth. Since ye will not permit me to live, do ye at least place my soul with her.

123.

"And thou, O city, which I leave at war, and thou, Priam, and ye, dear brethren, farewell, for I am going away beneath the ground, seeking the fair eyes of Cressida. And thou for whom sorrow doth so grip me and who dost send the soul from the body, do thou receive me;" Cressida he meant, with his sword already at his breast to suffer death,

124.

When she, recovering her senses, heaved a long, deep sigh, calling upon Troilus. To her he said: "O my sweet desire, dost thou still live?" And weeping he caught her up in his arms and alleviating her distress, as well as he might, with words, he comforted her. And her bewildered soul returned to her body, whence it had taken flight.

125.

All beside herself she stood awhile and spake no word. Then when she saw the sword, she began: "Why was that drawn forth from the sheath?" To her the weeping Troilus related what his life had been. Whereat she said: "What is this I hear? So, had I delayed a little longer, thou wouldst have slain thyself in this spot.

126.

Oimè dolente a me, che m' ha' tu detto!
  Io non sarei in vita stata mai
  Di dietro a te, ma per lo tristo petto
  Fitta l' avrei : or noi abbiamo assai
  A lodar Dio : per ora andiamo a letto,
  Quivi ragionerem de' nostri guai ;
  S' io considero il torchio consumato,
  El n' è di notte già gran pezzo andato.

127.

Come altra volta gli stretti abbracciari
  Érano stati, così furon ora,
  Ma questi fur più di lagrime amari,
  Che stati fosser di dolcezza ; ancora
  I piacevoli e tristi ragionari
  Fra loro incominciar senza dimora ;
  E cominciò Criseida : dolce amico,
  Ascolta bene attento quel ch' io dico.

128.

Poscia ch' io seppi la trista novella
  Del traditor del mio padre malvagio,
  Se Dio mi guardi la tua faccia bella,
  Nulla giammai sentì tanto disagio
  Quant' io ho poi sentito, come quella ;
  Ch' oro non curo, città nè palagio,
  Ma sol di dimorar sempre con teco
  In festa ed in piacere, e tu con meco.

129.

E voleami del tutto disperare
  Non credendo giammai più rivederti ;
  Ma poi che tu la mia anima errare
  Vedesti, e ritornar dinuovo, certi
  Pensier mi sento per la mente andare,
  Utili forse, i quali vo' che aperti
  Prima ti sien che noi più ci dogliamo,
  Che forse sperar bene ancor possiamo.

[348]

126.

"Alas, how grievous to me is all that thou hast told me! Never should I have remained alive after thee but I too should have plunged it through my sad breast. Now must we highly praise the gods. Now let us to bed and there shall we hold converse of our woes. If I consider the waning torch, a great part of the night hath already gone."

127.

As the close embracings had been once, so now they were, but these were more bitter with tears than the former had been joyous. Once again commenced without delay the bittersweet discourse between them. Cressida began: "Sweet my friend, give careful heed to what I say.

128.

"After I heard the sad news of my wicked father's treachery, an the gods may preserve thy fair face for me, no woman e'er felt as great distress as I felt then, since I care not for gold, city, or palace, but only to dwell always with thee in joy and pleasure and thou with me.

129.

"And I wished entirely to abandon myself to despair in the belief that I should ne'er see thee again. But since thou hast seen my soul wander and return again, I feel pass through my mind certain thoughts, useful peradventure, which I desire to be clear to thee before we yield to further grief, for perchance we may yet hope for good.

130.

Tu vedi che mio padre mi richiede,
   Al qual di girne non ubbidirei
   Se 'l re non mi strignesse, la cui fede
   Convien s' osservi, come saper dei;
   Per che andar mi conviene con Diomede,
   Ch' è stato trattator de' patti rei,
   Qualora tornerà : volesse Iddio
   Ch' el non tornasse mai nel tempo rio.

131.

Tu sai che qui è ogni mio parente
   Fuor che mio padre, e ciascuna mia cosa
   Ancora ci rimane ; e s' alla mente
   Mi torna ben, di questa perigliosa
   Guerra si tratta continuamente
   Pace tra voi e' Greci, e se la sposa
   Si rende a Menelao, credo l' avrete,
   Ed io so già che voi presso vi siete.

132.

Qui mi ritornerò se voi la fate,
   Perocchè altrove non ho dove gire ;
   E se per avventura la lasciate,
   Nel tempo delle tregue di venire
   Ci avrò cagione, e così fatte andate
   Sai che non s' usa alle donne disdire ;
   E i miei parenti mi ci vederanno
   Di buona voglia, e mi c' inviteranno.

133.

Allor potremo alcun sollazzo avere,
   Come che l' aspettar sia grave noia ;
   Ma conviensi apparare a sostenere
   Della fatica, chi vuol che la gioia
   Li venga poscia con maggior piacere ;
   Io veggio pur, che stando noi in Troia,
   Senza vederci più dì ci conviene
   Talor passar con angosciose pene.

130.

"Thou seest that my father demandeth my return. Yet I would not obey him in going hence, were I not constrained by the king, whose faith must be observed, as thou shouldst know. Wherefore I must go with Diomede, who hath been the negotiator of this cruel treaty, whenever he returneth. Would to the gods that he never return in the cruel time.

131.

"Thou knowest that every kinsman of mine, barring my father, is here, and that everything of mine still remaineth here. And if I remember rightly, there is ever talk between you and the Greeks of an end to this perilous war. If his wife surrender herself to Menelaus, I believe that you will have it, and I know that you are already near to it.

132.

"Hither will I return if ye make peace, since I have not other where to go. And if perchance ye make it not, there will be opportunity to come here in times of truce, and such passages thou knowest it is not customary to forbid the women, and my kinsmen will gladly see and invite me here.

133.

"Then shall we be able to have some solace, even though the waiting may be a sore vexation. But he who wisheth that joy come after with greater pleasure, must prepare to bear hardship. I see indeed that here in Troy we must sometimes pass many a day in grievous pain without seeing each other.

134.

Ed oltre a questo, maggiore speranza,
 O pace o no, mi nasce del tornarci;
 Mio padre ha ora questa disianza,
 E forse avvisa ch' io non possa starci
 Per lo suo fallo, senza dubitanza
 Di forza, o di biasmo ad acquistarci;
 Come saprà che io ci sia onorata,
 Più non curerà della mia tornata.

135.

Ed a che far tra' Greci mi terrebbe,
 Che come vedi son sempre nell' armi?
 E s' el non mi tien ivi, ove potrebbe
 In altra parte, io nol veggio, mandarmi?
 E se 'l potesse credo nol farebbe,
 Perciocchè a' Greci non vorria fidarmi;
 Qui dunque rimandarmi egli è opportuno,
 Nè ben ci veggio contrario nessuno.

136.

Egli è, come tu sai, vecchio ed avaro,
 E qui ha ciò che gli può fare udire
 Il che io gli dirò, s' egli l' ha* caro,
 Per lo miglior mi faccia qui reddire,
 Mostrandogli com' io possa riparo,
 Ad ogni cosa che sopravvenire
 Potesse, porre, ed el per avarizia
 Della mia ritornata avrà letizia.

137.

Troilo attento la donna ascoltava,
 Ed il dir suo gli toccava la mente,
 E quasi verisimil gli sembrava
 Dover ciò che diceva certamente
 Esser così, ma perchè molto amava,
 Pur fede vi prestava lentamente;
 Ma alla fin, come che vago fosse,
 Seco cercando, a crederlo si mosse.

* Savj-Lopez, *è*

134.

"And besides this, peace or no peace, there springeth up in me a greater hope of returning here. My father hath now desire of this and perhaps he imagineth that because of his evildoing I cannot abide here without fear of violence or of blame to be gained here. When he knoweth that I am honored here, he will no more care for my coming back.

135.

"And for what purpose should he keep me among the Greeks, who, as thou seest, are ever in arms? And if he keepeth me not there, where else he could send me I see not. And even if he could, I believe he would not, since he would have no desire to entrust me to the Greeks. Here then is it fitting to send me back, nor do I clearly see anyone opposed to it.

136.

"He is, as thou knowest, old and avaricious and here he hath that which, if he prizeth it, may make him pay heed to what I shall tell him, to have me brought back here as best he may, for I shall show him how I may find a remedy for aught that might happen against expectation, and he through avarice will take delight in my return."

137.

Troilus listened to the lady with attention and her speech produced an effect upon his mind. And it seemed to him reasonable to suppose that what she said so positively ought to be true. But because he loved much, only with hesitation did he give credence to it. Yet in the end, as one who is anxious for a thing, he brought himself to believe it, seeking reasons within himself for so doing.

138.

Laonde parte della grave doglia
Da lor partissi, e ritornò speranza;
E divenuti poi di men ria voglia,
Ricominciaron l' amorosa danza:
E sì come l' uccel di foglia in foglia
Nel nuovo tempo prende dilettanza
Del canto suo; così facean costoro,
Di molte cose parlando fra loro.

139.

Ma non potendo a Troilo passare
Dal cor, che questa partir si dovea,
Incominciò in tal guisa a parlare:
O Criseida mia, più ch' altra dea
Amata assai, e più da onorare
Da me, che dianzi uccider mi volea
Credendo morta te, che vita credi
Che fia la mia, se tosto tu non riedi?

140.

Vivi sicura, come del morire,
Che io m' ucciderei, se tu penassi
Nïente troppo di qui rivenire;
Nè veggio bene ancor com' io mi passi
Senza doglioso ed amaro languire,
Sentendo te altrove; e dubbio fassi
Novello in me, che el non ti ritegna
Calcas, e quel che parli non avvegna.

141.

Non so se pace fra noi si fia mai:
O pace o no, appena che tornarci
Credo che Calcas ci voglia giammai,
Perchè non crederia dovere starci
Senza infamia del fallo, che assai
Fu, se in ciò non vogliamo ingannarci,
E se con tanta istanza ti richiede,
Ch' el ti rimandi appena vi do fede.

138.

Whereat a part of this heavy grief departed from them and hope returned. And then becoming of a less bitter mind, they began again the amorous sport. And just as in the new season the bird taketh delight in his song from leaf to leaf, so did they, speaking the while to each other of many things.

139.

But since the thought could not pass from the heart of Troilus that this departure would have to be, he began to speak after this wise: "O Cressida mine, much loved beyond any other goddess and more to be honored by me, who just now would have slain myself when I thought thee dead, what manner of life thinkest thou mine will be if thou returnest not quickly?

140.

"Live as certain as thou art of death, that shouldst thou defer thy return here one moment too long, I would kill myself, nor do I clearly perceive yet how I shall get along without grievous and bitter sighing, when I feel thou art elsewhere. And a new apprehension ariseth in me lest Calchas may keep thee and that which thou sayest may not come to pass.

141.

"I know not whether peace shall ever be made between us. Peace or no peace, hardly do I believe that Calchas will ever desire to return here, for he would not believe that he could stay here without incurring the ignominy of his guilt, which was very great, if we do not wish to deceive ourselves in the matter. And if with so much insistence he demandeth thy return, hardly do I credit his sending thee back.

142.

E' ti darà fra li Greci marito,
  E mostreratti che stare assediata
  È dubbio di venire a rio partito;
  Lusingheratti, e farà che onorata
  Sarai da' Greci, ed el v' è riverito
  Sì come intendo, e molto v' è pregiata
  La sua virtù, perchè non senza noia
  Temo che tu giammai non torni in Troia.

143.

E questo m' è a pensar tanto grave,
  Che dir nol ti potria, anima bella;
  E tu sol' hai nelle tue man la chiave
  Della mia vita e della morte, e quella
  Sì, che la puoi e misera e soave
  Come ti piace fare, o chiara stella,
  Per cui io vado al grazioso porto;
  Se tu mi lasci pensa ch' io sia morto.

144.

Dunque, per Dio, troviam modo e cagione
  Che tu non vada, se trovar si puote;
  Andiamcene in un' altra regïone,
  Non ci curiam se le promesse vote
  Vengon del re, se la sua offensione
  Fuggir possiamo; e' son di qui remote
  Genti che volentieri ci vedranno,
  E per signori ancor sempre ci avranno.

145.

Fuggiamci dunque quinci occultamente,
  E là n' andiamo insieme tu ed io;
  E quel che noi abbiam di rimanente
  Nel mondo a viver, cor del corpo mio,
  Viviamlo con diletto insiememente;
  Questo vorrei, e questo ho in disio,
  S' el ti paresse; e questo è più sicuro,
  Ed ogni altro partito mi par duro.

142.

"He will give thee a husband among the Greeks and he will show thee that in being besieged there lieth danger of coming to evil pass. He will flatter thee and cause thee to be honored among the Greeks. And he is much revered there, as I understand, and his virtue highly esteemed. Wherefore not without disquiet do I fear that thou wilt never return to Troy.

143.

"And this thought is so grievous to me, fair soul, that I could not tell thee how much. Thou alone holdest in thy hands the key of my life and death, and the former so entirely that thou canst make it wretched or sweet as it pleaseth thee, O bright star by which I lay my course to the grateful port. If thou dost abandon me, bear in mind that I am dead.

144.

"So then in the name of the gods let us contrive a means and excuse for thy not going, if it can be done. Let us betake ourselves to some other region. Let us care not if the king's promises be unfulfilled, provided we may escape injury from him. There are, remote from here, peoples who will receive us gladly and who will besides ever hold us for lords.

145.

"Wherefore let us make our flight hence secretly, and let us go there together, you and I, and what time we have left to live in the world, heart of my body, let us live it together in delight. This I would wish and this is my desire, if it should accord with thine. This is the safer plan and every other course of action seemeth to me difficult."

146.

Criseida sospirando gli rispose:
    Caro mio bene e del mio cor diletto,
    Tutte potrebbon' esser quelle cose,
    Ed ancor più, nella forma c' hai detto;
    Ma io ti giuro per quelle amorose
    Saette che per te m' entrar nel petto,
    Comandamenti, lusinghe, o marito,
    Non torceran da te mai l'appetito.

147.

Ma ciò che d' andar via tu ragionavi,
    Non è savio consiglio al mio parere:
    Pensar si deve in questi tempi gravi,
    E di te e de' tuoi ti dee calere;
    Che s' andassimo via, come parlavi,
    Tre cose ree ne potresti vedere,
    L' una verrebbe per la rotta fede,
    Che porta più di mal ch' altri non crede:

148.

E ciò sarebbe delli tuoi in periglio,
    Che se per una femmina lasciati
    Gli avessi fuor d' aiuto e di consiglio,
    Darian paura agli altri degli aguati.
    E se io ben con meco m' assottiglio,
    Voi ne sareste molto biasimati,
    Nè vi saria il ver giammai creduto,
    Da chi n' avesse sol questo veduto.

149.

E se tempo nïun fede o leanza
    Richiede, quel della guerra par esso;
    Perocchè nullo ha tanto di possanza,
    Che guari possa per sè solo stesso:
    Aggiungonvisi molti ad isperanza
    Che quel che metton per altrui sia messo
    Per lor; che se in avere ed in persona
    Mettono, in ciò sperando s' abbandona.

146.

Cressida made answer to him with a sigh: "Dear joy of mine, my heart's delight, all this and even more might be just as thou hast said. But I swear to thee, by those shafts of Love that on thy account have entered into my heart, commands, flatteries, O husband, will never turn my desire from thee.

147.

"But what thou didst say of our going away is not in my opinion wise counsel. Thou shouldst take thought and care in these grievous times of thee and thine. For should we make our departure, as thou hast said, thou mightest see three dire results ensue therefrom. One would come for the broken faith, which causeth more evil than others believe.

148.

"And that would be dangerous to thy kinsfolk. For if for a woman thou shouldst have left them bereft of aid and counsel, they would by their plight arouse in others fear of stratagems, and if I see clearly in my mind, you would be much blamed for it, nor would the truth ever be believed by any who had seen only this part of it.

149.

"And if any time demandeth faith and loyalty, it seemeth to be the time of war. For no one hath such power that he may long stand by himself alone; many join forces in the hope that what they risk for others will be risked for themselves. For if they put their trust in property and person, ruin followeth upon their hopes.

150.

D' altra parte, che pensi tra le genti
  Della partita tua si ragionasse?
  E' non dirien ch' amor co' suoi ferventi
  Dardi a cotal partito ti menasse,
  Ma paura e viltà: dunque ritienti
  Da tal pensier se mai nel cor t' entrasse,
  Se el t' è punto la tua fama cara,
  Che del valor tuo suona tanto chiara.

151.

Appresso pensa che la mia onestate
  E la mia castità, somme tenute,
  Di quanta infamia sarien maculate,
  Anzi del tutto disfatte e perdute
  Sarieno in me, nè giammai rilevate
  Per iscusa sarieno, o per virtute
  Ch' io potessi operar, che ch' io facessi,
  Se anni centomila in vita stessi.

152.

Ed oltre a questo, vo' che tu riguardi
  A ciò che quasi d' ogni cosa avviene;
  Non è cosa sì vil, se ben si guardi,
  Che non si faccia disiar con pene,
  E quanto più di possederla ardi,
  Più tosto abominío nel cor ti viene,
  Se larga potestade di vederla
  Fatta ti fia, e ancor di ritenerla.

153.

Il nostro amor, che cotanto ti piace,
  È perchè far convien furtivamente,
  E di rado venire a questa pace;
  Ma se tu m' averai liberamente,
  Tosto si spegnerà l' ardente face
  Ch' ora t' accende, e me similemente;
  Perchè se 'l nostro amor vogliam che duri,
  Com' or facciam, convien sempre si furi.

150.

"On the other hand what thinkest thou might be said among the people of thy going? They would not say that Love with his hot darts had led thee to such a decision but rather fear and baseness. Therefore hold thyself aloof from such thoughts, should they ever enter thy heart, if thy repute for valor, which echoeth so loudly, is at all dear to thee.

151.

"Then consider with how much infamy mine honor and chastity, held in the highest esteem, would be stained, nay ruined quite and lost to me, nor would they ever be redeemed by excuse or virtue that I could bring to bear, whatsoever I should do, were I to remain in life a hundred thousand years.

152.

"And besides this, I desire thee to take thought to what happeneth in the case of almost everything. There is nothing so base that doth not, if it be guarded well, make itself ardently desired, and the more thou dost yearn to possess it, the sooner doth loathing spring in thy heart, if full power be granted thee to see it, and even more, to keep it.

153.

"Our love which pleaseth thee so much, pleaseth thee because thou must act secretly and seldom come to this place. But if thou wilt have me freely, soon will be extinguished the glowing torch which now enkindleth thee—and me likewise. For if, as now, we wish our love to last, it must ever lie concealed.

154.

Dunque prendi conforto, e la fortuna
　　Col dare il dosso vinci e rendi stanca;
　　Non soggiacette a lei giammai nessuna
　　Persona in cui trovasse anima franca:
　　Seguiamo il corso suo, fingiti alcuna
　　Andata in questo mezzo, e in quella manca
　　Li tuoi sospiri, ch' al decimo giorno
　　Senza alcun fallo qui farò ritorno.

155.

Se tu, allor disse Troilo, ci sarai
　　Infra 'l decimo giorno, i' son contento:
　　Ma in questo mezzo i miei dolenti guai
　　Da cui avranno alcuno alleggiamento?
　　Già non poss' ora, siccome tu sai,
　　Passare un' ora senza gran tormento
　　Se non ti veggio, come i dieci giorni
　　Passar potrò infin che tu non torni?

156.

Deh per Dio trova modo a rimanere,
　　Deh non andar, se tu vedi alcun modo:
　　Io ti conosco d' arguto sapere,
　　Se bene intendo ciò che da te odo;
　　E se tu m' ami, tu puoi ben vedere
　　Che pur di ciò pensar tutto mi rodo,
　　Cioè che tu te ne vada; e creder puoi,
　　Se te ne vai, qual fia mia vita poi.

157.

Oimè, disse Criseida, tu m' uccidi,
　　Ed oltre al creder tuo malinconia
　　Troppa mi dai, e veggio non ti fidi
　　Quant' io credea nella promessa mia;
　　Deh ben mio dolce, perchè sì diffidi,
　　Perchè a te di te toi la balía?
　　Chi crederia che uomo in arme forte,
　　L' aspettar dieci dì el non comporte?

154.

"Therefore take comfort and by turning thy back upon Fortune, conquer her and tire her out. No person in whom she might find a courageous soul would ever fall subject to her. Let us follow her course. In the meantime feign for thyself some journey and while upon it bate thy sighs, for on the tenth day shall I without fail make my return hither."

155.

"If," said Troilus then, "you are here on the tenth day, I am content. But in the meantime from whom shall my grievous woes have any solace? Since I cannot now, as thou knowest, pass one hour without great torment, if I see thee not, how then shall I contrive to pass ten days until thou returnest?

156.

"In God's name find some means to stay. Go not, if thou dost see any means. I know thee to be quick of wit, if I understand aright what I hear concerning thee. If thou lovest me thou mayest well perceive that I am all consumed with but one thought, that thou goest away, and if thou goest, thou mayest well believe what manner of life will then be mine."

157.

"Alas," said Cressida, "thou slayest me and beyond all belief of thine thou givest me excessive sadness. I see that thou dost not believe in my promise as much as I thought. Ah, dear my sweet, why art thou of so little faith? Why dost thou rob thyself of all self-mastery? Who would believe that a man strong in arms might not endure the ten days' wait?

158.

Io credo di gran lunga sia il migliore
  Di prendere il partito ch' io t' ho detto;
  Siine contento, dolce mio signore,
  E cappiati per certo dentro al petto
  Ch' el me ne piange l' anima nel core
  Di allontanarmi dal tuo dolce aspetto,
  Forse più che non credi o non ci pensi,
  Ben lo sent' io per tutti quanti i sensi.

159.

L' aspettar tempo è utile talvolta
  Per tempo guadagnare, anima mia:
  Io non ti son come tu mostri tolta,
  Perch' io al padre mio renduta sia;
  Nè ti cappia nel cor ch' io sia sì stolta,
  Che non sappia trovare e modo e via
  Di ritornare a te, cui io più bramo
  Che la mia vita, e vie più troppo t' amo.

160.

Ond' io ti prego, se 'l mio prego vale,
  E per lo grande amore il qual mi porti,
  E per quel ch' io a te porto, ch' è altrettale,
  Che tu di questa andata ti conforti;
  Che tu sapessi quanto mi fa male
  Veder li pianti e li sospir sì forti
  Che tu ne gitti, el te ne increscerebbe,
  E di farne cotanti ti dorrebbe.

161.

Per te in allegrezza ed in disio
  Spero di vivere e di tornar tosto,
  E trovar modo al tuo diletto e mio:
  Fa' ch' io ti veggia in tal guisa disposto
  Pria che da te io mi diparta, ch' io
  Non abbia più dolor, che quel che posto
  M' ha nella mente amor troppo focoso;
  Fallo, ten prego, dolce mio riposo.

158.

"I think it by far the better part of wisdom to adopt the plan of which I told thee. Be content with it, sweet my lord, and hold it for certain within thy breast that my soul in my body weepeth at the thought of going far away from the sweet sight of thee, perhaps more than thou dost believe or think. I feel it strongly through all my senses.

159.

"To bide time, my soul, is often useful in order to gain time. I am not reft from thee, as thou seekest to prove, because I am given back to my father. Nor think thou in thy heart that I am so stupid that I cannot find means and ways to return to thee, whom I desire more than my life—I love thee far too much.

160.

"Wherefore I pray thee, if my prayer availeth, both for the great love thou hast for me and for the love that I bear thee, that thou console thyself for this my departure. If only thou couldst know how much it paineth me to see thy laments and to hear the deep-fetched sighs thou utterest, thou wouldst feel regret for them and it would grieve thee to give vent to so many tears.

161.

"For thee in joy and love I hope to live and quickly to return and find a means to thy delight and mine. See to it that I may behold thee so set at rest before my departure from thee that I may have no more pain than that which too ardent love hath planted in my mind. Do this I pray thee, sweet balm of my heart.

162.

E pregoti, mentr' io sarò lontana,
Che prender non ti lasci dal piacere
D' alcuna donna, o da vaghezza strana;
Che s' io 'l sapessi, dei per certo avere
Che io m' ucciderei siccome insana,
Dolendomi di te oltra 'l dovere.
Mi lasceresti per altra, che sai
Che t' amo più che donna amasse uom mai?

163.

A quest' ultima parte sospirando
Rispose Troilo: s' io fare volessi
Ciò che tu ora tocchi sospicando,
Non so veder com' io giammai potessi;
Sì m' ha per te ghermito amore amando,
Non so veder com' io in vita stessi.
Questo amor ch' io ti porto e la ragione
Ti spiegherò, ed in breve sermone.

164.

Non mi sospinse ad amarti bellezza,
La quale spesso altrui suole irretire;
Non mi trasse ad amarti gentilezza
Che suol pigliar de' nobili il desire;
Non ornamento ancora, non ricchezza
Mi fe' per te amor nel cor sentire;
Delle qua' tutte se' più copïosa,
Che altra fosse mai donna amorosa;

165.

Ma gli atti tuoi altieri e signorili,
Il valore e 'l parlar cavalleresco,
I tuoi costumi più ch' altra gentili,
Ed il vezzoso tuo sdegno donnesco,
Per lo quale apparien d'esserti vili
Ogni appetito ed oprar popolesco,
Qual tu mi se', o donna mia possente,
Con amor mi ti miser nella mente.

162.

"And I pray thee, while I am afar, let thyself not be caught by the pleasure thou takest in any woman or by any strange fancy. For if I should know of it, thou must be sure that I would slay myself like a mad woman, grieving for thee beyond all duty. Wouldst thou leave me for another, thou who knowest that I love thee more than woman ever loved man?"

163.

To this last part Troilus answered sighing: "Had I the wish to do that which thou dost now touch on with some suspicion, I cannot see how I ever should have the power to do it. So by loving hath love for thee caught me in its grip, I cannot see how I could still live on. This love I bear thee and its reason shall I explain to thee and in few brief words.

164.

"Beauty, which is often wont to take others in its net, drew me not to love thee, nor did gentle birth, which is ever like to catch the desire of the noble, draw me to love thee, nor yet did ornaments nor riches, in all of which thou art more abundant than was ever amorous lady, make me feel love for thee in my heart;

165.

"But thy noble and princely manners, thy excellence and thy courtly speech, thy ways more high-bred than those of any other lady, and thy graceful ladylike disdain, whereby every low-born desire and action seemeth base to thee—such art thou to me, O sovereign lady mine—have enthroned thee in my mind with love.

166.

E queste cose non posson tor gli anni
  Nè mobile fortuna, laond' io
Con più angoscia e con maggiori affanni
  Sempre d' averti spero nel disio.
  Oimè lasso, qual fia de' miei danni
  Ristoro, se ten vai, dolce amor mio?
Certo nessun, se non la morte omai,
Questa fia sola fine de' miei guai.

167.

Poscia ch' egli ebber molto ragionato
  E pianto insieme, perchè s' appressava
Già l' aurora, quello hanno lasciato,
  E strettamente l' un l' altro abbracciava;
  Ma poich' e' galli molto ebber cantato,
  Dopo ben mille baci si levava
Ciascun, l' un l' altro sè raccomandando,
E così dipartirsi lagrimando.

166.

"And these things neither years nor fickle fortune can snatch away. Wherefore with much anguish and the greatest anxiety I place my hope ever in the desire of having thee always. Woe's me, alas! What solace shall there be for all my sorrows, if thou goest hence, sweet my love? None surely, if not death forever. This will be the only end of my woes."

167.

After they had long conversed and wept together, since dawn was drawing near, they left off and embraced one another closely. But when the cocks had long been crowing, after quite a thousand kisses, each arose, the one commending himself to the other, and thus they departed tearfully.

IL FILOSTRATO

DI

GIOVANNI BOCCACCIO

PARTE QUINTA

ARGOMENTO

Comincia la quinta parte del Filostrato, nella quale Criseida è renduta. Troilo l'accompagna, e tornasi in Troia; piagne solo, e appresso con Pandaro, per lo consiglio del quale, alquanti dì se ne vanno a dimorare con Serpedone. Tornasi in Troia, laddove ogni luogo rammenta Criseida a Troilo, ed egli per mitigare i suoi dolori, quelli medesimi canta, aspettando che'l dì decimo passi. E primieramente Criseida è renduta a Diomede, la quale Troilo accompagna infino fuori della città, e partita da lui, ell' è con festa ricevuta dal suo padre.

1.

Quel giorno istesso vi fu Diomede
    Per volere a' Troian dare Antenore,
    Perchè Priamo Criseïda li diede,
    Di sospiri, di pianti e di dolore
    Sì piena, che n' incresce a chi la vede;
    Dall' altra parte v' era il suo amadore
    In sì fatta tristizia, che alcuno
    Un simil non ne vide mai nessuno.

2.

Vero è che con gran forza nascondea
    Mirabilmente dentro al tristo petto
    La gran battaglia la qual' egli avea
    Con sospiri e con pianto; e nell' aspetto
    Niente o poco ancor gli si parea,
    Come ch' egli attendesse esser soletto,
    E quivi piangere e rammaricarsi,
    Ed a grand' agio seco disfogarsi.

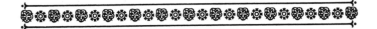

THE FILOSTRATO

OF

GIOVANNI BOCCACCIO

FIFTH PART

ARGUMENT

Here beginneth the fifth part of the Filostrato, in which Cressida is given back. Troilus accompanieth her and returneth to Troy. He weepeth alone and in the company of Pandarus, by whose advice they go to spend some days with Sarpedon. He returneth to Troy, where every spot remindeth him of Cressida, and in order to assuage his sorrows he giveth utterance to them in song, awaiting until the tenth day shall pass. And in the first place Cressida is delivered to Diomede. Troilus accompanieth her to the outskirts of the city and after he hath left her, she is joyfully received by her father.

1.

That same day was Diomede there for the purpose of surrendering Antenor to the Trojans. Into his hands therefore Priam delivered Cressida, so full of sighs and tears and grief that it stirreth sorrow in him that seeth her. On the other hand was the lover, in such distress that none did ever see his like.

2.

True it is that with great effort he made wondrous concealment within his breast of the great strife he had with sighs and tears. And in his face little or no sign of it did yet appear, although he yearned to be alone, and in solitude to weep and vent his bitterness and relieve himself by giving full rein to his affliction.

[371]

3.

Oh quante cose nell' altera mente
  Gli vennero, Criseida vedendo
  Rendere al padre! questi primamente
  D' ira e di cruccio tututto fremendo,
  Seco rodeasi, e dicea pianamente:
  O misero dolente, e che più attendo?
  Non è el meglio una volta morire,
  Che sempre in pianto vivere e languire?

4.

Che non turb' io coll' arme questi patti?
  Perchè qui Diomede non uccido?
  Perchè non taglio il vecchio che gli ha fatti?
  Perchè li miei fratei tutti non sfido?
  Che ora fosser ei tutti disfatti!
  Perchè in pianto ed in dolente grido
  Troia non metto? Perchè non rapisco
  Criseida ora, e me stesso guarisco?

5.

Chi 'l vieterà, s' io il vorrò pur fare?
  O perchè colli Greci non m' accosto
  Se mi volesser Criseida donare?
  Deh perchè più dimoro, che non tosto
  Corro colà e follami lasciare?
  Ma così fiero ed altiero proposto
  Gli fe' lasciar paura, non uccisa
  Criseida fosse in sì fatta divisa.

6.

E Criseida poi vide che partire
  Le convenia, qual' ell' era, dogliosa,
  Con quella compagnia che dovea gire,
  Sopra il caval montò, e dispettosa
  Con seco stesso cominciò a dire:
  Ahi crudel Giove, e fortuna noiosa,
  Dove me ne portate contro voglia?
  Perchè v' aggrada tanto la mia doglia?

3.

Ah, how many things came to his noble mind when he saw Cressida yielded to her father! Quivering in every limb with wrath and grief, he first chafed inwardly with very rage and said under his breath: "O miserable wretch that I am, what more do I wait for? Is it not better to die once and for all than ever in tears to live and languish?

4.

"Why do I not break up these pacts with arms? Why do I not slay Diomede on the spot? Why do I not put an end to the old man who hath made them? Why not hurl defiance at all my brothers? Would that they were all undone! Why do I not plunge Troy in lamentation and mournful wailing? Why at this moment do I not steal Cressida away and cure myself?

5.

"Who shall say me nay if I shall indeed wish to do so? Why not go to the Greeks and see if they will yield me Cressida? Alas, why do I delay longer? Why do I not quickly hasten thither and force them to surrender her to me?" But fear made him abandon a course so desperate and bold, lest Cressida should be slain in such a fray.

6.

When Cressida saw that she must, despite her grief, go with the company that was to depart, she mounted her horse and began angrily to say to herself: "Ah, cruel Jove and bitter fortune, whither do ye bear me against my will? Why doth my grief delight you so?

7.

Voi mi togliete, crudi e dispietati,
  Da quel piacer che più m'andava a core;
  E forse vi credete umilïati
  Esser con sacrificio e con onore
  Alcun da me, ma voi sete ingannati;
  In vostro vituperio e disonore
  Mi dorrò sempre, infin che non ritorno
  A riveder di Troilo il viso adorno.

8.

Quinci si volse disdegnosamente
  Ver Diomede, e disse: andianne omai,
  Assai ci siam mostrati a questa gente;
  La quale omai sperar può de' suoi guai
  Salute, se ben miran sottilmente
  All' onorevol cambio che fatt' hai,
  Che hai per una femmina renduto
  Un sì gran re e cotanto temuto.

9.

E questo detto, al caval degli sproni
  Diè, senza dire fuor che a' suoi addio;
  E ben conobbe il re e' suoi baroni
  Lo sdegno della donna: indi sen gio,
  Senza ascoltare comiato o sermoni,
  O riguardare alcuno, e se n' uscio
  Di Troia, nella qual giammai tornare
  Più non doveva, nè con Troilo stare.

10.

Troilo a guisa d' una cortesia,
  Con più compagni montò a cavallo
  Con un falcone in pugno, e compagnia
  Le fece infino fuor di tutto il vallo,
  E volentieri per tutta la via
  L' averia fatta insino al suo stallo,
  Ma troppo discoperto saria stato,
  E poco senno ancora riputato.

7.

"Ye in your cruelty and heartlessness take me away from the pleasure that was most dear to my heart. Perchance ye think yourselves humiliated by any sacrifice or honor from me. But ye are deceived. Ever shall I spend my days of grief in heaping upon you obloquy and dishonor, until I return and behold again the fair face of Troilus."

8.

Then scornfully she turned to Diomede and thus she spake: "Now let us be gone. Long enough have we exposed ourselves to the gaze of this people, who may now expect solace for their woes, if they will carefully consider the honorable exchange which thou hast made in surrendering so great and dreaded a king for a mere woman."

9.

And this said, she gave spurs to her horse, speaking no word save a farewell to her attendants. And well did the king and his barons take note of the lady's wrath. Forth she went nor would she listen to farewell or parting speech or cast a glance at anyone. Forth she went from Troy, whither she was never again to return or to be with Troilus.

10.

Troilus, as though to perform an act of courtesy, mounted his horse with many companions and with a hawk upon his fist did bear her company as far as the outer ring of the rampart, and gladly would he have done likewise all along the way even to her lodging, but it would have been too open and also thought of little sense.

11.

E tra lor già venuto era Antenore
  Dalli Greci renduto, e con gran festa
Ricevuto l' aveano e con onore
  I giovani troiani; e benchè questa
Tornata fosse a Troilo dentro al core
  Per Criseida data assai molesta,
Pur con buon viso il ricevette, e fello
Con Pandar cavalcar davanti ad ello.

12.

E già essendo per accomiatarsi,
  Egli e Criseida si fermaro alquanto,
E dentro agli occhi l' un l' altro guatarsi,
  Nè ritener potè la donna il pianto,
E poscia per le man destre pigliarsi,
  E a lei Troilo allor s' accostò tanto,
Che pian parlando, ella 'l potè udire,
E disse: torna, non mi far morire.

13.

E senza più, rivoltato il destriere,
  Tutto tinto nel viso, a Diomede
Non parlò punto, e di cotal mestiere
  Sol Diomede s' accorse, e bene vede
L' amor de' due, e dentro al suo pensiere
  Con diversi argomenti ne fa fede,
E di ciò mentre seco ne pispiglia,
Nascosamente di colei si piglia.

14.

Il padre la raccolse con gran festa,
  Come ch' a lei gravasse tale amore;
Ella si stava tacita e modesta,
  Sè stessa seco con grave dolore
Tutta rodendo, ed in vita molesta,
  Pure a Troilo avendo fermo il coro;
Che tosto si doveva permutare,
E lui per nuovo amante abbandonare.

11.

And Antenor, surrendered by the Greeks, had already come among them and with great festivity and honor had the young Trojans received him. And although this return was very grievous to Troilus' heart because of the surrender of Cressida, yet did he receive him with a good face, and made him ride before him with Pandarus.

12.

And when they were already on the point of taking leave, he and Cressida stopped for some moments, and gazed into each other's eyes, nor could the lady restrain her tears. And they then took one another by the right hand, and at that Troilus approached so near to her side that she could hear him as he spake low and said: "Come back again, cause me not to die."

13.

And without more ado, having turned his steed, with his face all flushed, he spake no word to Diomede. And of such behavior Diomede alone took note. Well he seeth the love of the twain and with diverse reasons maketh proof of it in his mind. While he whispereth of it to himself, secretly is he smitten with her.

14.

Her father welcomed her with great joy, although such show of affection lay heavy upon her. She was silent and subdued, consuming herself with heavy sorrow, and in wretched case, her heart being still faithful to Troilus, although she was soon to change and to forsake him for a new lover.

15.

Troilo in Troia tristo ed angoscioso,
   Quanto neun fu mai, se ne rivenne;
   E nel viso fellone e niquitoso,
   Pria ch' al palagio suo non si ritenne;
   Quivi smontato, troppo più pensoso
   Che stato fosse ancora, non sostenne
   Che da alcuno gli fosse nulla detto,
   Ma se n' entrò in camera soletto.

16.

Quivi al dolor che aveva ritenuto
   Diè largo luogo, chiamando la morte;
   Ed il suo ben piangeva, che perduto
   Gliel pare avere, e sì gridava forte,
   Che 'n forse fu di non esser sentuto
   Da quei che intorno givan per la corte;
   E in cotal pianto tutto il giorno stette,
   Che servo nè amico nol vedette.

17.

Se 'l giorno era con doglia trapassato,
   Non la scemò la notte già oscura,
   Ma fu il pianto e 'l gran duol raddoppiato,
   Così lo conducea la sua sciagura;
   El bestemmiava il giorno che fu nato,
   E gli dei e le dee e la natura,
   E 'l padre, e chi parola conceduta
   Avea che fosse Criseida renduta.

18.

Egli sè stesso ancor maledicea,
   Che sì l' aveva lasciata partire,
   E che 'l partito che preso n' avea,
   Cioè con lei di volersi fuggire,
   Non l' avea fatto, e forte sen pentea,
   E di dolor ne voleva morire;
   O che almen non l' aveva domandata,
   Che forse li saria stata donata.

15.

Troilus sad and distressed, as none was e'er before, turned back to Troy; and with a sullen and angry scowl upon his face, he tarried not until he reached his palace. Dismounting here, in mood much sadder than had e'er been his before, he suffered none to speak aught to him but entered his chamber in solitude.

16.

There he gave free vent to the grief that he had held in check, calling for death, and he bewailed his happiness which he thought he had lost, and so loudly did he cry that almost was he heard of those who were going about through the court. And in such weeping did he pass the whole day that neither servant nor friend saw him.

17.

If the day had passed in grief, the night, already dark, did not diminish it. But his lament and his great grief were redoubled, so did his misfortune gain the upper hand over him. He cursed the day upon which he was born and the gods and the goddesses and Dame Nature and his father and as many as had consented to the surrender of Cressida.

18.

He also cursed himself for having let her so depart and for not having carried out the decision that he had made, that is, to try to take flight with her. Bitterly did he repent of it, and he would willingly have died of grief because of it, or for not having at least asked for her, for perchance she might have been granted to him.

19.

E sè in qua ed ora in là volgendo,
  Senza luogo trovar per lo suo letto,
  Seco diceva talora piangendo:
  Che notte è questa! vogliendo rispetto
  Avere alla passata, s' io comprendo
  Qual' ora è; tal fiata il bianco petto,
  La bocca, e gli occhi, e 'l bel viso baciava
  Della mia donna, e spesso l' abbracciava;

20.

Ella baciava me, e ragionando
  Prendevam festa lieta e grazïosa;
  Or sol mi trovo, lasso, e lagrimando,
  In dubbio se giammai tanto gioiosa
  Notte deggia tornare; ora abbracciando
  Vado il piumaccio, e la fiamma amorosa
  Sento farsi maggiore, e la speranza
  Farsi minor, per lo duol che l' avanza.

21.

Che farò dunque, misero dolente,
  Aspetterò, pure che 'l possa fare?
  Ma se così s' attrista la mia mente
  Nel suo partir, come perseverare
  Io spero di potere? Egli è niente
  A chi ben ama il potersi posare,
  Perchè in tal guisa fece il simigliante
  La notte e 'l dì ch' era passato avante.

22.

Pandar non era il dì potuto andare
  A lui, nè alcun altro, onde il mattino
  Venuto, tosto sel fece chiamare,
  Per poter seco alquanto il cor meschino,
  Parlando di Criseida, alleggerare.
  Pandar vi venne, e bene era indovino
  Di ciò che quella notte fatto avea,
  Ed ancora di ciò ch' esso volea.

19.

And as he turned in his bed now here and now there, without finding any resting place, at such times would he in his weeping say to himself: "What a night is this! When I consider the past night, if I read the hour aright, such time as it now is did I kiss the white bosom, the mouth, the eyes, and the lovely face of my lady, and oft embrace her.

20.

"She would kiss me and we took a happy and gracious pleasure in conversing together. Now I find myself alone, alas, and weeping, in doubt whether so joyous a night is ever to come again. Now I keep embracing the pillow, and I feel the flame of love waxing greater, and hope becoming less on account of the grief that over-whelmeth it.

21.

"What then shall I do, miserable wretch that I am? Shall I wait if it so be that I can do so? But if my mind is so saddened by her departure, how shall I hope to be able to live on? To him who loveth well the power to rest is of no account, because in such wise did he* the like the night and day that had passed before."

22.

That day neither Pandarus nor any other had been able to come to him. Wherefore with the coming of day he at once had him summoned that he might be able somewhat to relieve his wretched heart by talking of Cressida. Pandarus came there and well could he divine what he had done that night and also what he desired.

* I.e., Troilus.

23.

O Pandar mio, disse Troilo, fioco
  Per lo gridare e per lo lungo pianto,
  Che farò io? che l' amoroso foco
  Sì mi comprende dentro tutto quanto,
  Che riposar non posso assai nè poco?
  Che farò io dolente, poichè tanto
  M' è stata la fortuna mia nemica,
  Ch' i' ho perduta la mia dolce amica?

24.

Io non la credo riveder giammai:
  Così foss' io allor caduto morto,
  Che io partir da me ier la lasciai!
  O dolce bene, o caro mio diporto,
  O bella donna a cui io mi donai;
  O dolce anima mia, o sol conforto
  Degli occhi tristi fiumi divenuti,
  Deh non ve' tu ch' io muoio, e non m' aiuti?

25.

Chi ti ved' ora, dolce anima bella?
  Chi siede teco, cor del corpo mio?
  Chi t' ascolta ora, chi teco favella?
  Oimè lasso più ch' altro, non io!
  Di' che fa' tu? or étti punto nella
  Mente di me, o messo m' hai in oblio
  Per lo tuo padre vecchio ch' ora t' have,
  Laond' io vivo in pena tanto grave?

26.

Qual tu m' odi ora, Pandaro, cotale
  Ho tutta notte fatto, nè dormire
  Lasciato m' ha quest' amoroso male;
  O pur se sonno alcun nel mio languire
  Trovato ha luogo, nïente mi vale,
  Perchè dormendo sogno di fuggire,
  O d' esser solo in luoghi paurosi,
  O nelle man di nemici animosi.

23.

"O Pandarus mine," quoth Troilus, hoarse with his cries and his long lament, "what shall I do? For the fire of love doth so enwrap me all within that neither much nor little may I rest. What shall I do in my woe, since Lady Fortune hath been so hostile to me that I have lost my sweet friend?

24.

"I do not believe that I shall ever again cast mine eyes upon her. Would therefore I had fallen dead, when yesterday I permitted her to depart. O sweet my love, O my dear delight, O lady fair, to whom I gave myself, O sweet my soul, O single solace of these sad eyes now turned to streams, alas, seest thou not I die, and givest thou not thine aid to me?

25.

"Who seeth thee now, fair sweet soul? Who sitteth with thee, heart of my body? Who listeneth to thee now, who holdeth speech with thee? Alas, not I, wretched beyond any other. Say, what doest thou? Hast thou now any thought of me in thy mind or hast thou forgotten me for thine aged father, who hath thee now, wherefore I live in so grievous pain?

26.

"As thou hearest me do now, Pandarus, so have I done all the night, nor hath this amorous woe let me sleep; or indeed, if any sleep hath found a place in my languishing, it availeth me naught, since when I sleep I do ever dream of flight or of being alone in fearsome places or in the hands of fierce enemies.

27.

E tanta noja m' è questo a vedere,
  E sì fatto spavento m' è nel core,
  Che vegghiar mi saria meglio e dolere :
  E spesse volte mi giugne un tremore
  Che mi riscuote e desta, e fa parere
  Che d' alto in basso io caggia, e desto, amore*
  Insieme con Criseida chiamo forte,
  Or per mercè pregando, ora per morte.

28.

A cotal punto, qual odi, venuto
  Misero sono, e duolmi di me stesso,
  E del partir, più che giammai creduto
  Io non avrei ; oimè che io confesso
  Che io deggia sperare ancora aiuto,
  E che la bella donna ancor con esso
  Verrà tornando, ma il core, che l' ama,
  Non mel consente, ed ognora la chiama.

29.

Poscia ch' egli ebbe in tal guisa gran pezza
  Parlato e detto, Pandaro, doglioso
  Di così grave e noiosa gramezza,
  Disse : deh dimmi Troilo, se riposo
  E fine dee aver questa tristezza,
  Non credi tu che il colpo amoroso
  Da altri mai che da te sia sentito,
  O di partenza sia stato al partito ?

30.

Ben son degli altri così innamorati
  Come tu se', per Pallade tel giuro ;
  E sonne ancor di quei che sventurati
  Son più di te, men pare esser sicuro ;
  E non si son però del tutto dati,
  Come tu se', a viver tanto duro,
  Ma la lor doglia, quando troppo avanza,
  S' ingegnan d' alleggiar con isperanza.

* Savj-Lopez, *desto, e Amore*

27.

"And so doth it vex me to see this, and such terror is in my heart that 'twere better for me to lie awake and grieve. And often there cometh upon me a trembling that shaketh and rouseth me and maketh it seem that I fall from a high place into the depths. And awakened I call loudly upon Love and upon Cressida, now praying for mercy and now for death.

28.

"To such a point as thou dost hear have I come in my misery and I grieve for myself and for that parting more than I could ever have believed. Alas that I confess I must still hope for help, and that the fair lady will yet come back with it. But the heart which loveth her, doth not allow me this and doth ever call on her."

29.

After he had spoken and discoursed a long time in such wise, Pandarus, sorrowing for a grief so heavy and vexatious, spake thus: "Alas, tell me, Troilus, an this sadness is ever to have surcease and end, dost thou not believe that the blow of love hath ever been felt by others than by thee, or that others have been put to the necessity of parting?

30.

"Truly others there are as enamored as thou art—by Pallas I swear it. And of them there be also some, I make no doubt, more stricken in fortune than thou. Yet have they not completely abandoned themselves, as thou hast, to the fate of so hard a life, but their grief, when it becometh too great, they seek to alleviate with hope.

31.

E tu dovresti il somigliante fare:
  Tu di' che ella infra 'l decimo giorno
  T' ha impromesso di qui ritornare;
  Questo non è tanto lungo soggiorno,
  Che tu nol debbi potere aspettare
  Senza attristarti, e star come musorno:
  Come potresti sofferir l' affanno,
  Se allontanar si convenisse un anno?

32.

I sogni e le paure caccia via,
  In quel che son lasciali andar ne' venti;
  Essi procedon da malinconia,
  E quel fanno veder che tu paventi;
  Solo Iddio sa il ver di quel che fia,
  Ed i sogni e gli augurii, a che le genti
  Stolte riguardan, non montano un moco,
  Nè al futuro fanno assai o poco.

33.

Dunque, per Dio, a te stesso perdona,
  Lascia questo dolor cotanto fiero;
  Fammi esta grazia, questo don mi dona,
  Levati su, alleggia il tuo pensiero,
  E dei passati ben meco ragiona,
  Ed ai futuri il tuo animo altero
  Dispon, che torneranno assai di corto;
  Dunque sperando ben prendi conforto.

34.

Questa città è grande e dilettosa,
  Ed ora è in tregua, siccome tu sai,
  Andianne in qualche parte graziosa
  Di qui lontana, e quivi ti starai
  Con alcun d' esti re, e la noiosa
  Vita con esso lui trapasserai,
  Mentre che passi il termine c' ha dato
  La bella donna che t' ha il cor piagato.

31.

"And thou shouldst do the like. Thou sayst that she hath given thee promises to return hither within the tenth day. This is not so long a tarrying that thou shouldst not be able to wait without putting on a long face and dawdling like a booby. How couldst thou suffer the torment if 'twere a question of a year's absence?

32.

"Drive away dreams and fears. Let them go into the winds that they are. They proceed from melancholy and cause thee to see what thou fearest. God alone knoweth the truth of what will be. Dreams and auguries, to which stupid people pay heed, amount to nothing nor have they little or much to do with the future.

33.

"So, then, in the name of the gods, have mercy upon thyself, leave off this so savage grief. Do me this favor, grant me this boon. Rise up, make thy thoughts light. Talk with me, if thou wilt, of the past but prepare thy noble soul for the future. For the past will come back again within a very short time. So take good comfort then in hoping.

34.

"This city is a great one and full of delights. Now, as thou knowest, there is a truce. Let us go hence to some pleasant place afar from here. There shalt thou be with some one of these kings and with him shalt thou beguile thy wearisome life, whilst thou passest the time set for thee by the fair lady who hath wounded thy heart.

35.

Deh fallo, io te ne prego, leva suso,
 Non è atto magnanimo il dolersi
Come tu fai, ed il giacer pur giuso;
 E s' e' tuoi modi sì stolti e diversi
Fuor si sapesson, saresti confuso;
 E diria l' uom, che tu de' tempi avversi,
Come codardo, e non d'amor piangessi,
O che d' essere infermo t' infingessi.

36.

Oimè! chi molto perde piange assai,
 Nè 'l può conoscer chi non l' ha provato
Qual è quel ben che io andar lasciai;
 Però non doverei esser biasmato
S' altro che pianger non facesse mai ;*
 Ma poichè tu, amico, m' hai pregato,
Conforterommi a tutto mio potere,
In tuo servigio e per farti piacere.

37.

Mandimi Iddio il dì decimo tosto,
 Sì ch' io mi torni lieto com' io m' era
Quando di render questa fu proposto:
 Non fu mai rosa in dolce primavera,
Bella, com' io a ritornar disposto
 Sono, come vedrò la fresca cera
Di quella donna ritornata in Troia,
Che m' è cagion di tormento e di noia.

38.

Ma dove potrem noi per festa andare
 Come ragioni? Andianne a Serpedone:
E come vi potrò io dimorare,
 Che io avrò sempre all' animo questione,
Non forse questa potesse tornare
 Anzi al dì dato per nulla cagione;
Che non vorrei non esserci, se avviene,
Per quanto il mondo vale e può di bene.

* Savj-Lopez, *facessi*

35.

"Ah, do this, I pray thee, rise up. To grieve as thou dost, is no courageous act. The same is true of thy lying down. If thy stupid and contrarious behavior should be known outside, thou wouldst be put to shame, and men would say that thou, like a coward, hadst been weeping for the adverse time, not for love, or that thou hadst been making pretense of illness."

36.

"Alas, he who loseth much, weepeth much, nor can he who hath not experienced it, know of what sort is that happiness which I let go. Wherefore I should not be blamed if ever I did naught but weep. But since thou, my friend, hast prayed me to do so, I will comfort myself to the best of my ability in order to serve thee and do thy pleasure.

37.

"May God soon send me the tenth day, so that I may again become as happy as I was when it was proposed to give her up. Never was rose in the sweet spring as fair as I am minded to become when I shall see again in Troy the fresh countenance of that lady who is the cause of all my torment and woe.

38.

"But where can we go for pastime, as thou dost suggest? Suppose we go to Sarpedon. How can I stay there, for I shall ever have anxiety in my soul lest she perchance return in vain before the day appointed. For I would not, if this should happen, be away for all the good things that life may buy or command."

39.

Deh io farò che senza indugio, alcuno,
  Se ella torna, fia per me venuto,
  Rispose Pandaro, e porrò qui uno
  Per questo sol, sicchè ben fia saputo
  Da noi; ch' or forse già non c' è nessuno
  Da cui come da me fosse voluto;
  Sicchè per questo già non lascerai;
  Andianne là dov' ora detto m' hai.

40.

I due compagni nel cammino entraro,
  E dopo forse quattromila passi
  Là dove Serpedone era arrivaro;
  Il quale come il seppe, incontro fassi
  A Troilo lieto, e molto gli fu caro.
  Li quali, avvegna che de'* fosser lassi
  Del molto sospirar, pur lietamente
  Festa fer grande col baron possente.

41.

Costui, siccome quel che d' alto cuore
  Era più ch' altro in ciascheduna cosa,
  Fece a ciascun maraviglioso onore
  Or con cacce or con festa grazïosa
  Di belle donne e di molto valore,
  Con canti e suoni, e sempre con pomposa
  Grandezza di conviti tanti e tali,
  Che 'n Troia mai non s' eran fatti eguali.

42.

Ma che giovavan queste cose al pio
  Troilo che 'l core ad esse non avea?
  Egli era là dove spesso il disio
  Formato nel pensier suo nel traea,
  E Criseida come suo iddio
  Con gli occhi della mente ognor vedea;
  Or una cosa or altra immaginando,
  Di lei e spesso d' amor sospirando.

* Savj-Lopez, *ched e'*

39.

"Ah, I shall see to it that someone, if she returneth, come for me without delay," replied Pandarus, "and I shall station one here for this sole purpose, so that it may be well known by us, since now indeed there is none perchance by whom it would be desired as by myself. So do not give up for this reason. Let us go where thou even now hast proposed to me."

40.

The two companions started forth upon the road, and after about four miles they reached the place where Sarpedon was. He, when he knew it, advanced joyfully to meet Troilus, and glad he was to do so. They, although weary from much sighing, joyfully made great festivity with the powerful baron.

41.

He, as one who was in all things more noble-hearted than any other, did marvelous honor to each, now with hunts and now with the gracious welcome of fair and very worthy ladies, with song and music, and always with grandeur of banquets of such number and sort that their like had never been held at Troy.

42.

But what availed all these things to the faithful Troilus who had no heart for them? He was in that place whither the love formed in his thoughts did often draw him, and Cressida as his god he did ever see with the eyes of his mind, imagining now one thing and now another, sighing for her and often for love.

43.

Ogni altra donna a veder gli era grave,
  Quantunque fosse valorosa e bella;
Ogni sollazzo, ogni canto soave
Noioso gli era non vedendo quella,
Nelle cui mani amor posto la chiave
Avea della sua vita tapinella;
  E tanto bene avea, quanto pensare
  A lei potea, lasciando ogni altro affare.

44.

E non passava sera nè mattina
  Che con sospiri costui non chiamasse,
  O luce bella, o stella mattutina;
  Poi, come s' ella presente ascoltasse,
  Mille fiate e più, rosa di spina
  Chiamandola che ella il salutasse,
  Pria ch' e' ristesse sempre convenia,
  Il salutar col sospirar finia.

45.

Nessuna ora del giorno trapassava
  Che non la nominasse mille fiate;
  Sempre il suo nome in la bocca li stava,
  E 'l suo bel viso e le parole ornate
  Nel cuore e nella mente figurava;
  Le lettere da lei a lui mandate
  Il dì ben cento volte rivolgea,
  Tanto di rivederle gli piacea.

46.

E' non vi furon tre dì dimorati,
  Ch' a Pandar Troilo cominciò a dire:
  Che facciam noi più qui? siam noi legati
  A dovere qui vivere e morire?
  Aspettiam noi d' essere accomiatati?
  A dirti il vero i' me ne vorre' ire:
  Deh andianne, per Dio, assai siam suti
  Con Serpedone e volentier veduti.

43.

However worthy and fair she might be, every other lady was tiresome in his sight. All diversions, every sweet song, were vexatious to him, since he saw not her in whose hands love had placed the key to his piteous life. He was happy only as he thought of her, forgetting every other matter.

44.

And there passed not evening nor morning that he did not cry out with sighs: "O lovely light, O morning star." Then as if she were present and listening, a thousand times he called her "thorn rose" in the hope of a salutation. But he always had to leave off in the middle; his salutations ended in sighs.

45.

No hour in the day passed by that he did not call her by name a thousand times; her name was ever upon his lips, and her fair countenance and graceful speech he pictured in his heart and mind. The letters sent to him by her he turned over a full hundred times a day, so did it please him to see them again.

46.

They had not tarried there three days when Troilus began to say to Pandarus: "What do we here any longer? Are we in duty bound to live and die here? Are we waiting to be sent on our way? To tell thee true, I would fain go hence. Let us go away in the name of the gods; we have been long enough with Sarpedon, who hath granted us willing hospitality."

47.

Pandaro allora: or siam noi per lo fuoco
   Venuti qui, o è 'l decimo giorno
   Venuto? Ancor deh temperati un poco,
   Che l' andarne ora parrebbe uno scorno.
   Dove n' andrai tu ora ed in qual loco
   Nel qual tu facci più lieto soggiorno?
   Deh stiamo ancor due dì, poi ce n'andremo,
   E se vorrai, a casa torneremo.

48.

Come che contra voglia Troilo stesse,
   Pur si rimase ne' pensieri usati,
   Nè valea perchè Pandar gliel dicesse.
   Ma dopo il quinto dì accomiatati,
   Quantunque a Serpedone non piacesse,
   Ver le lor case si son ritornati;
   Troilo dicendo pel cammino: o Dio!
   Troverò io tornato l' amor mio?

49.

Ma Pandar seco diceva altrimente,
   Come colui che conosceva intera
   L' intenzïon di Calcas pienamente:
   Questa tua voglia sì focosa e fiera
   Si potrà raffreddar, s' el non mi mente
   Ciò ch' io udii infin quand' ella c' era;
   Ed il decimo giorno, e 'l mese e l' anno,
   Pria la rivegghi, credo passeranno.

50.

Poi che furono a casa ritornati,
   Intramendue in camera n' andaro,
   Ed a seder si furono assettati
   E di Criseida molto ragionaro,
   Senza dar sosta Troilo agl' infiammati
   Sospir, ma dopo alquanto si levaro,
   Dicendo Troilo: andiamo, e sì vedremo
   La casa almen, poich' altro non potemo.

47.

Then quoth Pandarus: "Look you now, have we come hither to escape the hot pangs of love or hath the tenth day arrived? O restrain thyself but a little longer, for our going home would seem a slight. Whither now shalt thou go and to what place wherein thou mayest make a happier sojourn? Let us stay two days longer. Then shall we depart, and if thou dost wish it, homeward wend."

48.

Although against his will Troilus tarried, yet did he remain in his usual train of thought. Nor did Pandarus' words avail aught. But after the fifth day, having taken their leave, though to the displeasure of Sarpedon, they returned to their own homes, Troilus saying along the way: "O God, shall I find my love returned?"

49.

But Pandarus, as one who fully knew the whole intent of Calchas, spake otherwise with him. "This wish of thine, so fierce and fiery, may be cooled, if I be not deceived by what I heard even when she was here. I believe that the tenth day and the month and the year will pass before thou dost see her again."

50.

When they were returned home, both went into a chamber and when they had found a place to sit, much they talked of Cressida without Troilus' giving any respite to his hot sighs. But after a little while Troilus said: "Let us go and see the house at least, since else we cannot do."

51.

E detto questo, il suo Pandaro prese
   Per mano, e 'l viso alquanto si dipinse
Con falso riso, e del palagio scese,
   E varie cagïon con gli altri finse
Ch' eran con lui, per nasconder l' offese
   Ch' e' sentiva d' amor; ma poich' attinse
Con gli occhi di Criseida la magione
Chiusa, sentì novella turbazione.

52.

E' gli parve che il cor gli si schiantasse
   Poi veduta ebbe la porta serrata
E le finestre; e tanto di sè 'l trasse
   La passïon novellamente nata,
Ch' el non sapea se stesse o se andasse;
   E nella faccia sua tutta cambiata
N' averia dato segno manifesto,
A chi l' avesse riguardato presto.

53.

Con Pandar poi come potea doglioso
   Dalla sua nuova angoscia ragionava;
Poi dicea: lasso, quanto luminoso
   Era il luogo e piacevol, quando stava
In te quella beltà, che 'l mio riposo
   Dentro dagli occhi suoi tutto portava;
Or se' rimaso oscuro senza lei,
Nè so se mai riaver la ti dei.

54.

Quindi sen gì per Troia cavalcando,
   E ciascun luogo gliel tornava a mente;
De' quai con seco giva ragionando:
   Quivi rider la vidi lietamente;
Quivi la vidi verso me guardando:
   Quivi mi salutò benignamente;
Quivi far festa e quivi star pensosa,
Quivi la vidi a' miei sospir pietosa.

51.

And having said this, he took Pandarus by the hand. And his face wore something of a deceptive smile. He descended from the palace and to the others that were with him made various pretexts to conceal the assaults of love he felt. But when his eyes fell upon the closed house of Cressida, he experienced a new agitation.

52.

And it seemed to him that his heart would break when he beheld the locked door and the windows. So distracted was he by the newborn passion that he knew not whether he stood or walked. And his changed countenance would have given manifest tokens of it to anyone who had bestowed upon him even a casual glance.

53.

Grieving thus on account of his new anguish, he did his best to talk with Pandarus. Then he said: "Alas, how full of brightness and delight wert thou, O place,* when that beautiful lady was in thee, for she bore my peace entirely within her eyes! Now without her art thou left dark nor do I know whether thou art ever to have her again."

54.

Then he went forth riding through Troy. And every place recalled her to his mind. Of these places he continued to hold discourse with himself as he rode on. "There I saw her laugh happily; there I saw her cast her glance upon me; there she graciously saluted me; there I saw her rejoice and there turn thoughtful; there I saw her pitiful of my sighs.

* Note the anacoluthon in the Italian.

55.

Colà istava, quand' ella mi prese
  Con gli occhi belli e vaghi con amore;
Colà istava, quando ella m' accese
  Con un sospir di maggior fuoco il core;
Colà istava, quando condiscese
  Al mio piacere il donnesco valore;
Colà la vidi altiera, e là umile
Mi si mostrò la mia donna gentile.

56.

Poi ciò pensando, giva soggiugnendo:
  Lunga hai fatta di me amor la storia,
S' io non mi voglio a me gir nascondendo,
  E 'l ver ben mi ridice la memoria;
Dove ch' io vada o stia, s' io bene intendo,
  Ben mille segni della tua vittoria
Discerno, c' hai avuta trionfante
Di me, che scherníi già ciascuno amante.

57.

Ben hai la tua ingiuria vendicata,
  Signor possente e molto da temere:
Ma poi ch' a te servir l' alma s' è data
  Tutta, siccome chiaro puoi vedere,
Non la lasciar morire sconsolata,
  Ritornala nel suo primo piacere,
Stringi Criseida sì come me fai,
Sì ch' ella torni a dar fine a' miei guai.

58.

El se ne gia talvolta in sulla porta
  Per la qual' era la sua donna uscita:
Di quinci uscì colei che mi conforta,
  Di quinci uscì la mia soave vita;
Fino a quel loco le feci la scorta,
  E quivi da lei feci dipartita;
E quivi lasso le toccai la mano;
Seco dicea, piangendo a mano a mano.

55.

"There she was when with her fair and beautiful eyes she made me a captive with love; there she was when she enkindled my heart with a sigh of greater warmth; there she was when her ladylike worthiness condescended to my pleasure; there I saw her haughty, and there humble did my gentle lady show herself to me."

56.

Then as he thought of that, he went on to add: "Long hast thou made me a byword on the lips of men, O Love, if I do not wish to continue this self-deception, and memory well repeateth the truth to me. Wherever I go or stay, if I understand aright, I discern a full thousand signs of thy victory, which thou hast won in triumph over me, who once did mock at every lover.

57.

"Well hast thou avenged the insult put upon thee, powerful and very redoubtable lord. But since my soul hath devoted itself entirely to thy service, as thou mayest clearly see, let it not die disconsolate, restore it to its first pleasure; constrain Cressida as thou dost me, so that she may return to put an end to my woes."

58.

At times he went forth even to the city gate through which his lady had departed. "Hence issued she who comforted me, hence went forth my sweet life; and even to that place did I give her escort, and there did I make my parting from her, and there, alas, did I touch her hand." All these things he said to himself, bursting into tears at once.

59.

Quindi n' andasti, cor del corpo mio;
  Quando sarà che tu quindi ritorni,
  Caro mio bene e dolce mio disio?
  Certo io non so, ma questi dieci giorni
  Più che mill' anni fien; deh vedrott' io
  Giammai tornar colli tu' atti adorni,
  A rallegrarmi sì com' hai promesso?
  Deh fia omai, deh or foss' egli adesso!

60.

E gli parea a sè stesso nel viso
  Esser men che l' usato colorito,
  E per questo faceva in suo avviso
  D' esser talvolta dimostrato a dito,
  Quasi dicesser: perchè sì conquiso
  È divenuto Troilo e sì smarrito?
  Color che 'l dimostrassono e' non era,
  Ma sospica chi sa la cosa vera.

61.

Per che gli piacque di mostrare in versi
  Chi ne fosse cagione: sospirando,
  Quando era assai stanco di dolersi,
  Alcuna sosta quasi al dolor dando,
  Mentre aspettava nelli tempi avversi
  Con bassa voce sen giva cantando,
  E ricreando l' anima conquisa
  Dal soperchio d' amore, in cotal guisa:

62.

La dolce vista e 'l bel guardo soave
  De' più begli occhi che si vider mai,
  Ch' i' ho perduti, fan parer sì grave
  La vita mia, ch' io vo traendo guai;
  Ed a tal punto già condotto m' have,
  Che invece di sospir leggiadri e gai
  Ch' aver solea, disii porto di morte
  Per la partenza, sì me ne duol forte.

59.

"Hence thou didst depart, heart of my body. When shall it be that thou wilt return thence, dear joy of mine and sweet my love? Surely I do not know but these ten days will be more than a thousand years. Ah, shall I ever see thee return to delight me with thy comely ways, even as thou hast promised? Ah, will it ever be? Ah, would it were even now!"

60.

And it seemed to him that there was less than the usual color in his face, and for this reason he fancied that he was at times pointed at, as if men were saying: "Why hath Troilus become so submissive and so bemused?" There was none that pointed at him, but he who knoweth the truth is suspicious.

61.

Wherefore it pleased him to show in verses who was its cause. And sighing when aweary of grieving, giving some respite, as it were, to his sorrow—while he waited in luckless days—he went his way with a low-voiced song upon his lips, diverting his soul overborne with excess of love in such wise as this:

62.

"The sweet sight and the fair soft glance of the loveliest eyes that e'er were seen, which I have lost, make my life seem so wearisome that I go about heaving groans of woe. And so far have they led me that instead of the light, joyous sighs that I used to fetch, I yearn for death on account of thy going, so deeply doth it pain me.

63.

Oimè Amor, perchè nel primo passo
  Non mi feristi sì ch' io fossi morto ?
  Perchè non dipartisti da me lasso
  Lo spirito angoscioso che io porto ?
  Perciocchè d' alto mi veggio ora in basso.
  Non è amore al mio dolor conforto
  Fuor che 'l morir, trovandomi partuto
  Da que' begli occhi ov' io t' ho già veduto.

64.

Quando per gentil atto di salute
  Ver bella donna giro gli occhi alquanto,
  Sì tutta si disfà la mia virtute
  Che ritener non posso dentro il pianto ;
  Così mi van l' amorose ferute
  Membrando la mia donna, a cui son tanto,
  O lasso me, lontano a veder lei,
  Che se 'l volesse Amor, morir vorrei.

65.

Poichè la mia ventura è tanto cruda
  Che ciò ch' agli occhi incontra più m' attrista,
  Per Dio, Amor, che la tua man li chiuda,
  Poic' ho perduta l' amorosa vista ;
  Lascia di me, Amor, la carne ignuda,
  Che quando vita per morte s' acquista
  Gioioso dovria essere il morire,
  E sai ben dove l' alma ne dee gire.

66.

Ella n' andrà in quelle belle braccia
  Dove fortuna n' ha 'l corpo gittato :
  Non vedi tu che già nella mia faccia
  Io son del color suo, Amor, segnato ?
  Vedi l' angoscia che da me la caccia,
  Trannela tu, e nel seno più amato
  Da lei la porta, ov' ella attende pace,
  Che già ogni altra cosa le dispiace.

63.

"Alas, Love, why at the first step didst thou not wound me so grievously that I should have died? Why, alas, didst thou not separate from me the anguished spirit I bear, since from being aloft I now see myself brought low? There is no comfort, Love, to my griefs save only death, when I find myself parted from those fair eyes in which I have once seen thee.

64.

"When for the gentle act of salutation I turn mine eyes somewhat toward some fair lady, all my strength is so dissipated that I cannot check within me my lamenting. Thus do the amorous wounds remind me of my lady, from whose sight I am now so far, O woe is me, that if Love should wish it, I fain would die.

65.

"Since my fortune is so cruel that all that meeteth mine eyes saddeneth me the more, in the name of the gods, O Love, let thy hand close them, since I have lost the amorous sight. Leave, O Love, my naked flesh, for when life is acquired by death, dying should be joyous; and thou knowest well where the soul must go.

66.

"It will go to those fair arms into which fortune hath already cast the body. Dost thou not see, O Love, that I am already marked in the face with its* own color? See then the anguish that the pursuit giveth me, draw it forth, and bear it to the bosom most beloved by it, where it awaiteth peace, for every other thing displeaseth it."

* I.e., Death's.

67.

Poich' egli avea cantando così detto,
    Al sospirare antico si tornava;
    Il dì andando, e la notte nel letto,
    Di Criseida sua sempre pensava;
    Nè d' altro quasi prendeva diletto,
    E i dì passati spesso annoverava,
    Non credendo giammai giungere a' dieci,
    Ch' a lui tornasse Criseida da' Greci.

68.

Li giorni grandi e le notti maggiori
    Oltre all' usato modo gli parieno;
    El misurava dalli primi albori
    Infino allor che le stelle apparieno;
    Diceva: il sol è entrato in nuovi errori,
    Nè i cavai suoi come già fer corrieno:
    Della notte diceva il simigliante,
    E l' una, due, diceva tutte quante.

69.

Era la vecchia luna già cornuta
    Nel partir di Criseida, ed el l' avea,
    Da lei uscendo, in sul mattin veduta;
    Per che sovente con seco dicea:
    Allor che questa sarà divenuta
    Colle sue nuove corna, qual parea
    Quando sen gì la nostra donna, fia
    Tornata qui allor l' anima mia.

70.

El riguardava li Greci attendati
    Davanti a Troia, e come già turbarsi
    Vedendoli solea, così mirati
    Con diletto eran; e ciò che soffiarsi
    Sentia nel viso, sì come mandati
    Sospiri di Criseida solea darsi
    A creder fosser, dicendo sovente:
    O qua o quivi è mia donna piacente.

67.

When he had uttered these words in his song, he turned again to his former sighing. As he went about by day, and as by night he lay in bed, he did ever think upon his Cressida, nor took he pleasure in scarce any other thing. And often did he number o'er the days gone past, never believing that he would reach the tenth, when Cressida should return to him from the Greeks.

68.

Beyond the usual fashion the days seemed to him long and the nights longer. He measured from the first white gleam of dawn until the moment when the stars appeared. Thus would he say: "The sun hath entered upon new errors nor do his horses run as once they did." Of the night he would say the like: "one o'clock," "two o'clock," he'd repeat them all.

69.

The old moon was already horned at the going of Cressida, and he had seen it early in the morning when he departed from her house. Wherefore he often said to himself: "When it shall have become with its new horns just as it appeared when our lady went away, then will my soul have returned here."

70.

He gazed at the Greeks in their tents before Troy. And as formerly he was wont to be disturbed when he saw them, so now were they looked upon with pleasure. And that breeze which he felt blowing in his face, he was often wont to believe sighs wafted from Cressida. And as often would he say: "Either here or there is my gracious lady."

71.

In cotal guisa, e in altri modi assai,
   Il tempo sospirando trapassava;
   E con lui Pandaro era sempre mai,
   Che a ciò far sovente il confortava;
   Ed in ragionamenti lieti e gai
   A suo poter di trarlo s' ingegnava;
   Donando a lui ognor buona speranza
   Della sua vaga e valorosa amanza.

71.

In such wise and in many another fashion he passed the time away in sighs. And with him was ever Pandarus, who often comforted him in his lamenting. And in so far as he might, he endeavored to draw him into gay and gladsome talk, ever giving him good hope of his fair and worthy love.

IL FILOSTRATO

DI

GIOVANNI BOCCACCIO

PARTE SESTA

ARGOMENTO

Qui comincia la sesta parte del Filostrato, nella quale primieramente Criseida, essendo presso al padre, si duole d'esser lontana a Troilo. Viene a lei Diomede e favellale; biasimale Troia e i Troiani, e discuoprele il suo amore; al quale ella risponde, e lascialo in dubbio s'egli le piaccia o no; e ultimamente intiepidita di Troilo, il comincia a dimenticare. E primieramente si duole piangendo Criseida d'essere da Troilo lontana.

1.

Dall' altra parte in sul lito del mare,
   Con poche donne, tra le genti armate
   Stava Criseida, ed in lagrime amare
   Da lei eran le notti consumate,
   Che 'l giorno più le convenia guardare,
   Perchè le fresche guance e delicate
   Pallide e magre l' eran divenute,
   Lontana dalla sua dolce salute.

2.

Ella piangeva seco mormorando
   Di Troilo lo già preso piacere,
   E gli atti tutti andava disegnando
   Stati tra loro, e le parole intere
   Tutte con seco venia ricordando,
   Qualora ella n' avea tempo o potere;
   Perchè da lui vedendosi lontana,
   Fe' de' suoi occhi un' amara fontana.

THE FILOSTRATO

OF

GIOVANNI BOCCACCIO

❦

SIXTH PART

ARGUMENT

Here beginneth the sixth part of the Filostrato, in which, to begin with, Cressida, while at her father's tent, grieveth at her separation from Troilus. Diomede cometh to her and holdeth discourse with her. He disparageth Troy and the Trojans, and discovereth his love. To him she replieth and leaveth him in doubt whether he please her or not. Finally grown indifferent to Troilus, she beginneth to forget him. And in the first place Cressida weepeth grievously at her separation from Troilus.

1.

On the other side, by the seashore, with few ladies, among armed men was Cressida. In bitter tears were spent her nights, for by day it was more fitting for her to use precaution, for the fresh and delicate cheeks had grown wan and thin. She was far from her sweet well-being.

2.

She wept, whispering to herself the delight she had heretofore taken with Troilus, and she did ever and anon tell over to herself all that had happened between them and often did she call to mind their every word, whenever she had the time or power to do so. For when she saw how far from him she was, she made a bitter fountain of her eyes.

[409]

3.

Nè saria stato alcun sì dispietato
  Ch' udendo lei rammaricar dolente
  Con lei di pianger si fosse temprato.
  Ella piangeva sì amaramente,
  Quando punto di tempo l' era dato,
  Che dir non si potrebbe interamente;
  E quel che peggio ch' altro le facea,
  Era, con cui dolersi non avea.

4.

Ella mirava le mura di Troia,
  E' palagi, le torri e le fortezze,
  E dicea seco: oimè, quanta gioia,
  Quanto piacere e quanto di dolcezze
  N' ebb' io già dentro! ed ora in trista noia
  Consumo qui le mie care bellezze:
  Oimè, Troilo mio, che fa' tu ora,
  Ricordati di me niente ancora?

5.

Oimè lassa! or t' avess' io creduto,
  E insieme tramendue fossimo giti
  Dove e in qual regno ti fosse piaciuto;
  Ch' or non sarien questi dolor sentiti
  Da me, nè tanto buon tempo perduto:
  Quando che sia saremmo poi redditi;
  E chi di me avria poi detto male,
  Perchè andata ne fossi con uom tale?

6.

Oime lassa! che tardi m' avveggio
  Che 'l senno mio mi torna ora nemico:
  Io fuggii il male e seguitai il peggio,
  Onde di gioia il mio cuore è mendico;
  E per conforto invan la morte chieggio,
  Poi veder non ti posso, o dolce amico,
  E temo di giammai più non vederti;
  Così sien tosto li Greci diserti!

3.

Nor would anyone have been so heartless, when he heard her make bitter plaint in her sorrows, as to refrain from weeping with her. So grievous was her weeping, when a moment of time was given her, that it could not be described to the full. And that which afflicted her more than aught else, was that she had none to share her grief.

4.

She would gaze upon the walls of Troy, the palaces, towers, and fortresses, and to herself would she say: "Alas, what a deal of joy, pleasure, and sweetness had I once within them! And now here in sad distress do I consume my precious beauty. Alas, my Troilus, what doest thou now? Hast thou still any memory of me?

5.

"O woe, alas! Now would I had believed thee and together we had gone whithersoever and to whatsoever realm it had pleased thee. For now should I feel none of these sorrows, nor would so much good time be wasted. We should have returned at any time thereafter, and who would have said evil of me because I had gone away with such a man?

6.

"O woe, alas, that at this late hour I perceive how my judgment now turneth enemy to me! I turned from the bad and pursued the worse; wherefore my heart is bereft of joy. Vainly do I call upon death for solace, since I cannot see thee, O sweet friend. And I fear I shall never see thee again. May the Greeks full soon be as wretched as I.

7.

Ma mio poter farò quinci fuggirmi,
    Se conceduto non mi fia 'l venire
    In altra guisa, e con teco reddirmi
    Com' io promisi; e vada dove gire
    Ne vuole il fumo, e ciò che può seguirmi
    Di ciò ne segua; ch' anzi che morire
    Di dolor voglia, io voglio che parlare
    Possa chi voglia e di ciò abbaiare.

8.

Ma di sì alto e grande intendimento
    Tosto la volse novello amadore:
    Aoperava Diomede ogni argomento
    Che el potea per entrarle nel core;
    Nè gli fallì al suo tempo l' attento,
    E 'n breve spazio ne cacciò di fuore
    Troilo e Troia, ed ogni altro pensiero
    Che 'n lei fosse di lui o falso o vero.

9.

Ella non v' era il quarto giorno stata
    Dopo l' amara dipartenza, quando
    Cagione onesta a lei venir trovata
    Da Diomede fu, che sospirando
    La trovò sola, e quasi trasformata
    Dal dì che prima con lei cavalcando
    Di Troia quivi menata l' avea,
    Il che gran maraviglia gli parea.

10.

E seco disse nella prima vista:
    Vana fatica credo sia la mia;
    Questa donna è per altrui amor trista,
    Siccom' io veggio, sospirosa e pia;
    Troppo esser converria sovrano artista
    S' io ne volessi il primo cacciar via
    Per entrarv' io: oimè che male andai
    Per me a Troia quando la menai.

7.

"But I shall do all in my power to make my escape hence, if in no other way my coming to thee be permitted, and to return to thy side, as I promised, and let the smoke float where it listeth and any consequence that will, follow me. For rather than consent to die of grief I am nothing loath that he who wisheth, may speak of it in barking tones."

8.

But soon did a new lover turn her from so high and great intent. Diomede made use of every argument that he could to make way into her heart. Nor did the attempt fail him in due season. In brief space he drave forth from it Troilus and Troy and every other thought which she had of him, or false or true.

9.

She had not been there the fourth day after the bitter parting when honorable cause to come to her was found by Diomede, who found her weeping in solitude and almost a different woman from the day when first riding forth with her, he had conducted her thither from Troy. And this seemed a great marvel to him.

10.

And to himself he said when first he saw her: "I think this labor of mine an idle one. This lady is sad for the love of another, as I see her, full of the sighs of constancy. Too much the master artist should I have to be, if I would drive out the first in order to make my own way in. Alas, in what an evil hour did I go to Troy when I brought her away!"

11.

Ma come quei ch' era di grande ardire,
  E di gran cuor, con seco stesso prese,
  S' el ne dovesse per certo morire,
  Poi quivi era venuto, l' aspre offese
  Ch' amore gli facea per lei sentire
  Di dimostrarle, sì come s' accese
  Prima di lei; e postosi a sedere,
  Di lungi assai si fece al suo volere.

12.

E prima seco entrò a ragionare
  Dell' aspra guerra tra loro e' Troiani,
  Lei domandando quel che le ne pare,
  S' e' lor pensier credea frivoli o vani:
  Quinci discese poi a domandare
  Se le parien de' Greci i modi strani;
  Nè molto poi si tenne a domandarla,
  Perchè stesse Calcas di maritarla.

13.

Criseida, che ancor l' animo avea
  In Troia fitto al suo dolce amadore,
  Dell' astuzia di lui non s' accorgea,
  Ma sì come piaceva al suo signore
  Amore, a Diomede rispondea,
  E spesse volte gli passava il cuore
  Con grieve doglia, e talor li donava
  Lieta speranza di quel che cercava.

14.

Il qual come con lei rassicurato
  Fu ragionando, cominciò a dire:
  Giovane donna, s' io v' ho ben guardato
  Nell' angelico viso da aggradire
  Più ch' altro visto mai, quel trasformato
  Mi par veder per noioso martire,
  Dal giorno in qua che di Troia partimmo,
  E qui come sapete ne venimmo.

11.

But as one who had great daring and a stout heart, he made resolve, now that he had come hither, to disclose to her, even were he to die for it, the rough assaults that love had made him feel on her account, and how he was first enkindled with love for her. And after taking a seat he came gradually to his desires.

12.

And first he began to speak to her of the cruel wars between themselves and the Trojans, asking her opinion on the subject, whether she thought their designs frivolous or vain. Whence he went on to ask whether the ways of the Greeks seemed strange to her. Nor did he long refrain from asking her why Calchas delayed to seek her a husband.

13.

Cressida, whose mind still dwelt upon her sweet lover in Troy, did not perceive his cunning but answered Diomede as it pleased her master Love. Again and again she pierced his heart with grievous pain and now and then she gave him joyous hope of what he sought.

14.

He, gathering assurance as he talked with her, began to say: "O youthful lady, if I have looked well into the face that delighteth more than any other ever seen, meseemeth that I see it much changed, on account of cruel torment, from the day on which we started hither from Troy, and, as you know, came here.

15.

Nè so ch' esser si possa la cagione
   S' amor non fosse, il qual, se savia sete,
   Gittrete via, udendo la ragione,
   Perchè siccom' io dico far dovete.
   Li Troian son si può dire in prigione
   Da noi tenuti, siccome vedete,
   Che siam disposti di non mutar loco
   Senza disfarla o con ferro o con fuoco:

16.

Nè crediate ch' alcun che dentro sia
   Trovi pietà da noi in sempiterno;
   Nè mai commise alcuno altra follia
   O commettrà, se 'l mondo fosse eterno,
   Che assai chiaro esempio non gli fia,
   O qui tra' vivi, o tra' morti in inferno,
   La punizion ch' a Paride daremo,
   Della fatta da lui, se noi potremo.

17.

E se vi fosser ben dodici Ettori,
   Come un ve n' è, e sessanta fratelli;
   Se Calcas per ambage e per errori
   Qui non ci mena, parimente d' elli,
   Quantunque sieno, i disiati onori
   Avremo e tosto: e la morte di quelli,
   Che sarà in breve, ne darà certanza
   Che non sia falsa la nostra speranza.

18.

E non crediate che Calcas avesse
   Con tanta istanza voi raddomandata,
   Se ciò ch' io dico non antivedesse:
   Ben' ho io già con esso lui trattata
   Questa questione prima che 'l facesse,
   E ciascuna cagione esaminata;
   Ond' ei per trarvi di cotal periglio,
   Di rivolervi qui prese consiglio.

[416]

15.

"Nor do I know what may be the cause, if 'twere not love, which, if you be wise, you will cast aside when you listen to reason, because you must do as I say. The Trojans are, it may be said, imprisoned by us, as you see, for we are minded not to depart until we have destroyed Troy either with sword or fire.

16.

"Believe not that any in the city shall ever find pity in us. Neither ever did anyone nor ever, even if the world were eternal, shall any commit other folly without the punishment we shall mete out to Paris, if we may, for the deed he hath done, becoming a very shining example to him, either here among the living or among the dead in hell.

17.

"And were there indeed a dozen Hectors, as there is but one, and sixty brothers, we shall, even if Calchas doth not bring us to it by treacherous and deceitful speech, have, and that soon, the longed-for victory over them, one and all, no matter how many there be. And their death, which shall be within a very short space of time, will give us certainty that our hope is not ill-founded.

18.

"And believe not that Calchas would have demanded you back with such urgency had he not foreseen what I tell you. Well have I discussed this matter with him before he did so and taken every circumstance into consideration. Wherefore in order to draw you away from such dangers, he took counsel how to have you returned hither.

19.

Ed io nel confortai, di voi udendo
　Mirabili virtù ed altre cose;
　Ed Antenor per voi dargli sentendo,
　M' offersi trattator, ed el m' impose
　Ch' io il facessi, assai ben conoscendo
　La fede mia; nè mi fur faticose
　L' andate e le tornate per vedervi,
　Per parlarvi, conoscervi ed udervi.

20.

Chè vo' dir dunque, bella donna e cara,
　Lasciate de' Troian l' amor fallace;
　Cacciate via questa speranza amara
　Che 'nvano sospirare ora vi face,
　E rivocate la bellezza chiara,
　La qual più ch' altra a chi intende piace;
　Ch' a tal partito omai Troia è venuta
　Ch' ogni speranza ch' uom v' ha è perduta.

21.

E s' ella fosse pur per sempre stare,
　Sì sono il re, e' figli e gli abitanti
　Barbari e scostumati, e da apprezzare
　Poco, a rispetto de' Greci, ch' avanti
　Ad ogni altra nazion possono andare,
　D' alti costumi e d' ornati sembianti;
　Voi siete ora tra uomin costumati,
　Dove eravate tra bruti insensati.

22.

E non crediate che ne' Greci amore
　Non sia, assai più alto e più perfetto
　Che tra' Troiani; e 'l vostro gran valore,
　La gran beltà e l' angelico aspetto
　Troverà qui assai degno amadore,
　Se el vi fia di pigliarlo diletto;
　E se non vi spiacesse, io sarei desso,
　Più volentier che re de' Greci adesso.

19.

"And I did urge him, hearing of your marvelous virtues and other excellencies, and when Antenor learned that he was to be given in exchange for you, I made offer of myself as mediator. And he laid upon me the charge that I should take this part, knowing full well my fealty. Nor were the goings and comings to see you, speak to you, know you, and hear you wearisome to me.

20.

"Therefore I desire to say to you, fair dear lady, renounce the fruitless love for the Trojans, drive away this bitter hope which now maketh you to sigh in vain, and recover the resplendent beauty which more than anything delighteth him who is a man of understanding. For to such straits hath Troy now come that every hope that man hath there is lost.

21.

"And were it indeed to stand forever, yet are its king, its sons, and its inhabitants barbarous and rude in their ways, and to be held in little esteem in comparison with the Greeks, who surpass every other nation in goodly ways and mannerly appearance. You are among well-bred men, where formerly you were among drunken brutes.

22.

"And do not believe that there is not among the Greeks love nobler and more perfect than among the Trojans. And your great worth, exceeding beauty, and angelic aspect shall find here a very worthy lover, if you shall find pleasure in accepting him. And if it should not displease you, I would at this moment be he more gladly than king of the Greeks."

23.

E questo detto diventò vermiglio
  Come fuoco nel viso, e la favella
  Tremante alquanto; in terra bassò il ciglio,
  Alquanto gli occhi torcendo da ella.
  Ma poi tornò da subito consiglio
  Più pronto che non era, e con isnella
  Loquela* seguitò: non vi sia noia,
  Io son così gentil come uom di Troia.

24.

Se 'l padre mio Tideo fosse vissuto,
  Com' el fu morto a Tebe combattendo,
  Di Calidonia e d' Argo saria suto
  Re, siccom' io ancora essere intendo;
  Nè era stran nell' un regno venuto,
  Ma conosciuto, antico e reverendo,
  E, se creder si può, di Dio disceso,
  Sì ch' io non son tra' Greci di men peso.

25.

Pregovi dunque, se 'l mio prego vale,
  Che via cacciate ogni malinconia,
  E me, se io vi paio tanto e tale
  Qual si conviene a vostra signoria,
  In servidor prendiate; io sarò quale
  L' onestà vostra e l' alta leggiadria,
  Ch' io veggio in voi più ch' in altra, richiede,
  Sì che ancor caro avrete Diomede.

26.

Criseida ascoltava, e rispondea
  Poche parole e rade, vergognosa,
  Secondo che 'l di lui dir richiedea;
  Ma poi udendo quest' ultima cosa,
  Seco l' ardir di lui grande dicea,
  A traverso mirandol dispettosa,
  Tanto poteva ancor Troilo in essa,
  E così disse con voce sommessa:

* Savj-Lopez, *loquella*

23.

And when he had said this, he turned red as fire in his face and his voice did somewhat shake. His gaze he cast upon the ground, averting somewhat his eyes from her. But then he turned with sudden thought, readier of word than he had been, and with swift speech continued: "Let it not vex you; I am as gentle born as any man in Troy.

24.

"If my father Tydeus had lived—he was killed fighting at Thebes—I should have been king of Calydon and Argos, as I still intend to be, nor had I come into a kingdom a stranger but known, of ancient line, and honorable, and, if it may be believed, descended from the gods, so that I am not of least weight among the Greeks.

25.

"I pray you then, if my prayer availeth, that you drive away all melancholy and that you take me as your vassal, if I seem to be a man of such worth and excellence as befitteth your sovereignty. I shall be what is demanded by your high beauty—which I behold in you more than in any other—, so that you will also hold Diomede dear."

26.

Cressida listened and shamefaced made reply with words few and far between, according as his speech demanded. But when she heard this last remark, she said to herself that his daring was great. Askance she eyed him and in anger—so much power did Troilus still have over her—and thus in voice subdued she spake:

27.

Io amo, Diomede, quella terra
  Nella qual son cresciuta ed allevata,
  E quanto può mi grava la sua guerra,
  E volentier la vedrei liberata;
  E se fato crudel fuor me ne serra,
  Questo mi fa con gran ragion turbata,
  Ma d' ogni affanno per me ricevuto,
  Prego buon merto te ne sia renduto.

28.

Ben so ch' e' Greci son d' alto valore
  E costumati sì come ragioni;
  Ma de' Troian non è però minore
  L' alta virtù; e le lor condizioni
  L' hanno mostrate nelle man d' Ettore;
  Nè senno è credo per divisïoni
  O per altra cagione altrui biasmare,
  E poscia sè sopra gli altri lodare.

29.

Amore io non conobbi, poi morio
  Colui al qual lealmente il servai,
  Sì come a marito e signor mio;
  Nè Greco nè Troian mai non curai
  In cotal fatto, nè me n' è in disio
  Curarne alcuno, nè mi fia giammai:
  Che tu sia di real sangue disceso
  Cred' io assai, ed hollo bene inteso.

30.

E questo assai mi dà d' ammirazione,
  Che possi porre in una femminella,
  Come son io, di poca condizione
  L' animo tuo: a te Elena bella
  Si converria: io ho tribulazione,
  Nè son disposta a sì fatta novella;
  Non perciò dico che io sia dolente
  D' essere amata da te certamente.

27.

"I love, Diomede, the land in which I have been bred and reared and I am as distressed as may be by the war in which she is engaged, and would gladly see her free. And if cruel fate doth drag me forth from her, with good reason am I disturbed. But for every anxiety received on my account I pray good desert be rendered thee.

28.

"I know well that the Greeks are of high worth and well-mannered, as thou sayest, but the high virtue of the Trojans is no less on that account. Their qualities have they shown in the handiwork of Hector. Nor do I believe there is good judgment in disparaging others on account of strife, or for other reason, and then praising self above them.

29.

"Love I have not known since he died to whom loyally I rendered it, as to my husband and my lord. Nor did I ever care in such fashion for Greek or Trojan, nor is it in my desire ever to care for any or ever will be. That thou art descended of royal blood I believe readily enough and I have well understood it.

30.

"And this causeth me much wonder that thou canst place thy mind upon an insignificant woman, as I am, of low rank. For thee the fair Helen would be more fitting. I am in distress and not disposed to listen to such a declaration. I do not mean, however, that I am sorry to be loved faithfully by thee.

31.

Il tempo è reo, e voi siete nell' armi,
    Lascia venir la vittoria ch' aspetti,
    Allor saprò io molto me' che farmi;
    Forse mi piaceranno più i diletti
    Ch' ora non fanno, e potrai riparlarmi,
    E per ventura più cari i tuoi detti
    Mi fieno ch' or non son : l' uom dee guardare
    Tempo e stagion quand' altri vuol pigliare.

32.

Quest' ultimo parlare a Diomede
    Fu assai caro, e parveli potere
    Isperar senza fallo ancor mercede,
    Siccom' egli ebbe poi a suo piacere ;
    E risposele : donna, io vi fo fede
    Quanto posso maggiore, che al volere
    Di voi io sono e sarò sempre presto :
    Nè altro disse, e gissen dopo questo.

33.

Egli era grande e bel della persona,
    Giovane fresco e piacevole assai,
    E forte e fier siccome si ragiona,
    E parlante quant' altro Greco mai,
    E ad amor la natura aveva prona ;
    Le quai cose Criseida ne' suoi guai,
    Partito lui, seco venne pensando,
    D' accostarsi o fuggirsi dubitando.

34.

Queste la fer raffreddar nel pensiero
    Caldo ch' avea di voler pur reddire ;
    Queste piegaro il suo animo intero
    Che in ver Troilo aveva, ed il disire
    Torsono indietro, e 'l tormento severo
    Nuova speranza alquanto fe' fuggire :
    E da queste cagion sommossa, avvenne
    Che la promessa a Troilo non attenne.

31.

"The times are cruel and you are in arms. Let the victory that thou dost expect, come. Then shall I know much better what to do. Perhaps then I shall be much more content with the pleasures that now please me not, and thou mayest speak to me again. Perchance what thou sayest will be dearer to me then than it is now. One must regard time and season when one wisheth to capture another."

32.

This last speech was very pleasing to Diomede and it seemed to him that he might still hope without fail for some favor, such as he had afterward to his content. And he made answer to her: "Lady, I pledge you the greatest faith I can, that I am and always shall be ready to thy will." Nor aught else said he, and after this departed thence.

33.

Tall he was and well-favored in person, young, fresh, and very pleasing, and strong and haughty, as men say, graceful of speech as ever any other Greek, and he had a nature prone to love. Which things Cressida in the midst of her woes kept pondering to herself when he had departed, hesitating whether to approach or avoid him.

34.

These things cooled her in the warm thought she had of wishing only to return. These things turned her whole mind, which was intent upon seeing Troilus, and abated her desire, and a new hope put somewhat to flight her grievous torment. And it befell that, moved by these reasons, she kept not her promises to Troilus.

IL FILOSTRATO

DI

GIOVANNI BOCCACCIO

PARTE SETTIMA

ARGOMENTO

Qui comincia la settima parte del Filostrato, nella quale pri-mieramente Troilo il dì decimo attende Criseida alla porta; la quale non venendo, scusala, e tornavi l'undecimo, e più altri; e non venendo essa, alle lagrime ritorna. Con dolore consumasi Troilo; prima il dimanda della cagione, tacela Troilo. Sogna Troilo Criseida essergli tolta; dicelo a Pandaro, e vuolsi ucci-dere: Pandaro il ritiene, e stornalo da ciò. Scrive a Criseida. Deifebo s'accorge del suo amore. Giacendo lui le donne il visi-tano; Cassandra il riprende, ed egli riprende Cassandra. E pri-mieramente venuto il dì decimo, Troilo e Pandaro aspettano Criseida in sulla porta.

1.

Troilo, siccome egli è di sopra detto,
   Passava il tempo il dì dato aspettando,
   Il qual pur venne dopo lungo aspetto;
   Ond' egli altre faccende dimostrando
   In ver la porta se ne gì soletto,
   Con Pandaro di ciò molto parlando;
   E 'n verso il campo rimirando gieno
   Se in ver Troia alcun venir vedieno.

THE FILOSTRATO

OF

GIOVANNI BOCCACCIO

SEVENTH PART

ARGUMENT

Here beginneth the seventh part of the Filostrato, in which first of all Troilus on the tenth day awaiteth Cressida at the gate. Whom, when she cometh not, he excuseth, and returneth thither on the eleventh day and again on other days. And when she cometh not, he returneth to his tears. With sorrow Troilus consumeth himself. Priam asketh him the reason; Troilus keepeth silent. Troilus dreameth that Cressida hath been taken away from him. He relateth his dream to Pandarus and wisheth to kill himself. Pandarus restraineth and keepeth him back therefrom. He writeth to Cressida. Deiphoebus learneth of his love. While he lieth in bed, ladies visit him. Cassandra rebuketh him and he rebuketh Cassandra. And in the first place, when the tenth day hath arrived, Troilus and Pandarus await Cressida at the gate.

1.

Troilus, as hath been said above, was passing the time awaiting the appointed day, which arrived indeed after long waiting. Wherefore feigning other concerns, he went away alone toward the gate, discoursing much thereof with Pandarus. And toward the camp they went, gazing about to discover whether they might see anyone coming toward Troy.

[427]

2.

E ciascun che da loro era veduto
    Venir ver loro, solo o accompagnato,
    Che Criseida fosse era creduto,
    Finch' el non s' era a lor tanto appressato
    Che apertamente fosse conosciuto;
    E così stetter mezzodì passato,
    Beffati spesso dalla lor credenza,
    Siccome poi mostrava l' esperienza.

3.

Troilo disse : anzi mangiare omai,
    Per quel ch' io possa creder, non verrebbe ;
    Ella penrà a disbrigarsi assai
    Dal vecchio padre più che non vorrebbe :
    Per mio avviso tu che ne dirai ?
    Io pur mi credo che ella sarebbe
    Venuta, se venire ella potesse,
    E s' a mangiar con lui non si ristesse.

4.

Pandaro disse : io credo dichi il vero ;
    Però andianne, e poi ci torneremo.
    A Troilo piacque, e al fine così fero ;
    E lo spazio che stettero, assai stremo
    Fu, che tornar, ma gl' ingannò il pensiero,
    Siccome apparve, e trovaronlo scemo,
    Che questa gentil donna non venia,
    E già la nona su'n alto salia.

5.

Troilo disse : forse che impedita
    L' avrà il padre, e vorrà che dimori
    Infino a vespro, e però sua reddita
    Al tardi fia : omai stiamci di fuori,
    Sì ch' ella abbia l' entrata spedita ;
    Che spesse volte questi guardatori
    Soglion tenere in parole chi viene,
    Senza distinguere a cui si conviene.

2.

And everyone whom they saw coming toward them alone or in company was believed to be Cressida, until he had come so close to them that he could be easily recognized. And there they tarried until after midday, often deluded by this belief, as their later experience showed.

3.

Troilus said: "As far as I can believe she would not now come before mealtime. She will have difficulty in ridding herself of her old father—more than she would wish. What counsel wilt thou give me in this? I for my part believe that she would have come, if come she might and if she had not stopped to eat with him."

4.

Pandarus said: "I believe that thou speakest truly. But let us depart and then we shall return again." Troilus agreed and thus they did in the end. And the time that they tarried before returning, was very long, but the hope deceived them, as it appeared, and they found it empty, for this gentle lady came not, and already it was far gone in the ninth hour.

5.

Quoth Troilus: "Peradventure her father will have detained her and will desire that she stay until vespers and therefore her return will be somewhat late. Now let us stay on the outside so that her entrance be not delayed, for oftentimes these sentries are wont to hold in talk him who cometh, without making distinction for whom it is fitting."

6.

Il vespro venne, e poi venne la sera,
  E molti avevan Troilo ingannato,
  Il quale in ver lo campo sospeso era
  Istato sempre, e tutti riguardato
  Avea color che di ver la riviera
  Venieno a Troia, ed alcun domandato
  Per nuove circostanze, e non avea
  Nulla raccolto di ciò che chiedea.

7.

Perchè si volse a Pandaro dicendo:
  Fatto avrà questa donna saviamente,
  Se de' suoi modi meco ben comprendo;
  Ella vorrà venir celatamente,
  Però la notte attende, ed io 'l commendo;
  Non vorrà far maravigliar la gente,
  Nè dir: costei che fu raddomandata
  Per Antenor, c' è sì tosto tornata?

8.

Però non ti rincresca l' aspettare,
  Pandaro mio, io ten prego per Dio,
  Noi non abbiam or' altra cosa a fare,
  Non ti gravi seguire il mio disio:
  E s' io non erro veder la mi pare;
  Deh guarda in giù, deh vedi tu quel ch' io?
  Nò, disse Pandar, se ben gli occhi sbarro,
  Quel che mi mostri parea me un carro.

9.

Oimè che tu di' vero! Troilo disse,
  Or così va, cotanto mi trasporta
  Quel ch' io vorrei ch' al presente avvenisse.
  Era del sole già la luce morta,
  E stella alcuna in ciel parea venisse,
  Quando Troilo disse: El mi conforta
  Non so che pensier dolce nel desire,
  Abbi per certo ch' or ne dee venire.

6.

Twilight came and after that the evening, and many persons had deceived Troilus, who had ever stood in suspense, with eye riveted on the camp, and closely had he scanned all who came from the shore to Troy, and some had he questioned for further particulars, and naught had he gathered of that which he sought.

7.

Wherefore he turned to Pandarus and said: "This lady hath doubtless done wisely, if I have good understanding of her ways. Probably she desireth to come secretly and therefore waiteth for the night, and I commend it. Probably she hath no desire to make men wonder or say: 'Hath she who was demanded in exchange for Antenor returned here so soon?'

8.

"Therefore let not waiting displease thee, my Pandarus, I pray thee in the name of the gods. We have now naught else to do. Let not the attainment of my desire weigh heavily upon thee. If I mistake not, it seemeth to me that I see her. Ah, look yonder, ah, dost thou see what I do?" "No," said Pandarus, "if my eyes are really open, what thou showest me seemeth to me naught else but a cart."

9.

"Alas that thou sayest truly!" said Troilus. "Even as it now goeth, so much doth that which I would wish might now happen, transport me." Already had the sun's light grown dim and an occasional star appeared to have come into the heavens when Troilus said: "Some sweet thought comforteth me in my desire; believe it for certain that she is to come hither now."

10.

Pandaro seco, ma tacitamente,
 Ridea di ciò che Troilo dicea,
 E conosceva manifestamente
 La cagione che a ciò dire il movea;
 E per non farlo di ciò più dolente
 Che el si fosse, sembiante facea
 Di crederli, e dicea: di Mongibello
 Aspetta il vento questo tapinello.

11.

L' attendere era nulla, ed i guardiani
 Facean sopra la porta gran romore,
 Dentro chiamando cittadini e strani,
 Qual non volesse rimaner di fuore,
 Colle lor bestie ancor tutti i villani;
 Ma Troilo fe' tardar più di due ore;
 Infine essendo il ciel tutto stellato,
 Con Pandar dentro se n' è ritornato.

12.

E benchè in sè medesmo molte volte,
 Or con una or con altra il dì avesse
 Isperanza ingannato, intra le molte
 Voleva amor dover pur ch' el credesse
 Ad alcuna di quelle meno stolte;
 Per che da capo il suo parlar diresse
 Ver Pandaro, dicendo: stolti siamo,
 Che questo giorno aspettata l' abbiamo.

13.

Ella mi disse dieci dì starebbe
 Col padre, senza più starvi niente,
 E poscia in Troia se ne tornerebbe;
 Il termine è per questo dì presente:
 Dunque doman venir se ne dovrebbe,
 Sebbene annoveriam dirittamente,
 E noi siam qui tutto il dì dimorati,
 Tanto n' ha fatti il disio smemorati.

10.

Pandarus laughed to himself, but silently, at that which Troilus said and clearly understood the reason that moved him to say it. And in order not to make him more sorrowful on that account than he was, he made a semblance of believing and said: "This wretched youth expecteth a wind from Mongibello."

11.

The waiting came to naught, and the sentries were making a great clamor at the gate, calling within both citizens and strangers, whoever did not wish to remain outside, and also all the country people and their beasts. But Troilus made them wait more than two hours. At last when the sky had become all starry, he returned within, accompanied by Pandarus.

12.

And although he had many times beguiled the day by entertaining now one hope and now another, among the many Love wished that he should give credence to some one of those less foolish. Wherefore he again directed his speech to Pandarus, saying: "We are fools for having expected her today.

13.

"Ten days she told me she would tarry with her father, without delaying there a moment longer, and that she would after that return to Troy. The end of the time is set for this present day. Therefore she should be coming hither tomorrow, if we count correctly, and we have stayed here the entire day, so much hath desire made us unmindful of it.

14.

Domattina per tempo ritornare
   Pandar ci si vorrà; e così fero.
   Ma poco valse in su e 'n giù guardare,
   Ch' ad altro già ell' avea dritto il pensiero;
   Sì che costor dopo molto badare,
   Siccome fatto aveano il dì primiero,
   Fatto già notte dentro si tornaro;
   Ma ciò a Troilo fu soverchio amaro;

15.

E la speranza lieta ch' egli avea
   Quasi più non avea dove appiccarsi;
   Di che con seco molto si dolea,
   E forte cominciò a rammaricarsi
   E di lei e d' amor, nè gli parea
   Per cagion nulla che tanto indugiarsi
   Dovesse a ritornare, avendogli essa
   La ritornata con fede promessa.

16.

Ma 'l terzo, e 'l quarto, e 'l quinto, e 'l sesto giorno,
   Dopo 'l decimo dì già trapassato,
   Sperando e non sperando il suo ritorno,
   Da Troilo fu con sospiri aspettato:
   E dopo questi, più lungo soggiorno
   Ancor dalla speranza fu impetrato,
   E tutto invan, costei pur non tornava,
   Laonde Troilo se ne consumava.

17.

Le lagrime che erano allenate
   Pe' conforti di Pandaro, e' sospiri,
   Tornar senza esser da lui rivocate,
   Dando lor via i focosi disiri;
   E quelle che speranze risparmiate
   Aveva, usciron doppie pe' martiri
   Che 'n lui gabbato più si fer cocenti
   Che pria non eran, ben per ognun venti.

14.

"Tomorrow morning, Pandarus, we must return here betimes." But little availed their looking up and down, for to another had she directed her thought; so that, after long waiting, they returned within the walls, as they had done the day before, since 'twas already night. But that was over-bitter to Troilus.

15.

And the glad hope that he had, had almost nothing to which it might cling. Wherefore he grieved much within himself and began to complain more bitterly 'gainst her and Love, nor did it seem to him at all reasonable that she should so long delay in returning, since she had promised him faithfully to return.

16.

But the third, and the fourth, and the fifth, and the sixth day after the tenth, which had already expired, each was awaited with sighs by Troilus, now hoping and now ceasing to hope for her return. And after these a longer respite was again obtained of hope, and all in vain, for she did not return, whilst Troilus was pining away in expectation.

17.

The tears that had slackened under the encouragement of Pandarus, and the sighs as well, returned without having been recalled by him, giving free vent to fiery desire and those which hope had spared, poured forth in double quantity under the torments that became hotter in him, tricked as he was, than they had been before, a full score for every one.

18.

In lui ogni disio istato antico
 Ritornò nuovo, e sopra esso l' inganno
Che li parea ricevere, e 'l nemico
 Spirto di gelosia* gravoso affanno
Più ch' alcun altro è† di posa mendico,
 Come son‡ quei che già provato l' hanno;
Ond' el piangeva giorno e notte tanto,
Quanto bastavan gli occhi ed egli al pianto.

19.

El non mangiava quasi e non bevea,
 Sì avea pieno d' angoscia il tristo petto;
Ed oltre a questo dormir non potea
 Se non da' sospir vinto, ed in dispetto
La vita sua e sè del tutto avea,
 E come 'l fuoco fuggiva 'l diletto,
Ed ogni festa ed ogni compagnia
Similemente a suo poter fuggia.

20.

Ed era tal nel viso divenuto,
 Che piuttosto che uom pareva fera;
Nè l' averia alcun riconosciuto,
 Sì pallida e smarrita avea la cera;
Del corpo s' era ogni valor partuto,
 E tanta forza appena ne' membri era
Che 'l sostenesse, nè conforto alcuno
Prender volea che gli desse nessuno.

21.

Priamo che 'l vedea così smarrito,
 A sè alcuna volta lui chiamava,
Dicendo: figliuol mio che hai tu sentito?
 Qual cosa è quella che tanto ti grava?
Tu non par desso, tu se' scolorito,
 Che è cagion della tua vita prava?
Dimmel figliuolo, tu non ti sostieni,
E s' io discerno ben, tutto men vieni.

---

* Savj-Lopez, *comma* † Savj-Lopez, *e* ‡ Savj-Lopez, *san*

18.

In him every desire which had been ancient, returned afresh, and beside it the deceit which it seemed to him that he had suffered, and the hostile spirit of jealousy, a burden more than any other grievous and unrelieved by respite, as know those who have experienced it. Wherefore he wept day and night as much as his eyes and he were capable of weeping.

19.

He ate but little and naught did he drink, so full of anguish was his sad heart. And beside this he could not sleep, except his sleep were broken by sighs, and his life and himself he held utterly in contempt, and pleasure he shunned as fire, and likewise he avoided as much as he might every festivity and every company.

20.

And such had he become in his visage that rather seemed he beast than man; nor would anyone have recognized him, so wan and dispirited was now his face. All strength had departed from his body and scarce was there in his limbs vigor enough to sustain him, nor would he accept any consolation that anyone offered him.

21.

Priam, who saw him thus bewildered, did sometimes call him to himself and say: "My son, what hath ailed thee? What is it that grieveth thee? Thou seemest not the same, and pallid thou art. What is the cause of thy wretched life? Tell me, my son,—thou canst hardly stand, and, if I mistake not, thou art very faint."

22.

Il simigliante gli diceva Ettore,
    Paris e gli altri fratelli e sorelle;
    E domandavan d' onde esto dolore
    Sì grande avesse, e per quai ree novelle.
    Alli quai tutti diceva ch' al core
    Si sentia noie, ma quai fosser quelle,
    Niuno poteva tanto addomandare
    Che da lui più ne potesse apparare.

23.

Erasi un dì tutto maninconoso,
    Per la fallita fede, ito a dormire
    Troilo, e in sogno vide il periglioso
    Fallo di quella che 'l facea languire:
    Che gli parea per entro un bosco ombroso
    Un gran fracasso e spiacevol sentire;
    Per che levato il capo, gli sembrava
    Un gran cinghiar veder che valicava.

24.

E poi appresso gli parve vedere
    Sotto a' suoi piè Criseida, alla quale
    Col grifo il cor traeva, ed al parere
    Di lui, Criseida di così gran male
    Non si curava, ma quasi piacere
    Prendea di ciò che facea l' animale,
    Il che a lui sì forte era in dispetto,
    Che questo ruppe il sonno deboletto.

25.

Com' el fu desto, cominciò a pensare
    Sopra di ciò che in sogno avea veduto;
    E chiaro parve a lui considerare,
    Che volea dir ciò che gli era apparuto;
    E prestamente si fece chiamare
    Pandaro, il qual come a lui fu venuto,
    Piangendo cominciò: Pandaro mio,
    La vita mia non piace più a Dio!

22.

The like would Hector say to him, and Paris, and his other brothers and his sisters. And they would ask him whence he had so great a grief as this and on account of what cruel news. To all of whom he would say that he felt pain in his heart, but what it might be, none could question him so far that he could learn more of it from him.

23.

One day all melancholy on account of the broken pledge, Troilus had gone to sleep, and in a dream he saw the perilous sin of her who made him languish. For he seemed to hear a great and unpleasant crashing within a shady wood. Upon raising his head thereat he seemed to behold a great charging boar.

24.

And then afterward it seemed to him that he saw beneath its feet Cressida, whose heart it tore forth with its snout. And as it seemed, little cared Cressida for so great a hurt, but almost did she take pleasure in what the beast was doing. This gave him such a fit of rage that it broke off his uneasy slumber.

25.

When he was awake he began to reflect upon what he had seen in the dream. And he thought that he saw clearly the meaning of that which had appeared to him. And quickly he sent for Pandarus. And when the latter had come to him, weeping he began: "O Pandarus mine, my life no longer pleaseth the gods.

26.

La tua Criseida, oimè, m' ha ingannato,
  Di cui io più che d' altra mi fidava,
  Ell' ha ad altrui il suo amor donato,
  Il che più che la morte assai mi grava:
  Gl' iddii me l' hanno nel sogno mostrato:
  E quinci il sogno tutto gli narrava;
  Poi cominciò a dir quel che volea
  Sì fatto sogno, e così gli dicea:

27.

Questo cinghiar ch' io vidi è Diomede,
  Perocchè l' avolo uccise il cinghiaro
  Di Calidonia, se si può dar fede
  A' nostri antichi, e sempre poi portaro
  Per sopransegna, siccome si vede,
  I discendenti il porco. Oimè amaro
  E vero sogno! questi l' avrà il cuore
  Col parlar tratto, cioè il suo amore.

28.

Questi la tien, dolente la mia vita,
  Siccome aperto ancor potrai vedere;
  Questi impedisce sol la sua reddita;
  Se ciò non fosse, ben v' era il potere
  Di ritornar, nè l' avrebbe impedita
  Il vecchio padre nè altro calere;
  Laond' io sono ingannato, credendo,
  Ed ischernito invan lei attendendo.

29.

Oimè Criseida, qual sottile ingegno,
  Qual piacer nuovo, qual vaga bellezza,
  Qual cruccio verso me, qual giusto sdegno,
  Qual fallo mio, o qual fiera stranezza,
  L' animo tuo altiero, ad altro segno
  Han potuto recare? oimè fermezza,
  Oimè promessa, oimè fede e leanza,
  Chi v' ha gittate dalla mia amanza?

26.

"Thy Cressida, alas, in whom I trusted more than in any other, hath deceived me. She hath given her love to another, which grieveth me much more than death. The gods have shown it me in the dream." And thereupon he narrated to him all the dream. Then he began to tell him what was the meaning of such a dream; and thus he said to him:

27.

"This boar that I saw is Diomede, since his grandfather slew the boar of Calidon, if we may give credence to our ancestors, and ever afterward the descendants, as it is seen, have borne the swine as a crest. Alas, how bitter and true a dream! He must have robbed her of her heart, that is her love, with his speech.

28.

"He holdeth her, woe is me, as thou too mayest plainly see. He alone preventeth her return; if that were not so, it was well within her power to return, nor would her aged father nor any other care have been an obstacle. Whereby I have been deceived whilst I believed in her and mocked the while I awaited her in vain.

29.

"Alas, Cressida, what subtle wit, what new pleasure, what alluring beauty, what wrath against me, what just anger, what fault of mine, or what cruel strangeness have been able to bring thy noble mind to another aim? Alas constancy, alas promise, alas faith and loyalty! Who hath cast you forth from the object of my affection?

30.

Oimè, perchè andar mai ti lasciai?
   Perchè credetti al tuo consiglio rio?
   Perchè con meco non te ne menai,
   Com' io aveva, lasso, nel disio?
   Perchè i patti fatti non guastai,
   Come nel cuor mi venne, allora ch' io
   Ti vidi render? Tu non disleale
   Saresti e falsa, nè io tristo aguale.

31.

Io ti credetti e sperava per certo
   Santa esser la tua fede, e le parole
   Essere un vero certissimo e aperto
   Più ch' a' viventi la luce del sole;
   Ma tu parlavi ambiguo e coperto,
   Siccome egli ora appar nelle tue fole;
   Che solamente a me non se' tornata,
   Ma con altro uomo ti se' innamorata.

32.

Che farò Pandaro? io mi sento un fuoco
   Di nuovo acceso nella mente forte,
   Tal ch' io non trovo nel mio pensier loco:
   Io vo' colle mie man prender la morte,
   Che 'n tal vita più star non saria giuoco;
   Poi la fortuna a sì malvagia sorte
   Recato m' ha, il morir fia diletto,
   Dove il viver saria noia e dispetto.

33.

E questo detto, corse ad un coltello,
   Il qual pendea nella camera aguto,
   E per lo petto si volle con ello
   Dar, se non fosse che fu ritenuto
   Da Pandaro, il quale il tapinello
   Giovane prese, com' ebbe veduto
   Lui disperar nelle parole usate,
   Con sospiri e con lagrime versate.

30.

"Alas, why did I ever let thee go? Why did I believe in thy bad counsel? Why did I not bring thee away with me, as, alas, I had desire to do? Why did I not break the agreements made, as it came into my heart to do, when I saw thee surrendered? Thou wouldst not then have been disloyal and false, nor would I now be miserable.

31.

"I believed thee and I hoped in all certainty that thy faith would be sacred and thy words a most certain truth, a truth more open than the light of the sun to living men. But thou didst speak to me ambiguously and covertly, as it appeareth now in thy vanities. For not only hast thou not returned to me but thou hast fallen in love with another man.

32.

"What shall I do, Pandarus? I feel a great fire newly enkindled in my mind, such that I find no room in my thought for aught else. I desire to seize upon death with my hands, for it would be no sport to remain longer in such a life. Now that Fortune hath brought me to so evil a fate, dying will be a delight whenas living would be distress and despite."

33.

When he had said this, he ran to a sharp knife hanging in the room and would have stabbed himself in the breast with it, had he not been restrained by Pandarus, who caught the wretched youth when he had seen him vent his despair in the usual words, with sighs and the shedding of tears.

34.

Troilo gridava: deh non mi tenere,
 Amico caro, io ten prego per Dio,
 Poichè disposto sono a tal volere,
 Lascia seguirmi il mio fiero desio;
 Lasciami, stu* non vuoi prima sapere
 Qual sia la morte alla quale corr' io;
 Lasciami Pandar, che ti fediraggio
 Se non mi lasci, e poi m' uccideraggio.

35.

Lasciami tor del mondo il più dolente
 Corpo che viva: lasciami, morendo,
 Contenta far la nostra fraudolente
 Donna, la quale ancora andrò seguendo
 Tra l' ombre nere nel regno dolente:
 Lasciami uccider, che 'l viver languendo
 Peggio è che morte. E dicendo, sforzava
 Sè per lo ferro, il qual quel gli negava.

36.

Pandaro ancora faceva romore
 Con lui, tenendol forte, e se non fosse
 Che Troilo era debole, il valore
 Di Pandar saria vinto, tali scosse
 Troilo dava stretto dal furore;
 Pure alla fine il ferro gli rimosse
 Pandar di mano, e lui contra 'l volere
 Fece piangendo con seco sedere.

37.

E dopo amaro pianto, verso lui
 Con tai parole si volse pietoso:
 Troilo, sempre in tal credenza fui
 Di te ver me, che s' io stato fossi oso
 Di domandar per me o per altrui
 Che t' uccidessi, tu sì animoso
 Senza indugio nessun l' avessi fatto,
 Com' io farei per te in ciascun atto.

* Savj-Lopez, *se tu*

34.

Troilus cried out: "Ah, hold me not, dear friend, I pray thee in the name of the gods; since I am minded to desire such a thing, let me carry out my cruel intent; unhand me, if thou wilt not first learn what manner of death that is to which I hasten; unhand me, Pandarus, for I shall strike thee, if thou dost not, and then I shall slay myself.

35.

"Let me take away from the world the most sorrowful body alive; let me in my death give contentment to our deceitful lady, who will some day go following my footsteps through the dark shades in the realm of sorrow; let me kill myself, for a languishing life is worse than death." And saying this he strove again and again for the knife, which the other kept away from him.

36.

Pandarus still struggled with him, holding him straitly, and had it not been that Troilus was weak, the strength of Pandarus would have been overcome, such jerks did Troilus give, abetted by his mad rage. Yet in the end Pandarus removed the knife from the reach of his hand and made him against his will sit tearfully with him.

37.

And after bitter weeping he turned toward him in pity with such words as these: "Troilus, I have always had such faith in thy devotion to me that had I been bold enough to demand that thou shouldst kill thyself for me or for another, thou wouldst have done so immediately, as courageously as I would for thee in every case.

38.

E tu a' preghi miei non hai la morte
  Sozza e spiacevol voluta fuggire;
  E s' io non fossi stato ora più forte
  Di te, t' avrei qui veduto morire:
  Nol mi credea alle promesse porte
  Da te a me le mi veggia fallire,
  Benchè ancora questo emendar puoti,
  Se con effetto quel che dico noti.

39.

Per quel che paia a me, tu hai concetto
  Che Criseida sia di Diomede;
  E s' io ho ben raccolto ciò c' hai detto,
  Null' altra cosa di ciò ti fa fede
  Se non il sogno, il qual prendi sospetto
  Per l' animale il qual col dente lede,
  E senza più voler sentirne avanti,
  Finir volei con morte i tristi pianti.

40.

Io ti dissi altra volta, che follia
  Era ne' sogni troppo riguardare;
  Nessun ne fu, nè è, nè giammai fia
  Che possa certo ben significare,
  Ciò che dormendo altrui la fantasia
  Con varie forme puote dimostrare,
  E molti già credettero una cosa,
  Ch' altra n' avvenne opposita e ritrosa.

41.

Così potrebbe addivenir di questo;
  Forse che là dove tu l' animale
  Al tuo amore interpetri molesto,
  Ti fia utile, e non ti farà male
  Siccome stimi: parti egli atto onesto
  A nessun uomo, non che ad un reale,
  Come tu se', colle sue man s' uccida,
  O faccia per amor sì fatte strida?

38.

"And thou hast been unwilling at my prayers to shun ugly and displeasing death, and had I not been stronger than thou, I should have seen thee die here. I did not believe that I should see thee fail me in the promises thou gavest me, although thou canst still make amends for this, if thou note with profit what I say.

39.

"As far as I can see, thou hast formed the opinion that Cressida is Diomedes'. And if I have well understood what thou hast said about it, nothing else giveth thee proof of that but the dream, a suspicion which thou dost entertain on account of the animal which woundeth with his tushes, and being unwilling to think more about it beforehand, thou dost desire to end wretched weeping with death.

40.

"And I told thee once before that it was folly to look too deeply into dreams. No one there was nor is nor ever will be who can with certainty well interpret what fancy can show forth with varied forms in the sleep of another, and many indeed have believed one thing while another opposite and contrary thereto came to pass.

41.

"So might it turn out in respect to this. Perhaps where you interpret the animal as hostile to thy love, it will be beneficial to thee and will do thee no harm, as thou thinkest. Doth it seem to thee an honorable deed for any man—to say nothing of one of royal line, as thou art—to kill himself with his own hands, or utter such shrieks on love's account?

42.

Questa cosa era in tutt' altra maniera
  Da dover far, che tu non la facevi;
  Pria sottilmente si volea se vera
  Fosse saper, siccome tu potevi,
  E se falsa trovata, e non intera-
  Mente l' avessi, allora ti dovevi
  Dalla fede de' sogni e dallo inganno
  D' essi levar, che venieno a tuo danno.

43.

Se ver trovassi che tu per altrui
  Da Criseida fossi abbandonato,
  Non dovevi con tutti i pensier tui
  Per partito pigliar deliberato
  Pur di morire, ch' io non so da cui
  Giammai ne fossi se non biasimato;
  Ma si voleva prender per partito,
  Di schernir lei com' ella ha te schernito.

44.

E se pure a morire i pensier gravi
  Ti sospignean per sentir minor doglia,
  Non era da pigliar ciò che pigliavi,
  Ch' altra via c' era a fornir cotal voglia;
  E ben te la doveano i pensier pravi
  Mostrar, perciocchè avanti della soglia
  Della porta di Troia i Greci sono,
  Che t' uccidran senza chieder perdono.

45.

Andremo adunque contro a' Greci armati,
  Quando morir vorrai, insiememente:
  Quivi siccome giovani pregiati
  Combatterem con loro, e virilmente
  Loro uccidendo morrem vendicati,
  Nè vieterolti a loro certamente,
  Sol ch' io m' avveggia che cagion ti mova
  Giusta a voler morire in cotal prova.

42.

"This thing should have been done in quite another way than thou didst it. First was it desirable to find out cunningly, as thou couldst, whether it were true, and if thou hadst found it false, and yet not entirely so, then shouldst thou have raised thyself above faith in dreams and their deceit, which are harmful to thee.

43.

"If thou shouldst find it true that thou hast been abandoned by Cressida for another, thou shouldst not with all thy mind take deliberate counsel that there is nothing for thee to do but die; for I do not know by whom it was ever held in anything but blame. But 'twere well hadst thou taken thought to make mock of her as she hath made mock of thee.

44.

"And if indeed heavy thoughts drive thee to death to feel a lesser grief, that which thou didst choose should not have been chosen, for other way there was to accomplish such a wish. Verily thy wicked thoughts should have shown it thee, since the Greeks are before the threshold of the gate of Troy, and they will slay thee and ask no pardon.

45.

"So then we shall go together in arms against the Greeks whenever thou mayest wish to die; here shall we fight against them as honored youths, and like men shall we die avenged in slaying them, nor shall I forbid it thee at their hands certainly, provided I perceive that a just cause moveth thee to desire death in such fashion."

46.

Troilo ch' ancor fremea di cruccio acceso,
  Quanto potea, dolente, l' ascoltava;
  E poi che l' ebbe lungamente inteso,
  Qual esso ancor doglioso lagrimava,
  Ver lui si volse, il quale stava atteso
  Se dall' impresa folle si mutava,
  E in cotal guisa li parlò piangendo,
  Sempre il parlar con singhiozzi rompendo:

47.

Pandaro, vivi di questo sicuro,
  Che io son tutto tuo in ciò ch' io posso,
  Il vivere e 'l morir non mi fia duro
  Come ti piacerà, e se rimosso
  Dal furor fui da consiglio maturo,
  Poco davanti quando tu addosso
  Mi fosti per la mia propria salute,
  Non se ne dee ammirar la tua virtute.

48.

In tale error la subita credenza
  Del tristo sogno mi fece venire;
  Or men cruccioso, la mia gran fallenza
  Aperta veggio e 'l mio folle desire;
  Ma se tu vedi con che esperienza
  Di questa sospezione il ver sentire
  Io possa, dilla, per Dio ten richieggio,
  Ch' io son turbato e da me non la veggio.

49.

A cui Pandaro disse: al mio parere,
  Con iscrittura è da tentar costei;
  Perocchè s' ella non t' avrà in calere,
  Non credo che risposta abbiam da lei,
  E se l' avrem, potrem chiaro vedere
  Per le scritte parole, se tu dei
  Sperare ancor nella sua ritornata,
  O s' ella s' è d' altro uomo innamorata.

46.

Troilus, who still trembled in hot rage, listened to him as well as his grief might permit, and when he had heard him to the end, he wept as one still in distress. He turned to him, who stood waiting to see whether he was diverted from his mad intent, and in this wise spake to him through his tears, ever interrupting his speech with sobs:

47.

"Pandarus, live sure of this, that I am entirely thine in all that I can be. Living and dying will not be hard for me so long as thy pleasure is done, and if a little while ago, when thou didst belabor me for my own welfare, I was beyond the reach of wise judgment on account of my madness, thy prudence must not wonder at it.

48.

"Into such error sudden belief in the wretched dream made me come. Now in less angry mood do I see clearly my great delusion and my mad desire. But if thou dost see by what proof I can perceive the truth of this suspicion, do thou tell it me, I pray thee in the name of the gods, for I am confused and by myself I see it not."

49.

To whom Pandarus said: "In my opinion she is to be tested by writing, since if she careth no longer for thee, I do not believe that we shall have response from her, and if we have it, we may see clearly by the written words whether thou art to have further hope of her return, or whether she hath become enamored of another man.

50.

Poi si partì, giammai non le scrivesti,
  Nè ella a te, e del suo star cagione
  Potrebbe tale aver, che tu diresti
  Che ella avesse ben di star ragione;
  E potrebbe esser tal, che riprendresti
  Più tiepidezza ch' altra offensïone:
  Scrivile adunque, che se ben lo fai
  Chiaro vedrai ciò che cercando vai.

51.

Già incresceva a Troilo di sè stesso,
  Perchè 'l credette volentieri: e tratto
  Da parte, comandò ch' a lui adesso
  Da scriver fosse dato, ed il fu fatto;
  Ond' egli alquanto pensato sopra esso
  Che scrivere dovea, non come matto
  Incominciò, e senza indugio scrisse
  Alla sua donna, e in cotal guisa disse:

52.

Giovane donna, a cui amor mi diede
  E tuo mi tiene, e mentre sarò in vita
  Mi terrà sempre con intera fede,
  Perciocchè tu nella tua dipartita
  In miseria maggior ch' alcun non crede
  Qui mi lasciasti l' anima smarrita,
  Si raccomanda alla tua gran virtute,
  E mandarti non può altra salute.

53.

El non dovrà, come che divenuta
  Sii quasi Greca, la lettera mia
  Da te ancor non esser ricevuta;
  Perciocchè 'n poco tempo non s' oblia
  Sì lungo amor, qual tiene ed ha tenuta
  Nostra amistà congiunta, la qual sia
  Eterna prego, e però prenderaila
  E 'nfino alla sua fine leggeraila.

50.

"Since she departed, never hast thou written to her nor she to thee. And she might have such cause for her tarrying that thou wouldst say that she was right indeed to stay, and it might be such that thou wouldst take timidity to task rather than any other offense. Write to her then, for if thou doest it, thou wilt see clearly what thou art in search of."

51.

Already was Troilus disgusted with himself; therefore he believed him readily. And having withdrawn apart, he commanded that writing materials should be given him at once. And it was done. Wherefore after reflecting somewhat over what he ought to write, he began, not as one mad, and wrote without delay to his lady. And in this wise he said:

52.

"Youthful lady, to whom Love gave me and whose he holdeth me and, while I am alive, will ever hold me with faith unbroken, since thou in thy departure didst leave here in greater misery than any man believeth, my soul dismayed, it commendeth itself to thy great excellence and cannot send thee other salutation.

53.

"Although thou art become almost a Greek, my letter will not fail to be received by thee, since in a short time one forgetteth not so long a love as that which holdeth and hath held our friendship together, which, I pray, may be eternal. Therefore take it and read it even to the end.

54.

Se 'l servidore in caso alcun potesse
Del suo signor dolersi, forse ch' io
Avrei ragion se di te mi dolesse;
Considerando al tuo affetto pio,
La fede data, e le molte promesse,
Ed il giurato a ciascheduno iddio
Che torneresti infra 'l decimo giorno,
Nè fra quaranta ancor fatt' hai ritorno;

55.

Ma perciocchè a me convien piacere
Quanto a te piace, rammarcar non m' oso,
Ma quanto umile posso, il mio parere
Ti scrivo, più che mai d' amor focoso:
E similmente il mio caldo volere,
E la mia vita ancor, volonteroso
Di saper qual la tua vita sia stata
Poichè tra' Greci fosti permutata.

56.

Parmi, se 'l tuo consiglio ho bene a mente,
Che potuto abbiano in te le paterne
Lusinghe, o nuovo amor t' è nella mente
Entrato, o quel che rado ci si scerne
Vecchio divenir largo, che 'l tegnente
Calcas cortese sia, dove l' interne
Tue intenzion mi mostraro il contrario*
Nell' ultimo tuo pianto e mio amaro.

57.

Poi sì lontano oltre al nostro proposto
Se' dimorata, che tornar dovevi
Secondo le promesse così tosto;
Se 'l primo o 'l terzo fosse, mel dovevi
Significar, poi sai che io m' accosto
Ed accostava a ciò che tu volevi;
Che paziente l' avrei comportato,
Quantunque grave assai mi fosse stato.

* Savj-Lopez, *contraro*

54.

"If the servant might in any case complain of his lord, perhaps I should have reason to complain of thee, considering the faith I gave to thy devoted affection and the many promises and the oath thou madest to every god that thou wouldst return by the tenth day— and thou hast not yet made thy return within forty.

55.

"But since it is fitting that all that pleaseth thee, pleaseth me, I dare not complain, but as humbly as I can, I write thee my mind, more glowing with love than ever before, and likewise my ardent longing and my life as well, desirous, as I am, to know what thy life hath been since thou wert sent in exchange among the Greeks.

56.

"It seemeth to me, if I have not misinterpreted what is passing in thy mind, that the flatteries of thy father have had much influence upon thee, or a new lover hath entered thy mind, or, although for an old man to become generous is a phenomenon rarely remarked among us, that the avaricious Calchas may have turned liberal, though the intent* in thy heart led me to the contrary belief in thy last and bitter plaint.

57.

"And then thou hast tarried so far beyond our proposal, when thou wert according to thy promises under obligation to return so soon. If it were the first or the third reason, thou shouldst have made it plain to me, for thou knowest that I do and did agree to what thou didst wish. For I should have borne it patiently, however much grief it had caused me.

* I.e., to beguile her father.

58.

Ma forte* temo che novello amore
   Non sia cagion di tua lunga dimora,
   Il che se fosse, mi saria dolore
   Maggior ch' alcun ch' io ne provassi ancora;
   E se l' ha meritato il mio fervore,
   Nol devi avere tu a conoscer ora:
   Di questo vivo misero in paura
   Tal, che diletto e speranza mi fura.

59.

Questa paura dispietate stride
   Trarre mi fa, quand' io vorrei posarmi;
   Questa paura sola mi conquide
   Dentro al pensiero, ond' io non so che farmi;
   Questa paura, oimè lasso, m' uccide,
   Nè so nè posso più da lei atarmi;
   Questa paura m' ha recato in parte,
   Ch' a Venere non sono util nè a Marte.

60.

Gli occhi dolenti dopo il tuo partire
   Di lagrimar non ristetter giammai;
   Mangiar nè ber, riposar nè dormire
   Poi non potei, ma sempre ho tratti guai;
   E quel che più della mia bocca udire
   Potuto s' è, nomarti sempre mai,
   E chiamar te ed amor per conforto,
   Per questo credo sol ch' io non sia morto.

61.

Ben puoi pensare omai quel che farei
   Se certo fossi di ciò c' ho dottanza:
   Certo io credo ch' io m' ucciderei
   Di te sentendo sì fatta fallanza;
   Ed a che far dappoi ci viverei
   Ch' io avessi perduta la speranza
   Di te, anima mia, cui io attendo
   Per sola pace in lagrime vivendo?

* Savj-Lopez, *forte*

58.

"But much I fear that a new love may be the cause of thy long staying. And if this be true, it would be a greater pain than any I have yet experienced. And if my ardor hath deserved it,* thou shouldst not now have reason to know of it. On this account I live wretchedly in such fear that it robbeth me of pleasure and hope.

59.

"This fear maketh me utter heart-rending cries, when I would wish to be at my ease. This fear alone playeth the conqueror in my thoughts. Wherefore I know not what to do. This fear, alas and alack, slayeth me, and I have neither the knowledge nor the power to protect myself from it. This fear hath brought me to such a pass that I am useful neither to Venus nor to Mars.

60.

"My grieving eyes, after thy departure, never left off weeping; eat or drink, rest or sleep I could not thereafter. But always have I uttered bitter moans; and what could most often have been heard upon my lips was the constant naming of thy name and calling upon thee and upon love for comfort. On account of this only I believe that I am not dead.

61.

"Well mayest thou give thought, alas, to what I should do, were I certain of what I suspect. Surely I believe that I would take my life, if I were convinced of such defection on thy part. And to what purpose should I live on in this world, had I lost hope of thee, my heart's desire, whom I await for my only peace in this tearful life of mine?

* I.e., betrayal.

62.

Li dolci canti e le brigate oneste,
　　Gli uccelli e' cani e l' andar sollazzando,
　　Le vaghe donne, i templi e le gran feste,
　　Che per addietro solea gir cercando,
　　Fuggo ora tutte e sonmi oimè moleste,
　　Qualora vengo con meco pensando
　　Che tu di qui dimori ora lontana,
　　Dolce mio bene, e speme mia sovrana.

63.

Li fior dipinti e la novella erbetta,
　　Ch' e' prati fan di ben mille colori,
　　Non posson trarre a sè l' alma ristretta
　　Donna per te negli amorosi ardori;
　　Sol quella parte del ciel mi diletta,
　　Sotto la quale or credo che dimori,
　　Quella riguardo, e dico: quella vede
　　Ora colei da cui spero mercede.

64.

Io guardo i monti che d' intorno stanno,
　　Ed il luogo ch' a me ti tien nascosa,
　　E sospirando dico: coloro hanno,
　　Senza sentirla, la vista amorosa
　　Degli occhi vaghi per la quale affanno
　　Lontan da essi in vita assai noiosa:
　　Or foss' io un di loro, o sopra un d' essi
　　Or dimorass' io sì ch' io la vedessi!

65.

Io guardo l' onde discendenti al mare,
　　Alle qual' ora dimori vicina,
　　E dico: quelle dopo alquanto andare
　　Quivi verranno, dove la divina
　　Luce degli occhi miei n' è gita a stare,
　　E da lei fien vedute: oimè tapina
　　La vita mia! perchè in loco di quelle
　　Andar non posso siccome fann' elle?

62.

"Sweet songs and honest gatherings, birds and dogs and going about taking my pleasure, lovely ladies, temples, and great feasts, in search of which I once was wont to go, one and all I now avoid. Alas, they are hateful to me whenever I take thought that thou, my sweet felicity and my sovereign hope, now dwellest far away from here.

63.

"The bright colored flowers and the soft grass, which make the fields of quite a thousand colors, cannot charm my soul, constrained, O lady, on thine account, by the ardors of love. That part of heaven alone delighteth me under which I believe thou now dwellest, and upon that I gaze and say: 'That part now seeth her from whom I hope reward.'

64.

"I gaze upon the mountains that stand round about, and the place that holdeth thee hidden from me, and sighing I say: 'They have, though they know it not, the love-inspiring sight of the fair eyes for which I grieve far from them in a very distressful life. Now would I were one of them, or would I might now dwell upon one of them so that I might see it.'

65.

"I behold the waters descending to the sea, near which thou now dwellest, and I say: 'Those waters after some flowing will come thither where the divine light of mine eyes hath gone to stay and will be seen by her.' Alas, wretched life of mine! Why can I not go in their place as they do?

66.

Se 'l sol discende, con invidia il miro,
 Perchè mi par che vago del mio bene,
Cioè di te tirato dal disiro,
 Più dell' usato tosto se ne vene
A rivederti, e dopo alcun sospiro,
 Mi viene in odio, e crescon le mie pene,
Ond' io temendo ch' el non mi ti tolga,
La notte prego che tosto giù volga.

67.

L' udir talvolta nominare il loco
 Dove dimori, o talvolta vedere
Chi di là venga, mi raccende il fuoco
 Nel cor mancato per troppo dolere,
E par ch' io senta alcun nascoso giuoco
 Nell' anima legata dal piacere,
E meco dico : quindi veniss' io
Onde quel viene, o dolce mio disio !

68.

Ma tu che fai tra' cavalieri armati,
 Tra gli uomin bellicosi e tra' romori,
Sotto le tende in mezzo degli aguati,
 Sovente spaventata da' furori
Del suon dell' armi, e delle tempestati
 Marine, a cui vicina ora dimori ?
Non t' è el, donna mia, gravosa noia,
Ch' esser solei sì dilicata in Troia ?

69.

I' ho di te nel ver compassïone,
 Più ch' io non ho di me siccome deggio.
Ritorna adunque, e la tua promissione
 Intera fa' prima ch' io caggia in peggio :
Io ti perdono ogni mia offensione
 Per dimoranza fatta, e non ne chieggio
Ammenda, fuor vedere il tuo bel viso,
Nel quale è sol tutto il mio paradiso.

66.

"If the sun setteth, I watch him with envy, because it seemeth to me that enamored of my joy—that is, urged on by desire of thee—he returneth more quickly than he is wont, to see thee again. And after some sighing I begin to hate it and my sorrows increase. Wherefore, in fear lest he may take thee from me, I pray that night may fall again quickly.

67.

"Hearing sometimes men name the place where thou dost dwell or sometimes seeing one who cometh from there, rekindleth the fire in my heart, worn out by too much sorrowing, and it seemeth that I feel some secret joy in my pleasure-bound soul and to myself I say: 'Would I might go from here to that place whence he cometh, O sweet my desire.'

68.

"But what doest thou among armèd knights, among warlike men and the noise of war, under the tents in the midst of ambushes, often dismayed by the terrors of the clank of arms and of the storms along the coast near which thou dwellest now? Is it not, my lady, a grievous sorrow to thee, who wert wont to lead so pleasant a life in Troy?

69.

"I have indeed compassion upon thee more than upon myself, who am the properer object thereof. Do thou then return and keep thy promise wholly before I fall into a worse condition. I pardon thee every wound inflicted upon me by thy long tarrying and I ask no amends for it, except the sight of thy fair face, in which alone is my paradise.

70.

Deh io ten prego per quella vaghezza
  Che me di te e te di me già prese,
  E similmente per quella dolcezza
  Che li cuor nostri parimente accese;
  E poi appresso per quella bellezza
  La qual possiedi, donna mia cortese;
  Per li sospiri e pe' pietosi pianti
  Che noi facemmo insieme già cotanti.

71.

Pe' dolci baci e per quello abbracciare
  Che già ci tenne insieme tanto stretti;
  Per la gran festa e 'l dolce ragionare,
  Che più lieti facea nostri diletti;
  Per quella fede ancor la qual prestare
  Ti piacque già negli amorosi detti,
  Quando l' ultima volta ci partimmo,
  Nè più insieme appresso poi reddimmo;

72.

Che di me ti ricordi, e che tu torni:
  E se per avventura se' impedita,
  Mi scrivi chi dopo li dieci giorni
  T' ha ritenuta di qui far reddita.
  Deh non sia grave a' tuoi parlari adorni,
  In questo almen contenta la mia vita,
  E dimmi se io deggio più di spene
  In te avere omai, dolce mio bene.

73.

Se mi darai speranza, aspetteraggio,
  Come ch' el mi sia grave oltremisura;
  Se tu la mi torrai, m' uccideraggio,
  E darò fine alla mia vita dura.
  Ma come che si sia mio il dannaggio,
  La vergogna sia tua, ch' a così oscura
  Morte recato avrai un tuo soggetto,
  Non avendo commesso alcun difetto.

70.

"Ah, I pray thee by that desire which once seized me for thee and thee for me, and likewise by that sweetness which did equally enkindle our hearts, and moreover by that beauty which thou dost possess, gracious lady mine, by the sighs and piteous laments, so many in number, that once we made together,

71.

"By the sweet kisses and by that embrace which once held us so close bound, by the great joy and the sweet converse that made our delight the happier, by that faith as well which it once pleased thee to give to amorous words, when we parted the last time and came not together again thereafter,

72.

"I pray that thou wilt remember me and return. And if perchance thou art prevented, write to me who after the ten days hath hindered thee from making thy return here. Ah, let it not be grievous to thy sweet speech; in this at least content my life, and tell me if I am ever to have more hope in thee, sweet my love.

73.

"If thou wilt give me hope, I will wait, although it is beyond measure grievous to me; if thou wilt take it from me, I will slay myself and put an end to my hard life. But though the harm is mine, let the shame be thine, for thou wilt have brought a subject of thine, who hath committed no fault, to so inglorious a death.

74.

Perdona se nell' ordine dettando
   I' ho fallito, e se di macchie piena
   Forse vedi la lettera ch' io mando:
   Che dell' uno e dell' altro la mia pena
N' è gran cagion, perocchè lagrimando
   Vivo e dimoro, nè le mi raffrena
   Nullo accidente: adunque son dolenti
   Lacrime, queste macchie sì soventi.

75.

E più non dico, benchè a dire assai
   Ancor mi resti, se non che ne vegni;
   Deh fallo anima mia, che tu potrai,
   Se tu quanto tu sai pur te n' ingegni.
Oimè, che tu non mi conoscerai,
   Tal son tornato ne' dolor malegni;
   Nè più ti dico, se non Dio sia teco,
   E tosto faccia te esser con meco.

76.

Quinci la diede a Pandar suggellata,
   Che la mandò: ma la risposta invano
   Da essi fu per più giorni aspettata;
   Onde il dolor di Troilo più che umano
Perseverò, e fugli raffermata
   L' openïon del sogno suo non sano,
   Non però tanto ch' el non isperasse
   Che pure ancor Criseida l' amasse.

77.

Di giorno in giorno il suo dolor crescea
   Mancando la speranza, onde a giacere
   Por li convenne, che più non potea:
   Ma pur per caso un dì 'l venne a vedere
Deifebo, a cui molto ben volea;
   Il qual non vedendo el, nel suo dolere,
   Criseida, a dir cominciò pianamente,
   Deh non mi far morir tanto dolente.

74.

"Pardon if in setting down the words I have failed in the order, and if perchance thou dost behold the letter that I send covered with stains. For my pain is the great cause both of the one and of the other, since I live and abide in tears, nor doth aught that happens check them. Therefore these so frequent spots are grievous tears.

75.

"And more I say not, although there still remaineth much for me to say, except 'do thou come.' Ah, bring it about, my soul, for thou canst if only thou dost apply thereto all the wit thou art master of. Alas, for thou wilt not know me, so am I changed in my malignant sorrows. Nor do I say more to thee, save only the gods be with thee, and make thee soon to be with me."

76.

Then did he give it sealed to Pandarus, who dispatched it. But the reply was vainly awaited by them for many days. Wherefore the more than human grief of Troilus persisted and he was confirmed in his opinion of his insane dream, not however to such a degree that he ceased to hope that Cressida might indeed yet love him.

77.

From day to day his grief waxed greater with the decline of hope. Wherefore he had to take to his bed, for he was exhausted. But indeed by chance there came to visit him Deiphoebus, for whom he had much love. Not seeing him in his woe, he began to say in a low voice: "Alas, Cressida, make me not to die in such grief."

78.

Deifebo s' accorse allor, che quello
    Fosse che lo strignea, e fatta vista
    D' udito non l' aver, disse : fratello,
    Che non conforti omai l' anima trista ?
    Il tempo gaio viene e fassi bello,
    Rinverdiscono i prati, e lieta vista
    Danno di sè ; e il dì è già venuto
    Che della tregua il termine è compiuto.

79.

Sicchè 'l nostro valore al modo usato
    Potrem nell' armi a' Greci far sentire :
    Non vuo' tu più con noi venire armato,
    Che 'l primo solevi essere al ferire,
    E come pro' da loro esser dottato
    Tanto, ch' avanti a te tutti fuggire
    Ne solei fare ? Ettor n' ha già commossi,
    Che doman siam con lui di fuor da' fossi.

80.

Quale lion famelico, cercando
    Per preda, faticato si riposa,
    Subito su si leva i crin vibrando
    Se cervo, o toro sente o altra cosa
    Che gli appetisca, sol quella bramando ;
    Tal Troilo udendo la guerra dubbiosa
    Ricominciarsi, subito vigore
    Gli corse dentro all' infiammato core.

81.

E 'l capo alzato, disse : fratel mio,
    Io son nel vero alquanto deboletto,
    Ma io ho della guerra tal disio,
    Che rinforzato, tosto d' esto letto
    Mi leverò : e giuroti, se io
    Mai combattei con duro e forte petto
    Contra li Greci, or più combatteraggio
    Ch' ancor facessi, in sì grand' odio gli aggio.

78.

Deiphoebus then perceived what it was that constrained him, and affecting not to have heard, said: "Brother, why dost thou not now comfort thy sad soul? The gay season cometh and maketh itself fair; the meadows grow green again and afford a pleasing prospect of themselves; and the day hath already come when the term of the truce hath reached its end,

79.

"So that in the usual way we shall be able to make our valor felt by the Greeks. Dost thou no more desire to come in arms with us, for thou wert wont to be the first in dealing blows and as a warrior to be so feared by them that thou didst ever cause them all to flee before thee? Hector hath already given orders to be with him tomorrow outside the moat."

80.

Just as the hungry lion in search of prey that resteth when weary, suddenly starteth up, shaking his mane, if he perceiveth stag, bull, or other thing, desiring only that, so doth Troilus, when he heareth the doubtful battle begin again, vigor suddenly coursing through his inflamed heart.

81.

And raising his head he said: "Brother mine, in truth I am a trifle weak, but such desire have I for war that I shall soon rise with full vigor from this bed. And I swear to thee, if ever I fought with hard and stern heart against the Greeks, now shall I fight more than ever I did before, in so great hatred do I hold them."

82.

Intese ben Deifebo ove gieno
  Quelle parole, e confortollo assai,
Dicendogli che là l' aspetterieno,
  Però non s' indugiasse più omai
Al suo conforto, e addio si dicieno;
  Troilo rimase con gli usati guai,
Deifebo a' fratei sen venne ratto,
  Ed ebbe a lor tutto contato il fatto.

83.

Il che essi credetter prestamente,
  Per atti già veduti; e per non farlo
Tristo di ciò, di non dirne niente
  Fra lor diliberaro, e d' aiutarlo;
Perchè alle donne loro incontanente
  Fer dir ch' ognuna andasse a visitarlo,
E con suoni e cantori a fargli festa,
  Sì ch' obliasse la vita molesta.

84.

In poca d' ora la camera piena
  Di donne fu, e di suoni e di canti:
Dall' una parte gli era Polissena,
  Ch' un angela pareva ne' sembianti;
Dall' altra gli sedea la bella Elena,
  Cassandra ancora gli stava davanti;
Ecuba v' era, e Andromaca, e molte
  Di lui cognate e parenti raccolte.

85.

Ciascuna a suo potere il confortava,
  E tale il domandava che sentia;
Esso non rispondea, ma riguardava
  Or l' una or l' altra, e nella mente pia
Di Criseida sua si ricordava,
  Nè più che con sospir ciò discopria;
E pur sentiva alquanto di dolcezza
  E per li suoni e per la lor bellezza.

82.

Deiphoebus well understood what these words meant and much did he urge him on, telling him that they would await him there but that for his comfort he should not now delay longer. And they bade each other farewell. Troilus remained with his usual woes and Deiphoebus made swiftly away to his brothers and related the whole matter to them.

83.

This they readily believed because of the behavior already noticed. And in order not to make him sad on that account they took counsel together to make no mention of it and to give him relief. For they immediately sent messages to their ladies that each of them should go and visit him and make entertainment for him with melodies and singers, so that he should forget his irksome life.

84.

In but a little time the chamber was filled with ladies, and music, and song. On one side of him was Polyxena, who seemed an angel in looks; on the other sat the fair Helen; Cassandra, also, stood in front of them; Hecuba was there and Andromache, and many sisters-in-law and female relatives were gathered together.

85.

Each one comforted him as far as lay within her power, and someone asked him how he felt. He answered not, but regarded now one and now another, and in his faithful mind held remembrance of his Cressida. Nor more than with sighs did he disclose this, and yet some measure of delight did he feel both because of the singing and their beauty.

86.

Cassandra che per caso aveva udito
  Ciò che 'l fratel Deifebo aveva detto,
  Quasi schernendol perchè sì smarrito
  Si dimostrava, ed era nell' aspetto
  Disse: fratel, per te mal fu sentito,
  Siccome io m' accorgo, il maladetto
  Amor, per cui disfatti esser dobbiamo,
  Come veder, se noi vogliam, possiamo.

87.

E poichè pur così doveva andare,
  Di nobil donna fostu innamorato!
  Che condotto ti se' a consumare
  Per la figlia d' un prete scellerato,
  E mal vissuto e di piccolo affare:
  Ecco figliuolo d' alto re onorato,
  Che 'n pena e 'n pianto mena la sua vita,
  Perchè da lui Criseida s' è partita!

88.

Turbossi Troilo la sorella udendo,
  Sì perchè udiva dispregiar colei
  La quale el più amava, e sì sentendo
  Che 'l suo segreto agli orecchi a costei
  Era venuto, il come non sapendo,
  Pensò che per risponso degli dei
  Ella il sapesse; non pertanto disse:
  Ver parria questo se io mi tacisse;

89.

E cominciò: Cassandra, il tuo volere
  Ogni segreto, più che l' altra gente,
  Con tue immaginazioni antivedere,
  T' ha molte volte già fatta dolente;
  Forse più senno ti saria il tacere,
  Che sì parlare scapestratamente:
  Tu gitti innanzi a tutti i tuoi sermoni,
  Nè so che di Criseida ti ragioni.

86.

Cassandra, who had heard by chance what her brother Deiphoebus had said, almost as if she were making fun of him because he appeared so dispirited and wore so rueful a look, said: "Brother, by thee to thy great malease was felt, as I learn, the accursed love, by which we are all to be undone, as we may see if we but wish to.

87.

"And since, albeit, matters were thus to be, would that thou wert enamored of a noble lady, instead of having brought thyself to wasting away on account of the daughter of a wicked priest, a man of evil life and of small importance. Here is the honored son of a great king who leadeth his life in sorrow and weeping because Cressida hath departed from him."

88.

Troilus was disturbed when he heard his sister, both because he heard dispraise of her whom he loved most and because perceiving that his secret had come to her ears—not knowing how,—he thought that she must know it through the oracles of the gods. Nevertheless he said: "It might appear true, were I to keep silent."

89.

And he began: "Cassandra, thy desire to guess at every secret more than other people, with thine imaginings, hath already many times caused thee sorrow. Perhaps it would be wiser for thee to hold thy peace than to speak thus at random. Thou dost cast thy speech before all, nor do I know what thou meanest about Cressida.

90.

Perchè vedendo te soprabbondare,
 Io vo' far quel che io non feci ancora,
 Cioè la tua bestialità mostrare:
 Tu di' che per Criseida mi scolora
 Soperchio amore, e vuommel rivoltare
 In gran vergogna, ma infino ad ora
 Non t' ha di questo il vero assai mostrato
 Il tuo Apollo, il qual di' c' hai gabbato.

91.

Per tale amor Criseida giammai
 Non mi fu in piacer, nè credo sia
 Nessuno al mondo nè che fosse mai
 Ch' ardisse a sostener questa bugia:
 E se, siccome tu dicendo vai,
 Ver fosse, giuro per la fede mia,
 Mai non l' avrei di qui lasciata gire,
 Prima m' avria Priam fatto morire.

92.

Non che io creda che l' avria sofferto,
 Come sofferse che Paris Eléna
 Rapisse, onde abbiam ora cotal merto:
 Però la lingua tua pronta raffrena.
 Ma pognam pur che così fosse certo,
 Ch' io per lei fosse in questa grave pena,
 Perchè non è Criseida in ciascun atto
 Degna d' ogni grand' uom, qual vuoi sia fatto?

93.

Io non vo' ragionar della bellezza
 Di lei, che al giudicio di ciascuno
 Trapassa quella della somma altezza,
 Perocchè fior caduto è tosto bruno;
 Ma vegnam pure alla sua gentilezza,
 La qual tu biasmi tanto, e qui ognuno
 Consenta il ver se 'l dico, e l' altro il nieghi,
 Ma il perchè, il prego, ch' egli alleghi.

90.

"Wherefore when I see thee speak too much, I have a mind to do what I have not yet done, that is, to reveal thy ignorance. Thou sayest that excessive love for Cressida maketh me pale, and thou dost wish to turn it to my great shame. But thus far thine Apollo, the god thou hast mocked, hath not clearly shown thee the truth respecting this matter.

91.

"Cressida never pleased me by such love, nor do I believe that there is or ever was anyone in the world who would dare maintain this lie. And if, as thou dost keep saying, it were true, I swear by my faith I would never have let her go hence, unless Priam had slain me first.

92.

"Not that I believe he would have permitted it, as he permitted Paris to abduct Helen, of which we now have such reason to be proud. Therefore check thy ready tongue. But let me suppose indeed that it were established that, as thou sayest, I were in this grievous sorrow on her account, why is not Cressida in every respect worthy of any great man, of whatsoever sort thou wishest?

93.

"I do not wish to speak of her beauty, which, in the judgment of every man, surpasseth that of the highest, since the fallen flower is soon brown. But let us come simply to the matter of her nobility, which thou dost so much disparage, and now let everyone admit the truth, if I tell it, and should another deny it, I pray him to set forth the reason why.

94.

È gentilezza dovunque è virtute,
   Questo nol negherà niuno che 'l senta,
   Ed elle sono in lei tutte vedute,
   Se dall' opra l' effetto s' argomenta:
   Ma pur partitamente a tal salute
   È da venir, sol per lasciar contenta
   Costei che tanto d' ogni gente parla,
   Senza saper che sia quel ch' ella ciarla.

95.

Se non m' inganna forse la veduta,
   E quel ch' altri ne dice, più onesta
   Di costei nulla ne fia mai nè è suta;
   E se 'l ver odo, sobria e modesta
   È oltre all' altre, e certo la paruta
   Di lei il mostra; e similmente è questa
   Tacita ove conviensi e vergognosa,
   Che in donna è segno di nobile cosa.

96.

Appar negli atti suoi la discrezione,
   E nel suo ragionare, il quale è tanto
   Saldo e sentito e pien d' ogni ragione,
   Ed io ne vidi in parte uguanno quanto
   Fosse, in la scusa della tradigione
   Fatta per lei del padre, e nel suo pianto
   Del suo altiero e ben reale sdegno
   Con dicenti parole diede segno.

97.

I suoi costumi sono assai palesi,
   E perciò non mi par ch' abbian mestieri
   Nè d' altrui nè da me esser difesi;
   Nè credo in questa terra cavalieri,
   E siencen quanti voglin de' cortesi,
   Cui non mattasse in mezzo lo scacchieri
   Di cortesia e di magnificenza,
   Sol che in ciò far le basti la potenza.

94.

"Nobility is to be found wherever virtue is. This no one who understandeth it, will deny. And all virtues are to be seen in her if the effect may be argued from the cause. But also separately must one arrive at such felicity, just to satisfy this woman who speaketh of everybody without knowing what it is she chattereth of.

95.

"If perchance mine own eyesight and what others say of her deceiveth me not, none more chaste than she will ever be known or hath ever been. And if I hear the truth, unassuming and modest she is beyond others, and certainly her appearance showeth it. And likewise she is silent and retiring where it is fitting, which in woman is a sign of noble nature.

96.

"In her behavior appeareth her discretion and in her speech, which is so sound and judicious and full of all reason. And this year I saw in part how much she had of it in the excuse she made for the perfidy of her father. And in her weeping she gave evidence with eloquent words of her high-minded and very sincere scorn.

97.

"Her ways are very open and therefore meseemeth they need no defense either by me or by another. And I do not believe there are any knights in this city, be there as many courteous ones as you will, whom she would not mate in the middle of the chessboard in courtesy and liberality, provided only there should suffice her the means to do it.

98.

Ed io il so, che già istato sono
  Dov' ella me ed altri ha onorati
  Sì altamente, che in real trono
  Ne seggon molti alli quali impacciati
  Parria essere stati, e in abbandono
  Siccome vili n' avrien tralasciati:
  Se ella è stata qui sempre pudica,
  La fama sua lodevole lo dica.

99.

Che più, donna Cassandra, chiederete
  In donna omai? il suo sangue reale?
  Non son re tutti quelli a cui vedete
  Corona o scettro o vesta imperïale;
  Assai fiate udito già l' avete,
  Re è colui il qual per virtù vale,
  Non per potenza: e se costei potesse,
  Non cre' tu ch' ella come tu reggesse?

100.

Ben sapria meglio assai che tu tenerla,
  Io dico, stu m' intendi, la corona;
  Né saria, qual se' tu, donna baderla,
  Che dai di morso a ciascuna persona.
  Degno m' avesse Iddio fatto d' averla
  Per donna sì, come fra voi si suona,
  Ch' io mi terrei in grandissimo pregio
  Ciò che donna Cassandra ha in dispregio.

101.

Or via andate con mala ventura,
  Poi non sapete ragionar, filate;
  Ricorreggete la vostra bruttura,
  E le virtù d' altrui stare lasciate.
  Ecco dolore, ecco nuova sciagura,
  Che una pazza per sua vanitate
  Quello ch' è da lodar riprender vuole,
  E se non è ascoltata, le ne duole.

98.

"And this I know because I have already been where she hath honored me and others so highly that on royal thrones sit many who would have experienced a feeling akin to embarrassment at it and who, like base men, would have left them in neglect. If she hath always been modest here, let her praiseworthy renown declare it.

99.

"What more, Lady Cassandra, will ye now demand in a woman? Her blood to be royal? All those upon whom you see crowns or scepters or imperial robes are not kings. Already many times have ye heard, a king is he who is worthy for his virtue, not for his power. And if this lady might, dost thou not believe that she would rule as well as thou?

100.

"Much better than thou would she wear it, I mean, if thou understandest me, the crown. Nor would she be, as thou art, a silly and conceited woman, who snappest at every person. Would the gods had made me worthy to have her for my lady so that, as the report circulateth among you, I might hold in the highest praise what the Lady Cassandra holdeth in dispraise.

101.

"Now be off with a curse to you; since ye cannot talk with reason, spin. Correct your ugliness and let be the virtue of others. Lo here a new sorrow and a new misfortune that a mad woman for vanity's sake is minded to disparage what deserveth praise, and if she be not listened to, it grieveth her."

102.

Cassandra tacque, e volentieri stata
 Esser vorrebbe altrove quella volta;
 E tra le donne si fu mescolata
 Senz' altro dire, e come gli fu tolta
 Dal viso, così tosto ne fu andata
 Al palagio real, nè mai più volta
 Per visitarlo dievvi: non fu ella
 Sì ben veduta ed ascoltata in quella.

103.

Ecuba, Elena, e l' altre commendaro
 Ciò ch' avea detto Troilo; e dopo un poco
 Piacevolmente tutte il confortaro,
 E con parole, e con festa e con giuoco:
 E quindi insieme tutte se n' andaro,
 Ciascheduna tornandosi al suo loco;
 E poi più volte il visitaro ancora,
 Mentre in sul letto debol fe' dimora.

104.

Troilo sì per lo continuare
 D' essere in doglia, divenne possente
 Con paziënza quella a comportare;
 E sì ancora per l' animo ardente
 Che contro a' Greci avea di dimostrare
 La sua virtù, li fece prestamente
 Le forze racquistar, ch' avea perdute,
 Per le troppo agre pene sostenute.

105.

Ed oltre a ciò Criseida gli avea scritto,
 E mostrato d' amarlo più che mai;
 E false scuse al suo tanto star fitto
 Senza tornare aveva indotte assai,
 E domandato ancor nuovo rispitto
 Al suo tornar, che non doveva giammai
 Essere, ed el' gli avea dato sperando
 Di rivederla, ma non sapea quando.

102.

Cassandra held her peace and fain would she have been at that moment elsewhere. She mingled with the ladies without saying aught else. And when she was gone from his presence, she repaired straight to the royal palace. Nor did he ever again give her opportunity to visit him there. She was not so willingly seen and listened to in that place.

103.

Hecuba, Helen, and the others commended what Troilus had said. And after a while they all did comfort him in pleasing wise with words and with mirth and with sport. And then they all went forth together, each one returning to her house. And after that they did often visit him again as he lay weak upon his couch.

104.

With the continuance of his grief Troilus became strong enough to bear it patiently. And also on account of the ardent desire he had of displaying his valor against the Greeks, he shortly recovered the strength he had lost through the too bitter pains he had endured.

105.

And besides that Cressida had written to him and explained how she loved him more than ever. And many false excuses had she set down for her so long tarrying without return and requested still another delay for her home-coming, which was never to be, and he had granted it to her, hoping to see her again, but he knew not when.

106.

E 'n più battaglie poi con gli avversarj
   Fatte, mostrò quanto in arme valea;
   E' suoi sospiri e gli altri pianti amari,
   Che per loro operare avuto avea,
   Oltre ogni stima gli vendea lor cari,
   Non però quanto l' ira sua volea:
   Ma morte poi, ch' ogni cosa disface,
   Amore e la sua guerra pose in pace.

106.

And then in many battles fought with his adversaries he showed how great was his worth in arms. And his sighs and the other bitter laments which he had had to utter on account of these struggles, he sold to the enemy dear beyond all thought, though not so dear as his wrath desired. But afterward death, which dissolveth everything, set at peace love and the strife which love bringeth.

IL FILOSTRATO

DI

GIOVANNI BOCCACCIO

PARTE OTTAVA

ARGOMENTO

Incomincia la parte ottava del Filostrato, nella quale primieramente Troilo con lettere e con ambasciate ritenta Criseida,
la quale il mena per parole. Appresso per uno vestimento tratto
da Deifebo a Diomede, conosce Troilo uno fermaglio il quale
avea dato a Criseida, e Criseida dato a Diomede. Troilo si duole
con Pandaro, e del tutto di lei si dispera. Ultimamente uscendo
alla battaglia fu morto da Achille, e finiscono i suoi dolori. E
primieramente Troilo con lettere e con ambasciate ritenta la fede
e l' amore di Criseida.

1.

Egli era, com' è detto, a sofferire
   Già adusato, e più nel fece forte
   L' alto dolor, da non poter mai dire,
   Che 'l padre, ed egli e' fratei per la morte
   Ebber d' Ettor, nel cui sovrano ardire
   E le fortezze, e le mura e le porte
   Credean di Troia, il qual lunga stagione
   Gli tenne in pianto ed in tribolazione.

2.

Ma non per ciò d' amor si dipartia,
   Come ch' assai mancasse la speranza;
   Anzi cercava in ogni modo e via,
   Come suol' esser degli amanti usanza,
   Di potere riaver qual solea pria
   La dolce sua ed unica intendanza;
   Lei del non ritornar sempre scusando,
   Per non poter ciò esser estimando.

THE FILOSTRATO

OF

GIOVANNI BOCCACCIO

EIGHTH PART

ARGUMENT

Here beginneth the eighth part of the Filostrato, in which first of all Troilus with letters and with messages maketh further trial of Cressida, who beareth him in hand with words. Soon by means of a garment snatched by Deiphoebus from Diomede Troilus recognizeth a brooch which he had given to Cressida and Cressida to Diomede. Troilus grieveth with Pandarus and despaireth of his lady entirely. Last of all he was slain, as he issued forth to battle, by Achilles and his woes end. And first of all Troilus with letters and with messages maketh further trial of the fidelity and love of Cressida.

1.

He was, as hath been said, already acquainted with suffering, and more severe was it made for him by the profound sorrow, that man might never tell, which his father, he himself, and his brothers felt on account of the death of Hector, in whose sovereign courage the forts and walls and gates of Troy had faith. This for a long time kept him in sorrow and tribulation.

2.

But not for that reason did he take leave of love, although hope failed him sorely; rather he sought in every manner and fashion, as is wont to be the way with lovers, how he might be able to recover what formerly was wont to be his sweet and only thought, ever excusing her for her failure to return, believing that 'twas because she could not.

3.

Ei le mandò più lettere, scrivendo
   Quel che sentia per lei la notte e 'l giorno;
   E 'l dolce tempo a mente riducendo,
   E la fede promessa del ritorno:
   Spesse fiate ancora riprendendo
   Cortesemente il suo lungo soggiorno
   Mandovvi Pandar, qualora tra essi
   O tregue o patti alcun furon concessi.

4.

E simigliante egli ebbe nel pensiero
   Ancor più volte di volervi andare
   Di pellegrino in abito leggiero;
   Ma sì non si sapeva contraffare
   Che gli paresse assai cuoprire il vero;
   Nè scusa degna sapeva trovare
   Da dir, se stato fosse conosciuto,
   In abito cotanto disparuto.

5.

Nè altro aveva da lei che parole
   Belle, e promesse grandi senza effetto:
   Onde a presumer cominciò che fole
   Erano tutte, ed a prender sospetto
   Di ciò che era ver, siccome suole
   Spesso avvenire a chi senza difetto
   Riguarda in fra le cose c' ha per mano,
   Perchè non fu il suo sospetto vano.

6.

E ben conobbe che novello amore
   Era cagion di tante e tai bugie;
   Seco affermando che giammai nel core
   Nè paterne lusinghe mai nè pie
   Carezze avuto avrien tanto valore;
   Nè gli era luogo a veder per quai vie
   Più s' accertasse di ciò che mostrato
   Già gli aveva il suo sogno sventurato.

3.

He dispatched many letters to her, writing what he felt for her both night and day, reminding her of the sweet time and the troth plighted for her return. Often he sent Pandarus to her, reproaching her courteously for her long stay, whenever any truce or pact was granted between them.

4.

And likewise he had frequently in his mind the thought that he would like to go there in the light habit of a pilgrim. But he knew not how so to disguise himself that it would seem to him that he had sufficiently concealed the truth. Nor could he find an adequate excuse to offer, should he be recognized disguised in such a habit.

5.

Nor had he from her aught but fair words and great but ineffectual promises. Wherefore he began to surmise that they were all idle tales and to conceive the suspicion of what was the truth, as is often wont to happen to one who goeth over without omission all the evidence he hath in hand, for his suspicion was not an empty one.

6.

And well he knew that a new love was the cause of so frequent and so great lies. And he assured himself that neither paternal flatteries nor devoted caresses would ever have had so much effect in her heart. Nor was there opportunity for him to see by what ways he might become the surer of what his unlucky dream had shown him.

7.

Al quale amor raccorciata la fede
   Aveva molto, siccom' egli avviene,
   Che colui ch' ama mal volentier crede
   Cosa che cresca amando le sue pene;
   Ma che pur fosse ver di Diomede,
   Come pria sospettò, fè ne gli fene
   Non molto poi un caso, che gli tolse
   Ciascuna scusa, ed a crederlo il volse.

8.

Stavasi Troilo non senza tormento
   Del suo amore timido e sospeso;
   Quand' egli udì, dopo un combattimento
   Tra li Troiani e' Greci assai disteso
   Fatto, con uno ornato vestimento,
   A Diomede gravemente offeso
   Tratto, tornar Deifebo pomposo
   Di cotal preda, e seco assai gioioso.

9.

E mentre che portarlosi davanti
   Facea per Troia, Troilo sopravvenne,
   E molto il commendò fra tutti quanti,
   E per vederlo meglio alquanto il tenne:
   E mentre e' rimirava, gli occhi erranti
   Or qua or là d' intorno a tutto, avvenne
   Che esso vide nel petto un fermaglio
   D' oro, lì posto forse per fibbiaglio:

10.

Il quale esso conobbe incontanente,
   Siccome quei che l' aveva donato
   A Criseida, allora che dolente
   Partendosi da lei prese comiato
   Quella mattina, che ultimamente
   Era la notte con lei dimorato;
   Laonde disse: or veggio pur ch' è vero
   Il sogno, il mio sospetto, ed il pensiero.

7.

In her love his faith had lessened much, just as it happeneth that he who loveth ill, willingly believeth aught that increaseth his pains in love. But that it was indeed true of Diomede, as he at first suspected, he was assured not long after by a chance that deprived him of any excuse and forced him to believe it.

8.

Timid and in suspense on account of his love Troilus was not without torment, when, after a very prolonged engagement between the Trojans and Greeks, he heard that Deiphoebus, proud of such spoils and very well pleased with himself, had returned with an ornamented garment snatched from the grievously wounded Diomede.

9.

And while he was having it borne before him through Troy, Troilus came up unexpectedly, and among all he commended him highly, and the better to see it, he held it a time, and while he gazed at it, his eyes wandering now here now there all over it, it chanced that he saw upon the breast a brooch of gold, set there perchance as a clasp.

10.

Which he recognized at once as that which he had given to Cressida when in grief he took leave of her that morning, when for the last time he had passed the night with her. Wherefore he said: "Now do I see indeed that my dream, my suspicion, and my thought are true."

11.

Quindi partito Troilo, chiamare
    Pandar si fe', il quale a lui venuto,
    Si cominciò con pianto a rammarcare
    Del lungo amore il quale aveva avuto
    A Criseida sua, e a dimostrare
    Aperto il tradimento ricevuto
    Gli cominciò, dolendosene forte,
    Sol per ristoro chiedendo la morte.

12.

E cominciò così piangendo a dire:
    O Criseida mia, dov' è la fede,
    Dove l' amore, dove ora 'l desire,
    Dove la tanto gradita mercede
    Data da te a me nel tuo partire?
    Ogni cosa possiede Diomede,
    Ed io, che più t' amai, per lo tuo inganno
    Rimaso sono in pianto ed in affanno.

13.

Chi crederà omai a nessun giuro,
    Chi ad amor, chi a femmina omai,
    Ben riguardando il tuo falso spergiuro?
    Oimè che io non so, nè pensai mai
    Che tanto avessi il cuor rigido e duro,
    Che per altro uom io t' uscissi giammai
    Dell' animo, che più che me t' amava,
    Ed ingannato sempre t' aspettava.

14.

Or non avevi tu altro gioiello
    Da poter dare al tuo novello amante,
    Io dico a Diomede, se non quello
    Ch' io t' avea dato con lagrime tante,
    In rimembranza di me cattivello,
    Mentre con Calcas fossi dimorante?
    Null' altro far tel fe' se non dispetto,
    E per mostrar ben chiaro il tuo intelletto.

11.

Troilus, when he departed hence, sent for Pandarus, and when the latter had come to him, he began to complain of the long love he had had for his Cressida, and openly to disclose the treachery he had suffered, grieving bitterly on account of it, calling upon death alone for solace.

12.

And then he began to say in the midst of his tears: "O Cressida mine, where now is the faith, where the love, where the desire, where the so pleasing guerdon given me by thee at thy departure? Diomede possesseth all and I, who loved thee more, have been left in weeping and distress on account of thy deceit.

13.

"Who will ever believe in any oath, in any love, in any woman, when he looketh well to thy treacherous lying? Alas, for I know not. Nor did I ever think that thou hadst a heart so rigid and hard that for another man I should ever come forth from thy soul, for I love thee more than myself, and I did ever await thee in my deception.

14.

"Now hadst thou, while thou wert dwelling with Calchas, no other jewel that thou mightest give thy new lover, Diomede I mean, save that one that I had given thee with so many tears in remembrance of poor wretched me? Naught else but spite did make thee do it, that and to reveal right clearly thy mind.

15.

Del tutto veggio che m' hai discacciato
  Del petto tuo, ed io contra mia voglia
  Nel mio ancora tengo effigïato
  Il tuo bel viso con noiosa doglia:
  O lasso me, che 'n malora fui nato,
  Questo pensier m' uccide e mi dispoglia
  D' ogni speranza di futura gioia,
  E cagion émmi d' angoscia e di noia.

16.

Tu m' hai cacciato a torto della mente,
  Laddov' io dimorar sempre credea,
  E nel mio luogo hai posto falsamente
  Diomede; ma per Venere dea
  Ti giuro, tosto ten farò dolente
  Colla mia spada alla prima mislea,
  Se egli avviene ch' io 'l possa trovare,
  Purchè con forza il possa soprastare:

17.

O el m' ucciderà, e fieti caro;
  Ma spero pur la divina giustizia
  Rispetto avrà al mio dolore amaro,
  E similmente alla tua gran nequizia.
  O sommo Giove, in cui certo riparo
  So c' ha ragione, e da cui tutta inizia
  L' alta virtù per cui si vive e muove,
  Son li giusti occhi tuoi rivolti altrove?

18.

Che fanno le tue folgori ferventi,
  Riposan elle? O più gli occhi non tieni
  Volti a' difetti dell' umane genti?
  O vero lume, o lucidi sereni,
  Pe' quai s' allegran le terrene menti,
  Togliete via colei nelli cui seni
  Bugie e inganni e tradimenti sono,
  Nè più la fate degna di perdono.

15.

"I see that thou hast driven me quite out of thy breast and in mine I still hold against my will and with irksome grief the image of thy fair face. Oh, alas for me, born as I was in an evil hour!, this thought killeth me and spoileth me of any hope of future joy and is to me cause of anguish and distress.

16.

"Thou hast wrongfully driven me forth from thy mind, wherein I thought to dwell forever and in my place thou hast falsely set Diomede. But by the goddess Venus I swear to thee, I shall soon make thee sorrow for it with my sword, in the first encounter, if it happeneth that I may find him, provided I may overcome him in strength,

17.

"Or he will slay me and 'twill be dear to thee. But I hope indeed that divine justice will have regard to my bitter grief, and likewise to thy great iniquity. O highest Jove, in whom I know that justice hath a sure refuge and in whom beginneth entirely the noble virtue by which men live and move, are thy just eyes cast elsewhere?

18.

"What are thy burning thunderbolts doing? Do they repose? Or dost thou hold thine eyes no longer turned upon the faults of human kind? O true light, O bright skies by which earthly minds are cheered, put an end to her in whose bosom are lies and deceits and betrayals and deem her ever more unworthy of pardon.

19.

O Pandar mio, che ne' sogni aver fede
  M' hai biasimato con cotanta istanza,
  Or puoi veder ciò che per lor si vede,
  La tua Criseida te ne fa certanza:
  Hanno gl' iddii di noi mortai mercede,
  Ed in diverse guise dimostranza
  Ci fan di quello, ch' è a noi ignoto,
  Per nostro bene spesse volte noto.

20.

E questo è l' un de' modi, che dormendo
  Talor si mostra, io me ne sono accorto
  Molte fïate già mente tenendo;
  Or vorre' io allora essermi morto,
  Dappoi che per innanzi non attendo
  Sollazzo, gioia, piacer nè diporto;
  Ma per lo tuo consiglio vo' indugiarmi,
  A morir co' nemici miei coll' armi.

21.

Mandimi Iddio Diomede davanti
  La prima volta ch' esco alla battaglia!
  Questo disio tra li miei guai cotanti,
  Sì ch' io provar gli faccia come taglia
  La spada mia, e lui morir con pianti
  Nel campo faccia, e poi non me ne caglia
  Che mi s' uccida, sol ch' e' muoia, e lui
  Misero trovi nelli regni bui.

22.

Pandaro con dolor tutto ascoltava,
  E 'l ver sentendo, non sapea che dirsi:
  E da una parte a star quivi il tirava
  Dell' amico l'amor, d' altra a partirsi
  Vergogna spesse volte lo invitava
  Pel fallo di Criseida, e spedirsi
  Qual far dovesse seco non sapea,
  E l' uno e l' altro forte gli dolea.

19.

"O Pandarus mine, who hast blamed me with so much insistence for putting faith in dreams, now canst thou perceive what is found out through them; thy Cressida proveth it to thee. The gods have pity upon us mortals and in diverse wise do they make manifest to us that which is unknown to us, and very often known to our good.

20.

"And this is one of the ways, that showeth itself sometimes in sleep. Many times already have I remarked it, now that I come to think of it. Would indeed I had died then, since in future time I look forward to no solace, no joy, no pleasure, nor diversion. But by thy counsel I desire to wait, to die in arms with my enemies.

21.

"May the gods send Diomede in my way the first time that I go forth to battle. This do I desire among my great woes, that I may let him know by experience how my sword cutteth and put him to death with groans on the field of battle. And then I care not if I die provided only that he die and that I find him wretched in the realm of darkness."

22.

Pandarus listened to all with sorrow, and perceiving the truth, he knew not what to say. On the one hand, love of his friend inclined him to remain here; on the other, shame for Cressida's transgression did ofttimes invite him to depart. And he knew not in his own mind how to decide what he ought to do, and either alternative did grieve him sore.

23.

Alla fine così disse piangendo:
  Troilo, non so che mi ti debba dire:
  Lei quanto posso tanto più riprendo
  Siccome di', e del suo gran fallire
  Nïuna scusa avanti far n' intendo,
  Nè mai dov' ella sia più voler gire;
  Ciò ch' io fe' già il feci per tuo amore,
  Lasciando addietro ciascuno mio onore.

24.

E s' io ti piacqui, assai m' è grazïoso:
  Di quel ch' or fassi altro non posso fare,
  E come tu così ne son cruccioso;
  E s' io vedessi il modo d' ammendare,
  Abbi per certo io ne sarei studioso:
  Faccialo Iddio, che può tutto voltare,
  Pregolo quanto posso ch' el punisca
  Lei, sì che più 'n tal guisa non fallisca.

25.

Grandi furo i lamenti e 'l rammarchio,
  Ma pur fortuna suo corso facea;
  Colei amava con tutto il disio
  Diomede, e Troilo piangea;
  Diomede si lodava d' Iddio,
  E Troilo per contrario si dolea;
  Nelle battaglie Troilo sempre entrava,
  E più che altri Diomede cercava.

26.

E spesse volte assieme s' avvisaro
  Con rimproveri cattivi e villani,
  E di gran colpi fra lor si donaro,
  Talvolta urtando, e talor nelle mani
  Le spade avendo, vendendosi caro
  Insieme molto il loro amor non sani:
  Ma non avea la fortuna disposto,
  Che l' un dell' altro fornisse il proposto.

23.

Thus he spake at last, in tears: "Troilus, I know not what I ought to tell thee. I blame her, as thou dost say, as much as I can, and for her great misdeed I purpose to bring forward no excuse, nor do I wish ever to go again where she may be. What I did once, I did for thy love, putting behind all honor of mine.

24.

"And if I pleased thee, it is very grateful to me. I cannot do otherwise than what I am now doing, and, like thyself, enraged am I because of it. And if I should see any way of making amends, be assured that I should be zealous to do so. May the gods, who can change all, bring it to pass. I pray them with all my might to punish her, so that she may not again sin in like fashion."

25.

Great were the laments and the bitterness but Fortune still ran her course. She loved Diomede with all her heart and Troilus wept. Diomede thanked the gods and Troilus, on the contrary, grieved. Troilus did ever enter the battles and more than others did he seek Diomede.

26.

And many times did they come together face to face with ugly and vile reproaches, and great blows they exchanged with one another, now thrusting with lance and now with sword in hand, intemperately selling each other their love very dear. But Fortune had not ordained that one should work his will upon the other.

27.

L' ira di Troilo in tempi diversi
 A' Greci nocque molto senza fallo,
 Tanto che pochi ne gli uscien avversi
 Che non cacciasse morti da cavallo,
 Solo che l' attendesser, sì perversi
 Colpi donava; e dopo lungo stallo,
 Avendone già morti più di mille,
 Miseramente un dì l' uccise Achille.

28.

Cotal fine ebbe il mal concetto amore
 Di Troilo in Criseida, e cotale
 Fin' ebbe il miserabile dolore
 Di lui, al qual non fu mai altro eguale;
 Cotal fin' ebbe il lucido splendore
 Che lui servava al solìo reale;
 Cotal fin' ebbe la speranza vana
 Di Troilo in Criseida villana.

29.

O giovanetti, ne' quai coll' etate
 Surgendo vien l' amoroso disio,
 Per Dio vi prego che voi raffreniate
 I pronti passi all' appetito rio,
 E nell' amor di Troilo vi specchiate,
 Il qual dimostra suso il verso mio,
 Perchè se ben col cuor gli leggerete,
 Non di leggieri a tutte crederete.

30.

Giovane donna è mobile, e vogliosa
 È negli amanti molti, e sua bellezza
 Estima più ch' allo specchio, e pomposa
 Ha vanagloria di sua giovinezza;
 La qual quanto piacevole e vezzosa
 È più, cotanto più seco l' apprezza;
 Virtù non sente nè conoscimento,
 Volubil sempre come foglia al vento.

27.

The wrath of Troilus did not at diverse times fail to be very harmful to the Greeks, so that few came forth to oppose him that he did not topple in death from their horses, if only they would await him, such vicious blows he dealt. And one day, after a long stalemate, when he had already killed more than a thousand, Achilles slew him miserably.

28.

Such was the end that came to the ill-conceived love of Troilus for Cressida; and such was the end that came to his wretched grief, to which none other was ever equal; such was the end that came to the brilliant splendor that he held in store for the royal throne; such was the end of the vain hopes of Troilus in base Cressida.

29.

O youths, in whom amorous desire gradually riseth with age, I pray you for the love of the gods that ye check the ready steps to that evil passion and that ye mirror yourselves in the love of Troilus, which my verses set forth above, for if ye will read them aright and will take them to heart, not lightly will ye have trust in all women.

30.

A young woman is fickle and is desirous of many lovers, and her beauty she esteemeth more than it is in her mirror, and abounding vainglory hath she in her youth, which is all the more pleasing and attractive the more she judgeth it in her own mind. She hath no feeling for virtue or reason, inconstant ever as leaf in the wind.

31.

E molte ancor perchè d' alto lignaggio
   Discese sono, e sanno annoverare
   Gli avoli lor, si credon che vantaggio
   Deggiano aver dall' altre nell' amare;
   E pensan che costume sia oltraggio,
   Torcere il naso e dispettose andare;
   Queste schifate, ed abbiatele a vili,
   Che bestie son, non son donne gentili.

32.

Perfetta donna ha più fermo disire
   D' essere amata, e d' amar si diletta;
   Discerne e vede ciò ch' è da fuggire,
   Lascia ed elegge, provvede ed aspetta
   Le promission: queste son da seguire:
   Ma non si vuol però scegliere in fretta,
   Che non son tutte saggie, perchè sieno
   Più attempate, e quelle vaglion meno.

33.

Dunque siate avveduti, e compassione
   Di Troilo e di voi insiememente
   Abbiate, e fia ben fatto: ed orazione
   Per lui fate ad amor pietosamente,
   Ch' el posi in pace in quella regïone
   Dov' el dimora, ed a voi dolcemente
   Conceda grazia sì d' amare accorti,
   Che per ria donna alfin non siate morti.

31.

And many women also, because they are descended from noble lineage and can count their ancestors, believe that they deserve advantage over others in loving, and think that civility is an outrage, and that they can turn up their noses and go about with a disdainful air. Shun all such and hold them base, for beasts they are and not noble ladies.

32.

The perfect lady hath a stronger desire to be loved and taketh delight in loving; she discerneth and seeth what is to be eschewed; she avoideth and chooseth; foresight she hath and looketh to the fulfilment of her engagements. All such ladies are to be followed, but choice should not be made in haste, for they are not all wise, because they may be older and age lesseneth worth.

33.

Therefore be advised and have compassion upon Troilus and upon yourself at the same time and all shall be well. And piously make prayer for him to Love that Troilus may rest in peace in that region where Love dwelleth and that Love may kindly grant you the boon of loving so wisely that ye shall not die in the end for an evil woman.

IL FILOSTRATO

DI

GIOVANNI BOCCACCIO

✿

PARTE NONA

ARGOMENTO

Qui comincia la nona ed ultima parte del Filostrato, nella quale l' autore parla all'opera sua, e dicegli di cui e con cui debba andare, e quello ch' ella debbia fare; e qui pone fine.

1.

Sogliono i lieti tempi esser cagione
  Di dolci versi, canzon mia pietosa;
  Ma te nella mia grave afflizïone
  Ha tratta amor dall' anima dogliosa
  Contra natura, nè ne so ragione;
  Se non venisse da virtù nascosa,
  Spirata e mossa dal sommo valore
  Di nostra donna nel trafitto core.

2.

Costei, siccom' io so, che spesso il sento,
  Mi può far nulla, e molto più da fare
  Che io non sono, e quinci l' argomento
  Della cagion del tuo lungo parlare
  Credo che nasca, ed io me ne contento,
  Che più da ciò che dalle doglie amare
  Venuto sia; ma ciò che si sia stato,
  Noi siamo al fine da me disiato.

THE FILOSTRATO

OF

GIOVANNI BOCCACCIO

❀

NINTH PART

ARGUMENT

Here beginneth the ninth and last part of the Filostrato, in which the author addresseth his work. He instructeth it to whom it belongeth, and with whom it is expected to take its way, and what it is expected to accomplish. And at this point he bringeth his work to an end.

1.

"Happy times are wont to be the inspiration of sweet verses, my piteous song. But in my affliction Love hath unnaturally drawn thee from my grieving soul nor do I know the reason why, if it come not from hidden virtue, inspired and stirred in the piercèd heart by the supreme excellence of our lady.

2.

"She, as I know, for I often feel it, cannot forget my existence, and moreover she cannot think of me as another sort of man. And hence, I believe, ariseth the real reason for thy long speaking. And I am satisfied thereat, for more from that than from my bitter woes hath it come. But whatever it may have been, we are arrived at the end desired by me.

3.

Noi siam venuti al porto, il qual cercando
  Ora fra scogli ed or per mare aperto,
  Con zefiro e con turbo navigando
  Andati siam, seguendo per l' incerto
  Pelago l' alta luce e 'l venerando
  Segno di quella stella, che esperto
  Fa ogni mio pensiero al fin dovuto,
  E fe' poi che da me fu conosciuto.

4.

Estimo dunque che l' ancore sieno
  Qui da gittare e far fine al cammino;
  E quelle grazie con affetto pieno,
  Che render deve il grato pellegrino
  A chi guidati n' ha, qui rendereno;
  E sopra il lido, ch' ora n' è vicino,
  Le debite ghirlande e gli altri onori
  Porremo al legno delli nostri amori.

5.

Poi tu, posata alquanto, te n' andrai
  Alla donna gentil della mia mente:
  O te felice, che la vederai,
  Quel ch' io non posso far, lasso e dolente!
  E come tu nelle sue man sarai
  Con festa ricevuta, umilemente
  Mi raccomanda all' alta sua virtute,
  La qual sola mi può render salute.

6.

E nell' abito appresso lagrimoso
  Nel qual tu se', ti prego le dichiari
  Negli altri danni il mio viver noioso,
  Li guai, e li sospiri e i pianti amari
  Ne' quali stato sono e sto doglioso,
  Poichè de' suoi begli occhi i raggi chiari
  Mi s' occultaron per la sua partenza,
  Che lieto sol vivea di lor presenza.

3.

"We have reached the haven which we have come seeking, now among the rocks and now upon the open sea, sailing with zephyr and with stormy winds, following over the uncertain sea the noble light and the revered sign of that star which maketh every thought of mine quick and keen to the proper end, and then did make itself known by me.

4.

"Here then, I judge, the anchors are to be cast and an end put to our course and here shall we make offering, with complete good will, of those thanks which the grateful pilgrim is expected to render to him who hath guided us. And on the shore, which is now near by, shall we place upon the ship of our loves fitting garlands and other honors which are his due.

5.

"Then thou, a little rested, wilt go away to the gentle lady of my thoughts. O happy thou, for thou shalt see her, which I cannot do, weary and sorrowful that I am. And when thou art joyfully received into her hand, recommend me humbly to her high excellence, which alone can give me felicity.

6.

"And in the almost tearful habit in which thou art, I pray thee declare to her how wearily I live in the griefs of another, the woes, the sorrows, the sighs, and the bitter moans in which I am and have been sorrowful since the bright rays of her fair eyes were concealed from me by her departure, for I lived in happiness by their presence alone.

7.

Se tu la vedi ad ascoltarti pia
  Nell' angelico aspetto punto farsi,
  O sospirar della fatica mia,
  Pregala quanto puoi che ritornarsi
  Omai le piaccia, o comandar che via
  Da me l' anima deggia dileguarsi,
  Perocchè dove ch' ella ne deggia ire,
  Me' che tal vita m' è troppo il morire.

8.

Ma guarda che così alta imbasciata
  Non facci senza amor, che tu saresti
  Per avventura assai male accettata,
  Ed anche ben senza lui non sapresti.
  Se seco vai, sarai credo onorata:
  Or va': ch' io prego Apollo che ti presti
  Tanto di grazia ch' ascoltata sii,
  E con lieta risposta a me t' invii.

7.

"If thou dost see her make ready in her angelic face to listen respectfully to thee, or sigh for the hardships I have endured, pray her as earnestly as thou canst, that it may please her presently to return or to command my soul to flee from me, for wherever it is to go, much better is death than such a life.

8.

"But see to it that thou dost not make so high an embassy without Love, for thou wouldst be perchance quite ill received, and also thou wouldst not have understanding without him. If thou goest with Love, thou wilt, I believe, be honored. Now go, for I pray Apollo to lend thee so much grace that thou mayest be listened to and she may send thee back to me with a happy response."